About the Authors

Author **Ally Blake** loves strong hot coffee, fluffy white clouds, dancing in the car to a song she hasn't heard in ages, and the glide of a soft, dark pencil over really good notepaper. She also adores writing love stories. Having sold over four million copies of her books worldwide she is living the dream. Alongside one handsome husband, their three spectacular children, and too many animal companions to count, Ally lives and writes in the leafy western suburbs of Brisbane, Australia.

In 2002 **Janice Maynard** left a career as an elementary teacher to pursue writing full-time. Her first love is creating sexy, character-driven, contemporary romance. She has written for Kensington and NAL, and is very happy to be part of the Mills & Boon family – a lifelong dream. Janice and her husband live in the shadow of the Great Smoky Mountains. They love to hike and travel. Visit her at www.JaniceMaynard.com

USA TODAY bestselling author **Heidi Rice** used to work as a film journalist until she found a new dream job writing romance for Mills & Boon in 2007. She adores getting swept up in a world of high emotions, sensual excitement, funny feisty women, sexy tortured men and glamourous locations where laundry doesn't exist. She lives in London, England with her husband, two sons and lots of other gorgeous men who exist entirely in her imagination (unlike the laundry, unfortunately!)

Tropical Temptation

Tropical Temptation:
Exotic Love

ALLY BLAKE

JANICE MAYNARD

HEIDI RICE

MILLS & BOON

First Published in Great Britain 2020
By Mills & Boon, an imprint of HarperCollins*Publishers*
1 London Bridge Street, London, SE1 9GF

TROPICAL TEMPTATION: EXOTIC LOVE © 2020
Harlequin Books S.A.

Her Hottest Summer Yet © 2014 Ally Blake
The Billionaire's Borrowed Baby © 2011 Janice Maynard
Beach Bar Baby © 2014 Heidi Rice

ISBN: 978-0-263-29834-5

MIX
Paper from
responsible sources
FSC™ C007454

This book is produced from independently certified FSC™ paper to ensure responsible forest management.

For more information visit: www.harpercollins.co.uk/green

Printed and bound in Spain
by CPI, Barcelona

HER HOTTEST
SUMMER YET

ALLY BLAKE

This one is for all the long, hot Australian summers of my life; for all the memories and possibilities they hold.

With an extra dollop of love for Amy Andrews, one of my favorite writers and a sublime woman to boot.

CHAPTER ONE

AVERY SHAW BARELY noticed the salty breeze whipping pale blonde hair across her face and fluttering the diaphanous layers of her dress against her legs. She was blissfully deep in a whirlpool of warm, hazy, happy memories as she stood on the sandy footpath and beamed up at the facade of the Tropicana Nights Resort.

She lifted a hand to shield her eyes from the shimmering Australian summer sun, and breathed the place in. It was bigger than she remembered, and more striking. Like some great white colonial palace, uprooted out of another era and transplanted to the pretty beach strip that was Crescent Cove. The garden now teetered on the wild side, and its facade was more than a little shabby around the edges. But ten years did that to a place.

Things changed. She was hardly the naive sixteen-year-old with the knobbly knees she'd been the summer she was last there. Back when all that mattered was friends, and fun, and—

A loud whoosh and rattle behind her tugged Avery back to the present. She glanced down the curving sidewalk to see a group of skinny brown-skinned boys in board shorts hurtling across the road on their skateboards before running down the beach and straight into the sparkling blue water of the Pacific.

And sometimes, she thought with a pleasant tightening in her lungs, *things don't change much at all*.

Lungs full to bursting with the taste of salt and sea and expectation, Avery and her Vuitton luggage set bumped merrily up the wide front steps and into the lobby. Huge faux marble columns held up the two-storey ceiling. Below sat cushy lounge chairs, colossal rugs, and potted palms dotted a floor made of the most beautiful swirling mosaic tiles in a million sandy tones. And by the archway leading to the restaurant beyond sat an old-fashioned noticeboard shouting out: Two-For-One Main Courses at the Capricorn Café For Any Guests Sporting an Eye Patch!

She laughed, the sound bouncing about in the empty space. For the lobby was empty, which for a beach resort at the height of summer seemed odd. But everyone was probably at the pool. Or having siestas in their rooms. And considering the hustle and bustle Avery had left behind in Manhattan, it was a relief.

Deeper inside the colossal entrance, reception loomed by way of a long sandstone desk with waves carved into the side. Behind said desk stood a young woman with deep red hair pulled back into a long sleek ponytail, her name tag sporting the Tropicana Nights logo slightly askew on the jacket of the faded yellow and blue Hawaiian print dress, which might well have been worn in the seventies.

"Ahoy, there!" sing-songed the woman—whose name tag read Isis—front teeth overlapping endearingly. Then, seeing Avery's gaze light upon the stuffed parrot wiggling on her shoulder, Isis gave the thing a scratch under the chin. "It's Pirates and Parrots theme at the resort this week."

"Of course it is," Avery said, the eye patch now making more sense. "I'm Avery Shaw. Claudia Davis is expecting me."

"Yo ho ho, and a bottle of rum... The American!"

"That I am!" The girl's pep was infectious, jet lag or no.

"Claude has been beside herself all morning, making me check the Qantas website hourly to make sure you arrived safe and sound."

"That's my girl," Avery said, feeling better and better about her last-minute decision to fly across the world, to the only person in her world who'd understand why.

Tap-tap-tap went Isis's long aqua fingernails on the keyboard. "Now, Claude could be…anywhere. Things have been slightly crazy around here since her parents choofed off."

Choofed off? Maybe that was Aussie for *retired*. Crazy or not, when Avery had first called Claude to say she was coming, Claude had sounded giddy that the management of the resort her family had owned for the past twenty years was finally up to her. She had ideas! Brilliant ones! People were going to flock as they hadn't flocked in years!

Glancing back at the still-empty lobby, Avery figured the *flocking* was still in the planning. "Shall I wait?"

"*No* ho ho," said Isis, back to tapping at the keyboard, "you'll be waiting till next millennium. Get thee to thy room. Goodies await. I'll get one of the crew to show you the way."

Avery glanced over her shoulder, her mind going instantly to the stream of messages her friends had sent when they'd heard she was heading to Australia, most of which were vividly imagined snippets of advice on how best to lure a hot, musclebound young porter "down under."

The kid ambling her way *was* young—couldn't have been a day over seventeen. But with his bright red hair and galaxy of freckles, hunching over his lurid yellow and blue shirt and wearing a floppy black pirate hat that had seen better days, he probably wasn't what they'd had in mind.

"Cyrus," Isis said, an impressive warning note creeping into her voice.

Cyrus looked up, his flapping sandshoes coming to a slow halt. Then he grinned, the overlapping teeth putting it beyond doubt that he and Isis were related.

"This is Miss Shaw," warned Isis. "Claudia's friend."

"Thanks, Cyrus," Avery said, heaving her luggage onto the golden trolley by the desk since Cyrus was too busy staring to seem to remember how.

"Impshi," Isis growled. "Kindly escort Miss Shaw to the Tiki Suite."

Avery's bags wobbled precariously as Cyrus finally grabbed the high bar of the trolley and began loping off towards the rear of the lobby.

"You're the New Yorker," he said.

Jogging to catch up, Avery said, "I'm the New Yorker."

"So how do *you* know Claude anyway? She never goes *anywhere*," said Cyrus, stopping short and throwing out an arm that nearly got her around the neck. She realised belatedly he was letting a couple of women with matching silver hair and eye-popping orange sarongs squeeze past.

Avery ducked under Cyrus's arm. "Claude has been all over the place, and I know because I went with her. The best trips were Italy…Morocco… One particular night in the Maldives was particularly memorable. We first met when my family holidayed here about ten years back."

Not *about* ten years. *Exactly.* Nearly to the day. There'd be no forgetting that these next few weeks. No matter how far from home she was.

"Now, come on Cyrus," Avery said, shaking off the sudden weight upon her chest. She looped a hand through the crook of Cyrus's bony elbow and dragged him in the direction of her suite. "Take me to my room."

Kid nearly tripped over his size thirteens.

One wrong turn and a generous tip later the Tiki Suite was all hers, and Avery was alone in the blissful cool of

the soft, worn, white-on-white decor where indeed goodies did await: a basket of warm-skinned peaches, plums
and nectarines, a box of divine chocolate, and a huge bottle of pink bubbly.

But first Avery kicked off her shoes and moved to the
French doors, where the scent of sea air and the lemon trees
that bordered the wall of her private courtyard filled her
senses. She lifted her face to the sun to find it hotter than
back home, crisper somehow.

It was the same suite in which her family had stayed
a decade before. Her mother had kicked up a fuss when
they'd discovered the place was less glamorous than she'd
envisaged, but by that stage Avery had already met Claude
and begged to stay. For once her dear dad had put his foot
down, and Avery had gone on to have a magical, memorable, lazy, hazy summer.

The last simple, wonderful, innocent summer of her life.

The last before her parents' divorce.

The divorce her mother was about to celebrate with a
Divorced a Decade party, in fact; capitals intended.

Avery glanced over her shoulder at the tote she'd left
on the bed, and tickles of perspiration burst over her skin.

She had to call home, let her mother know she'd arrived.
Even though she knew she'd barely get in a hello before
she was force fed every new detail of the big bash colour
theme—*blood*-red—guest lists—exclusive yet extensive—
and all-male live entertainment—no, *no*, NO!

Avery sent a text.

I'm here! Sun is shining. Beach looks splendiferous. I'll call
once jet lag wears off. Prepare yourself for stories of back-
yard tattoos, pub crawls, killer spiders the size of a studio
apartment, and naked midnight beach sprints. Happy to
hear the same from you. Ave xXx

Then, switching off her phone, she threw it to the bed. Then shoved a pillow over the top.

Knowing she couldn't be trusted to sit in the room and wait for Claude without turning her phone back on, Avery changed into a swimsuit, lathered suncreen over every exposed inch, grabbed a beach towel, and headed out to marvel at the Pacific.

As she padded through the resort, smiling at each and every one of Claude's—yes, Claude's!—pink-faced guests, Avery thought about how her decision to come back had been purely reactive, a panic-driven emotional hiccup when her mother had broached the idea of the Divorced a Decade party for the very first time.

But now she was here, the swirl of warm memories seeping under her skin, she wondered why it had never occurred to her sooner to come back. To come full circle.

Because that's how it felt. Like over the next few weeks she'd not only hang with her bestie—or nab herself a willing cabana boy to help get the kinks out—but maybe even be able to work her way back to how things had been here before her family had flown back to Manhattan and everything had fallen apart. To find the hopeful girl she'd once been before her life had become an endless series of gymnastic spins from one parent to the other and back again. Cartwheels to get her absent father's attention. Cheerleading her way through her mother's wild moods.

She'd never felt quite as safe, as secure, as *content* since that summer.

The summer of her first beer.

Her first beach bonfire.

Her first crush…

Avery's feet came to a squeaking halt.

In fact, wasn't *he*—the object of said crush—in Crescent Cove, right now?

Claude had mentioned him. Okay, so she'd bitched and

moaned; that he was *only* in the cove till he and Claudia sorted out what they were going to do with the resort now that their respective parents had retired and left the two of them in charge. But that was about *Claude's* history with the guy, not Avery's.

Her history was nice. And at that moment *he* was there. And *she* was there. It would be nice to look him up. And compared to the supercharged emotional tornado that was her family life in New York, this summer Avery could really do with some *nice*.

Jonah North pushed his arms through the rippling water, the ocean cool sliding over the heat-baked skin of his back and shoulders, his feet trailing lazily through the water behind him.

Once he hit a sweet spot—calm, warm, a good distance from the sand—he pressed himself to sitting, legs either side of his board. He ran two hands over his face, shook the water from his hair, and took in the view.

The town of Crescent Cove was nestled behind a double row of palm trees that fringed the curved beach that gave the place its name. Through the gaps were flashes of pastel—huge resorts, holiday accommodation, locally run shops, as well as scattered homes of locals yet to sell out. Above him only sky, behind and below the endless blue of the Pacific. Paradise.

It was late in the morning for a paddle—there'd been no question of carving out enough time to head down the coast where coral didn't hamper actual surf. Who was he kidding? There was never any time. Which, for a lobsterman's son, whose sea legs had come in before his land legs, was near sacrilege.

But he was here now.

Jonah closed his eyes, tilted his face to the sun, soaked in its life force. No sound to be heard bar the heave of his slowing breaths, the gentle lap of water against his thighs, a scream—

His eyes snapped open, his last breath trapped in his lungs. His ears strained. His gaze sweeping the gentle rolling water between himself and the sand, searching for—

There. A keening. Not a gull. Not music drifting on the breeze from one of the resort hotels. Distress. Human distress.

Muscles seized, every sense on red alert, he waited. His vision now locked into an arc from where he'd heard the cry. Imagining the reason. Stinger? No, the beach was protected by a stinger net this time of year so it'd be tough luck if they'd been hit.

And then he saw it.

A hand.

His rare moment of quietude at a fast and furious end, Jonah was flat on his belly, arms heaving the ocean out of his way before he took his next breath.

With each swell he glanced up the beach to see if anyone else was about. But the yellow and red flags marking out the patch of beach patrolled by lifesavers were farther away, this part cleared of life bar a furry blot of brown and white dog patiently awaiting his return.

Jonah kept his eyes on the spot, recalculating distance and tidal currents with every stroke. He'd practically been born on the water, reading her as natural to him as breathing. But the ocean was as cruel as she was restorative, and if she decided not to give up, there wasn't much even the most sea-savvy person could do. He knew.

As for the owner of the hand? *Tourist.* Not a single doubt in his mind.

The adrenalin thundering through him spiked when sunlight glinted off skin close enough to grab. Within seconds he was dragging a woman from the water.

Her hair was so long it trailed behind her like a curtain

of silk, so pale it blended with the sandy backdrop behind. Her skin so fair he found himself squinting at the sun reflecting off her long limbs. And she was lathered in so much damn sunscreen she was as slippery as a fish and he could barely get a grip.

And that was before she began to fight back. "No!" she spluttered.

"Hell, woman," Jonah gritted out. "I'm trying to rescue you, which will not be possible unless you stop struggling."

The woman stopped wriggling long enough to shoot him a flat stare. "I'm an excellent swimmer," she croaked. "I swam conference for Bryn Mawr."

Not just a tourist, Jonah thought, her cultured American accent clipping him about the ears. *From the whole other side of the world.*

"Could have fooled me," he muttered. "Unless that's what passes for the Australian Crawl stateside these days."

The stare became a glare. And her eyes... A wicked green, they were, only one was marred with a whopping great splotch of brown.

And while *he* stared at the anomaly, her hand slipped. Lucky she had the smarts to grab the pointy end of his board, leaving him to clench his thighs for all he was worth.

"Honey," he growled, by then near the end of his limited patience, "I understand that you're embarrassed. But would you rather be humbled or dead?"

Her strange eyes flinted at the *Honey*, not that he gave a damn. All he cared was that she gave a short nod. The sooner he dumped her back on the sand and got on with his day, the better. And if a dose of reality was necessary to get it done, then so be it.

"Good. Now, hoick yourself up on three." When her teeth clamped down on her bottom lip to suppress a grimace, and her fair skin came over paler again, he knew there'd be no hoicking. "Cramp?"

Her next grimace was as good as a yes.

Damn. No more finessing. In for a penny, Jonah locked his legs around the board, hooked his elbows under her arms, and heaved.

She landed awkwardly in a mass of gangly limbs and sea water. Only Jonah's experience and strength kept them from ending up ass up, lungs full of sea water, as he slid her onto his lap, throwing her arms around his neck where she gripped like a limpet. He grabbed her by the waist and held her still as the waves they'd created settled to a gentle rock.

Jonah wondered at what point she would become aware that she was straddling him, groin to groin, skin sliding against him all slippery and salty. Because after a few long moments it was just about all he could think about. Especially when with another grimace she hooked an arm over his shoulder, the other cradling the back of his head, and stretched her leg sideways, flexing her foot, easing out the cramp, her eyes fluttering closed as her expression eased into bliss.

He ought to have cleared his throat, or shifted her into a less compromising position, but with those odd eyes closed to him he got a proper look. Neat nose, long curling lashes stuck together with sea water, mouth like a kiss waiting to happen. If he had to have his paddle disturbed, might as well be by a nice-looking woman…

Tourist, he reminded himself.

And as much as the tourist dollar was his life's blood, and that of the entire cove, he knew that with all the Hawaiian shirts and Havana shorts they packed, it didn't leave much room for common sense.

And those were just the uncomplicated ones. The ones who were happy to come, and happy to go home. Lanky

Yankee here—a city girl with clear dibs on herself—had *complication* written all over.

"You all right?" Jonah asked.

She nodded. Her eyes flicked open, and switched between his and finally she realised she was curled around him like seaweed.

Light sparked in the green depths, the brown splodge strangely unmoved. Then, with a quick swallow, she slid her gaze down his bare chest to where they were joined at the hip. Lower. She breathed in quick, rolling as if to separate only to send a shard of heat right through him as she hit a sweet spot with impressive precision.

"May I—?" she asked, rolling again as if to disentangle.

Gritting his teeth, Jonah grunted in response. Having a woman be seaweed on him wasn't necessarily a bad thing. But out here? With a tourist on the verge of cramp? Besides which she was a bossy little thing. Skin and bone. Burn to a crisp if he didn't get her indoors. Not his type at all.

"This is nice and all," he said, boredom lacing his voice, "but any chance we could get a move on?"

"*Nice?* You clearly need to get out more."

She had him there.

With that she got to it, lifting a leg, the edge of a foot scraping a line across his bare belly, hooking a hair or two on the way, before her toes hit the board, mere millimetres from doing him serious damage. He shifted an inch into safe territory and breathed out. And finally they were both facing front.

Not better, he realised as The Tourist leant forward to grip the edges of his surfboard, leaving nowhere for him to put his hands without fear of getting slapped.

Especially when, in place of swimmers, the woman was bound in something that looked like a big-girl version of those lacy things his Gran used to insist on placing on every table top—all pale string, and cut-out holes, the stuff lifted and separated every time she moved, every time she breathed.

"Did you lose part of your swimmers?"

With a start she looked down, only to breathe out in relief. "No. I'm decent."

"You sure about that?"

The look she shot him over her shoulder was forbearing, the storm swirling in her odd eyes making itself felt south of the border.

"Then I suggest we get moving."

With one last pitying stare that told him she had decided he was about as high on the evolutionary scale as, say, *kelp*, she turned front.

Jonah gave himself a moment to breathe. He'd been on the receiving end of that look before. Funny that the original looker had been an urbanite too, though not from so far away as this piece of work, making him wonder if it was a class they gave at Posh Girls' Schools—*How to Make a Man Feel Lower Than Dirt*.

Only it hadn't worked on him then, and didn't now. They bred them too tough out here. Just made him want to get this over with as soon as humanly possible.

"Lie down," he growled, then settled himself alongside her.

"No way!" she said, wriggling as he trapped her beneath his weight. The woman might look like skin and bone but under him she felt plenty female. She also had a mean right elbow.

"Settle," Jonah demanded. "Or we'll both go under. And this time you can look after your own damn self."

She flicked him a glance, those eyes thunderous, those lips pursed like a promise. A promise he had no intention of honouring.

"Now," he drawled, "are you going to be a good girl and

let me get you safe back to shore, or are you determined
to become a statistic?"

After a moment, her accented voice came to him as a
hum he felt right through his chest. "Humility or death?"

He felt the smile yank at the corner of his mouth a second too late to stop it. Hers flashed unexpected, like sunshine on a cloudy day.

"Honey," he drawled, "you're not in Kansas any more."

One eyebrow lifted, and her eyes went to his mouth and
stayed a beat before they once again looked him in the eye.
"New York, actually. I'm from New York. Where there
are simply not enough men with your effortless charm."

Sass. Bedraggled and pale and now shaking a little from
shock and she was sassing him. Couldn't help but respect
her for that. Which was why the time had come to offload
her for good.

Jonah held on tight and kicked, making a beeline for
the beach.

He did his best to ignore the warmth of the woman beneath him, her creamy back with its crazy mass of string
masquerading as a swimsuit.

As soon as they were near enough, he let his feet drop
to the sand and pushed the board into the shallows.

She slid off in a gaggle of limbs. He made to help, but
she pulled her arm away. Didn't like help this one. Not
his at any rate.

Hull stood at their approach, shook the sand from his
speckled fur, then sat. Not too close. He was as wary of
strangers as Jonah was. Smart animal.

Jonah took note and moved his hand away. "Stick to the
resort pool, next time. Full-time lifeguards. Do you need
me to walk you back to the Tropicana?" Probably best
to check in with Claudia, make sure she knew she had a
knucklehead staying at her resort.

"How on earth do you know where I'm staying?" asked said knucklehead.

He flicked a dark glance at the Tropicana Nights logo on the towel she'd wrapped tight about her.

"Right," she said, her cheeks pinkening. "Of course. Sorry. I didn't mean to suggest—"

"Yeah, you did."

A deep breath lifted her chest and her odd eyes with it so that she looked up at him from beneath long lashes clumped together like stars. "You're right, I did." A shrug, unexpectedly self-deprecating. Then, "But I can walk myself. Thanks, though, for the other. I really am a good swimmer, but I… Thanks. I guess."

"You're welcome." Then, "I guess."

That smile flickered for a moment, the one that made the woman's face look all warm and welcoming and new. Then all of a sudden she came over green, her wicked gaze became deeply tangled in his, she said, "Luke?" and passed out.

Jonah caught her: bunched towel, gangly limbs, and all.

He lowered himself—and her with him—to the sand, and felt for a pulse at her neck to find it strong and even. She'd be fine. A mix of heatstroke and too much ocean swallowed. No matter what she said about how good a swimmer she was, she was clearly no gym junkie. Even as dead weight she was light as a feather in his arms. All soft, warm skin too. And that mouth, parted, breathing gently. Beckoning.

He slapped her. On the cheek. Lightly.

Then not so lightly.

But she just lay there, angelic and unconscious. Nicer that way, in fact.

Luke, she'd said. He knew a Luke. Was good mates with one. But they didn't look a thing alike. Jonah's hair was darker, curlier. His eyes were grey, Luke's were…buggered if he knew. And while Luke had split Crescent Cove the first chance he had—coming home only when he had no choice—nothing bar the entire cove sinking into the sea would shift Jonah. Not again.

Literally, it seemed, as he tried to ignore the soft heat of the woman in his arms.

Clearly the universe was trying to tell him something. He'd learned to listen when that happened. *Storm's a coming: head to shore. A woman gets it in her head to leave you: never follow. Dinner at the seafood place manned by the local Dreadlock Army: avoid the oysters.*

What the hell he was meant to learn from sitting on a beach with an unconscious American in his arms, he had no idea.

Avery's head hurt. A big red whumping kind of hurt that meant she didn't want to open her eyes.

"That's the way, kid," a voice rumbled into her subconscious. A deep voice. Rough. Male.

For a second, she just lay there, hopeful that when she opened her eyes it would be to find herself lying on a sun lounge, a big buff cabana boy leaning over her holding a tray with piña coladas and coconut oil, his dark curls a halo in the sun…

"Come on, honey. You can do it."

Honey? Australian accent. It all came back to her.

Jet lag. Scorching heat. A quick dip in the ocean to wake up. Then from nowhere, cramp. Fear gripping her lungs as she struggled to keep her head above water. A hand gripping her wrist: strong, brown, safe. And then eyes, formidable grey eyes. Anything but safe.

Letting out a long slow breath to quell the wooziness rising in her belly, Avery opened her eyes.

"Atta girl," said the voice and this time there was a face to go with it. A deeply masculine face—strong jaw covered in stubble a long way past a shadow, lines fanning from the corners of grey eyes shaded by dark brows and thick lashes, a nose with a kink as if it had met with foul play.

Not a cabana boy, then. Not a boy at all. As his quick-silver eyes roved over her, Avery's stomach experienced a very grown-up quiver. It clearly didn't care that the guy was also frowning at her as if she were something that had washed up from the depths of the sea.

So who was he, then?

Luke? The name rang in her head like an echo, and her heart rate quickened to match. Could *this* be him?

But no. Strong as the urge was to have her teenage crush grow up into *this*, he was too big, too rugged. And she'd had enough updates about Claude's family friend over the years to know Luke had lived in London for a while now. Worked in advertising. If *this* guy worked in an office she'd eat her luggage.

And as for *nice*? The sensations tumbling through her belly felt anything but. They felt ragged, brusque, hot and pulsey. And oddly snarky, which she could only put down to the recent oxygen deficit.

On that note, she thought, trying to lift herself to sitting. But her head swam and her stomach right along with it.

Before she had the chance to alter the situation, the guy barked, "Lie down, will you? Last thing I need is for you to throw up on me as well."

While the idea of lying down a bit longer appealed, that wasn't how she rolled. She'd been looking after her-self, and everyone else in her life, since she was sixteen.

"I think I'm about done here," she said.

"Can I get somebody for you?" he asked. "Someone from the resort? Luke?"

Her eyes shot to his. So he wasn't Luke, but he knew him? How did he know *she* knew him…? Oh, my God. Just before she'd passed out, she'd called Luke's name.

Heat and humiliation wrapped around her, Avery untwisted herself from Not-Luke's arms to land on the towel. She scrambled to her feet, jumbled everything into a big ball and on legs of jelly she backed away.

"I'm fine. I'll be fine." She pushed the straggly lumps of hair from her face. "Thanks again. And sorry for ruining your swim. Surf. Whatever."

The brooding stranger stood—sand pale against the brown of his knees, muscles in his arms bunching as he wrapped a hand around the edge of the surfboard he'd wedged into the sand. "I'm a big boy. I'll live."

Yes, you are, a saucy little voice cooed inside her head. But not particularly *nice*. And that was the thing. She'd had some kind of epiphany before she'd gone for a swim, hadn't she? Something about needing some sweet, simple, wholesome, *niceness* in her life compared with the horror her mother was gleefully planning on the other side of the world.

"Take care, little mermaid," he said, taking a step back, right into a slice of golden sunlight that caught his curls, and cut across his big bronzed bare chest.

"You too!" she sing-songed, her inveterate Pollyanna-ness having finally fought its way back to the surface. "And it's Avery. Avery Shaw."

"Good to know," he said. Then he smiled. And it was something special—kind of crooked and sexy and fabulous. Though Avery felt a subversive moment of disappointment when it didn't reach his eyes. Those crinkles held such promise.

Then he turned and walked away, his surfboard hooked under one arm, his bare feet slapping on the footpath. And from nowhere a huge dog joined him—shaggy and mottled with deep liquid eyes that glanced back at her a moment before turning back into the sun.

Definitely not Luke. Luke Hargreaves had been taller,

his hair lighter, his eyes a gentle brown. And that long-ago summer before her whole world had fallen apart he'd made her feel safe. To this day Avery could sense the approach of conflict as tingles all over her skin, the way some people felt a storm coming in their bad knees, and Mr Muscles back there made her feel as if she'd come out in hives.

She blinked when she realised she was staring, then, turning away, trudged up the beach towards the road, the resort, a good long sensible lie-down.

"Avery!"

She glanced up and saw a brilliantly familiar blonde waving madly her way from the doorway of the Tropicana: navy skirt, blinding blue and yellow Hawaiian shirt, old-fashioned clipboard an extension of her arm. *Claudia.* Oh, now *there* was a sight for sore eyes, and a bruised ego and—

Avery's feet stopped working, right in the middle of the street. For there, standing behind Claudia and a little to the left, thumb swishing distractedly over a smartphone, was Luke Hargreaves—tall, lean, handsome in a clean-shaven city-boy kind of way, in a suit she could pin as Armani from twenty feet away. If that wasn't enough, compared to the mountain of growly man flesh she'd left back there on the beach, not a *single* skin prickle was felt.

With relief Pollyanna tap danced gleefully inside her head as Avery broke out in a sunny smile.

CHAPTER TWO

A CAR HONKED long and loud and Avery came to. Heat landed in her cheeks as she and her still wobbly legs made their way across the road.

She wished her entrance could have been more elegant, but since in the past half an hour she'd near drowned, passed out, woken up looking into the eyes of a testosterone-fuelled surfer who made her skin itch, she had to settle for still standing.

Avery walked up the grassy bank to the front path of the resort where Claudia near ploughed her down with a mass of hugging arms and kisses and relieved laughter. When Avery was finally able to disentangle herself she pulled back, laughing. Compared with the stylishly subdued Mr Hargreaves, Claudia with her bright blue eyes and wild shirt was like sunshine and fairy floss.

"What happened to you?" asked Claudia. No hellos, no *how was your flight*. The best kind of friendship, it always picked up just where it left off.

"Just been out for a refreshing ocean dip!"

Avery shot a telling glance at Luke. Claudia crossed her arms and steadfastly ignored the man at her back. Avery raised an eyebrow. Claudia curled her lip.

They might have lived on different continents their whole lives but with Skype, email, and several overseas trips together, their shorthand was well entrenched.

Finally Claudia cocked her head at the man and with a brief flare of her nostrils said, "Luke, you remember Avery Shaw."

Luke looked up at the sound of his name. Avery held her breath. Luke just blinked.

Rolling her eyes, Claudia turned on him. "My *friend* Avery. The Shaws stayed at the resort ten odd years ago."

Still nothing.

"They booked out the Tiki Suite for an entire summer."

"Right," he said, a flare of recognition *finally* dawning in his seriously lovely brown eyes. "The Americans."

Claudia clearly wasn't moved by it. Something he'd said, or the way he said it, had Claudia bristling. And Claudia wasn't a bristler by nature; she was as bubbly as they came.

Avery didn't have a problem with him seeming rather... serious. Serious was better than hives, any day. And like the worrying of a jagged tooth her mind skipped back to the scratch of the other man's leg hairs on her inner thighs. To the hard heat of his hands gripping her waist, calloused fingers spanning her belly, big thumbs digging uncomfortably into her hips. Those cool grey eyes looking right through her, as if if he could he would have wished her well away...

She shook herself back to the much more pleasant present where Claude snuggled up to her with love. Waiting till she had Luke's distracted attention, she brought out the big guns—a smile that had cost her parents as much as a small car. "Nice seeing you again, Luke. Hopefully we'll bump into one another again. Catch up on old times."

He blinked again, as if he thought that was what they'd just done. But it was early days. She had time. To do what, she was as yet undecided, but the seeds were there.

"I'm off duty as of this second, Luke," Claude said, not even deigning to look his way. "We'll talk about that *other stuff* later."

"Soon," he said, an edge to his voice.

Claude waved a dismissive hand over her shoulder, offloaded Avery of half her gear as they headed up the stairs into the resort.

"Are you sure?" Avery said. "You must be so busy right now, and I don't want to get in the way. I can help! Whatever you need. I have skills. And they are at your disposal."

"Relax, *Polly*," Claude said, using the nickname she'd given Avery for when she got herself in a positivity loop. "*You* are never in my way."

"Fine, *Julie*," Avery shot back. Claude's nickname had sprung from an odd fascination with *The Love Boat* that Avery had never understood. Though when Claude instantly perked up as a seniors tour group from the UK emerged from behind a pylon—amazingly remembering everybody by name—it couldn't have been more apt.

Cyrus—who'd been leaning on the desk staring out at nothing—straightened so quickly his pirate hat flopped into his eyes.

Claudia frowned at Cyrus, who moved off at quite a pace. "Welcome to Crescent Cove," she said to Avery, "where heat addles the hormones."

"Is that in the town charter?" Avery asked, grinning. "Did I read it on the sign driving in?"

"Unfortunately not. Do you think it would work? As a marketing ploy?" Claude looked more hopeful than the idea merited.

Avery, whose business was public relations and thus who paid to create goodwill, gave Claude's arm a squeeze. "It couldn't hurt."

They reached the Tiki Suite and Claudia dumped Avery's stuff on a white cane chair in the corner, oblivious to the bucketload of sand raining onto the floor. "Now, refreshing dip, my sweet patooty. What happened to you out there?"

"You should see the other guy," Avery muttered before landing face down on the bed.

Claudia landed next to her face up. Then after a beat she turned on her side, head resting in her upturned palm as she loomed over Avery, eyebrows doing a merry dance. "What other guy?"

Avery scrunched up her face. Then rolled onto her back and stared up at the ceiling. "My leg cramped, and a guy on a surfboard dragged me out of the ocean. I'd have been fine, though. I am a very good swimmer."

Claudia landed on her back and laughed herself silly. "I've been locked inside with Luke all morning, forced to listen to him yabber on about figures and columns and hard decisions and I missed it! Who was the *guy*?"

Avery opened her mouth to give his name, then realised he hadn't given it. *Barbarian.* "I have no clue."

Claude flapped a hand in the sky. "I know everybody. What did he look like?"

Avery tried a shrug, but truth was she could probably describe every crinkle around those deep grey eyes. But knowing she would not be allowed to sleep, till Claudia knew all, she said, "Big. Tanned. Dark curly hair. Your basic beefcake nightmare."

Claudia paused for so long Avery glanced her way. Only to wish she hadn't. For the smile in her friend's eyes did not bode well for her hope that this conversation might be at an end.

"Grey surfboard with a big palm tree on it? Magnificent wolf dog at his heels?"

Damn. "That's the one."

Claude's smile stretched into an all-out grin. "You, my sweet, had the pleasure of meeting Jonah North. That's one supreme example of Australian manhood. And he rescued you? Like, actually pulled you out of the ocean? With his bare hands? What was that like?"

Avery slapped her hands over her face to hide the rising pink as her skin kicked into full-on memory mode at the feeling of those bare hands. "It was mortifying. He called me *honey*. Men only do that when they can't be bothered knowing your name."

"Huh. And yet I can't even remember the last time a guy called me honey. Raoul always called me Sugar Puff."

"Raoul?"

"The dance instructor I was seeing. Once upon a million years ago."

"Well, Sugar Puff is sweet. Toothache inducing, maybe, but sweet."

Truth was Avery usually loved an endearment. They always felt like an arrow to the part of her that had switched to maximum voltage the day her parents had told her they were getting divorced. *Like me! Love me! Don't ever leave me!*

Maybe the fact that she'd responded unfavourably to the barbarian meant she'd grown. "Either way, the guy rubbed me the wrong way."

"I know many a woman who'd give their bikini bottoms to have Jonah North rub them any which way."

"Are you one of them?"

Claude blinked, then laughed so hard she fell back on the bed with a thump.

"That's a no?"

Claude just laughed harder.

"What's so funny?" *Honestly.* Because even while it had been mortifying, it had been one of the more blatantly sensual experiences of her recent memory: the twitch of his muscles as she'd slid her foot across his flat belly, the scrape of longing she'd felt when she'd realised he was holding his breath. Talk about addled.

Claudia brought herself back under control, then shrugged. "Aside from the fact that Jonah really learned how to pull off 'curmudgeonly' the past few years? He's a born and bred local, like me. You know what it's like when you know a guy forever?"

"Sure. Pretty much everyone in my social circle will end up with someone they've known forever."

Claudia's eyes widened. "That's…"

"Neat?"

"I was going to say 'demoralising,' but neat works too."

"It's the Park Avenue way. Dynastic. Families know one another. Finances secured. Much like if you and Luke ended up together. It would keep the resort all in the family."

Claudia flinched, and shook her head. "No. Don't even… But that's *my* point. Anyway, I don't want to talk about Luke. I don't like him very much at the moment."

"I have no idea why. He's grown into quite the dish. And he seems perfectly nice." There was that word again. It had sounded quite wonderful before, all poignant and time-gone-by lovely. This time it fell kind of flat. But that was just semantics. She'd find another word.

In the meanwhile Claude shot her a look that said she'd quite like to lock the man up and throw away the key, but not before she'd lathered him in pollen and set a pack of bees on him. She might look like rainbows and sunshine, but there were clever, cunning, dark places inside Claude. Places she tapped into if those she loved were under threat. While Avery had shut her touchy tendencies away in a box with a big fat lock, oh, about ten years ago, in fact.

"Well, then," said Avery, finding her smile, "how do you feel about my getting to know him a little better while I'm here?"

"Jonah? Perfect! He used to be such a cool guy, so chilled. But he's been so damn broody nowadays. Laughs at my jokes only three times out of ten. Go shake him up, for all our sakes."

"Actually…" Avery said, then cleared her throat. "I meant Luke."

Claude's eyes snapped wide, then settled back to near normal. "Hargreaves?"

"*Yes*, Hargreaves."

Claude thought about this a moment. A few moments. Long enough Avery began to wonder if Claude's irritation with the man was the flipside of something quite the other. In which case she'd back-pedal like crazy!

Claude put her mind to rest when she said, "You do re-alise he has a stick up his backside? Like, permanently?"

"So says you." Avery laughed. "I thought he seemed perfectly—"

"*Nice?* Okay, then. You have my blessing. Shake that tree if it floats your boat. Just don't get hurt. By the stick. Up his—"

"Yes, thank you. I get it."

"In fact have at them both if you so desire. *Neither* Jonah Broody North or Luke Bloody Hargreaves are my type, that's for sure."

Avery swallowed down the tangled flash of heat at thought of one and focused on the soothing warmth that settled in her belly at thought of the other. "So what *is* your type these days, Miss Claudia?"

Claude's hand came to rest on her chest as she stared at the ceiling. "A man who in thirty years still looks at me the way my dad looks at my mum. Who looks at me one day and says, 'You've worked hard enough, hon, let's go buy a campervan and travel the country.' Who looks at me like I'm his moon and stars. Hokey, right?"

Avery stared up at the ceiling too, noticing a watermark, dismissing it. "So hokey. And while you're at it, could you find me one of those too, please?"

"We here at the Tropicana Nights always aim to please. Now," Claude said, pulling herself to sitting and reaching for the phone, "time to tell me why you are really here. Because I know you too well to know an impromptu month off had nothing to do with it."

Then she held up a finger as someone answered on the other end. And while Claudia ordered dinner, a massage, and a jug of something called a Flaming Flamingo, Avery wondered quite where to start.

Claude knew the background.

That after the divorce Avery rarely saw her dad. Mostly at monthly lunches she organised. And thank goodness they honestly both loved baseball, or those meetings would be quiet affairs. Go Yanks!

As for dear old Mom, she'd turned on Avery's father with such constant and unceasing venom when he'd left it had been made pretty clear to Avery that once on her mother's bad side there was no coming back.

In order to retain any semblance of the family she had left, what could Avery do but become the perfect Park Avenue daughter?

Until the moment her mother had announced her grand plans for her Divorced a Decade party. And Avery—being such a great party planner—*of course* was to be in charge of the entire thing! After a decade of smiling and achieving and navigating the balance between her less-than-accommodating parents, Miss Park Avenue Perfect had finally snapped.

"*You* snapped?" Claude asked as Avery hit that point of the story, her voice a reverent hush. "What did Caroline say when you told her *no*?"

Okay, so this was where it kind of got messy. Where Avery's memory of the event was skewed. By how hard she'd worked to retain a relationship with her distant dad. And how readily her mother had expected she'd be delighted to help out.

"I didn't exactly say…that. Not in so many words."

"Avery," Claude growled.

Avery scrunched her eyes shut tight and admitted, "I told her I couldn't help her because I was taking a sabbatical."

"A sabbatical. And she believed you?"

"When she saw the mock-up I quickly slapped together of my flight details she did. Then I just had to go ahead and call you and actually book the flights. And let all my clients know I was on extended leave from work and couldn't take any new jobs. And close up my apartment and turn off my electric and water and have my mail diverted for a couple months. And voilà!"

"Voilà!" Claude repeated. "Good God, hon! One of these days you're going to have to learn to say the word *no*!"

Avery pish-poshed, even though she and Claude had had the same argument a dozen times over the years.

"Starting now," said Claude. "Repeat after me—*No.*"

"No," Avery shot back.

"Good girl. Now practise. Ten times in the morning. Ten times before bed."

Avery nodded, promised and wondered why she hadn't brought up the fact that she hadn't had a problem saying "no" to Jonah North. And that saying "no" to *him* had felt good. Really good. So she had the ability. Buried somewhere deep down inside perhaps, but the instinct was there when she really meant it.

But Claude was right. She should have told her mother "no." Well, considering there were more venomous snakes in the world's top ten here than any other place on earth, if she was ever going to toughen up, this was the place.

The Charter North Reef Cruiser was on its way to Green Island. In the engine room everything looked shipshape, so Jonah headed up the companionway to the top deck.

The crew ought to have been used to him turning up on a skip unannounced; he did it all the time. There was no point having a fleet of boats with his name on them if they weren't up to his standards. Besides, his father had been a boatman before him and he knew an extra pair of hands was always welcome.

But the moment he entered the air-conditioned salon, the staff scattered. He caught the eye of one—a new girl, by the starched collar of her Charter North polo shirt, who wasn't as quick off the mark as the others. With a belated squeak she leapt into action, polishing the silver handrails with the edge of her sand-coloured shorts. Odd. But industrious.

So he walked the aisles. The passenger list was pretty much as per usual—marine biologists researching the reef, Green Island staffers, a group of girls who looked as if they'd closed one of the resort bars the night before, a toddler with a brown paper bag under his chin.

His gaze caught on a crew of skinny brown boys, skateboards tucked on their laps, eyes looking out of the window as if urging the island nearer. Part of the Dreadlock Army who lived in these parts, kids who survived on sea water and fresh air. A lifetime ago he'd been one of them.

Fast forward and this day he'd been awake since five. Gone for a five-kilometre run. Driven the half-hour to Charter North HQ in Port Douglas. Checked emails, read the new safety procedures manual he'd paid a small fortune to set up, negotiated the purchase of a new pleasure cruiser he had his eye on in Florida. No time for sticking a toe in the ocean, much less taking it on.

As the captain began his spiel over the speaker system about the adventures available once they hit the island, Jonah slid his sunglasses in place and headed aft.

A few customers had staked out prime positions in the

open air, laughing as they were hit with ocean spray. He didn't blame them. It was a hell of a day to be outside.

When they said Queensland was beautiful one day and perfect the next, they were talking about Crescent Cove. The Coral Sea was invariably warm, a slight southerly bringing about a gentle swell. The sky was a dome of blinding blue with only a smattering of soft white streaks far away on the horizon. And soon they'd hit the edge of the Great Barrier Reef, one of the natural wonders of the world.

He was a lucky man to have been born here. Luckier still to remain. He breathed deep of the sky and salt and sun. He didn't need surf. All he needed was never to take the place for granted again.

He nodded to the staff keeping watch on deck and made to head back inside when someone caught his eye. Not just any someone, it was his waterlogged mermaid herself.

She lifted a hand to shield her eyes and turned her gaze to Crescent Cove. She had nice hands. Fine. Her nails were the colour of her dress—a long flame-orange thing flapping against her legs—and her hair was twisted up into a complicated series of knots atop her head making her look as if she were about to step out onto the French Riviera not a small island on the edge of the Pacific.

Jonah glanced at his own hands knowing they'd be less than fine. Burly brown with many a war wound, and motor oil under his chipped nails. He rubbed his fingers across his rough chin. How long since he'd shaved? Three days? Four?

He shoved his hands deep into the pockets of his long shorts, his forehead pinching. What did he care about all that?

Unfortunately, in the time he'd spent *caring*, she'd turned to face him, all elegant stance and plaintive eyes.

Caught out, his breath found itself caught somewhere

in the region of his gut. And then her eyes narrowed. As if he'd done anything to her other than save her ass.

Then the boat hit a swell, the bow lifting and crashing to the water with a thud.

Squeals of excitement ricocheted through the cabin. But, facing him, his mermaid had no purchase. She lost balance, knocked a hip against the side of the boat, and began to topple—

From there everything happened in slow motion— Jonah's leap over a bench, his canvas shoes landing on the slippery deck then sliding him towards her. He reached for her hand, grabbed, caught, and dragged her back to safety and into his arms.

Her hands fisted into his shirt, the scrape of nails through cotton hooked his chest hair, pulling a couple right from the roots. At the sharp tug of pain, he sucked in a breath. And her eyes lifted swiftly to his. Those odd mismatched eyes. Seriously stunning in such an otherwise quiet face.

"Seriously?" he growled. "I'm going to start thinking these moments are all for my benefit."

She gave him a shove. Strength in those lean arms. "Seriously?" she shot back. Then heaved up a hunk of her skirt, flapped it at him accusingly and shot him a look that said that if she had the superpower, she'd have set him on fire. "All that I know is that thanks to you, I'm soaked!"

"Stick around here, princess, and chances are you're gonna get wet."

She opened her mouth…but nothing came out. Instead high spots of pink burned into her cheeks creating hollows beneath her elegant cheekbones, pursing those kissable lips, and bringing wild glints to those eyes. Not such a quiet face after all. "Maybe next time you decide to go all He-Man, try not to rip the victim's arm from its socket."

She rubbed her arm as if to prove as much, only bringing his attention to the fact that her skin was covered in goosebumps. With the temp edging into the high thirties, that was some feat. Only one other reason Jonah knew for a woman to go goosey when locked in a man's arms...

Testing his theory, Jonah leaned an inch her way, caught the intake of breath, the widening of her eyes, the fresh pink staining her cheeks. Seemed Miss Yankee Doodle Dandy here wasn't as unaffected by him as she was making out.

She swallowed and shoved, with less oomph this time. "Oh, go peddle your He-Man act to someone else for a change."

"No one else seems to need it." The fact that nobody else had ever brought out the urge he kept to himself.

Yeah, he'd heard the chatter since he'd come home; heard himself called hell-bent, a lone wolf. But the truth was even before that, as a kid with all the freedom in the world, he'd known he could count the people he could truly depend upon on one hand. He was glad of that instinct now. Less chance he'd make the mistake of counting on the wrong someone again.

And yet, with this one, it took someone else to wrench him away.

"Mr North?"

Jonah turned to find one of his staff standing in the doorway, wringing his hands, swallowing hard, as if his head might be bitten off for disturbing the boss.

"Sir," said the kid, "we have a Code Green."

"Right." Awesome. He'd asked the crew before they'd taken off to grab him in the event of any major incidents so that he could watch any of the new policies and procedures in action. Code Green was otherwise known as Puke Patrol.

"I'll be there in a sec."

The kid disappeared so fast into the salon he practically

evaporated. Leaving Jonah to turn back to Avery, whose eyes were locked onto his chest.

"Twenty minutes till touchdown, Avery," he said.

She blinked, looked up, then pinked some more. He'd never much been one for girls who blushed, but it suited her. Took the edge off her sharp tongue. Heaven help the guy who fell for one before he was witness to the other.

"You might want to get out of the sun. Get something to drink. Complimentary sunscreen's inside. Whatever you do, get something between you and the big blue. One of these days I won't be around to save you."

Not intending to stick around to see how that went down, Jonah slipped inside.

It was a little under twenty minutes before Green Island came into view: a sliver of land on the horizon that grew into a small atoll of forest-green with a long crooked jetty poking out into the ocean. The cruiser slipped through the reef to park and the passengers staggered off; some clutching snorkels ready for a close encounter with tropical fish, others planning to head straight to a bar.

Jonah caught a flash of orange out of the corner of his eye and turned to find Avery now with a huge sunhat covering her face. Lifting her long dress, she stepped onto the gangplank, her shoe caught and she tripped. Jonah near pulled a muscle in an effort not to grab her. Chin tilted a mite higher, she walked steadily along the jetty, where all sorts of adventures awaited.

Adventures…and dangers. Things happened to tourists all the time—swimming too far, diving too deep, getting knocked off by ingenious spouses.

"Avery!" he called.

She turned, surprise lighting her features. "Yes, Jonah?"

She knew his name. A thick slide of satisfaction washed through him—then he remembered the Code Green. *Down boy.* "Take care."

She blinked, those odd eyes widening, then softening in a way that made him want to howl at the moon.

Hence the reason he added, "Don't get eaten."

The next look she shot him might as well have said, *Bite me*. But when she realised they had an audience, she found a sweet-as-pie smile, and said, "Oh, *don't* get eaten. Thanks for the advice. I'll keep it in mind."

And he found himself laughing out loud.

With a frown and twitch of her mouth, she disappeared into the crowd.

Leaving Jonah to use the respite to remind himself that despite the lush mouth, and the bewitching eyes and the rich vein of sexual attraction she'd unearthed, he didn't much *like* her.

Because he'd known a woman like her once before.

He hadn't realised *why* Rach had stood out to him like bonfire on a cloudy night from the first moment he'd seen *her* until it was too late. Turned out it was because despite her attestations that a sea change was exactly what she needed she'd never left the city behind enough to really fit in. Too late by the time he'd seen it to stop her leaving. Too late to convince himself not to follow. Until he'd woken up in Sydney, cut off, miserable, realising what he'd given up for her, and that he'd lost her anyway.

Returning to Crescent Cove after that whole disaster had been hard. Returning to find *he* no longer quite fitted in the place he'd been born had been harder still. He'd had to remake his life, and to do that remake himself. As if the cove had needed a sacrifice in order to take him back, in order to make sure he'd never take her for granted again.

So no, for however long Avery Shaw flitted about the periphery of his life she'd mean no more, or less, to him than a pebble in his shoe.

Because this time his eyes were wide-open and staying that way. This time he wouldn't so much as blink.

CHAPTER THREE

Jonah wasn't looking for Avery, not entirely.

He found her anyway, on the beach. Her big hat, so wet it flopped onto her shoulders. Half in, half out of a wetsuit that flapped dejectedly against her legs as she jumped around slapping at her skin as if fighting off a swarm of bees.

Jonah picked up his pace to a jog.

"Avery," he called when near enough, "what the hell's wrong now?"

She didn't even look up, just kept on wriggling, giving him flashes of bare stomach through a silver one-piece with great swathes of Lycra cut away leaving the edges to caress a hip, to brush the underside of a breast, keeping Jonah locked into a loop of double takes.

"I'm stung!" she cried, jogging him out of his daze. "Something got me. A box jellyfish. Or a blue bottle. Or a stone fish. I read about them on the flight over. One of them got me. I sting. *Everywhere.*"

"Bottles don't come this far north, the suit protects from jellies, and the flippers from stone fish."

Avery jumped from flippered foot to flippered foot as if something terrible was about to explode from out of the sand at her feet. "Then what's wrong with me?"

Jonah made a mental note to have a talk with Claudia. She always had some crazy theme going on at her resort, with games and the like—surely she could keep the woman indoors and out of his sight.

But until then he had to make sure she wasn't actually hurt. Meaning he had to run hands down her arms, ignoring as best he could the new tension knotting hard and fast inside him.

He spun her around to check behind, wrapping the fall of hair about his hand to lift it off her neck, doing his all to avoid the mental images *that* brought forth. He swept his gaze over the skin the swimsuit revealed round back. Then grabbed her by the chin and tilted so he could see her face under the ridiculous hat. Her very pink face.

"Hell, woman," he growled, snapping his hand away. "You're sunburnt."

Her mismatched eyes widened. "Don't be ridiculous."

He took off the hat to make sure, and with a squeak her hand swept to her hair. Jonah rolled his eyes and slapped the hat back on her head. "Did you bring anything for sunburn?" *Sunscreen perhaps?*

He glanced at her silver bag to find its contents already upended and covered in a million grains of white sand. Clearly she'd been looking in the hopes of a remedy herself. *A remedy for stone fish*, he reminded himself, biting back a smile.

"Don't you dare laugh at me!"

Only made him smile all the more. "Don't tell me you were All Conference in Sun Protection at Brown Mare too?"

"Bryn Mawr," she bit out. And, whoa, was that a flicker of a smile from her? The one that lit her up brighter than the sun?

Jonah looked away, tilting his chin towards the jetty. "There's aloe vera on the boat. It'll soothe it at the very least. At least until the great peel sets in."

"I don't peel."

"You will peel, princess. Great ugly strips of dead skin sloughing away."

Muttering under her breath, she shoved all her bits and pieces back into her bag—including, he noted, a dog-eared novel, a bottle of fancy sparkling water, and, yep, sunscreen.

He plucked the sunscreen from her fingers and read the label. "American," he muttered under his breath.

"Excuse me!" she shot back, no muttering there.

"Your SPF levels are not the same as ours. With your skin you can't get away with this rubbish."

"What's wrong with my skin?" she asked, arms wide, giving him prime view of her perfectly lovely skin. And neat straight shoulders, lean waist, hips that flared just right. As for her backside, he remembered with great clarity as she bent over on his board...

Jonah closed his eyes a moment and sent out a blanket curse to whatever he'd done to piss off karma enough to send him Avery Shaw.

"I'm well aware I'm not all golden bronzed like the likes of you," she said, "which is why I bought a bottle from home. *Ours* are stronger."

"Wrong way around, sweetheart," Jonah drawled. "Aussies do it better."

She coughed and spluttered. That was better than having her eyes rove over his *golden-bronzed* self while standing there all pink, and pretty, and half-naked.

Then, feeling more than a little sorry for herself, she slowly went back to refilling her bag, now with far less gusto. Her drooping hat dripped ocean water down her pink skin, she had a scratch on her arm that could do with some antiseptic and a couple of toes had clearly come out badly in a fight with some coral before she'd remembered her flippers.

Suddenly she threw the bag on the sand, slammed her

hands onto her hips and looked him right in the eye. "In New York we have cab drivers who don't know the meaning of the words *health code*. Rats the size of opossums. Steam that oozes from the subways that could knock you out with its stench. I live in a place it takes street smarts to survive. But this place? Holy Jeter!"

After a sob, she began to laugh. And laugh and laugh. It hit the edge of hysteria, but thankfully it never slipped quite that far.

Jonah ran a hand up the back of his neck and looked out at the edge of the jetty visible around the corner of the beach where his boat and the bright blue sea awaited. Basic, elemental pleasures. Enduring... Then glanced back at the tourist whose safety had clearly, for whatever reason, been placed in his hands.

Whatever problems he had with her kind, there was no denying the woman was trying. Enough that something slipped inside him, just a fraction, just enough to give her a break.

"Come on, princess," he said, holding out a hand. "Let's get you a drink."

She glanced at his sand-covered hand and her nose crinkled. "I don't need a drink."

Knowing it was only a matter of time before he regretted it, Jonah took a moment to brush the sand from his hand before holding it out again. It looked so dark near her skin. Big and rough near all that softness. "Well, I do," he said, his voice gruff. "And I'm not about to resort to drinking alone."

Avery watched him from beneath her lashes. Then, taking her bag in one hand and the arms of her wetsuit in the other, she flapped her way back up the beach, leaving him to catch up. "So long as drink doesn't mean beer. Because I don't do beer."

Jonah watched her walk away, flinching every third step

in fear of having unearthed some other Great Australian Wildlife intent on taking her down. Shaking his head, he dug his hands into the pockets of his shorts and did what he'd promised himself he'd never do again—follow a city girl anywhere. "Pity, princess, you really are missing out on one of the great experiences of an Australian summer."

She cut him a look—straight, sure, street smart indeed—and said, "I'll live."

And for the first time since he'd met the woman Jonah believed she just might.

When her straw slurped against the bottom of the coconut shell, dragging in the last drops of rum, coconut milk, and something she couldn't put her finger on, Avery pushed the thing away and looked up with a blissful sigh to find that the fabulous outdoor bar that Jonah had escorted her to some time earlier was empty.

Jonah North of Charter North. About halfway through the cocktail she'd put two and two together and figured the boat was his. She was clever that way, she thought, fluffing up her nearly dry hair, the happy waves in her head making it feel nice. She liked feeling nice.

Now what about Jonah? Big, gruff, handsome, bossy Jonah. Oh, yeah, he'd left her a few minutes ago to go and do…something. She looked around, shielding her eyes against the streak of bright orange cloud lighting up the dark blue horizon. Oops. Since when had the sun begun to set?

She found her phone in her bag and checked the time. Holy Jeter, she'd missed the boat! With a groan she let her head fall into her hands.

She knew the guy had only taken her for a drink because he'd got it into his thick He-Man head that she'd perish without supervision, but now the cad had damn well left her on an island in the middle of the Pacific, with night falling, and nowhere—

"Everything okay?" a familiar deep voice asked.

Avery peeled one eye open and looked through the gaps between her fingers to find Jonah standing by the table, his hands in the pockets of his khaki shorts, his white Charter North shirt flapping against the rises and falls of his chest in the evening breeze, the sunlight pouring over his deeply browned skin.

The guy might be wholly annoying in an I Told You So kind of way, but there was no denying he was Gorgeous—capital G intended. What with that handsome brown face all covered in stubble. And those shoulders—so big, so broad. Those tight dark curls that made a girl want to reach out and touch. And the chest she'd had her hands all over when he'd pulled her out of the ocean, all muscle and golden skin and more dark curling hair. In fact there was plenty about him that made a girl want to touch…

But not her, she reminded herself, sinking her hands down onto the chair so that she could sit on them before they did anything stupid.

If anybody was going to get the benefit of her touch on this trip, it would be that unsuspecting cabana boy—and, boy, did that sound seedy all of a sudden. So maybe not. Maybe, ah, Luke! Yes, dashing, debonair, dishy Luke Hargreaves. *There you go, that was way better than* nice—

"You okay there, Avery?"

"Hmm? Sorry? What?"

Jonah's laugh was a deep low *huh-huh-huh* that she felt in the backs of her knees.

"How many of those have you had?" he asked.

"Just one, thank you very much." A big one. "I'm fine."

"You say that a lot. That you're *fine*."

She did? Funny, she could hear it too, like an eerie echo inside her head. *I'm fine! All good! Don't worry about me!*

Now what can I do to make you *feel better? Cheer-cheer, rah-rah-rah!*

"I say it because I am." *Mostly.* "And I am. Fine. Just too much sun. And those cocktails have quite a kick, don't they? And—" she pointed one way, and then turned and pointed the other, not quite sure which direction was which "—I do believe I'm meant to be on a boat heading back to the mainland right about now."

Jonah pulled out a chair and straddled the thing, like he needed extra room between his legs to accommodate…you know. Avery blinked fast at the direction of her thoughts, before lifting her eyes quick smart to his, only to connect with all that quicksilver. Cool and hot all at once. As if he knew exactly where her eyes and thoughts had just been.

She swallowed. Hard. Tasted rum and coconut and… whatever the other thing was. The deadly wicked other thing that seemed to have made her rather tipsy.

"Avery."

"Yes, Jonah."

The quicksilver shifted, glints lighting the depths. "Our boat left about the time you started filling me in on why you came to the cove."

Avery swallowed, wondering just how much rum she'd imbibed. She'd told him? What exactly? How she'd been a big chicken and fled New York so as to avoid her mother's mortifying divorce anniversary party?

"To catch up with Claudia," Jonah reminded her when she'd looked at him blankly for quite some time.

"Right! Of course. For *Claude.* We're friends, you know? Have been a *lo-o-ong* time."

No laugh this time, but a smile. An honest-to-goodness smile that made his eyes glow and his eye crinkles deepen. Sheesh; the man didn't need to have a sexy smile to go along with the sexy laugh and all the other sexy bits. But there it was. Talk about a potent cocktail.

"I've secured a room at a local resort, the Tea Tree—"

"Wow. It was decent of you to buy me a drink—" *a kicker of a cocktail* "—in order to ease the sunburn—" *embarrassment* "—and all, but a room's rather presumptuous, don't you think?"

A few more glints joined the rest and his next smile came with a flash of white teeth. The rare and beautiful sight made her girl parts uncurl like a cat in the sun.

"Avery," he said, and she kind of wished he'd called her princess, or honey, because her name in that drawl from that mouth was as good as ten minutes of concentrated foreplay. "The room is for you. Just you. Alone."

"Oh," she said. Then several moments too late, "Of course. I knew that. I just— How do you even know that I could pay? I might be broke. Or tight with the purse strings. Or—"

"We're more than a tourist town. The cove is a real community. All I had to do was drop Claude's name and it was comped."

"Really?" Oh, how lovely! They loved Claude enough to look after *her*? Oh, she loved this resort already. Belatedly she wondered why they wouldn't simply comp it for *him*. Probably because Jonah North was a big scary bear. Or maybe he wasn't big on favours. *She* certainly owed him a few.

"I also let Claudia know I'd make sure you got home safe and sound tomorrow."

Avery's eyes shot back to his. A drink. A room. A ride. Maybe he wasn't such a jackass after all. Huh. Did that mean she had to try harder to be nice to him now too? Saying "no" had actually been fun, like being outside her own skin rather than curled up tight inside…

He pushed back his chair and held out his hand to her, and not for the first time. And not for the first time, she baulked.

She glanced up into his eyes to find him watching her, impatience edging at the corner of his mouth. Not wanting to start an international incident, she placed her hand in his to find it warm—as she'd expected—and strong—as she'd imagined—and roughly calloused—which sent a sharp shot of awareness right down her arm.

"Sorry," she said in a rush of breath as he tugged her to her feet, "my manners seem to fly right out the window where you're concerned. I can't seem to figure out why."

His pale grey eyes now shadows in the falling light, he said, "Can't you?"

Avery's belly clenched at the intensity of his gaze, and her heart beat so hard she could hear it behind her ears.

Such a simple question, with such a simple answer: she could.

She was obnoxious when he was around because he flummoxed her. He made her feel as if she had to keep her emotional dukes up, permanently, lest he find a way in and knock her out.

And if the past few days far away from the drama of her real life had told her anything, it was that she sorely needed a break. A return to simpler times. Like the summer when the most important thing that had ever happened to her had been a smile from the dreamy brown-eyed boy across the other side of the beach bonfire.

"The thing is," she said, regretting opening her mouth even as the words poured out, "I'm currently…thinking about… seeing someone."

"Someone?" he asked, everything in him suddenly seeming very still.

"Well, a man, to be more specific."

Jonah looked about the bar where an islander was putting chairs onto the tables so he could sweep the floor. He hooked a thumb in the guy's direction.

"No!" said Avery, grabbing his thumb and pulling it

down by his side. It brought her within inches of his chest, so that she could feel the steady rise and fall of his breaths, the heat of his skin, could count his individual eyelashes, all one million of the gorgeous things. She let go. Backed away. Breathed. "Someone *else*. Someone I met here years ago. Someone I'm hoping to…*reconnect* with."

"So then you're *not* here to help out Claudia." His words were tinged with such depths of boredom she wondered how she'd even come to think it was any of his business in the first place.

"Of course I am." Avery lifted her chin. And she was. Or at least she would be. But since their big girlie talk, she hadn't been able to pin her friend down long enough for a coffee, much less a conversation. *Go play tourist!* Claude would say on the fly. *Swim, drink cocktails, take a boat to Green Island.* Look how that turned out.

"You city girls," said Jonah, his voice dropping into a by now familiar growl. "Can't relax. Can't do one thing at a time. Can't settle your damn selves for love or money."

"That's a pretty broad brush."

"Am I wrong?"

Well…no. Back home "busy-busy" or "can't seem to get anything done" was akin to "fine, thanks."

"Yeah," he said, ducking his head as he ran a hand up the back of his neck and through those glorious curls. "That's what I thought. Come on, princess, let's get you checked in."

He jerked his chin in the direction of the exit, and this time he didn't hold out a hand.

Feeling strangely bereft, Avery collected her sandy, sodden gear and followed in her wet clothes and bare feet as at some point she'd lost her shoes. Beneath the shadows of the palm trees that grew everywhere in this part of the world, up the neat paths nearly empty of tourists now most had headed off the island.

And her mind whirled back to how that mortifying conversation had begun.

Can't you? he'd asked, when she'd admitted not knowing why she pushed his buttons. But then why did he insist on pushing hers? Maybe, just maybe, she rubbed him the wrong way too. That very particular kind of wrong way that felt so right.

At that moment Jonah looked back, and she offered up her most innocuous smile.

"All okay?"

"Fine, thanks. You?"

The edge of his mouth twitched, but there was no smile. No evidence he thought she was hot stuff too. He merely lifted a big arm towards a small building with a thatched roof—the Tea Tree Resort and Spa—and they headed inside into blissful air-conditioned luxury.

Once she'd got her key and thanked the guy at Reception profusely for the room, promising him payment, free PR services, a night in a hotel in New York if he was ever in town—all of which he rejected with a grin—she headed in the direction of her bungalow.

The clearing of a male throat brought her up short, and she turned to find Jonah leaning against the wall.

"You're not staying here?" she asked, and the guy's jaw twitched so hard she worried he'd break a tooth. "I mean in another room?"

"I have a place on the island."

"Oh." She waited for more. A description would have been nice. A little shanty hidden from view in the mangroves on the far side of the island? A towel on the sand, nothing between him and the stars? But no, he just stood there, in the only patch of shadow in the entire bright space.

"Think you'll be okay here?" he asked, his voice rough

around the edges, and yet on closer inspection…not so much. Much like the man himself.

"You tell me. You're the one who seems to think I can't walk out the door without facing certain death."

"I'll make you a deal," he said, his expression cool, those eyes of his quiet, giving nothing away. "If you're still alive in the morning, I'll change my tune."

"Till the morning, then," Avery said, taking a step outside the force field the guy wore like a second skin. "Now I'm going to take a long cold shower."

His gaze hardened on hers, and she felt herself come over pink, and fast.

"For the sunburn."

At her flat response, his mouth kicked into a smile, giving her another hint of those neat white teeth. A flash of those eye crinkles. A flood of sensation curled deep into her belly.

"Good night, Jonah."

He breathed in deep, breathed out slow. "Sleep tight," he said, then walked away.

Yeah right, Avery thought, watching the front doorway through which he'd left long after he was gone.

When she got to her room it was to find a fruit basket, a bottle of wine, and a big fat tub of aloe vera with a Post-it note slapped on top that read, "For the American who now knows Aussies do it better."

CHAPTER FOUR

Avery woke to an insistent buzzing. Groaning, she scrunched one eye open to find herself in a strange room. A strange bed. Peering through narrowed eyes, she saw the pillow beside her was undisturbed. That was something, at least.

She let her senses stretch a mite and slowly the day before came back to her... Green Island. Jonah. Sunburn. Jonah. Cocktail. Jonah. And lusting. Oodles of coconut-scented lusting. *And Jonah.*

And she rolled over to bury her face in a pillow.

When the buzzing started up again, she realised it was the hotel phone. She smacked her hand around the bedside table till she found it. "Hello?" Her voice sounded as if she'd swallowed a bucket of sand.

The laughter that followed needed no introduction.

"Don't. Please. It hurts."

"I don't doubt it," Jonah rumbled, his voice even deeper through the phone. "How long till you can be ready to leave?"

"A week?"

She felt the smile. Felt it slink across her skin and settle in her belly. "Half an hour."

"I'll meet you in Reception in forty-five minutes. And don't forget the sunscreen. Australian. Factor thirty. Buy some from the resort shop."

"Where are we going?"

"Home," he said, then hung up.

Avery heaved herself upright and squinted against the sunshine pouring through the curtain-free windows. The scent of sea air was fresh and sharp, the swoosh of the water nearby like a lullaby. It was a fantasy, with—thanks to rum—glimpses of hell. But it sure wasn't home.

Home was blaring horns and sidewalks teeming with life, not all of it human. City lights so bright you could barely see the stars. It was keeping your handbag close and your frenemies closer. It was freezing in New York right now. And heading into night. The storefronts filled with the first hints at hopeful spring fashion even while the locals scurried by in scarves and boots and coats to keep out the chill.

As soon as she turned on her phone it beeped. Her mother had sent a message at some point, as if she could sense her beloved daughter was about to have less than positive thoughts.

Hello, my darling! I hope you are having a fabulous time. When you get a moment could you please send me Freddy Horgendaas's number as I have had a most brilliant idea. I miss you more than you can know. xXx

Freddy was a *most brilliant* cake-maker, famous for his wildly risqué creations. Avery pressed finger and thumb into her eye sockets, glad anew she wouldn't be there when her mother revealed a cake in the shape of her father's private parts with a whopping great knife stuck right in the centre.

She sent the number with the heading 'Freddy Deets' knowing the lack of a complete sentence would make her mother twitch. It wasn't a *no*. More like passive aggression. But for her it was definitely a move in the right direction.

Forty minutes later—showered and changed into the still-damp bikini she'd found on the bathroom floor—

she made a quick stop to the resort gift shop where she picked up an oversized It's Easy Being Green! T-shirt, a fisherman's hat, and flip-flops to replace the shoes she'd somehow lost along the way, and slathered herself in *Australian* sunscreen and handed her key in to the day staff at Reception.

The girls behind the desk chattered about the shock of Claudia's and Luke's parents suddenly heading off into the middle of nowhere, and asked how Claudia was coping. Avery said her friend was coping just great, all the while thinking *shock* and *coping* were pretty loaded words. Making a deal with herself to pin Claude down asap, Avery still knew the moment Jonah had arrived, for she might as well have turned invisible to the two women behind the desk.

"Hi, Jonah!" the girls sing-songed.

"Morning, ladies," he said from behind her, his deep Australian drawl hooking into that place behind Avery's belly button it always seemed to catch. Then to Avery, "Ready to go?"

And the girls' eyes turned to her in amazement and envy.

Avery shook her head infinitesimally—*I get the lust, believe me, but don't panic, he's not the guy for me.*

Then she turned, all that denial ringing in her head as it got a load of the man who'd arrived to take her away.

It shouldn't have been a surprise that Jonah was *still* unshaven, and yet the sight of all that manly stubble first thing in the morning did the strangest things to her constitution. As did the warm brown of his skin against the navy blue shirt, and the strong calves beneath his long shorts, and the crystal-clear grey eyes.

"Shall we?" he asked.

We shall, she thought.

"Bye, Jonah!" the girls called.

Avery, who was by then five steps ahead of Jonah, rolled her eyes.

When they hit sunlight, she stopped, not knowing which way to go.

"What time's the boat?"

"No boat today. Not for us anyway." And then his hand strayed to her lower back, burning like a brand as he guided her along the path, leaving nothing between his searing touch but the cotton of her T-shirt and her still-damp swimmers.

"This way," he said, guiding her with the slightest pressure as he eased her through a gate marked Private then down a sandy path beneath the shade of a small forest, and back out into the sunshine where a jetty poked out into the blinding blue sea. And perched on a big square at the end—

"A helicopter?" A pretty one too, with the Charter North logo emblazed across the side.

"It was brought here this morning on a charter. They don't need it back till four. Quickest way off the island."

"No, thanks," she said, crossing her arms across her chest, "I'll wait for the boat."

"You sure?" he asked, his eyes dropping to where her crossed arms had created a little faux cleavage. Her next breath in was difficult. "It'll be a good eight hours from now, the sea rocking you back and forth, all that noise from a bunch of very tired kids after a long hot day at the beach—"

Avery held up a hand to shush him as she swallowed down the heave of anticipatory post-cocktail seasickness rising up in her stomach. "Yes, thank you. I get your point. So where's our pilot?"

At the twist of his smile, she knew.

Before she could object, Jonah's hands were at her waist, shoving her forward. Her self-preservation instincts actually propelled her away from his touch and towards the contraption as if it were the lesser danger.

When he hoisted her up, she scrambled into her seat with less grace than she'd have liked. And then suddenly he was there, his silhouette blocking out the sun, the scent of him—soap and sea and so much man—sliding inside her senses, the back of his knuckles scraping the T-shirt across her belly...

Oh, he was plugging her in.

"That feels good," she said. Then, cheeks going from sunburned to scorched in half a second flat, added, "The *belt* feels good. Fine. Nice and tight." *Nice and tight?*

A muscle in Jonah's cheek twitched, then without another word he passed her a set of headphones, slid some over his dark curls, flipped some dials, chatted to a flight-control tower, and soon they were off, with Avery's stomach trailing about ten feet below.

It didn't help that Jonah seemed content to simply fly, sunlight slanting across the strong planes of his face, his big thighs spread out over his seat.

Three minutes into the flight Avery nearly whooped with relief when she found a subject that didn't carry some unintentional double entendre. She waved a hand Jonah's way.

He tapped her headphones. *Right.*

"I hope you found someone to look after your dog," she said, her voice tinny in her ears. "I was thinking about it before I fell asleep last night. I mean, since it was my fault you couldn't go home to him last night."

"Hull'll be fine."

Hull. It suited the huge wolfish beast. Like something a Viking might call his best friend.

Then Jonah added, "But he's not my dog."

"Oh. But I thought... Claude said—"

"He's not my dog."

Okay, then.

An age later Jonah's voice came to her, deep and echoey through the headphones. "Want to know what I was thinking about when I finally fell asleep?"

Yes... But she was meant to be getting better at saying no. And this seemed like a really good chance to practise. "No," she lied, her voice flat even as her heart rate shot through the roof.

He shot her a look. Grey eyes hooded, lazy with heat. And the smile that curved at his mouth was predatory. "I'm going to tell you anyway."

Oh, hell.

"I wondered how long it will be before I have to throw myself between you and a drop bear."

Avery wasn't fast enough to hide the smile that tugged at her mouth. Or slow enough not to notice that his gaze dropped to her mouth and stayed. "I may be a tourist, Jonah, but I'm not an idiot. There's no such thing as a drop bear."

His eyes—thankfully—slid back to hers. "Claudia tipped you off, eh?"

"She is fabulous that way."

At mention of her friend another option occurred to her! Sitting up straighter, she turned in her seat as much as she could, ignoring the zing that travelled up her leg as her knee brushed against his.

"Speaking of Claudia," she said. *Here goes.* "She thinks you're hot."

A rise of an eyebrow showed his surprise. "Really?" And for a moment she thought she had him. Then he had to go and ask, "What do *you* think?"

Her stomach clenched as if taking a direct hit. "That's irrelevant."

"Not to me."

"Why do you even care?"

His next look was flat, intent, no holds barred. "If you don't know that yet, Ms Shaw, then I'm afraid that fancy education of yours was a complete waste."

She tried to blink. To think. To come up with some fabulous retort that would send him yelping back into his man cave. But the pull of those eyes, that face, that voice, basking in the wholly masculine scent of him filling the tiny cabin, she couldn't come up with a pronoun, much less an entire sentence.

And the longer the silence built, the less chance she had of getting herself off the hook.

It took for him to break eye contact—when a gust of wind picked them up and rocked them about—for her to drag her eyes away.

With skill and haste, he slipped them above the air stream and into calmer air space. While her stomach still felt as if it were tripping and falling. All because of a little innocent flirting.

Only it didn't feel innocent. It *felt* like Jonah was staking a claim.

But he scared the bejesus out of her. Not *him* so much; the swiftness of her attraction to him. It was fierce. And kind of wild. And she was the woman who calmed the waters. Not the kind who ever went chasing storms.

Even while she knew she was about to admit she understood exactly what Jonah meant, she said, "I told you— I'm interested in someone else." *Considering becoming interested, anyway.*

Then, as if it just didn't matter, he said, "You didn't answer my question."

"Because it's a ridiculous question!"

"You brought it up."

So she had. How had this suddenly gone so wrong?

Avery risked a glance to find Jonah's eyes back on her mouth. His jaw was tight, his breaths slow and deep. And his deep grey eyes made their way back to hers.

"Good Lord, Jonah, first the girls at the hotel were all swoony over you—"

"You noticed?" The smile was back. And a sheen of perspiration prickled all over her skin.

She held up a hand to block his face from sight. "Then Claude mentions in passing that she thinks you're a 'supreme example of Australian manhood—'"

His laughter at *that* echoed through the tiny space till her toes curled. But still she forged on.

"You really need *me* to be in the line-up too? Are you really that egotistical?"

"No, Avery. I'm really that interested. I want to hear you admit you're as attracted to me as I think you are," he said, and not for a second did he take his eyes from hers.

If she hadn't been strapped up like a Thanksgiving turkey she'd have been on him like cranberry sauce. But she was, and she couldn't. And the conversation had become such a hot mess, Avery wished she could go back in time. Perhaps to the very beginning when all that mattered in life was sleep, food, and a safe place in which to hide from pesky dinosaurs.

"You want to know what I *want*?" she asked, proud of the fact that her voice wasn't quavering all over the place. "What I want is for you to keep your eyes on the sky! No matter what you think of my survival skills, I have no intention of dying today."

She waited, all air stuck in her lungs, for him to say something like *I'd rather keep my eyes on you*. But he merely smiled. As if he knew that she was a big fat liar. Deep down in the dark places inside her that she avoided at all costs. The place where Pollyanna had been born: always positive, not a bother, things would get better, they would! No wonder she worked in PR.

When Jonah's smile only grew, she muttered, "Oh, shut up."

"I didn't say a thing."

"Well, stop *thinking*. It doesn't suit you."

The smile turned into a laugh—*huh-huh-huh*. Then,

easy as you please, he shifted eyes front and left her alone for the rest of the flight.

Disappointment and temptation rode her in equal measure, so much so she clenched her fists and let herself have a good internal scream. Because she didn't need this, feeling all breathless and weightless with all the hot flushes and the like. Avery wasn't looking for sparks. Sparks were incendiary. Their sole purpose was to start fires. And fire burned.

She couldn't have been more relieved when the helicopter finally came to rest on a helipad at the end of a jetty belonging to one of the bigger resorts just north of Crescent Cove.

Even better when she saw Claudia waving as if Avery had been rescued from some deserted island.

And, bless his shiny black shoes, there was Luke, leaning against the Tropicana Nights shuttle bus in the car park at the far end of the jetty. Tall, and handsome, with half an eye on his phone.

Hull was there too. The beast sat apart, upright on a cluster of rocks in the shadow of a tilting palm tree at the end of the jetty. Not Jonah's dog? Maybe somebody should tell the dog that.

Avery managed to get herself unstrapped without help. But getting down was another matter.

Strong hands at her waist, Jonah dropped her to the ground. She didn't dare breathe as all that hard muscle and sun-drenched skin imprinted itself upon her and good. The second her feet hit terra firma, she peeled herself away.

"Here's hoping that's the last time you feel the need to come to my salvation."

Jonah didn't second that thought. In fact, even as he stood there, like some big hot, muscly statue, the look in his eyes told her he wasn't on the same page at all. With a shake of her head, she turned and walked away.

"Avery," he called.

She scrunched her eyes tight a second, held her breath. And when she looked back, she saw he was holding out her missing shoes.

Meaning at some point after he'd dropped her at the Tea Tree he must have gone looking for them. Which was actually...really...nice.

She walked to him, hating every second of it. And when she slid her fingers into the straps, her fingers brushed his. And there was the spark. Hard, fast, debilitating.

Their eyes met. One corner of his sexy mouth lifted. *Deny that*, he said without saying anything at all. And her heart thumped so hard against her ribs she dared not look down in case it was leaving a mark.

"Aaaaaveryyyy!" Claudia's voice carried on the air.

Jonah's eyes followed the sound, and lit up with an easy-going smile, one not fuelled with sex appeal and intent. When his eyes once again found hers, he caught her staring. And the next smile was all sex, all intent, all for her.

"Don't say it," she said, walking backwards, using her dangly sandals as a shield. "Don't even think it. The end."

And then she turned, looped her arm through Claudia's and swung her away from the crazy-making guy at her back.

"You okay?" Claude asked. "You looked all flushed."

"Sunburn," Avery deadpanned. Then bumped shoulders with her friend. "Now did you guys *really* drive out here just to get me?"

"Of course we did. When Jonah rang to say you'd nearly been eaten by a giant squid I had to find out the real story!"

"Funny man," she mumbled, "that friend of yours."

"Seems he's becoming quite the friend of *yours*. I've never been on his chopper before. Not once."

Avery turned back to find Jonah leaning on his helicopter watching her. The big wolf dog now sitting at his heels was watching her too.

"What is with the dog anyway?" she asked, distracting Claudia. "Jonah says it's not his."

"And yet there they are, their own private little wolf pack. It's kind of romantic really, in a tragic, Heathcliffian loner-type way."

"Except instead of cold, wet, English moors he wanders a sunny Aussie beach?"

"Exactly."

"Not quite so tragic, then."

Claude grinned. "If you're going to wander anywhere the rest of your days, might as well be here."

Avery opened her mouth to ask if there'd been a "Catherine" to send him wandering the moors/beach in the first place. Then snapped it shut tight. Jonah North was none of her business. Hopefully she could get through the rest of her holiday without tripping over the guy or she'd go back home even more tightly wound than when she left.

They neared the end of the jetty and Avery looked up and saw Luke watching them from his position at the shuttle bus. She stood straighter, smiled big, and lifted her hand in a cheery wave.

Luke shot her a nod. A smile. Just looking at him she knew he'd know his way around a wine cellar. That he knew a Windsor knot from a Prince Albert. He'd slip into any dinner party with her friends back home as if he were born there. And yet she could still feel Jonah behind her, even at twenty paces away.

"Thanks for the offer of a lift," she said to Claude, backing away, "but I think I'll walk back. Stretch my legs. Lunch later? Just you and me?"

"Lunch would be great."

Avery gave Claude a big hug, then wiggled her fisherman's hat tighter on her head, the strap of her bag digging into the sunburn on her shoulder, and headed off.

* * *

Hull padding along warm and strong beside him, Jonah ambled down the jetty towards Luke.

While he waited for his old mate to finish up his phone call, Jonah's eyes slid to the retreating back of the crazy-making blonde in the oversized green T-shirt that stopped just short of her backside. And he brooded.

With Claude the woman was like some kind of puppy dog, all floppy and happy and bright. Waving to Luke she'd practically preened. While with *him* she was a flinty little thing, all snappy and sharp. It was as if she didn't know who she was. Or that she felt a need to be different things to different people. And *then* there was all that talk of her 'reconnecting' with some other guy... And Jonah was a man who appreciated good faith above all. And yet there was no denying her physical response any time he came near. Or, for that matter, his. It had been a while since he'd felt that kind of spark. Real, instant, fiery. And like a fish-hook in the gut, it wasn't letting go. Every touch, every look, every time he caught her staring at him with those stunning odd eyes it dug deeper.

He should have known better. He *did* know better. Seemed his hormones didn't give a flying hoot. They wanted what they wanted. And they wanted restless little tourist Avery Shaw.

Rach had been a tourist too. Even while she'd *insisted* she wanted to be more. Even when her actions hadn't backed it up, even when she'd never really tried to fit in.

Not that he'd let himself see it. He'd been too caught up in the fantasy of a girl like her seeing something worthy in a drifter like him.

When *she'd* had enough of playing tourist and moved back to Sydney, he'd followed. She'd let him, probably for no stronger reason than that it felt good to be chased. While Jonah had given up everything, leaving his home, his friends, his way of life, selling his father's boat, getting a job on the docks as if water were water. Unable to admit he was wrong…

When he'd had run out of money and finally admitted to himself that it was all a farce, she was happily ensconced in her old life, while his was in tatters.

Lesson learned.

His biggest mistake had been thinking something was more than what it was.

Meaning he had to decide what this was, and soon. A spark. Attraction. A deep burn. Nothing more. So long as he owned it, he could use it. Enjoy it. Till it burned itself out.

Yeeeah, mind made up between one breath and the next. Next time he saw Avery Shaw it was game on.

As for her mysterious 'reconnect'? If it wasn't all some story she'd made up and the guy hadn't manned up by now, fool had missed his chance.

"Jonah, my man," Luke called, jerking Jonah from his reverie.

Jonah moved in and gave his old friend a man hug.

"Funny," said Luke, "riding in the resort van got me to thinking about that summer I used to hitch rides in your Kombi, driving as far as it took to find the best surf of the day."

"Ah, the surf. I remember it well."

"And the girls."

"That too," Jonah added, laughing. They'd spent long summers surfing and laughing and living and loving with no thought of the future. Of how things might ever be different.

Look at them both now. Luke, in his suit and tie, phone glued to his palm, a touch of London in his accent. Jonah the owner of a fleet of boats, a helicopter, more. Successful, single…satisfied.

"Found any wave time since you've been back?" Jonah

asked. If he had it'd be more than Jonah had seen in a long time.

Luke bent down to give Hull a quick scoff about the ears, which Hull took with good grace. "Nah," he said, frowning. "Not likely to either."

Maybe not completely satisfied, then.

"Aww, young Claude have you wrapped around her little finger, does she?"

Luke straightened slowly and slid his hands into his pockets, his gaze skidding to their sunny little friend at the end of the jetty. "Let's just say it's taking longer than I might have hoped for us to...set the tone of our new business relationship."

Jonah laughed. Luke had been one of the big reasons he'd even been able to carve a new life for himself in the cove after Rach. He owed him more than money could repay. But not enough he'd take on Claudia Davis. He patted his friend on the back and said, "Good luck there."

"And good luck there," Luke said, the tone of his voice shifting. Jonah followed the shift in Luke's eyeline to find him watching Avery shuffle off into the distance, her thongs catching at the soft sand, her ridiculously inappropriate city-girl shoes dangling from one hand—the shoes he'd spent an hour the night before combing the moonlit beach to track down.

"Cute," Luke added, both men watching till she disappeared into a copse of palms.

Jonah admitted, "She is that."

"She was here once before, you know," said Luke. "Ten odd years ago. With her family. Odd couple, I remember—father quiet, mother loud, dripping money. And Avery? Skinny little thing. Shy. Overly well-bred. Had a crush on me too, if memory serves. Big eyes following me up and down the beach. If I'd known then she'd turn out like that..."

Jonah missed whatever Luke said next as blood roared between his ears and a grave weight settled in his gut, as if he'd swallowed a load of concrete.

Luke.

Avery planned to 'reconnect' with Luke.

The way she'd bounced on her toes as she'd waved to the guy just now, fixing her hair, smiling from ear to ear, the sunshine smile and all. Hell, she'd called out Luke's name that day on the beach, hadn't she?

The concrete in Jonah's gut now turning his limbs to dead weights, he turned to face his old friend to find Luke's gaze was on the water now, following the line of white foam far out to sea. Avery clearly not on his mind. As the guy hadn't a single clue.

Hull whimpered at his side. Jonah sank a hand into the dog's fur before Hull lifted his big snout and pressed it into Jonah's palm, leaving a trail of slobber Jonah wiped back into his fur.

It had been Luke who'd put up the money to buy back his father's boat when Jonah had come back home to the cove with his tail between his legs, calling it 'back pay of petrol money' from the times he'd hitched rides in that old Kombi. From there Jonah had worked day and night, fixing the thing up, accepting reef charters to earn enough money to buy the next boat, and the next, and the next. Becoming a grown-up, forging a future, one intricately tied to the cove, his home.

He'd paid Luke back within a year. But he *owed* him more than money could ever repay.

Which was precisely why, even while the words tasted like battery acid on the back of his tongue, he said, "You should ask her out."

"Who?" Luke's phone rang, then, frowning, he strolled away, investing everything into the call. Leaving Jonah to throw out his arms in surrender.

Which was when Claudia stormed up. "No getting through to him now." Then, shaking her head, she turned to Jonah with a smile. "Now that you've brought my girl home safe, what's the plan?"

"Work," Jonah said. "Haircut, maybe."

"Don't you dare! Your curls are gorgeous."

Jonah glanced down at the petite bundle of energy at his side. A woman who was as much a part of the landscape as he was. A local. Someone who'd stick around. "Your little friend told me you think I'm hot."

"She did not!"

Jonah smiled back.

Claudia gaped at him a moment before she burst out laughing. "Of course I think you're hot. The entire region of females thinks you're hot. Anyone else simply hasn't met you yet." She squeezed his biceps, gave a little a shiver, and then went back to walking congenially at his side.

And *that* was why he'd never gone there with her. Because while Claudia was cute as a button, and local, and available, there'd never been that spark. That all-out, wham-bam, knock-the-wind-from-your-sails spark that he knew was out there for the having.

He knew because he'd felt it.

Twice.

The first woman who'd made him feel that way had made him believe it was real, until the day she woke up and decided it wasn't.

The other one had convinced herself she wanted to 're-connect' with his best mate.

To think, his week had started with such high hopes.

CHAPTER FIVE

FEELING BETTER ABOUT the world after having just signed a lucrative contract to keep his newest luxury yacht on call for clients of the Hawaiian Punch Hotel, Jonah set off through the outdoor Punch Bowl Bistro, Hull meeting him at the door and padding along beside him.

He'd nearly hit the path between resorts when Hull whimpered, ran around in front of him, and nudged his hand with his nose.

"What's up, boy?" Jonah asked, right at the moment he realised it wasn't a what, it was a *who*.

For there at a table sat Avery Shaw.

It had been days since he'd set eyes on her. After the Luke revelation, he'd figured total avoidance was the safest bet.

Now as he watched her sit at the table doing nothing more seductive than swirl a straw round and round in a pink drink the staunched heat clawed its way through his gut like some creature kept hungry way too long, settling with a discomforting ache in his groin.

Before he even felt his feet move Jonah was threading his way towards her.

Hull got to her first, curling around the base of her table and lying down as if he was expected.

"Hey!" Avery said, her face lighting up with surprised laughter. With sunshine.

Then he saw the moment she knew what Hull's sudden appearance meant. Her head whipped up, her eyes locking onto his, lit by an instant and wild flicker of heat, before she tilted her chin as if to say, *I refuse to admit my cheeks are flushed because of you.*

Yeah, honey, he thought, *right back at ya.*

Then her eyes slid past him, to the empty doorway leading inside the hotel. And all sunshine fled to leave way for sad Bambi. What scrape had she gotten herself into now?

His vision expanded to notice her knife and fork were untouched. The bread basket mere crumbs.

And he knew.

Luke. She'd made plans to have lunch with Luke. And for whatever reason, the goose had clearly failed to show.

That was the moment Jonah should have walked away. Considering how much he owed Luke, how long a friendship they'd enjoyed, and the fact that being anywhere near Avery made him feel like a rubber band stretched at its limit, it was the only honourable option.

And yet he dragged out a chair and—blocking Ms Shaw's view of the front door—sat down.

Luke not carving out time for a surf during his first time in the cove for years was one thing. But not knowing when a gorgeous woman wanted to get to know him better? Unforgivable.

And she was gorgeous. Her pale hair clipped neatly away from her face in some kind of fancy braid, eyes soft and sooty, lips slicked glossy pink, ropes of tiny beads draping over a black-and-white dress that made her look like a million bucks. If he ever needed a reminder she was not from here, that whatever spark was between them had *no* future…

Then she had to go and say, "Oh, you're *staying*?"

And that was it. He was hunkered in. His voice was

one notch above a growl as he said, "Nice to see you too, Miss Shaw."

She pointed over his shoulder. "I'm actually—"

"Thrilled to see me?"

She swallowed, clearly undecided as to whether to admit why she was there alone. In the end she kept her mouth shut.

"Saw you sitting here all alone and figured it was the gentlemanly thing to rescue you from your lonesomeness," he said, casually perusing the menu he already knew by heart. He put the menu down, and settled back in his chair, sliding a leg under the table, navigating Hull's big body. Only to find himself knocking shoes with Avery. Her high-heel-clad foot slipped away.

"Really?"

"Hand to heart," he said, action matching words.

Her eyes flickered to his hand, across his chest, over his shoulders, to his hair, pausing longest of all on his mouth, before skimming back to his eyes. And while he knew it was not smart, was *traitorous* even, he enjoyed every second of it.

"Is your dog even allowed in here?" she said, pointing under the table.

He lifted a shoulder, let it fall. "Not my dog."

She leaned forward a little then. Her mouth kicked into a half-smile.

"Well, whoever's dog he is," that mouth said, "he's sitting on my foot. And my toes are now officially numb. He's enormous."

"Huge," said Jonah, lifting his eyes to hers to find them darkened, determined, as if making some kind of connection between man and beast. Enough that he had to fight the urge to adjust himself.

Wrapping her lips around her straw in a way that was

entirely unfair, she asked, "So how did you and Hull meet?"

"Found him on the beach when he was a pup—a tiny, scrawny, shivery ball of mangy, matted fluff, near dead with exhaustion and hunger. Odds on he wasn't the only one in the litter dumped. Probably tied up in a sack full of rocks and thrown overboard. He's been crazy afraid of water ever since. Took him home, cleaned him up, fed him, and that was it."

"You saved his life and that doesn't make him your responsibility?"

"Never bought him, never sought him. Don't get me wrong, he's a great dog. And if he thinks you're a threat to me, he'd like nothing better than to tear you limb from limb."

"Me?" she said, flicking a quick glance at the now-snoring lump under the table. "A threat?"

Jonah shot her a flat look. She was the biggest threat he'd met in a long time.

By the rise and fall of her chest she got his meaning loud and clear.

Then, frowning, she slipped her fingers down the length of beads and stared at the little bits of pineapple bobbing on top of her drink. Most likely because of the elephant in the room. Or *not* in the room as he hadn't showed up.

Rubbing a hand up the back of his neck, Jonah wished he'd simply called Luke and asked where the hell he was. Or at the very least what his intentions towards her were, if any. Hell, he'd done such a fine job avoiding the woman, for all Jonah knew she and Luke could have been dating for days.

That thought clouded his vision something mad, but didn't put a dent in the attraction that rode over him like a rogue wave. The only right thing to do was leave. Walk away. Avoid more. At least until he knew where they all stood.

He quietly schooled his features, looked casually over the restaurant, towards the still-empty doorway. And set his feet to the floor as he made to leave her be.

When the waiter came shuffling up. "Oh, good, your company's finally arrived. Are you ready to order now?"

Jonah glanced back at Avery to find her blushing madly now, nose buried in the menu.

"Um…he's… I guess. Just… Can I have a second, please? Sorry!"

When she looked up at the waiter she shot him her sunshine smile, catching Jonah in its wake. The effect was like a smack to the back of the head, rattling his thoughts till he could no longer quite put them back in order.

"This is my first time here," she said. "What would you recommend?"

Jonah jabbed a finger at the rump steak. "Rare." Motioned to his friend under the table and said, "Two."

"Make it three," said Avery, picking out a pricey glass of red wine to go along with it.

When the waiter wandered off, she lowered the menu slowly, frowned at it a second, before taking a breath and looking up at him. Clearly bemused as to how they'd got there. Just the two of them. Having lunch.

He wished he knew himself.

Avery shuffled on her chair and said, "So, Jonah, did you always want to work with boats growing up?"

"Boats? We're really heading down that path?"

"Boats. The weather. You pick!" She threw her arms out in frustration. "Or you can just sit there all silent and broody for all I care. I was perfectly happy to have lunch on my own before you came along."

"Were you, now?"

She glared at him then, the truth hovering between them.

She grabbed her pink drink and slugged the thing down till it was empty. The fact that she thought she needed booze to get through lunch with him was actually kind of comforting. Then she licked her lips in search of stray pink drink. And Jonah had never felt less comfortable in his life.

He rubbed a hand over his jaw, hoping the prickle of stubble might wake him the hell up, but instead finding his cheeks covered in overly long scruff. The lack of a close shave was just about the only throwback to his old life. When the idea of lunch with a pretty girl was as normal to him as a day spent in the sea, not something fraught with malignant intentions and mortal peril.

He dropped his calloused fingers to his lap, so like his father's fingers.

She wanted to talk boats? What the hell. "My father worked on boats."

"Oh, a family tradition."

Jonah coughed out a laugh. His father wouldn't have thought so. As brutally proud as Jonah was of everything Charter North had become, he knew his father wouldn't have understood. The types of boats, or the number. Karl North had only ever owned the one boat, the *Mary-Jane*, named after Jonah's mother. And in the end she'd killed him.

"He was a lobster man," Jonah went on. "A diver. Over the reefs. Live collection, by hand." No big hauls, just long hours, negligible conversation, even less outward displays of affection, not much energy left for anything not on the boat.

Avery picked up on the *"Was?"*

"He died at sea when I was seventeen. He'd taught me a thing or two about boats before then, though. I could pull a boat engine apart and put it back together by the time I was fourteen."

"You think that's impressive? At fourteen I could speak French and create a five-course menu for twenty people."

"You cook?"

"I created the *menu*. Cook cooked it."

"Of course."

She grinned. *Sunshine.* And when she slid her fingers over the rope of beads, this time he felt the slide of those fingers somewhere quite else. "And your mother?"

"She left when I was eleven. I haven't seen her since. Hard being married to a man whose first love is big and blue. When the summer storms threaten to turn every boat inside out and upside down. When quotas laws changed, or the crops just weren't there. He went back out there the next day and tried again, because that's what men did."

And there you have it, folks, he thought, dragging in a breath. Most he'd said about his own folks…probably ever. Locals understood. Rach hadn't ever asked. While Avery dug it out of him with no more than a look.

Jonah shifted on his chair.

"My turn?" she said.

"Why the hell not?"

Grinning, this time less sunshine, more sass, she leaned down to wrap her lips around the edge of her glass, found it empty, left a perfect pink kiss in their place.

"My parents are both still around. Dad's an investment banker, busy man, Yankees fan—" A quick fist-pump. "Go Yanks! My mother earned her living the Park Avenue way—divorce—and is a fan of spending Dad's money. While I am the good daughter: cheerful, encouraging, conciliatory."

Jonah struggled to imagine this caustic creature being *conciliatory.* Until he remembered her snuggling up to Claude, bouncing on her heels as she waved to Luke. *Luke.* He frowned. Forgot what he was thinking about, or more likely shoved it way down deep inside.

"Even my apartment is equidistant from both of theirs," she went on.

"You're Switzerland?"

She laughed.

Chin resting on her upturned palm, she said, "Between you and me and this dog who's not yours, being Switzerland is exhausting. I didn't realise how much Switzerland needed a break till I came here. You know what my mother is doing right this second? Organising a *party* to celebrate the tenth anniversary of the divorce. Manhattan rooftop, over a hundred guests, yesterday she called to tell me about the comedian she's hired to roast my father, who won't even be there."

The waiter came back with her wine, which she wrapped her hands around as if it were a life ring. "Worst part? She actually thought I'd be dying to help. As if my relationship with my father—such as it is—means nothing."

Her eyes flickered, a pair of small lines creasing the skin above her nose. And when she shook her head, it was as if a flinty shell had crumbled to reveal a whole different Avery underneath. A woman trying to do the right thing in her small way against near impossible odds.

He got that.

With a shrug and an embarrassed twist of her sweet lips Avery gave him a look.

He opened his mouth to say…something, when Hull sat up with a muffled woof, saving him from saying anything at all. Seconds later the waiter arrived in a flurry. Hull's raw steak had been pounded into mush by the chef. Avery's and Jonah's sat in sweet and juicy seas of mushroom pepper sauce.

After the waiter left, Jonah said, "You know what Switzerland should do next?"

"What's that?" she asked, her hand flinching a little as she put her napkin on her lap.

"Eat," he said, shoving a chunk of steak in his mouth.

Her smile was new—soft, swift, and lovely. And Jonah breathed through the realisation that there couldn't *possibly* be any more last-minute saves.

The next time he nearly did something with this woman it would be all on him.

"So what's the plan for the afternoon?" Jonah asked later as they ambled onto the palm-tree-lined path that curled between the resorts and led back to the main street.

"Tropicana, I guess. Track down Claude. Sit on her so that we can get more than two minutes together in a row."

"How's she doing?" *Another scintillating question.* And yet he couldn't let her go. Not yet. The rubber-band feeling was back, tugging him away even as it pulled him right on back.

"Great. I think. Truth is, she's been so busy running the resort I've probably spent more time with you this holiday than her."

Her cheeks flushed as she realised what she'd said. And something swelled hot and sudden inside him. She'd spent more time with *him*. Not *Luke*. Meaning nothing had happened between them. Yet.

"Come on," he growled, pressing a hand to her back as he shielded her from a group of oblivious teenagers taking up the whole path as they headed towards the Punch Bowl.

Jonah kept his hand at her back as they continued along the now-secluded path. And she let him.

When they reached a fork in the path—one way headed straight to the beach, the other hooking back to the rear entrance to the Tropicana Nights—she turned towards him, and his hand slid naturally to her waist.

Wrong, he told himself, *on so many levels.* And yet it felt so right. His hand in the dip of her waist. Her scent curling beneath his nose. Her mismatched eyes picking up the earthy colours around her.

Her voice was breathless as she said, "Thanks for lunch. It was nice to have company."

Streaks of sunlight shot through the palm leaves above and shone in her pale hair and the pulse that beat in her throat. Through the thin dress he felt the give of her warm flesh beneath his rough palm. She leaned into his touch without even knowing it.

It finally drove him over the edge.

"Even if it wasn't the company you wanted?"

Her eyes flashed. Her cheeks flushed pink. Before she could move away, his second hand joined his first at her waist. And he pressed an inch closer. Two. Till their hips met. Her breath shot from her lungs in a whoosh and her top teeth came down over her bottom lip.

He lifted a hand to run his thumb over the spot, tugging the pink skin, leaving the pad of his thumb moist. "Luke is a fool," Jonah said, his voice so rough his throat hurt.

Her eyes widened, but she didn't deny it. Then they widened even more as she lifted her hands to press against his chest. "Is *that* why you had lunch with me? He couldn't come and sent you to soften the blow?"

"Hell, no," Jonah barked. "I'm nobody's flunky. And Luke's a stand-up guy. Doesn't mean that sometimes he doesn't know a good thing when it's right under his nose."

What the hell was he doing? Trying to talk her into the guy's arms? No. He was making sure she was sure. Because he was beyond sure that he wanted to kiss her. Taste her. Hell, he wanted to throw her over his shoulder and take her back to his cave and get it on till she cried out *his* name.

"He's your friend," she said, her fingers drifting to lie flat against his chest. Jonah's heart rocked against his ribs.

"Which gives me the right to call him out. And if the guy thought any place was better than being right here, right now, with a woman like you, who feels like you feel, and smells as good as you smell, and is into team sports as much as you—"

She laughed at that one, a dreamy gleam in her darkening eyes.

"He's worse than a fool," Jonah finished. "He's too late."

Avery's hands curled against his chest. He held his breath as he waited for her to take them away. Instead they gripped his polo shirt, her fingernails scraping cotton against skin, sending shards of heat straight to his groin. And he pressed back until she bumped against the white stuccoed wall beneath the palms.

Then, hauling Avery against him, with an expulsion of breath and self-control, Jonah laid his lips on hers.

He'd expected sweetness and experience—a woman couldn't be that gorgeous and not make the most of it.

What he didn't expect was the complete assault on his senses. Or the searing thread of need that wrapped tight about him, following the path of her hands as they slid up into his hair, deepening where her body arched against his, throbbing at every pulse point on his body.

Not a pause, or a breath, her lips simply melted under his, soft and delicious. And he drank her in as if it had been coming for days, eons, forever. He had no idea how long that kiss kept him in its thrall before he eased back, the cling of their lips parting on a sigh.

Slowly the rest of the world came back online until Jonah felt the warmth of the sunlight dappling through the trees, and the sound of the nearby waves lapping gently against the sand, and Avery, soft and trembling in his arms.

Then she looked up at him, shell-shocked. As if she'd never been kissed that way in her life. It was such an ego surge, it took everything in him not to wrap his arms around her, rest his forehead against hers, and just live in the moment. To forget about anything else. Anyone.

Hell, he thought, reality hitting like a Mack truck.

How readily he'd just caved. And kissed her. Avery Shaw. Claude's friend. Luke's…who the hell knew what? And until that point pain in his proverbial ass.

He dug deep to find whatever ruthlessness he'd once upon a time dredged up to take a dilapidated old lobster boat and turn it into an empire, and used it to put enough physical distance between himself and Avery that she wrapped her arms about her as if she was suddenly cold.

Her voice was soft as she said, "That was…unexpected."

Not to him. She'd been dragging him back to his old self—when he'd been wild, unfocused, all that mattered was following the sun—for days. Not that he was about to tell her so.

He looked at her sideways. "What was I supposed to do with you looking up at me like that?"

She blinked. "Like what?"

"Like Bambi when his mother died."

Her eyes opened as wide as they could go. "You kissed me to…*cheer me up*?"

"Did it work?"

Snapping back to factory settings, her hands jerked to her hips and her eyes narrowed to dark slits. "What do you think, smart guy? Do I *appear* cheerful?"

She *appeared* even more kissable now, her hair a little dishevelled, her lips swollen, and all those waves of emotion coursing his way. She also looked confused. And a little hurt.

Not so much it stopped him from saying, "I don't know you well enough to rightly say."

She reared back as if slapped. "Wow," she said. "I knew you were a stubborn son of a bitch, Jonah. But until right now I had no idea you were a coward."

And without once looking back she stormed away.

Rubbing a hand up the back of his head, he dragged his

eyes from her retreating back to find trusty Hull sitting at his feet, looking adoring as ever. No judgment there.

"She's partly right," he said. "I am a son of a bitch."

But he wasn't a coward. Not that he was about to chase her to point that out. In fact, considering that kiss, he considered himself pretty frickin' heroic for walking away. Until that point he'd been thinking all about him; why he should stay the hell away from her. Not once had it occurred to him she ought to stay away from him. Not until he'd felt her trembling in his arms.

While he'd made the decision to remain cemented in Crescent Cove for the rest of his natural life, emotionally he would always be a nomad. It was in his blood. Passed down from his flighty mother. His voyager father. To all intents and purposes he'd been on his own since before he was even a teen. Walked himself to school. Lived off what he could cook. Skating. Surfing. Nothing tying him to anything, or any place, except choice.

When Rach had sashayed into town he'd been twenty-three, living like a big kid in his father's house on the bluff, life insurance on the verge of gone. She'd been this sophisticated outsider, come from Sydney for a week, and he'd done everything in his power to win her over. The life might not have been enough for his mum, but if this woman could stay, to him it was incontrovertible proof that *his* was the best life on earth.

She'd moved in with him after three days, and stayed for near a year.

Inevitably, she'd grown bored.

And when she left he'd been left completely untethered. Banging about inside the old house like a bird with broken wings.

After his disastrous move to Sydney with its noise, and smog, and crush of people—he'd taken control of his life. Delivering on the promise of his father's hard work.

He might not have time to connect with the better parts of his old life—with the sun, and the sea, and the big blue—but he felt otherwise fulfilled. Better, he felt *redeemed*.

And he wasn't willing to risk that feeling for anything or anyone. No matter how kissable.

Avery was in such a red-hot haze she couldn't remember how she made it back to the resort. But soon the white steps were loud beneath her high heels as she made her way into the lobby.

Mere days before she'd been delighting in her ability to say *no* to the guy, as if it were some kind of sign that with a little R and R under her belt she might have the where-withal to say the same to her folks one of these days. But *no*. One touch, one deep dark look, and she'd practically devoured him.

She lifted fingers to lips that felt bruised and tender, knowing that not being able to say no and wanting to say yes were two wholly different things, but it was hard to think straight while she could still *feel* those big strong arms wrap tight about her, his heart thundering beneath her chest, his mouth on hers.

Suddenly feeling a mite woozy, she slowed, found a column and banged her forehead against the cool faux marble. It felt so good she did it again.

"Avery."

Avery looked up, rubbing at the spot on her head as she turned to find Luke Hargreaves striding towards her in his lovely suit with his lovely face and that lovely way he had about him that didn't make her feel as if she were being whipped about inside a tornado.

Her invitation to lunch *had* been casual. An honest-to-goodness catch-up. Nothing more. As picture-perfect as he appeared she'd struggled to whip up the kind of enthusiasm required to campaign for more. Yet maybe this whole thing had been a sign. That she needed to up her game.

"Luke!" she said, leaning in for an air kiss.

"Don't you look a million bucks." He looked her up and down, making her feel...neat. If Jonah had done the same she'd have felt stripped bare. "Don't tell me today was meant to be our lunch date."

Yeah, buddy, it was. "Not to worry! I bumped into Jonah." *Argh!* "So he sat with me, and we ate. Steak." *Oh, just shut up now.*

"Was it any good?"

"I'm sorry?" she squeaked.

"The steak."

"Oh, the *steak* was excellent. Tender. Tasty." *Please shoot me now.* "If you get the chance to eat there, try it."

Nodding as if he just might, Luke ran a hand through his hair leaving tracks that settled in attractively dishevelled waves. Even that didn't have her hankering to run her fingers in their wake. Yet every time she saw a certain head full of tight dark curls it was a physical struggle not to reach out and touch.

"You know what? What are you doing right now?" he asked.

Trying not to make it obvious that my knees aren't yet fully functional after your friend kissed me senseless. You?

He glanced at his watch, frowned some more. "Miraculously I have nothing on my plate right this second, if you'd like to grab a coffee."

"No," she said, rather more sternly than she'd intended. But Avery was a Shaw. And Shaws didn't know the meaning of giving in. Look at her mother! She softened it with a smile. Then said, "Dinner. Tomorrow night. A proper catch-up." *A proper setting to see if something nice can be forged.*

"Perfect." He smiled. "Catch you then." It was a perfectly lovely smile. Her blood didn't come close to rushing; in fact it didn't give a flying hoot.

Avery made to give him a quick peck on the cheek, but instead found herself patting him chummily on the arm. Then he headed off, always with purpose in his stride that one. Unlike Jonah who, even as he got things done, had this air about him as if he had all the time in the world.

With a sigh Avery didn't much want to pick apart, she looked up and caught the eye of young Isis behind the reception desk. The girl waggled her eyebrows suggestively.

If only, Avery thought. Even Pollyanna gave a little yawn. By the time Avery slipped back to her room she collapsed on her bed and had the first nap she'd had since she was a kid. All it took to finally find the limit to her exhaustion was making a date with one man while the kiss of another still lingered on her lips.

CHAPTER SIX

JONAH SAT AT the small backstreet pub the tourists always seemed to miss—probably because it wasn't suffocated by a surfeit of palm trees and Beach Boys music. Self-flagellation being a skill he'd honed during the long months spent in Sydney, he'd invited Luke to join him.

"Thanks for filling in at lunch with Avery today, mate," Luke said.

And there went Jonah's hopes for a quiet beer.

Frosty bottle an inch from his mouth, Luke added, "I bumped into her in the lobby after I finally extricated myself from one of Claudia's presentations. All cardboard signs and permanent markers. She has a dislike for PowerPoint I'll never understand." His eyes shifted Jonah's way. "So how was lunch?"

"They do a good steak," Jonah rumbled, then chugged a third of his beer in one hit.

"So I heard."

He and Luke might only see one another once every couple of years these days, but they'd been mates long enough for Jonah to know he'd been made. *Dammit.*

He held his ground, counting the bottles of spirits lining the shelves behind the bar. Luke shifted on his chair to face Jonah. Until, thumb swishing over the face of his phone, Luke said, "In fact we have dinner plans for tomorrow night. Avery and I."

Jonah gripped his beer, even as he felt his cheek twitch in a masochistic grin. He tipped his beer in Luke's direction as he caught his old friend's gaze. "You're going, right?"

Luke pushed his phone aside, a huge smile creasing his face. "Any reason I shouldn't?"

"You stood her up once before."

Luke's smile fell. "Hardly. She'd told me she was having lunch at the Punch if I was around."

"Luke. Man. Come on. She thought it was a date."

"I don't think so, mate. You've got your wires crossed somewhere."

When had his old mate morphed from his wingman into this blinkered, workaholic monkey with a phone permanently attached to his palm? In fairness, it was probably about the time his ex-wife took his heart out with a fork.

Luke watched him a few long seconds before slowly leaning back in the leather chair. "Should be a fun night, though. Those legs. That smile. And that accent? It just kills me."

Jonah tried to sit still, remain calm, and yet he could *feel* the steam pouring from his ears. Luke clearly noticed, as suddenly he laughed as if he'd never seen anything so funny.

With a tip of his beer bottle towards Jonah, Luke said, "So, you and Miss Manhattan, eh?"

"There is no me and Miss Manhattan."

Luke grinned like a shark as he parroted back, "Jonah. Man. *Come on.*"

Jonah settled his hands around his beer and stared hard into the bubbles. "I'm right there with you on the legs. And the smile. And the accent." And the eyes. He'd had dreams about those eyes, locked onto his, turning dark with pleasure as she fell apart in his arms. "But she's my worst nightmare."

The raised eyebrow of his old friend told him he didn't believe it for a second. "From what Claude tells me, she's from money. So high maintenance, maybe."

"It's not that. She's…" Stunning, sexy, yet despite the big-city sophistication still somehow compellingly naive. She could swipe his legs out from under him if he wasn't careful. "A pain in the ass."

Luke thought on it a moment. "Then again, aren't they all?"

Jonah tapped the neck of Luke's beer bottle with his own.

"I've been around the block a few times now," Jonah went on. "I've made mistakes. I'd like to think I've learned when to trust my gut about such things."

"Since You Know Who?"

Jonah raised an eyebrow in assent. "And yet, I can't seem to…not."

"Then lucky for you the man she clearly wants is me."

At that, whatever morbid little tunnel Jonah had been staring down blinked out of existence. He leant back in his chair, and smiled at his friend. "Not as much as she thinks she does."

"Now what makes you think my charms aren't all-encompassing?"

"I have it on good knowledge that she's…in flux."

Luke's laughter rang through the bar. He sat forward. All ears. And, thankfully, not a lick of rivalry in his gaze. "I've been out of circulation too long. Since when does 'steak' stand for something else?"

"Calm down. Steak meant steak," Jonah rumbled.

"But *something* happened."

When Jonah didn't answer, Luke slammed the table so hard their beers bounced. "Jonah North, pillar of the Crescent Cove community, made out with *my* dinner date who is also apparently his worst nightmare. Was this before or after she asked me to dinner?"

Jonah's cheek twitched and his head suddenly hurt so much he couldn't see straight. "Hell."

Luke's laughter was so loud it echoed through the small bar till the walls shook. "Man, you have no idea how much I'm enjoying this. The number of times girls came up to me only to ask if the dude with the palm-tree surfboard was single... And then along comes a sophisticated out-of-towner, not instantly bowled over by your—to my mind—*deeply* hidden charms, and—"

Luke's words came to an abrupt halt as the parallel with the last great—not so great—relationship of Jonah's life came to light. Luke slapped Jonah hard on the back. "Walk away. Walk away now and do not look back."

"Sounds fine in theory."

"Yet far better in practice. Trust me," Luke said with the bitter edge of first-hand knowledge.

Jonah nodded. The *other* outsider had shaken up his whole life until it had never been remotely the same again.

But he'd been a different man back then. Barely a man at all. Alone for so long, with nothing tethering him to his life, that he'd mistaken lust for intimacy. Company for partnership. The presence of another body in his house for it finally feeling like a home again.

His foundations were stronger now. He was embedded in his life. There was no way he'd make the same mistake twice. If something happened between Avery and him, he'd be just fine. Which meant the decision was now up to her.

"You haven't heard a word I said, have you?" Luke grumbled.

"About what?"

"Battening down the hatches. And several other good boating analogies."

"What the hell do you know about boats? Or women, for that matter."

Luke stared into the middle distance a moment before grinding out an, "Amen."

Avery stood outside the elegant Botch-A-Me restaurant Luke had picked for their date, and took a moment to check her reflection in the window. Her hair was twisted into a sleek sophisticated up-do. Her platinum-toned bustier was elegant and sexy, her wide-legged black pants floaty and sensual. Her favourite teardrop diamond earrings glinted in the light of the tiki torches lighting the restaurant with a warm golden glow.

The man didn't stand a chance.

Pity then that as her focus shifted as she looked through the window, she imagined for a second she'd seen a head of darkly curled hair.

Seriously? After the way Jonah had acted as if that kiss was some kind of *consolation* prize. Forget *him*. It was why she was here tonight after all. Only her damn heart wouldn't give up on him. Pathetic little thing couldn't think past the kiss at all.

Suddenly the dark curls moved and Luke's face came into view, and Avery's stomach sank. She wasn't imagining things. Jonah was there. With Luke. And they were clearly a couple of drinks down. Avery's stomach trembled even as it fell to her knees.

"Hey, kiddo! Sorry I'm late."

Avery turned to find Claudia beside her, peering through the window, her wispy blonde hair caught back in a pretty silver clip, and—for once out of uniform—looking effortlessly lovely in an aqua maxi-dress that made her blue eyes pop.

"Late for what?"

"Ah, dinner? I begged Luke to use the Grand Cayman

back at the Tropicana—the new chef I just hired is fantasmagorical. But *he* insisted *we* need to check out the competition. Everything okay? You look a little unwell."

"No. Everything's fine," Avery said, while the truth was she now shared Claude's urge to slap Luke across the back of the head. As for Jonah? Knees and soft body parts came to mind. All four of them at the same table was going to be a disaster.

Her usual MO would be to bounce about, create some cheery diversion to keep every faction distracted before it escalated into something she couldn't control. It was what she'd do back home.

Or she could face the music.

Taking a deep breath, Avery slipped a hand into the crook of Claudia's elbow and dragged her inside. Avery motioned to the host so that she could see her dining party and made a beeline for the table near the edge of the room, her heart beating so hard she could hear the swoosh of it behind her ears.

Luke saw her coming first, and gave her an honest-to-goodness smile that started in his mouth before landing in his lovely brown eyes. She might have forgiven him if not for the fact that she knew the moment his companion noticed it too. Jonah's buff brown forearm with white shirtsleeves rolled to his elbows moved to slide across the back of his chair, as his head turned and his eyes found hers.

Nothing like a polite smile there. In fact, Jonah was scowling at her as if the fact that he'd trapped her into a kiss gave him some kind of right to be upset with her for making a date with another man.

Gripping her sparkly purse so he couldn't see her trembling, Avery dragged her eyes from his and found Luke standing. Such a gentleman, unlike certain others who were giving her a once-over that made her feel as if her sophistication had been peeled all the way back to skin.

"Lovely to see you, *Luke*," she said.

"Evening, Avery. Don't you look stunning?"

"Thank you. As do you."

Jonah coughed beside her.

With a smile she leant into Luke for a kiss. With a light hand on her hip, he pressed his lips to her cheek. *Nice lips,* she thought. *Firm.* The hand on her hip brief but sure. And he smelled great. When he pulled away she waited for that lovely feeling of bereftness that came when a lover was no longer close enough to touch.

And realised with a sense of impending doom she'd be waiting forever.

"Good evening, Avery," said a deep voice to her left.

Avery looked into the deep grey eyes of Jonah North. He'd stood. *Belatedly.* And yet she had to knock her knees together to hold back the tide of heat that swept over her at the mere sight of him.

"Jonah," she managed.

All she got for her effort was a flicker of an eyebrow, and a slow smile. She leant in for a perfunctory kiss, trying not to remember with quite so much clarity the other kiss. Failing spectacularly as his hand landed on her hip like a brand. The touch of his stubble against her cheek was a delicious rasp that she felt at the backs of her knees. And when he pulled away she felt not so much bereft as bulldozed.

She blinked. And when a smile finally reached his eyes, making them crinkle, making them gleam, she realised that she probably looked exactly like she felt.

"Claude," said Luke, "looking just as lovely."

Claudia stood behind her chair at that, her lips tightening as if she was waiting for the "but." But when it didn't come she gave Luke a quick nod. His eyes darkened, before, with a tilt of his lips, he returned the nod.

Then, Mr Oblivious proceeded to help *Claudia* into her

chair. Meaning Avery had to put up with Jonah doing the same for her, leaving her feeling every inch of exposed skin in her shimmery strapless top.

Then Luke sat on one side of Avery looking intently at the menu, Jonah sat on the other staring her down, while Claudia's eyes smiled in relief over the top of a cocktail she must have ordered before she'd ever arrived.

Oh, well. She'd admit romantic defeat where it came to the estimable Luke Hargreaves, but that didn't mean she couldn't have a very nice catch-up with the boy she'd once known.

And if that pissed off the man on the other side of the table, well, he could lump it.

An hour later, Avery was so exhausted from being charming she could barely sit up straight. Taking a breather, she let the fifties torch song in the background and the chatter of the three friends float over her.

"You okay, Ave?" Claudia asked, the second Avery closed her eyes.

"Shh," she said, opening one eye, "I love this song."

Claudia listened. Then hummed in agreement. "Don't make 'em like they used to."

When the men had nothing to say to that, Claude jabbed them both in the arm. "Talk about not making 'em like they used to… Come on. One of you please ask the poor woman to dance."

"Claude—" Avery blushed. And blushed some more when Luke pushed his chair back and held out a hand. With a cock of his head towards the dance floor he invited her to join him.

She felt Jonah's eyes on hers, but stopped herself from looking his way. With a smile she put her hand in Luke's and lifted to her feet before following him to the dance floor to find they were the only ones there.

Without preamble he swung her out to the end of one arm before hauling her back. She grabbed him tight, breathless with laughter, her fingers gripping his upper arms. And then with a grace she couldn't have hoped for he calmed them into a perfect sway.

She glanced over his shoulder to find Jonah watching her, his white shirt doing its best to cage all that well-earned muscle, the collar slightly askew as if he'd torn the top button open in a hurry, his eyes dark and shadowed in the low lighting. Her stomach sparked, her skin tightening. When he lifted his drink in salute, she knew she'd been staring.

Luke felt…nice, safe. He smelled…clean. He danced…really well. The tiki torches about the edges of her vision wavered and gleamed, catching on jewellery, on sparkles in women's clothes. It would have been such a nice story to one day tell their grandchildren…if only she didn't find it easier to wax lyrical about her surroundings than the man in her arms.

Luke started, and turned them both to find Jonah behind him, a finger raised to tap Luke's shoulder. Yet the interloper's deep grey eyes were only on Avery's as he said, "May I cut in?"

Eyebrows raised, a not-so-surprised smile on his face, Luke turned back to Avery for an answer. "What do you think?" he asked. "Should I release you into the clutches of this ragamuffin?"

Should he? Avery felt as if her world were tipping on its axis. But when her eyes slid back to Jonah's and she felt her entire body fill to the brim with sparks, she knew with a finality that tightened her stomach into a fist that nice and safe weren't in her near future.

She must have nodded, or maybe she simply drifted into Jonah's arms. Either way, she didn't even feel Luke slip away, just that Jonah was there. She had one hand in his, his other hand burning a palm-print into her lower back—her whole body melted.

On the edge of her consciousness, the song came to an end. But they didn't stop swaying. Her eyes didn't leave Jonah's. And his didn't leave hers.

He pulled her closer still, till—without either of them breaking any indecency laws—every bit of her that could touch every bit of him did. When he lowered his hand so that his little finger dipped below the waistline of her pants, her breath hitched in her throat.

"Avery," he said, his voice rough and low.

"I know," she said, and as his arms folded around her she leant her head on his chest, the deep thundering of his heart more than a match for hers.

Whether it was the cocktails Claude was knocking back or Avery's sudden rose-tinted view of the world, she couldn't say—but the rest of the night Luke and Claude seemed to get along without sniping at one another. Which was *nice*. Or it would have been if Jonah hadn't kept finding ways to touch Avery. The slide of his foot against hers, resting his hand on her knee, drifting a finger over her shoulder. At that point *nice* was no longer in her vocabulary.

When the last dessert plate was cleared, and the bill had been paid, Claude sat back with a hand over her stomach. "Who's going to roll me back to my big beautiful home that I adore so very much?" She glanced at Avery before her gaze slid to Jonah. "Forget that. I'll be just fine on my own."

With a sigh, Luke pushed back his chair before collecting Claude with a hand under her elbow. She whipped her elbow away as if burned. But Luke took her hand and threaded it through his elbow and locked it there tight. "Come on, sunshine. Let's get back to our crumbling white elephant before it falls into the sea."

"She's not crumbling. She has…elegant patina."

Luke shot Avery a smile, Jonah a told-you-so look, then, with Claude babbling about fresh paint and passion, they disappeared through the door.

Jonah stood and held out a hand. This time there was no hesitation as Avery put her hand in his.

Outside the air was still and sweet, the road back from the beach devoid of crowds, the moon raining its brilliant light over the world. And as soon as Avery's eyes met Jonah's they were in one another's arms.

The moment their lips met, she felt parts of herself implode on impact. Heat sluiced through the gaps, her nerves went into total meltdown until she was a trembling mass of need, and want, and unhinged desire.

The sweet clinging kiss of the day before was a mere memory as Jonah plundered her senses with his touch, with the insistent seduction of his lips, the intimate rhapsody of his tongue.

Desperation riding them both, Avery's back slammed against a wall, the rough brick catching on her top, her hair, her skin. But she didn't care. She merely tilted and shifted until the kiss was as deep as it could be.

It wasn't deep enough.

All those clothes in the way. She tugged his shirt from his jeans and tore the thing open, her eyes drinking in the sight of him as her hand slid up his torso, through the tight whorls of hair, palming the scorching-hot skin, loving the harsh suck of his breath and the way the hard ridges of muscle jumped under her touch.

With a growl he lifted her bodily, till she wrapped her legs around him, her head rolling back as his mouth went to her neck, to her shoulder, the sweet spot behind her ear.

When he tugged her top down an inch, his nails scraping her soft skin, his tongue finding the edge of her nipple, she froze, the tiniest thread of sense coming back to her from somewhere deep down inside. It might be near midnight, but they were in a public place, her legs around his waist, one arm cradling his head, the other beneath his shirt and riding the length of his back.

"Jonah," she said, her voice a whisper on the still night air.

She felt him tense, then relax, just a fraction, but enough that he lifted his head to rest it against her collarbone, his deep breaths warming her bone deep.

Avery opened her eyes to the sky.

When Jonah had asked her to dance Luke hadn't been surprised. He'd been waiting for it. Which meant it hadn't been spur of the moment. Hadn't been some kind of He-Has-Girl-So-I-Want-Girl reaction.

This big, beautiful, difficult, taciturn, hard-to-crack man had staked his claim.

And scary as the feelings tumbling about inside of her at that knowledge were, the brilliance of them won out.

"Take me home, Jonah."

He held his breath, his chest pressing hard into hers so that she could feel the steady thump of his big strong heart.

"You sure?"

She slid a hand into the back of his hair, the tight curls ensnaring her fingers.

He growled, and she trapped the sound with her kiss as she strove to make the best mistake of her life.

CHAPTER SEVEN

AVERY'S FIRST GLIMPSE inside Jonah's place—a shack tucked away in the hills behind the cove—held no surprises; the place was a total man cave.

Surfboards and a kayak lined up on hooks in the entrance hall. Battered running shoes lay discarded on a small pile of sand under a top-of-the-range road bike. A slew of mismatched barstools shoved under an island bench in the utilitarian kitchen the only dining option, and along with a big dark sprawling lounge were a recycled timber coffee table covered in boating magazines and mug rings and a projector screen taller than she was.

Avery glanced back towards the front door; but as the last time she'd checked there was still no sign yet of the man himself.

Right in the middle of a pretty full-on make-out session on his porch, Hull had let out a gut-curdling yowl before taking off into the forest. And if Avery's heart hadn't already been racing like the Kentucky Derby from that kiss, the sight of big brawny Jonah staring in distress after his dog—sorry, not *his* dog—had made her heart flip twice and go splat.

She'd given him a shove. "Go."

After a brief thank-you kiss he'd gone, leaping off the porch, grabbing a man-sized torch from his big black muscle car, and run off into the forest like some kind of superhero.

No telling how long he'll be, she thought as she distracted her nerves by scoping out the rest of his home. Down the solitary hall was one seriously cool bathroom with a fantastic sunburst mosaic covering an entire wall and an old brass tub—the kind you sat in with your knees up to your chin. Leaning against the doorjamb of his small office, with its big wooden desk, a wall of shelves filled with books and knick-knacks, another covered in old maps, star charts, pictures of boats, she admitted that, while the house might be a total bachelor pad, with not a feminine touch in sight, it was seriously appealing. Simple and raw, woodsy and warm. Lived in.

It was Jonah.

Pushing herself away from the wall, she walked unthinkingly through the last door to find herself standing in a bedroom.

Jonah's bedroom.

Her next breath in was choppy, her palms growing uncommonly warm as her eyes skittered over the chair in the corner covered in man clothes. The bedside table—singular—had at one time been a beer barrel, and now boasted a lamp with a naked bulb, a book—pages curled, face down—and a handful of loose change. No curtains shielded the windows, which were recycled portholes looking out over what would no doubt be a spectacular Pacific view.

Her heart beat wildly as her eyes finally settled on the biggest thing in the room: Jonah's bed. It was big. *Huge.* And unmade, the white sheets a shambles. It wasn't hard to imagine his long brown limbs twisted up in the bedding.

Never in her wildest dreams would she have imagined that she'd be in such a position with a man like Jonah North. A man who made her twitch. And scramble. And think twice. And want. The *want* she felt around him was crazy, wild, and *corrupting*.

A man who couldn't even commit to a dog…

Insides twisting, Avery knew the smart thing to do would be to walk away, before the want became something else, something more. She could already feel it happening, encroaching. Heartbreak loomed with this one. Way better to find herself that cabana boy and piña colada and spend the rest of the summer in blissed-out inactivity.

Too late, she thought as warmth skittered over her skin. Jonah was back.

She turned to find him standing in the bedroom doorway, his broad shoulders blocking out the light from the hall. He'd ditched his shoes, and his shirt, and his eyes were as dark as coals.

Any doubts she might have harboured about what she was doing there went up in a puff of smoke. "Everything okay?" she asked, her voice so husky it was barely intelligible.

"All sorted."

"No baby birds to check on? Stray cats to nurture? Just saying I could go watch a DVD or something till you're… ready."

Jonah's smile was swift. Sexy as hell. And predatory.

And Avery was done thinking. The sound of a zipper rent the air; and when Avery's bustier sank forward into her arms she let it dangle from two fingers before dropping it to the floor.

Jonah's smile disappeared. And Avery's stomach quivered as his dark gaze raked her from head to toe.

When her hand went to the side zip of her floaty pants, Jonah shook his head. Just once, but it was enough for her fingers to fall away.

All man, this one. Never asked permission—not to rescue her, not to kiss her. The only time he'd asked was when he'd wanted to dance. As if he'd known that her acceptance was as significant as kicking down a brick wall.

When Jonah took a step her way, her breath caught in her throat, and in the low light his mouth hitched into a grin. She scowled back, which only made him laugh; that deep masculine *huh-huh-huh* that near took her knees out from under her. Lucky for her, suddenly he was there, an arm at her back, his nose rubbing gently against hers.

Then with a nudge he tilted her chin and captured her mouth with all the ease and honeyed smoothness of a man who'd done so a million times before.

Sparks flittered prettily at the edges of her vision before morphing into a deep delicious warmth that curled down her back and into her limbs. And without another thought Avery's hungry hands roved over all that smooth bare skin. The man was beyond beautiful. He was pure, raw, masculine heat, as if he'd trapped thirty years' worth of sun beneath his skin, till the heat of it pulsed inside him.

She moved, just a fraction, sliding her belly against the erection burning between them, breathless with expectation that she'd be thrown back onto the bed and ravished senseless. Then whimpered when Jonah pulled back. Not entirely, just enough to add air between them, allow breath to escape. Till she was left hyper-aware of the smallest touch, every erratic change to the beat of her pulse.

Then his lips were on her neck, and gone.

On her collarbone, then gone.

On the edge of her mouth, coaxing, teasing, then *gone*.

All the while his hands didn't stop touching, sliding over her back, his rough, calloused thumbs riding the curve of her waist, slipping under the edge of her bra, heading south…

Just when she thought she might melt into a puddle of tormented lust, Jonah took advantage. Completely. His tongue dipping into her sighing mouth to slide along hers, one warm hand cupping her backside pitching her closer, the other delving deep into her hair, capturing her until she was in his complete thrall.

Then his thumbs dipped into the waistband of her pants, finding a heretofore unknown sweet spot at the edge of her hipbones until she curled away from him, gasping. Leaving him all the room he needed to lick his way down her neck, her collarbone, his teeth grabbing the edge of her bra and tearing it away so that he could take her breast in his mouth.

She slipped a bare foot around his calf, keeping him hooked; she dug her hands into his hair, keeping him there, keeping him from ever leaving—ever—as his tongue and teeth and hot breath drove her wild. Until he pulled the other half of her bra away with his fingers, his rough, warm, sure fingers, and, caressing her as if she were something precious, sent the most intense pleasure looping inside her belly it near lifted her off her feet.

When his mouth once more found hers, he kissed her till she felt on the verge of drowning. And her knees finally gave way from under her and she landed on his bed with a thud and a bounce. She flung an arm over her closed eyes in an effort to find her balance.

When she opened them it was to find Jonah standing at the end of the bed, half-cocked grin on his gorgeous face. All golden-brown rippling abs. And dark whorling chest hair. Ropey muscle across his shoulders, veins slicing down his smooth brown arms. A deep tan line from his diving watch wrapping about his wrist.

"You are something else, Jonah North," she said, shaking her head back and forth.

The grin deepened, and his eyes roved over every inch of her. "When you find a name for it, let me know. As I'm totally in the dark about you, Avery Shaw."

And crazy as it sounded, that felt perfectly all right with her.

She hauled herself up, curled her fingers into his open fly to drag him closer only to discover the tan line at his wrist was matched by another. This one was a perfect horizon that split the dark trail of hair leading into his pants.

She kissed the demarcation, relishing his sharp intake of breath. She kissed a little lower to find his skin there scorching hot. She pulled back and licked her lips as if burnt to find they tasted like sun and salt and sharp sea air. Like him. When she went in for another lick he slid his finger to her chin, lifted it so she'd look him in his smoking-hot eyes, then bent towards her.

It seemed forever before his lips found hers. Enough time for all her compressed want to collide with what felt like years and years of unmet need and rustle up a very real shot of fear. Fear that this was about to be so good she might never recover.

Then he unhooked her bra with a practised flick, and the fear was smothered to death.

"Done that before have we, champ?"

Her hands sank into his springy curls as he smiled against her ear before taking her lobe between his teeth for a nip. "One of my many skills."

"Many?"

He lifted his head, moonlight through the porthole window slanting shadows across his crooked nose, his hooded eyes, his beautiful mouth. "You asking me to list them?"

"You seem more like a doer than a talker to me."

She got a grin, a slash of white teeth in his swarthy face, before he lifted an eyebrow in mercurial promise and set to it.

Avery wrapped herself about him as he kissed his way down her belly, his chest hair skimming her bare breasts, then he rid her of her pants and G-string in one smooth yank, and his mouth was on her inner thigh, his teeth grazing her hip, his tongue dipping into her navel.

"Lie still, woman," he demanded, his deep grey, eloquent eyes boring into hers.

She bit her lip and tried, really she tried. But the deep scraping pleasure was nearly too much to bear. And then she completely lost control—her control anyway; she was clearly helpless under his—as his rough hands skimmed over her sensitised breasts, caressed her flinching waist, dug into that sweet spot at her hips, then easy as you please pressed her thighs as far apart as they would go.

As soon as he broke eye contact her eyes slammed shut, red and black swirls of light and dark beating the backs of her eyelids as his breath fanned over her a split second before his tongue dipped deep inside.

That was where thought was lost to her as her world distorted into beats of purest pleasure. Of breath, touch, taste. The near painful rasp of his stubble on her most sensitive skin, the gentle wash of his warm breath, the glorious graze of his tongue, and her own heat, collapsing in on itself until all sensation balanced on the head of a pin before exploding into shards of light to every corner of her universe.

He gave her a scant few seconds to just enjoy it, to bask in the wonderment of such a bone-melting orgasm; enough time to get naked and sheath himself in protection before he kissed and nipped his way up her belly, her overwhelmed nerves crying out, her tenderised muscles jumping at every touch.

When he positioned himself over her, she had the ambitious thought to flip him over and give him the ride of his life, but he'd rendered her so completely limp all she could do was slink her body against his, to rain a series of soft kisses along the spiky underside of his jaw, and run her hands down his back till she found two handfuls of glorious male backside.

Then, wrapping her legs about him, she nudged her sensitised centre against his remarkable erection, and kissed him long and hard and wet and deep while she took him deep inside.

Her gasp was lost as he kissed her back, taking more, taking everything as he deepened the connection. Deeper, deeper, filling her with sensation so intense, she was absorbed. Lost in him.

When her eyes caught on his, she felt herself swirling, tumbling, drowning. She held him tighter, drew him deeper, his intense gaze her only anchor. As they—

"Oh, God!" she cried as she split apart before she even felt it coming.

When Jonah pushed himself to the hilt, and again, and again, finding sweet spots the likes of which Avery had never known, every ounce of pleasure was wrung from her. Too vast, too much… She found yet another peak as Jonah's muscles hardened beneath her touch, heat reaching a fever pitch as he came with a roar that shook the walls.

"Hell, Avery," he said an eon later, his voice muffled in the mess of sheets at her back.

"You're telling me."

He laughed, the sound still muffled. While she ran a quick finger under one eye before smoothing a hand down his back, biting her lip to stop any more tears from falling. Pure emotion, exhaustion, the last threads of tension that had built over the past few weeks back home finally finding a way out.

With a manly groan, Jonah rolled away, one arm flung above his head, the other lying between them. After a long moment he moved his arm closer, close enough his pinky finger spun sweet lazy circles at her hip.

Breathing deep, Avery took his hand, lifted it, and

kissed the palm till the heat of him sank into her like a brand. And then empty, like a vase just waiting to be filled, and wrapped up in layers of delicious afterglow, she fell deeply asleep.

Jonah woke slowly, dragging himself out of a deep sleep with the feeling that he'd been in the middle of a really good dream. When he shifted to find the sheets at his hips rather resembled a teepee, he knew; whatever he'd dreamt it would have been nothing on the very real delights of one Avery Shaw.

With a groan that told of muscles well used he rolled over, only to find the other side of his bed wasn't only empty, it was cold. Meaning she'd been up for a while.

Jonah yawned, scratched his belly, then lifted onto his elbow and listened for sounds of her. Felt with his subconsciousness for a sense of her. That particular snapping heat that sizzled about her like an electric current. But there was nothing.

"Avery!" he called, his voice husky, his legs not quite ready for dry land. "Come back to bed, woman!"

When his voice echoed off the walls and he got no response, the warmth in his limbs started to dissipate.

"Avery?"

In the distance he heard a scratching. Hull at the front door. He'd locked the dog inside the night before, after the odd run for the hills that had worried Jonah something fierce. But that scratching was coming from *outside*.

Avery. She'd let him out. When she'd left.

Jonah lowered himself back to the bed, laid a forearm over his eyes, slid another to the aching bulge between his legs and swore.

Of course she was gone. What had he expected—to be woken with coffee and bagels? That all it would take was one night to render his flinty little American all sweetness and light?

No. He hadn't. But he also hadn't expected her to run for the hills.

The myriad reasons why he'd managed to keep his hands off her till now had meant that instead of going at it like rabbits, they'd got to know one another in the past couple of weeks. While he wouldn't say they were *friends*—the word was a little too beige for the kinds of feelings the woman engendered—they knew enough about one another he'd have expected a little respect.

Jonah opened his eyes and stared at the first tinges of gold shifting across the ceiling. It had taken him months to realise Rach hadn't respected him. That while he'd been imagining a future, she'd seen him as free board and great lay. A man suitable for a season, not forever.

One night together and Avery had skulked out at God knew what time without having the grace to say *Thank you and good night*.

"Dammit," he swore, hauling himself upright to run two hands through his hair. And despite himself he couldn't help going to that place inside himself he'd worked his ass off to leave behind. The part of him that would always be small town, a lobsterman's son. That knew no matter how many boats he owned, how many homes, how many helicopters or tourism awards or dollars in the bank, to a city girl like Avery Shaw he'd never be enough.

Rachel. A girl like *Rachel*. He'd lived with *her* for a year. He'd slept with Avery once. There was no comparison. None at all.

Punching out enough oaths to make a boxer blush, Jonah hit the floor, tore the sheets off the bed, threw them down the hall to be washed. He didn't want to hit his bed that night and catch her scent, even if it was all he deserved for letting her in. To his head and his home. Thankfully his heart was tough as an old boot.

Still didn't mean it wasn't a smart idea to scrub her scent from his skin, her image from his head, and her presence from his heretofore perfectly fine life. If he saw Avery Shaw again in the weeks she spent in town it would be too soon.

When the cab dropped Avery at the Tropicana, the sun was barely threatening to spread its first golden streaks across the dawn sky.

She slid her room card into the slot at the front of the resort, opened the door and padded across Reception, which, due to the hour, was even more quiet than usual.

Except that Claudia was behind the reception desk.

Before Avery could think up an alternative escape route, Claudia looked up with a start; slamming shut her laptop, and looking as guilty as Avery felt.

"Hi!" said Claude.

"Morning!" chirped Avery. "What are you doing down here so early?"

"Oh, nothing. Just…bookings. *So-o-o* many bookings."

Claude's hair was a little askew, her eyes a little pink. She had gone hard at the cocktails the night before and yet here she was pre-sunrise, hours before check in, and all decked out in her polyester Tropicana Nights finest.

More importantly, though, she seemed distracted enough not to notice Avery's walk of shame.

"Okay, well, I'll catch you later then—"

"Wait."

Dammit. Avery turned to find Claudia looking anything but distracted, her eyes roving over Avery's shimmery top, her swishy black dress pants, the ankle breakers dangling from her fingers.

"Yo ho ho! Avery Shaw, you hot dog. You got yourself some Jonah!"

"Shh."

"Who's going to hear? The pot plants? Come," said Claude, scooting from behind the desk to drag Avery over to a sumptuous leather couch where sunlight was starting to hit patches of once-plush rug. "So what happened? Why the pre-dawn crawl home? After all that sexy touching and tractor-beams eyes you two had going on last night I'd have thought you'd have set the bed ablaze. Was it terrible? All smoke no fire?"

Avery sniffed out a laugh. Then laughed some more. Then laughed so hard she got a stitch. Clutching at her side, she bent from the waist and let her head fall between her knees. Nose an inch from an old wad of gum stuck on the underside of the couch, she sighed. "It was…spectacular. Claude, I can't even begin to describe the things that man did to me. On a cellular level."

"Ha!" Claude clapped her hands so loud it echoed through the gargantuan space. "Awesome. But if it was so spectacular why aren't you at Jonah's shack doing the wild thing with that man right now?"

Because it was only ever going to be a one-night thing? Because her itch for him had finally been scratched? Because she knew Jonah well enough to know he'd give his right pinky not to have to go through a talky-talky morning after?

Avery heaved herself to sitting and stared into nothingness. "Because I am a common-or-garden-variety coward."

Claudia took Avery's hand between hers, and waited till Avery's eyes were on hers. "You, my friend, are generous and kind. To a *fault*. But even the best of us trip over ourselves once in a while. Find your feet again, and you'll be fine."

Avery plucked a mint leaf—left over from some cocktail or other from the night before—from Claude's hair. She just had to figure out which direction her feet ought to be going.

She wondered if he was awake yet. If he knew she was gone. If the decision as to what her summer entailed was already out of her hands.

"So it's all over for you and Luke," Claude said, "one would think."

Avery laughed, then cringed. "Do you think he had any idea that I had…intentions?" Vague, and reactionary, as they'd been.

Claude's mouth twisted in an effort not to smile. "If it makes you feel any better I had a huge case of the hero-worships for the guy when I was a kid."

"Re-e-eally?"

Claudia slapped her on the arm at her saucy tone. "That was, of course, until I realised he was a robot. Thank goodness for Jonah or you might yet have married Luke and moved to wet old London and made robot babies."

Claudia shivered—but whether it was the thought of London weather or making babies with Luke, Avery couldn't be sure.

"What about you? Seeing anyone? Since Raoul?"

"Too busy," Claude said with a wistful sigh. "No time. No energy. Especially for the likes of Raoul."

"Stuff Raoul. Stuff Luke. You should have a fling with some hot blond surfie type, who has big brown muscles and never wears shoes and says dude a lot."

"Not leaving much room for movement there."

"It's a beach. In Australia. Walk outside right now and you'll trip over half a dozen of them."

Claudia checked her phone as if checking the time to see if she could squeeze in a quick fling, then saw she'd missed a message. And her whole demeanour changed:

back stiffening, her eyebrows flying high. "It's Luke," she said. "He's gone."

"What? Where?"

"London."

"When?"

"Some time between when he dropped me back at the resort last night and now. *Dammit.* We had the best conversation we've had all summer last night. About the old days, the mischief we used to get up to behind the scenes in this place, and the crazy plans we made for when we got to take over the resort, and how we used to watch *The Love Boat*…. And *then* he ditches me…*us* faster than a speeding bullet?" Frowning, Claudia pressed a thumb to her temple. "Jerk."

"Why?"

"Why is he a jerk? Let me count the ways—"

"No, why did he leave?"

Claudia waved her phone at Avery, too fast for her to catch a word. "'Important Work.' More important than here? His birthright? This place is the entire reason he's as successful as he is!" Claudia nibbled at a fingernail, her right knee shaking so hard it creaked, and stared over at the desk. "I'd better get back."

Avery's eyes glanced off her friend's less than perfect chignon, the dark smudges under her sunny blue eyes. The curve of her shoulders since Luke's message. It was obvious things weren't as peachy as Claude was making out; even Avery could see the resort wasn't as busy as it ought to have been at the height of summer. But she knew her stubborn little friend well enough to know that Claude would come to her in her own time.

Till then, Avery worked her magic the way she best knew how. She took Claude's stressed little face in her hands, removed a bobby pin, smoothed the errant hair into place, and slid the pin back in. "There, there. All better. Now, my clever, inventive, wonderful friend, go get 'em."

Claude sighed out a smile, and then tottered off, her hips swinging in her shiny navy capris, the yellow and blue Hawaiian-print shirt somehow working for her.

Good deed for the day done, Avery lay back on the couch. Unfortunately the second she closed her eyes the night she'd been holding at bay came swarming back to her.

Jonah's mouth on hers, tasting her as if she were precious, delicious, a delicacy he couldn't get enough of. His calloused touch making paths all over her body.

She snapped her eyes open, early morning light reflecting off the white columns and walls.

At least Luke had had the good grace to let Claudia know when he'd done a runner. Avery had dressed in the dark, called a cab and split. Even if none of her expensive schools had given classes on Mornings After, she was well aware that it was just bad form.

She pulled herself up and padded back to her room. She needed a shower. She needed a coffee. Then, as usual, it was up to her to put the world back to rights.

CHAPTER EIGHT

AVERY REALLY GOT the hang of the right-hand drive in Claudia's car—a bright yellow hatchback named Mabel with Tropicana Nights's logo emblazoned over every possible surface—about the time she hit Port Douglas.

The GPS on her phone led her to Charter North's operations, down a long straight road past a bright green golf course, million-dollar homes, and ten-million-dollar views.

She eased through the high gate and pulled to a halt by a security guard in a booth.

To her left was a car park big enough to fit fifty-odd cars, with a dozen gleaming sky-blue Charter North charter buses lined up beside a neat glass and brick building. Oceanside was a perfect row of crisp white sheds, as big as light airplane hangars, the Charter North logo on each catching glints of sunshine.

She knew the guy owned a few boats. And a helicopter. And a shack. Now nautical empire didn't seem such a stretch.

"Ma'am?" the security guard said, bringing her back to earth.

"Sorry. Ah, Avery Shaw to see Jonah North."

He took down her licence plate and let her through with a smile. She pulled into a car park in time for a super-friendly man in chinos and a navy polo shirt—who introduced himself as Tim the office manager—to point the way to a big white building hovering over the water. To Jonah. She would have known anyway, as right in a patch of sun outside lay Hull.

The sun beat down on her flowy shirt, and her bare legs beneath her short shorts. Her silver sandals slapped against the wood of the jetty and Hull lifted his speckled head at her approach.

"Hey, Hull," she whispered. His tail gave three solid thumps—meaning he at least wasn't about to eat her alive for dissing his master—then he went back to guarding the door. Her heart took up the rhythm; whumping so loud she feared it might echo.

The door was open a crack so she snuck inside—and understood instantly why Hull was stationed outside. Jonah had said the dog hated water, and inside huge jetties criss-crossed the floor and a ways below the ocean bobbed and swished against the pylons holding the building suspended above the waves.

A few boats were hooked to the walls by high-tech electrical arms, one in the process of being fixed. Yet another was getting a wash, and spray flew over the top and onto the jetty.

Not seeing any other movement, Avery eased that way, taking care where she stepped as the wood beneath her feet grew wet.

Until against one wall she saw a familiar surfboard. Silvery-grey, like its owner's eyes, with the shadow of a great palm tree right down the middle, and her heart beat so hard it filled her throat.

Because she knew why she'd fled in the middle of the night. Somehow in the odd sequence of meetings that had led her to Jonah's bed, she'd got to know the guy. And despite his ornery moods she even *liked* him.

She'd woken up terrified that those feelings would unleash her Pollyanna side upon him—*Like me! Love me!*—

like some rabid pixie hell-bent on smothering the world with fairy dust. Not quite so terrified, though, as what it might mean if Pollyanna still didn't show up at all.

Her feet felt numb as she came upon a curled-up hose, water trickling from its mouth. Then around the bow of the boat she found suds. And at the end of a great big sponge was Jonah. Feet bare, sopping wet jean shorts clinging to his strong thighs, T-shirt clinging wet to the dips and planes of his gorgeous chest.

As Avery's gaze swept over him, over his roguish dark hair, over the curve of his backside, his athletic legs, she didn't realise how dry her mouth had become until she opened it to talk. "You could hire people to do that, you know."

Jonah stilled. Then his deep grey eyes lifted and caught on her. She felt the look like a hook through the belly—yet he gave nothing away.

A moment later, he turned off the hose, threw the sponge into a bucket at his feet, wiped his forearm across his forehead, and slowly headed her way.

And when he spoke his deep Australian drawl twisted the hook so deep inside she was sure it would leave a scar. "I have hired people to do this." A beat, then, "But today I find being around water a damn fine release of tension."

Avery considered picking up the sponge herself. "Well, that's why I'm here, actually."

"To wash my boat?" His voice skittered down her arms like his touch—coarse and gentle all at once. How did the guy make even *that* sound sexy?

"To apologise."

"For?"

He was going to make her say it, wasn't he? *Not nice.* Not nasty either, though. Just…plain-spoken. Direct. True.

"For leaving. This morning. After—" She waved a hand to cover the rest.

"After you fell asleep in my bed, exhausted from all the hot lovin'."

"Jonah North," she muttered, throwing her hands in the air in despair, "last of the great romantics."

"It was sex, Avery," he said, walking towards her again. "Good sex. Nothing to apologise for."

He didn't stop till he was close enough she could feel his warmth infusing the air around her. Could see his eyelashes all spiked together with water, as they had been that first day. And that his face was a picture of frayed patience, also as it had been that first day.

But the difference between that day and now was vast.

"It was more than good," she said, her voice as jerky as a rusty chainsaw.

One eyebrow lifted along with the corner of his mouth.

"It was freakin' stupendous."

His mouth tilted fully into a smile so sexy it made her vision blur. Then he ran a hand up the back of his hair and said, "Yeah. I'll give you that."

Then he moved nearer, near enough to touch. But instead of touching her, he reached out for a towel draped over a mossy post near her feet. She closed her eyes and prayed for mercy, lest she drool and lose the high ground completely.

Jonah wiped the towel over his face, and down his arms, smearing the sweat and suds.

"Why, then, did you run?"

"I didn't run. I caught a cab."

By the way his brow collapsed over his eyes, she was pretty sure that being flip wasn't going to cut it. But there was no way on God's green earth she was about to tell him she ran because of *how* much she wanted to stay. She'd been very careful till now not to let anyone have that much sway over her desires. Keeping things light, happy, above the surface. The flipside was unthinkable.

"Just hit me with it, Avery," he said, throwing the towel over the back of his neck and holding onto the ends, his biceps bulging without any effort at all. "It's about Luke."

"What? No! Luke was…a brief flirtation with finding a way to distract myself from the goings-on back home by dipping my toes back into the past. But from pretty much the moment you hauled me out of the ocean and manhandled me back to shore and glared down at me with your steamy eyes…" Okay, heading off track now. She breathed deep, her cheeks beginning to heat with a slow burn that showed no signs of stopping, and said, "I want you."

Jonah didn't so much as twitch. He let her sway in the wind. Getting his money's worth. Till finally he said, "Okay, then."

"Okay, then?" That was it? That was all she got? For basically telling the guy he turned her to putty?

He took a step her way but Avery planted her feet into the floor so as not to sway back. "Was there something else?"

"Yeah. You're an ass, Jonah North. A gorgeous ass, one I can't seem to get out of my head no matter how much I try, but still an ass. I'll see you 'round."

She turned and walked away, waving a hand over her shoulder that might have had a certain finger raised. But she'd given her apology and *that* was all that was important. She had the high road. He only had her pride.

Then suddenly he was walking beside her.

"So," he said, "I was just about to head up to the Cape to check on a tour-boat operation I'm thinking of buying."

"How nice for you."

"Avery," he said, his voice a growl as he slid a hand into her elbow, forcing her to stop and look at him. She crossed her arms and glared, as if facing all that sun-soaked skin, and those deep grey eyes, and that pure masculine beauty were some kind of chore.

He tipped his face to the ceiling and muttered, "God, I'm going to regret this. Would you care to join me?"

Pollyanna showed up long enough to flip over and waggle her happy feet in the air. But Avery's dark side, her careful side, pulled Pollyanna's plaits and told her to shut the hell up for a second.

This wasn't as simple as being forgiven. *This* was the tipping point. Her chance to hole up with her heart and spend her summer reading, and swimming, and refilling her emotional well; or to dive into uncharted waters with no clue as to the dangers that lay beneath.

"Are you asking me on a date, Jonah North?"

He watched her for a few seconds, his eyes sliding to settle on her mouth, then with a hard heavy breath he said, "I'll let you decide when we get there."

Because there was no choice really. She *was* going with him. He knew it, and she knew it too.

Avery leant against the battered Jeep that had brought them to the edge of the crumbling jetty on the side of the marshy river, watching Jonah grumble his way through a business call.

He shot her the occasional apologetic glance, but honestly she could have stayed there all day, watching him pace, listening to that voice; it was nearly enough for her to forgive him the hat—a tatty Red Sox cap that he'd foraged from who knew where, as if the fates one day knew she'd be owed some payback.

Avery turned when she heard a boat. It appeared through the tall reeds; not as fast and streamlined as the boat to Green Island, or sleek and sexy as the one Jonah had been washing down back at Charter North HQ. This was squat, low riding, desperately in need of a paint job.

And had Cape Croc Tours written on the side.

While Jonah chatted with the tour operator, Hull—

who'd been pacing back and forth by the Jeep, one eye on the water the other on the man-who-was-not-his-master—huffed at her with a definite air of *You asked for it.*

Jonah rang off, slid the phone into the back pocket of his shorts, and came to her, long strides eating up the dusty ground. While she subjugated her panic beneath a smile.

"You okay?" he asked, and she dialled the smile back a notch.

"Fine! What girl doesn't dream about the day a guy offers to take her on a croc tour? Okay? No. I'm not okay. Are you freakin' kidding me?"

A grin curved across his mouth. Then he reached into the cabin of the Jeep and pulled out an old felt hat and slapped it on her head. Not the most glamorous thing she'd ever worn.

"Can they climb in the boat?"

"The crocs? No."

Hull huffed as if to say Jonah was pulling her leg. Avery glanced back to find him lying in a patch of shade by the Jeep, his head lying disconsolately on his front paws. In fact, maybe she ought to keep him company—

"Ready?" Jonah asked.

"As I'll ever be."

Avery took Jonah's hand as she stepped into the boat, gripping harder as the boat swayed under her feet. Jonah didn't let go till he sat her on a vinyl padded bench at the rear of the vessel.

Feeling a little less terrified, she caught his eye and smiled. "I like your shirt, by the way."

He glanced down at the faded American flag with the eagle emblazoned across it, pulling it away from his chest for a better look and giving her an eyeful of his gorgeous brown stomach.

"Were you thinking of me when you picked it out this morning?"

His deep eyes slunk back to hers, then in a voice deeper than the water below he said, "Believe it or not, princess, I go entire minutes without thinking of you."

Her smile turned into a grin. "Good for you."

He flipped some keys into the air, and caught them, then moved to sit on what looked like a modified barstool up near the helm.

"You're driving?" she called.

"Yep."

"Shouldn't we have a chaperone?" She earned a lift of two dark eyebrows for her efforts. "I mean because the boat's not yours."

Jonah glanced back at the dock. "If we go down he can have the Jeep. And the dog."

"The dog that's not your dog."

His eyes slid back to hers with a sexy smile.

"Fine. Whatever," she said, tipping her hat lower on her head and squinting against the sun. Just the two of them, heading off into the wilderness, where crocs were near guaranteed. She *really* hoped he'd forgiven her for sneaking out on him.

The engine turned over and the boat shifted in the water, giving her a fair spray of river water in the face. Gripping the bench, she looked back over her shoulder and saw how low the boat actually was. The edges of the thing looked real easy to scale. With an agility she wasn't aware she had she scuttled up to take the stool next to Jonah's.

"Happier there?"

"Better view." Her disobedient gaze landed on his muscular arms as he put the boat in gear, eased it into the middle of the thin river, and took the thing along at a goodly pace. *Yep, much better.*

"So, feel like a date yet?" he asked, and her insides gave a hearty little wobble.

"This is textbook. In New York a date isn't really a date if there aren't wild animals involved."

And just like that she and Jonah North were officially on a date. And she was okay. Not deeper than her limits. Just…about…right. Feeling unusually content about her world and everything in it, Avery propped her feet on the dash; the wind whipping at her hair, the sun beating down on her nose, the deep rumble of the engine lulling her into a most relaxed state. Till the hum, and the heat, and *eau de Jonah* had her deep in memories of the night before.

"I hate to think what you're conjuring up over there, Ms Shaw."

She nearly leapt out of her skin. "Nothing. Just soaking it all in. Thinking."

"Dare I ask what about?"

To say it out loud would be pornographic. "I really liked your shack."

A surprised smile kicked up the corner of his mouth. "It's hardly the Waldorf."

"Why would you want it to be? It's unique. And cool. It suits you."

After a few beats, Jonah added, "It was my father's house."

"Were you brought up there?"

He nodded. "Never lived anywhere else." He frowned. "Not true. I spent three months in Sydney a few years back."

"You? In Sydney?" She was already laughing at the idea by the time she noticed the twitch in his jaw and the sense that the air temperature had slipped several degrees towards arctic. *Okay…* "Was it for work? Play? Sea change…in reverse?"

"My ex-fiancée lived there."

Well, she'd had to go and ask!

A deep swirly discomfort filled her up and she struggled

to decipher if her reaction was shock at the fact a woman had managed to put up with him for any length of time, or that she'd been wrong about his lone-wolfdom. There was a woman out there that this man had at one time been prepared to *marry*. A fiancée. *Ex*-fiancée, her subconscious shot quickly back.

"I'm assuming things didn't turn out so well," she said, her daze evident in her hoarse whisper.

But he was clearly caught up in thoughts of his own. She jumped a little when after some time he answered.

"She came here on holidays and stayed. Then she left. I followed. Got a position with a shipping company to manage their freight in and out of the harbour. Told myself water was water."

Clearly it hadn't been, as here he was. Mr Not Quite So Thoroughly Unattainable After All.

On a date.

With her.

"Wow," she croaked, "Sydney." Yep, she was focusing on the easier of the two shocks. "Try as I might I can't picture you living in the big smoke."

Storm clouds gathered in his eyes, his jaw so tight he looked liable to crack a tooth.

"Jonah—"

"Don't sweat it, Avery. You're not the first woman to think me provincial."

And *that* came from so far out of left-field Avery flinched. "Hold on there, partner, that's not what I meant at all. I'm sure you made a huge splash in Sydney."

"I didn't, in fact." He took the boat down a gear so that the change in engine swept his words clean away.

"Rubbish," she scoffed, imagining the looks on her friends' faces if she'd ever turned up with this guy on her arm. Those Manhattan blue bloods would take one look at those delicious eye crinkles, those big shoulders, and drop their jaws like a row of cartoon characters. And it wasn't just the way the guy looked—it was in his bearing, how obviously he lived his life to as high a standard as any man ever had. "I don't believe that for a second."

Jonah glanced up, the storm clouds parting just enough for a spark to gleam from within. A spark that met its twin in her belly.

"What I *meant*," she said, *now* choosing her words with care, "about me not being able to imagine you in *Sydney*, is that you seem like you were made for this place—the scorching sun, the squalling sea, the immense sky. Sydney would be a big grey blur in comparison. Which sounds ridiculous now I've put it into words—"

"No," Jonah said, frowning and smiling at the same time. "No."

"Okay." Avery hugged her arms around her belly to contain the tumbly feelings as they softened down to a constant hum. "So what happened with you and—"

"Rach? Real life."

"It has a way of getting in the way of things."

"You ever come close?" Jonah asked. "Marriage. Kids. The whole calamity."

"Me? No. Not unless you include Luke, of course, and he wasn't even aware of our impending plans."

Jonah laughed. An honest laugh. Confident, this man. Why wouldn't he be, though? Look at him. One hand resting casually on the wheel, a shoe nudged against the foot of the helm, eyes crinkling in the sunshine as he eased the boat around the reeded bends of the river.

This was a man who knew where he belonged.

The boat hit a wider stretch and Jonah slowed the engine to a throaty hum.

Maybe she still had to figure out where she really belonged. Not here. A ride on a dilapidated old boat at the top of Australia was probably a bit of a stretch considering where she'd come from. But here, so far away, made her realise how much of her life she spent trying to sort out her parents' lives. And the seed was now sown; to find her place. It would be hard. It would mean unravelling a decade's worth of ties before weaving them into something new. Something better.

Later, she thought as her throat began to constrict with the thought of it. Right now, the summer was hers. All hers. Nobody else's. And she no longer had any doubts about how she wanted to spend the time she had left.

Avery slipped off her stool and slipped under Jonah's arm, finding a perfect spot for herself between his knees. She rested a hand on his chest; the other took the cap from his head. His slow intake of breath and the darkening of his eyes created pools of heat low in her belly.

"So, Jonah North, what do you say we put all that behind us and just have some damn fun? No promises. No regrets. Do you want to be the man who makes my summer holiday one to remember?"

A muscle ticced in his jaw a moment before he grabbed her by the waist and drew her into him, covering her mouth with his. No finesse this time, no interminable teasing, just pure unleashed desire.

Lust rushed through her, unfettered, thick and fast, and she kissed him back, the heat of his mouth, the slide of his tongue driving every thought from her head but *more, now, yes*!

She threw his hat away—the man was hot but kissing a Sox fan would be sacrilege—and tucked her hands under his T-shirt, revelling in the warm skin, the rasp of hair, the sheer size of him. He was so big and hot and so much man he made her feel so light, like a breath of fresh air. As if nothing else mattered but here, now, this.

He tugged her closer, the ridge of his desire pressed

against her belly, and her head fell back as anticipation shivered through her with the surety of what was to come.

"What time do you have to have the boat back?"

Holding her close with one hand, Jonah grabbed his phone with the other, punched in a message, waited a long minute for a response, then with a wolfish grin said, "Never. The boat's mine."

Avery's knees near gave out. In her life she'd been wooed with bling, with tables at impossible-to-get-into restaurants, *never* had she had a man want her so much he'd bought the real estate under his feet in order to have her.

In one swift move he lifted her floaty top over her head, taking the hat with it. "Hell," he said, spying her bikini top which was made of mostly string a shade or two paler than her skin.

"You like? I found it in this wicked boutique in the Village—*oh*..."

Jonah proceeded to show her just how much he liked it by yanking it down to take her breast in his mouth. When she thought herself filled with more pleasure than she could possibly bear, his mouth slowly softened, placing gentle kisses over the moist tip.

And the thumb at her hip dipped below the beltline of her shorts. He found her button, snapped it open; the slide of her zip rent the quiet river air like a promise.

His hand slid an inch within. Her breath hitched, then he lifted his hand to run the backs of his knuckles over her stomach and her breath trembled out of her.

When his hand sank into the back of her shorts, the calloused pads of his palm cradling her backside with such gentleness, such reverence, she bit her lip to stop from crying out.

Using his teeth, he pulled the other half of her bikini top free, and took her nipple in his mouth, his tongue circling the tip but not quite touching. Right as his hand dived into her shorts and a finger swiped over her, once, then twice, then found her centre with the most perfect precision.

She gave in then, crying out. The crocodiles, wherever they might be, would just have to deal.

The gentle moans that followed sounded as if they were coming from a mile away but they were all her. Coming as they did with every slide of his finger, every lathe of his tongue.

Warmth spread through her, building to a searing heat where he touched, where he caressed, where he coaxed her higher, higher, till she reached a peak of insane pleasure. And there she stayed hovering, aching, for eons. And as she felt herself tip, as she began to spill over the other side he took her mouth, his tongue and touch guiding her all the way until she was left shaking in the strongest arms.

He held her there long after while she found herself gripped by mighty aftershocks. He pulled back only when she had stilled. Lifted her face with a finger to her chin, and kissed her. Eyes open. Such deep, absorbing eyes.

She reached between them, caressed the impressive length of him, wondering how on earth she'd coped with all that the night before. Her pulse quickened with anticipation at doing so again.

Grunting, he pulled his wallet from his back pocket, produced a small foil packet, which she snapped out of his grip. And with as much reverence as he'd shown her, she peeled away his pants and sheathed him, stopping every now and then for a sweet kiss, a swipe of her cheek, a lick.

With a growl he pulled her back upright, turned and backed her up against the dash. His eyes were like mercury, all slippery silver as he rid her of her bikini top and her shorts, leaving her naked.

The sun beat down on her shoulders, the dials dug into her back, and there was the occasional splash, the occasional bump of the hull, a possible deadly beast coming to say hello—but she didn't care.

All that mattered was Jonah, eyes roving over her as if he couldn't quite believe it. His hands followed, running over her so gently, tenderly, as if he was memorising her shape.

With a hand to his shoulder, she pulled him close, lifted a leg to hook around his hip, and then with a bone-deep sigh he was inside. Filling her slowly, achingly slowly, a sweet scrape that built till she couldn't stand it. He pulsed inside her, deeper, deeper, deeper than she'd ever been touched.

He came with a ferocity that made her head spin, and half a second later she followed right behind. Sensation imploding until all she could feel was the pulse between her legs. In her belly. In her heart. And Jonah's heart, thundering beneath her ear as she rested her head on his chest.

As they both struggled to drag in breaths, Jonah laughed, and Avery joined him. She lifted her head to find something fleeting and warming lighting his eyes.

Before she could pin it down he shook his head, hitched his shorts into place, then slumped back on the floor of the boat and lifted his face to the sun. "You're not the only one having a summer to remember, Miss Shaw."

Avery kneeled down to kiss him, then stood and spun about the boat butt naked. While Jonah lifted onto one elbow to watch, appreciation and wonder playing about his face.

And Avery wondered where she'd been her whole life.

Jonah took his time heading back.

One hand on the wheel, the other resting on Avery's lower back as she leant over the dash in her wild bikini top and short shorts. Sunlight flickering over her through the trees lining the marshy bank; her eyes otherwise cloaked in shadows from the brim of his ancient Akubra, her lush mouth tilted up at the corners.

It was so quiet out on the river, the scenery so rugged and raw they could have been the last two people on earth.

Then a telltale splash tugged at his instincts, and he squinted against the sun beating off the water. "Look," he said, his voice rough from under-use.

Avery blinked, followed the line of his arm, and saw. A croc. Its long brown body floating below the water snout, beady eyes, and a few bumpy scales cutting through the surface.

She stood taller, her fingers gripping the console till her nail beds turned bright pink. "It's huge."

"Twelve feet. Fourteen maybe."

She tipped back her hat—which had left a red mark slicing across her forehead. "It's looking right at me. No doubt thinking 'there's lunch.'"

"Don't blame him."

She flicked Jonah a glance, then licked her lips to cover a grin that made itself felt right in the groin. Then she turned, leant her backside against the dash, her long legs crossed at the ankles. "If, heaven forbid, I fell in right now you'd save me, right?"

"From a croc? Not on your life, princess. If he took you under that'd be it. They don't call it a death roll for nothing."

Her laughter was shocked, but the gleam in her eye was not. "How do the ladies resist you, Jonah North?"

"Resist me? Why do you think I let Hull skulk at my heels? Without him I'd be beating them away with a stick."

Her eyes narrowed a fraction, as if the idea of hordes of women coming after him was not one of her happier thoughts. "Ye-ea-a-ah," she said. "I actually half believe you. It's counterproductive, though, you know. Only adds to the tragic Heathcliffian mien you have going on."

"The what?"

"Nothing," she deadpanned.

Laughing under his breath, he ran a thumb along the red line on her forehead left by the hat. When her eyes flared at the touch, her breath hitching, her cheeks filling with blood, he tucked his hand back around the wheel.

His parents hadn't been demonstrative. Till then he'd figured he'd inherited the same. But the urge to touch Avery was strong. Too strong. So he did something he understood, reaching and slipping a hand around her waist, pulling her into the cradle between his legs.

His voice was rough as he said, "I notice Hull didn't scare you away."

"I notice you didn't beat me away with a stick."

The noticing beat between them like a pulse, until he pulled her in for a kiss. Her hand dived into the back of his hair, tugging till his skin thrummed with the sweet pleasure of her touch.

It took him longer than was smart to remember he was navigating croc-infested waters. He pulled away, thoughts all crooked. The intimacy part of this thing with Avery was so fresh, after keeping off every touch like an electric shock.

And yet he already found himself thinking towards the day her summer ended, while his simply kept on keeping on. Which was all he'd ever wanted. To belong here. In this paradise on earth. Where too much of a good thing was daily life.

The boat finally bumped against the riverbank back where they'd started, and Avery stretched away from him, yawning, leaving him to tie off. And get some space. Not that it seemed to help any. Her imprint lingered. Would do so for some time.

"Well, that was way more fun than I'd expected."

"Can I quote you for the website?"

The yawn turned into a grin. "Your slogan can be Satisfaction Guaranteed."

The tour operator called out a cheery welcome back, which stopped Jonah from giving her any kind of comeback. Leaving him to watch her head to the back of the boat to collect her stuff, her short shorts giving him a view of a hell of a length of leg.

She might have felt satisfied, but he felt as if his balls were in a vice.

The taste of her, the scent of her, the feel of her stamped on his senses like a brand. So much so he couldn't remember what any other woman of his experience felt like. Eyes on Avery, it was as if the rest had never existed.

But they did exist. And had taught him valuable life lessons. That things like this always ended. That advance bruise he felt behind his ribs was a good thing. Because this time he knew what was coming. This time it was in his control.

"Hull?" Avery said.

Yanked from his trance by the hitch in Avery's voice, Jonah looked past her to find Hull, not at the Jeep, but at the edge of the river, pacing back and forth so close to the edge his paws kept slipping into the water.

"Hey, boy," he called out. "No panic. We're back safe and sound." But Hull's whimpers only increased.

Jonah leapt off the boat the second he had it tied off. But instead of coming to sniff his hand Hull bolted to the Jeep, big paws clawing at the doors.

Flummoxed, Jonah looked to Avery, who hopped off the boat behind him and shrugged. He didn't know anything about dogs. He'd never had one as a kid—his father had never been home enough for it to be possible.

Jonah eased up to the dog, asked him to sit, which he did, which crazily made his heart squeeze. Then he ran gentle hands down Hull's legs, over his flanks, under his belly, checking to see if he might be hurt. Red-bellied black snakes liked water. Hull was tough. He'd survived being dumped. Survived where his brothers and sisters hadn't. He'd be fine.

"He doesn't look hurt to me," said Avery behind him. "He looks like he's pining."

"What?"

Avery's mouth twisted, then her eyes brightened. "Do you think he's found a lady friend?"

Jonah spun on his haunches, ready to shoot her theory down in flames. "He's three. A little over."

"That's twenty-one in dog years."

Jonah thought of himself at twenty-one and rocked back on his heels. "Aww hell."

"Unless of course he's neutered."

Jonah winced. "Hell, no!"

"Well, then, if your dog has knocked up some poor poo-dle, it's as much your responsibility as it is theirs."

"He's *not my dog*." But even as he said it he remembered the way he'd run after Hull into the forest the night before, panic like a fox trap around his chest. Thoughts catching on the burr of how blank his life would be without Hull in it. "You really think that's all it is?"

Avery snorted. "When the impulse can no longer be denied..."

Jonah's eyes swung back to the woman behind him. Her eyes liquid from the bright sun. Her clothes askew. Her skin pink from his stubble rash. Living proof of impulse no longer denied.

He looked back to his furry friend. "Hull." The dog looked up as he heard his name; all gentle eyes, wolfish profile, wildly speckled fur. "You missing your girl? Is that the problem?"

Hull licked his lips, panted, and Jonah swore beneath his breath. "What am I going to do with you, mate?"

Avery made snipping sounds that had Jonah clenching his man bits for all his might.

He whipped open the car door, and with a growl said, "Get in."

Hull leapt first, Avery followed.

Jonah took the keys back to the operator waiting in the hut, gave him Tim's card, and explained his man would get the lawyers together, then jogged back to the Jeep where a hot blonde and a hot-to-trot canine awaited him.

And he wondered at what point his well-managed life had gone to the dogs.

CHAPTER NINE

HALFWAY THROUGH AN early morning run up the beach path, Hull at his ankles, Jonah pulled up to jog on the spot. In the far distance he spied the ice-cream van that lived permanently on blocks in front of one of the dilapidated old beachfront homes that housed a half a dozen happy surfers.

Not that he felt like a half-melted ice cream. It was the blonde leaning into the thing that pulled him up short. Long lean legs, one bent so that her backside kicked out behind her, fair skin that had taken on the palest golden glow, long beach-waved hair trailing down her back.

Gone were the huge hat and fancy shoes that had been Avery's hallmark when she'd first arrived. In their place she wore the odd little fisherman's hat she'd picked up on Green Island and rubber thongs the local chemist sold for two bucks a pair. But the wild swimwear was all her—this one was strapless, the top a marvel of modern engineering, the bottom barely anything but a saucy frill that bounced as she lifted onto her toes to talk to the ice-cream guy who was now leaning out of the window, grinning through his dreadlocks.

And there but for the grace of God went he. Once upon a time *he'd* been one of those surfers who sat on that same porch, doing not much at all. It sounded nice in theory. Truth was it had been nice, and for a good while. Until it hadn't been enough.

Now he tried to carve an hour out of his work day every few weeks for a paddle, the way this kid no doubt carved an hour out of his surf time to put in an appearance at the dole office. The same kid who had all the time in the world to chat to a pretty tourist. And for the first time in years Jonah wondered who really had the better life.

Avery's laughter tinkled down the beach, and adrenalin poured through Jonah as he took off at a run.

She'd been in his bed near every day for the past week. Staying over more nights than not. And even while it was just a fling, Dreadlocks over there needed to know he wasn't in with a hope in hell. It was only neighbourly.

In fact *"just a fling"* had become somewhat of a mantra around his place, during those moments he found himself wondering when next he'd find her sitting at his kitchen table, draped in one of his shirts, one foot hooked up on a chair, hair a mussed mess as she smiled serenely out of the window at the forest-impeded ocean views beyond.

Unlike Rach, who'd set her treadmill up in his office, a small TV hooked to the front of it so she could watch the Kardashians, Avery soaked *every* moment in. Whether it was sitting on the jetty at Charter North watching him tinker with a dicky engine or on a bed of sketchy beach grass on Crescent Cove beach throwing a stick to Hull. She'd immersed herself in Crescent Cove.

Watching the cove through her eyes reminded him why he'd worked so hard to work himself back into the fabric of the place. And how little time he spent savouring it. What was the point of living in the most beautiful place on earth if you never even noticed?

Avery turned as he neared, hands wrapped around a cone. At the sight of her tongue curling about the melting ice cream, he missed a step and near ended up ass up. She looked up as he righted himself, grinned, and lifted her melting ice cream in a wave.

Hull peeled away to say hello and she crouched down to give the dog a cuddle about the ears. Even offered him a lick of the ice cream from her wrist and laughed when he took it.

When she stood Hull bounded back to join Jonah but from that point Avery's eyes were all on him as he jogged on the spot. He knew her odd eyes were dilated, even from the other side of the street. Knew they coursed over him, paused on the parts of him she liked best.

The urge to go to her, to kiss her, to throw her over his shoulder, and lock her up in his shack on the cliff was so thick, so all-encompassing, so *disquieting* he gave her a quick wave then kept running, just to prove he could.

"You!" said a woman who appeared as if from nowhere—her face red as a tomato.

Jonah only pulled up when he realised she wasn't talking to him, she was talking to Hull. "Ma'am, can I help you?"

"Don't you *Ma'am* me, sonny! Is this your dog?"

Jonah's cheek twitched with the urge to say no, but when Hull started whimpering in a way that made Jonah's insides go all squidgy, he heard himself say, "I'm his...main person."

"What the hell does that mean?"

It's all I've got for you, lady.

"Whatever you are, your...mongrel has been sniffing around my Petunia and you need to make him stop."

"Your—"

At that moment Avery appeared at his side. He caught her scent, her warmth, the zing of her travelling down his left arm before she even said a word.

"Hey, little thing. Petunia, is it?" she cooed, leaning towards the crazy woman's handbag where Jonah only just noticed a bald-headed little thing so overbred it could barely be labelled canine. Avery reached out to pat the thing's head, but it grew fangs and went in for a nip. She pulled back and sank down an arm around Hull's head, muttering loud enough for all to hear, "Really, Hull. Her?"

Jonah barely had a moment to note how much calmer Hull was with Avery all snuggled up to him before the woman stuck herself back into his line of sight. "Petunia is in heat."

Jonah snapped back to the present. "Do not tell me she's knocked up."

"No, she's not *carrying*! Thank goodness. And the last thing she needs is for your mutt to ruin her chances of producing champion offspring."

"My dog's not a mutt. While yours is—"

"Cute as a button," said Avery, standing at his side. "And champion, hey? Wowee. If she was my dog I'd take extra special care to keep her away from lusty male suitors. They can be temptation incarnate when they're all big and hairy like this guy."

Her voice was so kind, consoling, with that sophisticated New York measure, that the woman's face twitched as though she had a glitch in her regular programming. Then eyes slid away from Avery and back to Jonah. And she looked at him as if she hadn't really seen him before. More precisely, looked hard at his big and hairy chest.

Jonah took a step back and the woman shook her head as if coming out of a trance. "Just keep your mutt on a leash. Or I'll sue. Or I'll have him put down."

At that Jonah regained his lost step and more, leaning in and forcing the woman to look up and up and up. "Hang on a second, lady. If you kept your Pansy—"

"Petunia," Avery muttered.

"Petunia—*whatever*—at home while she's in heat rather than schlepping her out in your bloody handbag, then my dog wouldn't have looked twice at her. And I'll have you know he's not a mutt. He's a superb dog. A smart dog. A loving, loyal, kind dog. You and your little rat would be lucky to have him in your life!"

The other woman stormed off with her shivering critter in tow.

"Wow," Jonah said, running a hand over his sweat-dampened hair, knowing not all the sweat had been from the running. He glared down at Hull, who looked up at him with a kind of despair as the object of his affection was whisked away.

"Your dog."

Jonah glanced at Avery to find her back to licking her ice cream, a rogue smile gleaming deep within her mismatched eyes.

"I'm sorry?"

"You said Hull was *your* dog. There's no going back from that."

She tipped up onto her toes, placed a cool hand on his bare chest, and kissed him, a seriously hot lip lock that tasted like summer and ice cream and everything sweet and wholesome. Everything about the cove that made it feel like home. Then her hand trailed down his chest, her nails catching in his chest hair in a way that was the opposite of wholesome.

She walked backwards, back towards the resort, the frill of her bikini bottom bouncing up and down as if it were beckoning him to follow. Then said, "Your dog's a big softie, Jonah North. Just like his owner."

"Didn't I just hear you tell that woman I was temptation incarnate?"

She didn't even pretend she was talking about Hull. "I'm in PR. Which more often than not means taking not naturally pleasant products and talking them up till they smell like roses. Now you know I'm good at it."

Hips swinging, hair swaying, cheap thongs slapping on the hot concrete, she left him feeling anything but soft.

With a growl he turned and ran. And ran. And ran.

* * *

Avery headed into the Tropicana Nights, all aglow after her little run-in with Jonah.

Intending to take a long cool shower to wash off the sunscreen and ice cream and smirk before checking in with her mother, she took a short cut past the pool. Middle of the day and there was nobody there. So she gave her sticky hands a quick wash in the crystal-clear pool, then nearly fell in when she saw she wasn't alone—Claudia was all curled up on a white sun lounge.

"Hey, stranger!" Avery called out as she neared.

Claudia came to as if from far away. "Hey, kiddo! What's the haps?"

Avery parked her backside in the lounge next to Claudia's and filled her in on the unlikely Petunia.

"So you and Jonah are getting along quite well, then," Claude asked.

"We are," said Avery, and even she heard the sigh in her voice. So she qualified, "I mean, if you could create the perfect man for a summer fling, he'd be it, right?"

Claudia nodded wistfully. "Can't fault your logic there."

Avery nudged Claude's chair with her foot. "Which is why it kind of shocks me that he was *engaged* once upon a time."

"That he was," Claude said, the nods slowing. "Are you digging?"

"Frantically," Avery admitted.

"Her name was Rachel."

"Got that."

"She lived here, with him, for several months."

Months? Several?

"She was gorgeous, too. Uber-tanned, luscious dark hair, legs that went on forever. Amazonian, really. Like a half-foot taller than you. Fitness freak too, a body that would make you weep. And charismatic! Reserves of energy like nobody I've ever met—"

"Right, okay," Avery said, leaning over and slamming a hand over Claude's now-laughing mouth. "I get it. She was perfect."

Claude ducked away, grin intact. "She was a cool chick. But she was totally wrong for Jonah."

"How?" she asked, wondering how much it had to do with her being a city girl, him being a beach boy. Wishing she didn't care about the answer so very much.

"Turned out she was only waiting out her time here till her boss back in Sydney offered up a big enough package to lure her back."

"But weren't they engaged?"

"I think she'd have happily taken him back to Sydney and kept him there if he didn't do that big, strong, tree man thing better than any man I've ever known. She never saw beyond the hotness and the stubbornness to his big heart." Claude's eyes narrowed a fraction, then she said, "You see it, though, don't you?"

"What?" Well, sure she did, but that was beside the point. "No. Don't you go getting ideas now."

"I had to try."

"Wouldn't be you if you didn't."

Claudia took Avery's hands and squeezed, as if making sure Avery was paying attention before she said, "You need to know, though, that I've never seen him smile as much as when he's with you. While you…" Claude's eyes roved over Avery's face. "You, my friend, are glowing."

Avery flapped a "shut up" hand at Claude, and lay back in her sun lounge. Staring up at the cloudless blue sky, more questions came to her only when she looked over at Claude it was to find tears streaming down her face. She leapt to Claude's sun lounge, wrapping an arm about her shoulder. "Claude! Are they happy tears? Tell me they're happy tears!"

Claudia perked up, swiped under her eyes, and smiled. It was a pathetic effort. At least now her friend might be ready to tell her what the hell was really going on.

"That's it," Avery said, "enough of this stoic crap. Tell me. Are your parents okay?"

Claude shook her head so hard her wispy ponytail slapped her in the cheeks. "No, nothing like that. It's just while you're having the best summer of your life I can safely say this has been my worst. The resort... You must have noticed how quiet we are."

Avery looked across the vast pool that curled beneath the balconies of dozens of empty rooms. "When I said I was coming you said something about renovating, so I just thought—"

Claudia laughed, and sniffed. "We can't renovate. We have no money. The resort's bust, or near enough. I've been scraping by since I took over, but so much needs fixing and there's nothing left to fix it."

"Why didn't you tell me all this before?"

"Because I wanted you to have a good time. And I'm pissed off at my parents for not being here to give me any advice. And now I just don't know what else I can do."

Avery's stomach turned at the fear in Claudia's big blue eyes. "Luke's the advertising guru, right? What plans has he put in place?"

"Robot just sent me an email," Claude said, flashing her phone at Avery before curling it back into a tight grip. "He's given me an ultimatum. Get the resort in the black or he's taking over."

"What?"

"He wants to turn it into some flashy Contiki-style resort with a swim-up bar, and toga parties catering to hordes of drunken twenty-somethings."

"He does not!"

"He has figures, graphs, a business plan."

"But that's not what the Tropicana Nights is about. It's kitsch. Family fun. Like a cruise ship without the seasickness."

"Yes! You get it and you've only been here twice. He grew up here and still—" She couldn't get the words out.

"What an ass," Avery said.

And Claude coughed out a laugh. Her laughter turned to more tears, but it was better that than staring into space as she had been the past minute. "Wasn't this the same man you were set to ride off into the sunset with not that long ago?"

"I saw the error of my ways just in time."

"Thank goodness for Jonah."

Yeah, thank goodness for Jonah. But she didn't have time for that now. In fact she'd been a horrible friend all summer, letting Claude get this far without bringing her into the loop.

Avery took Claude by the arms and gave her a shake. "What do you need me to do?"

"You can't do anything."

"I can do quite a lot, as it turns out. I didn't get a first-class education for nothing."

"There's no time."

"Not for a complete turnaround, sure. But what if we could stall Luke? To convince him to give you a stay of execution?"

A flicker of hope came to life in Claude's eyes. "But you're busy."

"Doing what?"

"Jonah."

"Funny girl."

Claude gave a watery smile.

"Claude, I'm not about to walk away from you for some

hot summer loving. You're family." *And family comes first.* How many times had her mother said that, using it as a hook to drag Avery back into the fold any time she looked ready to stray? This time it was true.

Claude's mouth flashed into its first full smile. "Is it as hot as I imagine?"

"Hotter. And yet, here I am. What do you need?"

Sighing long and hard as her glassy gaze wafted over the huge, near-empty resort surrounding them all sides, Claude admitted, "A miracle."

"A party," Jonah repeated as Avery used his warm bare chest as a pillow. Together they lay on a massive hammock strung between two leaning palm trees down on his secluded private beach at the base of his cliff while the tide lapped a lullaby against the big black rocks cradling the small patch of sand.

"Not just a party," Avery said on a blissful sigh. "*The* party. I'm a New Yorker, Mr North. One who has spent nearly every August of my life in the Hamptons. My mother is on so many charity boards it would make you wince. And I am quite the PR savant. So I, Mr North, *know* how to throw a party."

Ironic, considering a party was why she'd fled her home country in the first place. Another reason why the party to relaunch the Tropicana Nights Resort was going to be the most upbeat party ever thrown.

"And it's you, young Jonah, who gave me the idea."

"I seriously doubt that," he murmured, his deep voice reverberating through her chest.

"Way back when, you told me the cove was more than a tourist town—it's a real community. I figured, why not let that community rally around the idea of an 'under new management' icon? So we've invited everyone who has any influence on where people stay in this town. And, using one of the great secrets of the human condition, we'll make them desperate to come by charging an absolute packet for tickets, thus giving Claude's coffers an immediate boost! We are going to put the Tropicana Nights Resort back on the map."

He lifted his head and cupped her chin so he could look her in the eye, clearly less excited than Claude had been. "So what you're really telling me is that you'll be busy the next couple of weeks."

Oh, that's why. "Some."

"Hmm," he growled, lowering himself back down. And wrapping her up tighter. She was near sure of it.

And even while every inch of her craved nothing more than to spend every second of her summer she had left in the arms of this man—converting him to her beloved Yankees—Go Yanks!—watching him let himself love Hull, and just swimming deep in the tumble of feelings she'd never come close to feeling before, Claude was her oldest friend.

And thus, miles from home, she'd once again found herself caught in the perennial tug of war between responsibility and aspiration.

In the past responsibility won, every time. It wasn't even a question. She'd lost count of the dates she'd broken because her mother had called her on her way to a nervous breakdown. But far from the epicentre of that life, she could see that she'd been perfectly happy to indulge in her mother's emotional blackmail. The ready excuse had been a *relief.* Beneath the Pollyanna effervescence, she'd been paralysed by fear of getting hurt.

But here, now, for the first time in memory she felt as if the choice was totally up to her. And while helping Claude in her time of greatest need was a no-brainer, she was all in with Jonah for as long as she had him.

"I'll be busy," she said, shuffling till she fell deeper into his grooves. "But not all the time."

Getting her meaning loud and clear, Jonah ran a lazy finger up and down her bare back, making her spine curl.

"In fact, I foresee many more days like this before my time here is at an end."

His hand stopped its delicious exploration as she felt him harden beneath her, and not in a good way. She shifted to look at his face to find the muscles in his jaw working overtime and his eyes glinting with silver streaks.

She took a careful breath, and had even more careful thoughts. They didn't ever talk about her leaving, but only because they hadn't needed to. It was simply there, a big beautiful prophylactic against the times she found her softer self wondering if being "all in" was less about time and more about the connection between them. Those moments when she caught him looking at her in a way that made her feel something sweet and painful, when it bloomed so sudden and bright within her it took her breath away.

Needing to change the subject, Avery said, "Speaking of hammocks."

"Were we?"

"Yes," she said, waiting for him to agree to pretend they hadn't both been thinking about The End.

With a short expulsion of breath he nodded. "Hammocks."

"Can we borrow yours?"

"For what?"

"The party! Have you not been listening to a word I've said?"

"Hard when you keep wriggling against me like that."

This they could do, Avery thought, curving her spine to meet his hand, breathing out long and hard when it went back to its lazy trawls up and down her back. The sexy stuff left little room for thinking, much less over-thinking.

"That's not the only way you're going to help, either," she said, running a hand over his pecs, his beautiful brown skin rippling under her palm.

"Who said I was going to help at all?"

"I did. You are buying tickets for the entire Charter North office. And I've already messaged Tim a list of the boating decor you'll be loaning us for the evening."

The sexy touching stopped as he moved to glare into her eyes. She wondered how she'd ever found that look infuriating. It was seriously hot. "You sidestepped me to go through Tim?"

"He's nicer than you are. He doesn't argue. He compliments me on my shoes. I think he likes me more than you do too."

"Not possible," he said without thinking, and the bittersweet bloom of feelings inside her ratcheted up to cyclonic levels. "He's gay, you know. Tim. Has a boyfriend. Going on three years now."

"Fabulous. Buy the boyfriend a ticket too."

At that Jonah laughed—finally!—the glare easing to a gleam. Then, by way of an answer, he kissed the corner of her mouth, then the other one, with a gentleness that the gleam in his eyes concealed. Grouchy Jonah was hot, but gentle Jonah, the one who snuck up on her at the least expected moments, was the one who could tear her apart.

She'd miss him when she left—more than it bore thinking about—but she'd never regret leaping into the wild wonderful world of Jonah North. And *that*, she decided in a brilliant epiphany, was the key. It wasn't the looming sense of loss that would define life after this summer, but how she dealt with it. She would not feel sorry for herself. She would not harp on it. And life would go on.

She pulled back to trace the bump on his nose, the ridge

of his cheekbone, the crinkles at the edge of an eye. His skin was so hot, so real.

Jonah's eyebrow raised in question.

Since she knew the surest way to have him leaping from the hammock and running for his life was to give him any indication what was going through her head, she scored her hands through his hair, his glorious dark curls, and drew his mouth back to hers. And with the ocean clawing its way onto the beach below, the sun baking the earth around them, she kissed him till she felt nothing but him. But this. All this.

For now...

Later that evening, curled up in a big round cane chair on Jonah's back porch, Avery found herself thinking more and more about home. Wondering if the best thing to do would be to book her flight back so that it was done.

Instead—as if *that* were the lesser of two evils—she Skyped her mother. She'd been avoiding it all week. Ever since she and Claude had started organising the party, in fact. Because it would come up. And then so would the *other* party. And distraction and avoidance had worked brilliantly so far, so why mess with it?

By the time her mother answered—her neat ash-blonde bob and perfectly made-up face flitting onto the screen—Avery's throat was so tight she wondered if she'd get a word out at all.

Lucky her mother was on song. "Who are you and what have you done with my daughter?"

Avery glanced at the small version of herself in the bottom of the screen, and realised for the first time since she'd arrived it hadn't occurred to her to dress up for the call. She had shaggy beach hair, freckles on her nose, wore a bikini and nothing else.

But that wasn't why she couldn't drag her eyes away

from her own image. Her mouth was soft. Her shoulders relaxed. Her eyes content. Somehow in the past few weeks she'd shed her air of quiet desperation and she looked... happy.

The tapping away of a computer keyboard in the office behind the open window farther down the porch brought her back to the present.

Blinking, she dragged her gaze back to the main screen. "You hate the tan, right?"

Caroline Shaw—she'd kept her ex-husband's name— rolled her eyes, careful not to wrinkle. "So long as you're using sunscreen. And moisturiser. And toner. And—"

"I'm having a fabulous time, thanks for asking."

When her mother smiled at the hit, Avery went on to fill her in on the happenings around the cove—about Claude, and Isis and Cyrus, and Hull and his lady friend. Not about the party, though. Or the man taking up most of her time.

"What about that man?" her mother asked, glancing away to grab a china cup hopefully filled with tea as Avery jumped.

It took everything in her power now to glance towards the glow of Jonah's window as she asked, "What man?"

"The hotelier. We came to know his parents all those years ago."

"The... *Luke*?"

"Mmm. I Googled him when you brought him up at one time. Handsome fellow. Eminently eligible. Divorced," she said with the usual hiss that implied, "but redeemable, one might hope. You haven't mentioned him in a while so I wondered, if perhaps..."

Avery had forgotten that her mother was like a human tuning fork, trembling in aggravation any time she thought her only daughter might be cast aside by some evil man as she herself had once been.

It would have been easy to pretend, just as it had been

easier to walk away from every romantic relationship than to think about why that was. But, for the first time in re-callable history, she said to her mother: "No. I'm actually seeing someone else."

Her mother paused with the teacup halfway to her mouth. "And who is this lucky young man?"

Avery's heart beat hard as she watched her mother's every facial movement for signs of a meltdown. "His name is Jonah. He's a local. We met in the ocean. Hull—the dog with the lady-friend—is his."

Good grief. Could she have offered a less interesting version of the man? But this was a watershed moment and she was doing her best.

"As handsome as the other one?" her mother asked gently as if she knew that Avery was struggling not to gush.

"More."

Her mother smiled softly, sadly, and Avery suddenly wished she hadn't said anything at all. Dealing with her mother as she raged at the world was one thing, seeing her wistful was like a knife to the heart.

Avery heard the shower start up, meaning Jonah was done with whatever he'd been working on in his office and was getting ready for bed. This *handsome* man she was seeing. Hearing it inside her head she saw how vanilla that sounded, how weak a description for what had happened to her this summer.

And she felt with a sharp keening deep inside her how little of that summer was left.

She feigned a yawn.

Her mother attempted to raise an eyebrow, which, considering the years of Botox, was a near impossibility. "Sleepy, darling? You'd be heading out now if you were back here."

The idea of heading out paled into insignificance compared with what was awaiting her by staying in. "Life's different here. It's slower. Gentler. It revolves around the sun. It's…" This time she couldn't stop herself glancing towards the window down the way, the light spilling out onto the rough wood and mixing with the unimpeded moonlight. "It's curative."

When Avery looked back at her mother's image on the screen, it was to find her mouth open, her forehead pinched, as if she was about say something; something Avery wouldn't like. Avery's stomach clenched. *Please*, she begged silently, not sure what she was pleading for. Time? Understanding? Amnesty? Release…?

Then her mother said, "Love you, baby girl. Take care. Come home soon." And signed off.

Avery breathed out hard.

She put Jonah's tablet on the kitchen bench inside and padded into his bedroom to find his en-suite shower—hot the way he liked it, filling both rooms with steam. And the man himself stripping bare.

Her eyes trailed his beautiful form, the movement of muscles across his back, the perfect pale backside between the deep golden-brown of his back and his thighs, like a hint of sweetness amidst all that raw testosterone.

She went to him and ran a hand over each cheek, kissing her way across his shoulder blades, grinning against him as his muscles clenched deliciously at her touch.

"You all done out there?" he asked, turning, his scrunched up T-shirt warm and soft between them.

"Mmm-hmm," she said, trailing fingers over the bumps of his biceps.

"All good?" he asked, his voice tight.

She glanced up to find his eyes were dark. His energy reined in. She couldn't wait for the moment it wasn't.

"As good as can be expected. My mother did wonder one thing…"

"What's that?"

"She wondered why I wasn't planning on going out."

"What did you tell her?"

"We're close, but we're not that close." With that she lifted onto her toes, sank her hands into his hair, and kissed him, melting from the outside in when he dropped the T-shirt and held her, his naked heat against her bikini-clad skin.

Lifting her lanky self into his arms as if she weighed nothing at all, he walked her into the bathroom, and dumped her in the shower, her head right under the hot spray. Laughing, she pushed her hair out of her eyes and grinned up at him. The grin fading to a sigh, when she caught the heat in his eyes.

Curative, she thought as he enfolded her in his strong arms, and kissed her till she saw stars. Making her wonder just what Jonah North might be curing her of.

CHAPTER TEN

AVERY NEVER DID get the chance to book that plane ticket home as the next week and a half of her life was consumed by the organising of The Party.

Claude had picked the theme—*Beyond the Sea*. Leaving room for exactly the kind of kitsch fun of the Tropicana Nights she had in mind along with a hefty dose of glamour, elegance, and old-world nostalgia, Avery Shaw style.

Dean Martin crooned smoothly beneath the sounds of laughter and chatter of the guests. Champagne, locally brewed beer, and pineapple punch flowed, served by a cute-as-a-button mermaid and a total hottie merman. Frangipani flowers and silver tea lights floated in the pool and above it all hung a web of lobster nets from which glinted strings of pure white fairy lights.

Jonah—by way of Tim the office manager—had donated the nets, life-preservers for the wait staff, and life rings for decorations, and the dozen vintage rum barrels currently serving as occasional tables. But the yacht? That was pure Jonah. A gorgeous black and silver thing reposing with lazy elegance on stumps in one corner of the pool deck, it had arrived at the resort the day before, complete with a crane to put it into place. There'd been no word as to where it had come from, just a note: "Raffle it. Knock 'em dead, kiddo." From the raffle tickets alone Claude had already made enough money to keep the resort afloat for a month.

Claudia leaned her head on Avery's shoulder as they took a rare breather from hostess duties. "I couldn't afford to throw a beach ball much less a party, but look at this."

Avery lifted her beer bottle in salute. "And this is only the beginning. Once the travel bloggers start trickling in for their free stays word will really get out that you offer something really special here, Claude. And people will come."

"I don't know how I can do all that without you, Avery."

Avery held her hand. Hard.

She'd always thought her attraction to PR was a natural extension of all those years playing Pollyanna with her mom and dad. But standing there with her best friend in the whole world, seeing their efforts about to come to fruition, felt pretty different from… What had she said to Jonah? *Taking not naturally pleasant products and talking them up till they smelled like roses.*

Avery drew Claude's arm close. "Go mingle. Thank. Drum up clients. A hotelier's work is never done."

Claudia pulled herself up straight, and went to do just that.

Which was when Avery felt a hand land on her lower back. She knew instantly it didn't belong to Jonah—no spark, no warmth, no drizzle of sensation that hit the backs of her knees and stayed even after his touch was gone.

She spun to find Luke—clean-shaven, neat as a pin, resplendent in his slick suit.

"Luke!" She leaned in and kissed his cheek. "Wow. No tie. It must be a party. Does Claude know you're here? She'll be thrilled you made it back in time to see her glory unfold."

"Sure about that?"

"Absolutely. And this is only a taste of the kinds of ideas

she has going forward. So you need to cut our girl some slack or you'll have me to deal with. Don't even think I'm kidding. I'm a New Yorker, remember. I know people."

Luke tapped the side of his nose. "I'll take it into consideration. Where is she?"

"She was heading to... Oh."

Avery caught sight of Claudia's wispy blonde ponytail. She was dancing with a dark-haired, dark-eyed, snake-hipped man who held her very, very close. It could only be Raoul.

Avery turned to Luke to point her out. By the look in Luke's eyes she didn't need to.

Tunnel vision down to an art form, Luke said, "Nice to see you, Avery," then made a beeline for his business partner.

Avery made to follow, to play intermediary, till she felt a pair of hands encircle her waist from behind, and this time there was no doubting who they belonged to. She leant into Jonah's warmth, sighing all over as she sank into his touch.

"How's Luke?" he asked in that deep, sexy, *sexy* voice of his.

"Had you worried there, did I?"

"Not for a New York second."

"A New York second, eh? You do know that's like a tenth the length of a Crescent Cove second."

"You're really going there?" His tone was joking, but the dark thread wavering beneath it curled itself around Avery's heart and pulled tight. But the thing was, the time was coming when she *would* be going there. They couldn't avoid it forever.

Beer, adrenalin, and the fact that she wasn't looking into his eyes gave her the guts to say, "Afraid you'll miss me so desperately when I go?"

He sank a kiss into her hair, his lips staying put. "No point. Without me around the moment you get home you'll fall down a sewer hole and never be seen again. And then I'll have to console Claudia. She'll insist we build a memorial. And I'm a busy man, don't you know?"

She knew. And she also knew how much time he'd carved out for her these past few weeks. The late starts, the early afternoons, the long delicious nights. Avery's stomach clenched so hard she put a hand on her belly. Jonah's hand landed quietly over the top. And there they stayed a few minutes, simply soaking in one another's warmth.

Then Jonah's chin landed on her shoulder, his breath brushing her ear. "Ms Shaw, are you actually drinking a beer?"

Avery lifted the bottle to her mouth and took a swig. Jonah growled in appreciation.

"I'd have thought you'd like women with a bit of tomboy in them. Women who can hoist a rigging. And swing an anchor. And lift a... No. I'm done."

There was a beat, like a moment lost in time, before he murmured, "I like you."

And while Avery's heart near imploded, she somehow managed to say, "Took your sweet time."

He laughed, the *huh-huh-huh* tripping gorgeously down her arms, before casual as you please he unwound his arms and ambled away.

Avery's breath shuddered through her chest as she stared after him. Watching him ease through the multitude, stopping to chat whenever anyone called his name. Such a man. A *good* man, she thought, her gaze glancing off all the extras he'd donated without having been asked. The yacht he'd given simply because he could. No fanfare. No drama. Just honest, down-to-earth decency.

And this man *liked* her.

She liked him too. She felt full around him—light and safe and important. She felt desired. She felt raw. In fact she liked the Avery she was around him. The one who didn't have to try so hard all the time.

The sexy, pulsing thrum of The Flamingos' "I Only Have Eyes For You" hummed from the speaker near Avery's feet. A burst of laughter split the night from somewhere to her right. A drip of condensation slid from the cold beer bottle clasped gently in her grip to land on her foot.

As just like that, between breaths, between beats, between one second and the next, Avery Shaw fell in love for the first time in her life.

Jonah watched Avery laughing it up with Tim and his boyfriend, Roger. Playing referee between Luke and Claude. Mesmerising the ice-cream-van guy and the rest of the Dreadlock Army who'd managed to wangle tickets from who knew where—though by the number of nubile young female tourists fluttering around them it had probably been a smart move to bus them in.

Not that he did any more than notice the others. Not with the way Avery seemed to fill his vision. Her dress a shimmery cream concoction of ruffles that made her skin gleam. Her hair a shining waterfall down her back. String of tiny silver beads sparkled on her wrist throwing off light every time she moved.

And it took every bit of self-restraint he had not to drag her away and find somewhere quiet, somewhere private, even if just to mess her up some.

Instead he downed a goodly dose of beer.

For these feelings were not fun. They were bloody terrifying. For this Avery wasn't the one he knew. In her place was some kind of professional miracle worker. What she'd done in whipping the slow-moving folk of the cove into a near frenzy to throw the bash of the century in such a short space of time was nothing short of miraculous.

She was something else—not that *his Avery* hadn't tried to tell him as much on many an occasion: competitive swimmer, life spent travelling the world, PR whiz in what was no doubt the toughest market in the world, with a life bigger, brighter, snazzier than he could possibly know.

Like knocking on a brick wall with a feather, it had been. Because he hadn't wanted to see it. Preferring to focus on her futile resistance to his charms. How readily she'd made room for him in her life. The ease with which she'd fitted into his. And how, for the first time in a half-dozen years, he'd found a reason big enough to carve time away from his business.

But tonight there was no hiding from the stark reality before him.

The Avery who'd snuck under his skin, made herself right at home, who looked as if she were born in a bikini, was at her heart a social butterfly, a Park Avenue Princess. She *glowed* out there, under the bright lights and attention.

While at his very essence he was a beach bum who'd had no plans beyond living off his father's meagre life insurance until a kick in the pants had brought his life to the very crux of survival.

Like a hard tug on the cord of an abandoned outboard motor, that resting survival instinct coughed and spluttered back to life, and Jonah took a step back, near tripping over a vintage rum barrel. One of his. Collector's items; he'd seen them, wanted them, and just had to have. So he'd made them his.

An offshoot of thriving so stridently. He'd become cocky. Proven by the fact that he'd seen Avery, wanted her, and hadn't let anything stand in the way of having her. Not the fact that she was a tourist. Not the fact that she drove him around the bend. Not even when her ridiculous notion of Luke had given him the best possible out.

All signs he'd ignored; when Avery and her kisses and

sweet skin and nothing to do but him were gateway drugs back to the old days. When he'd taken pleasure for pleasure's sake. When he'd had no responsibilities. When he'd had nobody left in his life to set him any boundaries. When things had felt simple, and easy, and free.

As if she'd sensed him watching, whatever she'd been saying came to a halt. Her cheeks pinked as her eyes lit on his and sparkled. She lifted the beer in salute. And by the time someone stepped in between them, blocking her from view, Jonah's lungs felt as if they were filling with water.

Avoiding the rum barrel, Jonah turned and walked away. Stopping only when he found a place he could think straight. He found it amongst the girls from the Tea Tree Resort of Green Island. They clearly didn't care that he didn't join in their conversation, which was something about men in boots.

Charming girls, he thought, their familiar accents earthing him. Charming like the cove. But the cove was too far away from the rest of the world to hold any but the most determined, the most dug in, forever. Avery would go back where *she* belonged and he'd be left rattling around in his big house. His big life. His full life.

A life that had felt like more than enough.

Until he'd gone looking for something he felt was missing that fateful morning, and found Avery.

His survival instincts were roaring now, propelling him fast and hard in the right direction. The other stuff, the stuff he didn't want to think about any more, he shut down piece by piece.

It was a trick he'd learnt after his mother had left. A trick he'd utilised, every night after, waiting past dark for his father to come home, never entirely sure that he would. Until the night he'd not come home at all.

In that state of numbed relief he'd remain. At least until the day Avery Shaw finally flew out of his life. And then, as before, he'd claw his way back out, using the restorative air of his home to bring him back to life again.

It was near three in the morning when Avery made it back to the Tiki Suite and floated inside, the gratification of success, a couple of late cocktails with an ebullient Claudia, and the wild blow of feelings for Jonah giving her wings.

She wished he were there to help her work off her adrenalin, but he'd disappeared at some point around midnight. Once the girls from Green Island had imbibed enough cocktails to start following him around and calling him Captain Jack, she'd known he'd only last so long.

Instead she decided to call her mother. It would be the afternoon before the other party. The flipside. Evil to Avery's Good. Even as it made her tummy flutter, it would be heartless not to let her mother know she was thinking about her, hoping it went…not disastrously. So why not do so while she was full of beer and joy?

Lying on her bed, moonlight pouring through the window, she pressed the phone to her ear.

"Hey," Avery said when her mother answered, her voice croaky from all the *talking, talking, talking*.

"Darling," her mother said, her voice so weary Avery quickly checked her phone to make sure she hadn't got the time wrong. "What time is it there?"

"Middle of the night. But that's okay. I'm just home from a party Claude and I threw. A Tropicana reboot. And it was fabulous."

"I have no doubt."

Avery swallowed. "Are you all ready for yours?"

"Hmm?"

"Your party?"

"Oh. Didn't I mention…? I cancelled it."

Didn't she…? *What?* Wow! And no. But good, right? Maybe even a breakthrough! The very idea of which swam through Avery like a wave of hope, of possibility that maybe things were changing on both sides of the world—

"Are you sitting down?" her mother asked, breaking into her reverie.

"Um, sure," Avery lied, lifting up onto her elbow at least.

"I have some news I was hoping to save until your return, but I don't want you to hear it on the grapevine, so… Darling, your father's getting remarried."

Avery's elbow shot out from under her.

"Darling?"

"I heard." Avery dragged herself to sitting, leaning forward over her crossed legs, the back of a hand on her suddenly spiking-hot forehead. Her father…getting remarried? "Oh, Mom."

"You seemed so happy when we Skyped last week, so content, I couldn't… But you had to know some time, so there it is. Phillip's getting *married*," her mother said again, and this time Avery heard more than just the words. She heard the deep quiet, the gentle sorrow, the *fresh* heartbreak. *Oh, Mom.* "Are *you* okay?"

"I'll be fine. Aren't I always?"

Avery could have begged to differ, but she let that one lie. Saying no to her mother was a lesson she had to learn, but that was not the time.

"Maybe this is a good thing…" Avery offered up, feeling sixteen all over again as she squeezed her eyes shut tight. "Maybe now you can move on."

"Sweet girl," said Caroline, making no promises.

And for the first time since their family fell apart, Avery kind of understood. There was a fine line between love and…not *hate* so much as exasperation. Avery knew how that felt. Jonah had taken her there these past weeks, right to the tipping point and back again, with his stubbornness, self-assuredness, neutrality. How long it had taken for him to even admit he *liked* her?

It was a scary thing, the tipping. But the reward so was worth it. Every time she saw in his eyes and felt in his touch that what was happening between them was so much bigger than *"like."*

Maybe that was why her mother had hung on as long as she could. Not out of some kind of predisposition to hysteria, but because when it had been good it had been beyond compare.

Avery bit her lip to stop the emotion welling up inside her.

"Darling," said her mother, into the silence, "just this one last thing. Something to tuck away for one day. When you find the one it's not all hearts and flowers—it's two separate people trying to fit into one another's lives. Which can feel nearly impossible at times. But no matter how hard it might be to live with them, it's far harder to live without them."

One day? Avery thought. Wondering if across the miles her mother had a single clue that her *one day* was *this day*. So much philosophy from her mother to take in at three in the morning, Avery pressed her fingers to her eyes.

"Now, just forget about it. Go back to enjoying your holiday. Is it sunny there?"

Avery looked at the moonlight shaving swathes into the darkness. "Sunny like no place on earth."

"Cover up. Hats and sunscreen. Don't ruin that gorgeous skin of yours. You're only young once. Blink and it's gone."

That was when the tears came. Big fat ones that left a big wet patch on her party dress.

"Love you, Mom."

"Love you too, baby girl."

Avery hung up her phone and held it in her lap. Shoulders hunched, she looked out at the moonlit sky. The same moon that would rise over New York the next night.

She imagined herself standing outside JFK airport, icy wind slapping her coat against her legs, the sharp scent of the island making her nostrils flare, the sound of a million cabs fighting for space.

Shaking her head she replaced the view with the angel in Central Park, with the stairs of the New York Public Library, with her favourite discount shoe shop deep in the canyons of the financial district. The colour of Broadway. Her favourite cocktail bar in the Flatiron. Laughing with her friends, sharing stories about people they all knew, had known all their lives.

She blinked and suddenly saw Jonah's face, his eyes crinkling, white teeth flashing in his brown face, his dark curls glistening with ocean water, sun pouring over his skin. She closed her eyes on a ragged sigh and felt his hand on her waist, sliding over her ribs, scraping the edge of her breast. She opened her mouth to his taste. His heat. His desire.

And his difference. Everyone took Avery at face value. Happy go lucky. Always with the smiling. With Jonah she'd never been anything but herself. Good, bad. Delighted, irate. Whatever that was at any given moment.

And her heart clenched with such a beat of loneliness, a foreshadowing of what she'd be—who she'd be—without him in her life.

Because she'd soon find out.

Her mother might be putting on a brave face, but, for all the drama of the past decade, this would be the hardest thing she'd gone through. And Avery had to be there. Not to do cartwheels and tell her everything was going to be okay. But to give her mother a hug. And let her know *she* was loved. Just the way *she* was.

Not because it would keep the peace, but because it felt like the right thing to do.

She opened her eyes, and lay slowly back on her bed, wrapping her arms about her stomach.

It was time for Avery to go home.

Late the next morning, Avery hung up from her dad.

He'd sounded…if not *over the moon* about his upcoming nuptials, about as close to as Phillip Maxwell Shaw ever got when not talking about the Dow Jones or the Yankees batting line-up.

She'd also discovered that he *knew*. He knew her mother still pined for him, had known for the past ten years that her feelings hadn't flagged, which was probably why he hadn't put out a cease and desist order the times she'd gone past the edge of reason.

Avery sank her face into her hands, letting the darkness behind her eyelids cool her thoughts.

Maybe the life lesson she'd been meant to learn from them *wasn't* that love was a perfect storm of emotional vertigo teetering on the precipice of destruction. Maybe it was just to be *honest* about it. Because if her mother and father had just had a candid conversation in the past ten years they could have saved themselves a hell of a lot of trouble. And *her*.

Her phone beeped. She breathed in a lungful of air, eyes refocusing.

You up for a swim? I can practically guarantee your survival.
Jonah.

Seeing his name was like an electric shock, shooting her from nonplussed to high alert. She'd wondered if the barrage of news, and the bright light of day, might dim her feelings. But if anything they'd taken on a new sharpness. A new veracity.

And the thought of going home, of saying goodbye, of never seeing him again, made her hurt. But she was going home. It was what happened after that that remained a big gloomy blur.

Her palms felt slick as she answered.

Meet you on the beach in ten.

She couldn't feel her feet as she made her way through the halls, through Reception, and outside.

She found Jonah leaning against his sleek black car, his naked torso gleaming in the shadows, his surfboard leaning beside him, Hull making circles in the grass beneath a palm tree before he sat with a *hurumph*.

Jonah looked up, took in her short white shorts, slinky black wraparound top, her strappy sandals. Her lack of a towel.

He pushed away from the car, his mouth kicking into a half-smile even as his eyes remained strangely flat. "I get that you're a city girl, but earrings?"

He looked so gorgeous. Her heart slammed against her ribs and she perched on his bumper to catch her breath.

Jonah joined her. Close enough to catch his scent, his warmth, far enough not to touch. As if he knew she was leaving. And how much she didn't want to.

She turned to find him looking back towards the Tropicana. "Jonah, I've booked my flight home."

Air filled his chest, his nostrils flaring, a frown darting across his brow before he looked down at his bare toes. Then finally, finally he looked her way, his grey eyes unreadable. His mouth so grim she could have been mistaken for thinking it had never learned to smile at all. "When?"

"Early this morning."

"No, when do you leave?"

"Oh." Her cheeks pinked. She felt so raw, so terrified by his reaction or lack thereof.

"Three days."

He breathed out. Nodded once. As if it was no surprise. And yet a world-weariness settled over him, adding a grey tinge to the golden halo that made him always seem more than a mere mortal. She could only hope that it was because he felt some fraction of what she felt for him. One way or the other, she'd soon find out.

"I'd like to come back. Soon." Deep breath. *Be honest.* "I'd like to come back to see you."

He didn't comment. Didn't even blink. A muscle ticing once in his jaw as he looked across the road.

"Or maybe you'd like to come visit me."

She shrugged, as if it didn't matter either way. When really her heart was now desperately trying to take its leave of the space behind her ribs and jump into his hands and say, *Do with me as you please, because I'm all yours!*

"I can show you around Manhattan. I think you'd love the park. And Liberty Island is a pretty special place. I promise not to drag you around Saks.'

As the words spilled out of her mouth she even began to see how it might work. How a long-distance relationship was actually...not impossible. They both had the means.

They both just had to want it enough.

Her want was palpable, running about inside her with such speed she had to hug herself so it didn't escape. All that aching hope was what finally woke Pollyanna. She gave a yawning stretch, stood to attention, brushed the dust from her hands, about to say, *Right, let's get this thing done!* But before she could open her mouth, Jonah came to.

"Avery," he said, his voice ocean-deep. "This has been fun. But we both knew it was only going to last until it was time for you to go."

Avery uncurled her spine and sat up straight, all the better to breathe. "That was the plan, sure. But plans can change. I'm saying…I'd like the plan to change."

There, Avery thought, breathing out hard.

Jonah shot her a glance, so fleeting it brushed past her eyes and away, but long enough she caught the heat, the ache, the want. Then said, "Not going to happen."

"Why?"

"Because I have a job here, Avery. One that's been getting short shrift of late. I have ties here. Because I have responsibilities I'm not about to turn my back on. Because *this* is where I want to be."

Avery flinched as his voice rose. "I know that. I'm not asking you to *move*. Or give up anything. Or change who you are. Just to spend some time. With me."

The look he shot her told her he didn't believe her for a second. Been there, done that, lived to regret every second.

"Jonah—"

"Avery. Just stop," he said, exasperation ravaging the edges of his voice.

She shifted on the bumper bar till her knees bumped his, the scoot of heat nothing in the quagmire of frustration and fear riding her roughshod. "This," she said, "from the man who came over huffy when he thought I had intimated he might be parochial! The cove is wonderful. I give it that. But I've travelled. I've seen a hundred places equally gorgeous. So why are you *really* hiding out at the end of the earth?"

His expression was cool, his voice cooler, as he said, "I'm not hiding, Avery. I'm home."

She snorted. Real ladylike.

But at least it seemed to snap him from his shell. "I've tried it out there, Avery. It's not for me."

The urge to scoff again was gone before it ever took

hold once she realised—by *out there* he didn't mean Sydney. He meant *love*.

He'd put his heart *out there*, and had it sent spinning right on back. She wanted to tell him she wouldn't do that. Wouldn't leave him like his mother. Wouldn't pretend to feel something as his ex had. Wouldn't let him flounder while she got on with her life like his dad had done.

But by the stern set of his jaw she realised he wouldn't believe her.

No snorting then. Just a sudden constriction in her chest as she saw the raw honesty in Jonah's clear grey eyes. The determination. The conviction that this was no different. She was no different.

God, how she wanted to hit him! To thump his big chest till he got it. That for them summer could go on forever. They…both…just…had…to…want…it.

And then it hit her, like a smack to the back of the head. She might want it enough for the both of them. But—as proven by events on the other side of the planet—it would never be enough.

"This can't be it," she said, the words tearing from her throat.

"Honey," he said, and this time it felt so much like a real endearment she opened her eyes wider to halt the tears. He saw. Right through her, as always. But instead of doing what the twitch in his jaw told her he wanted to do—to run his thumb underneath her eye, to slide his big hand over her shoulder, to haul her in tight—he sniffed out a breath of frustration and ran two hands down his face. And said, "This summer has been a blast. But like every summer before it has to end. It's time for you to go home. And soon you'll look back and thank your lucky stars you did."

Avery shook her head, her fingers biting into the hot metal at her backside.

Not having Jonah in her life would *not* be better than having him in it. She hadn't needed to hear her mother say it to know *that* for sure. But he looked at her with such clarity, such resolution.

"How can you just switch off like that? Tell me. Because I really want to know how to make this feeling—" She slammed a closed fist against her ribs, the surface hurt nothing on the tight ball of pain inside. "How can you make it just go away?"

"Avery—"

"I'm serious. *Can* you turn it off? Just like that? Honestly?"

He looked at her. Right into her eyes. As tears of frustration finally spilled down her cheeks. He looked right into her eyes, not even a flicker of reaction to her pain. And he said, "I can."

Then he leaned over, wrapped an arm about her shoulders, kissed her on top of her head, lifted himself from the back of his car, grabbed his surfboard, and took off for the water at a jog.

CHAPTER ELEVEN

HE COULDN'T.

The night of the party Jonah had convinced himself that the only way not to feel like crap at being left was by doing the leaving himself. As if *that* was the common denominator of the shittiest times of his life; the fact that they had been out of his control.

Turned out it didn't matter a lick. Two days on, walking away from Avery still bit. Like a shark bite, a great chunk of him missing, the wound exposed to the salty air.

"Storm's a coming."

"What?"

Tim backed up to the office door, two hands raised in surrender. "Nora said you were in a snit. I said, 'More than usual?' She said, 'Go poke the bear and you'll find out.'"

Jonah pinned his second in charge with a flat stare. "Consider me poked."

Tim lolloped into the office and sat. "Want to talk about it?"

"I'll give you one guess."

"Avery," Tim said, nodding sadly.

Right guess, wrong answer. Knowing Tim well enough to know the only way out of this was through, Jonah ran two hands over his face and turned his chair to look out over the water. The sun glinted so fiercely through a mass of gathering grey clouds he had to squint.

"She's really leaving, huh?" Tim asked.

A muscle twitched in Jonah's cheek. "You'll find that's what holidaymakers do. Keeps the tourist dollars spinning. Pays your wage and mine."

A pause from Tim. Then, "She's been doing the rounds of the entire town. Saying goodbye. And leaving little gifts." Tim held up his hand, a plaited friendship bracelet circling his arm. "It matches Roger's."

"Lucky Roger."

"What did she leave you?"

The knowledge that he'd been knocked around more times than he could count in his thirty-odd years on earth and hadn't learned a damn thing.

Jonah pushed himself to standing and grabbed his keys from the fish hook by the door. "I have to go. Appointment. Tell Nora to transfer calls to my mobile."

Tim saluted. "Aye-aye, Cap'n."

Jonah jogged through the offices. His staff were smart enough to leave him be.

Truth was he did have an appointment; one he'd made a week before. Once outside and at the Monaro, as he pressed the remote lock Hull apparated from nowhere to appear at his heels, his liquid eyes quietly sad, as if he knew what he was in for.

When the sorry truth was he was probably pining for Avery. Whole damn east coast was apparently pining for Avery.

Jonah clicked his fingers and Hull jumped in the back of the car. Jonah gunned the engine, the wild rumble of the muscle car matching his mood to perfection. He wound down the windows, thumbed the buttons till he found a song on the radio that had a hope in hell of numbing his mind. Then he set off for the vet.

For big Hull was getting the snip.

He'd be better off castrated. For one thing he could go

through life never again noticing the Petunias of the world. No more urges that were as helpful as a hole in the head.

For half a second Jonah was envious. An operation might be pushing it, but he'd take a pill if it meant ridding himself of the ache behind his ribs that refused to let up.

With a rumble of gears, he hit the freeway leading down the coast towards the cove.

Towards Avery. Yeah, she was still out there somewhere—lazing on the beach, drinking those coconutty things she couldn't get enough of, wearing some delectable excuse for swimwear, laughing in that loose sexy way of hers—

She hadn't been laughing, or smiling, when he'd last seen her. He'd been harsh. He'd had to. Even as she'd floated the idea to keep it going, he'd felt the same pull so strongly it had threatened to take him under. Because what he'd had with her was better than anything he'd ever had with another human being in the entire history of his life on earth.

But he'd had to make a clean break.

He lifted a hand to shield his face from the burning sun shining through the driver's side window, and pulled into the fast lane to overtake a semi-trailer. The road shook beneath him, rattling his teeth.

After his mother left, his childhood had been waylaid by waiting for the other shoe to drop. By the expectation that more bad things were to come. And they had, when his father had died. He'd realised too late that waiting for it to happen hadn't made it any easier. So with Rach, instead of waiting he'd leapt in, held on tighter. Not because *her* leaving had been that much of a shock—but because he was looking for a connection, *any* connection, something to prove he was more than a dandelion seed caught on the wind.

Half an hour later he pulled up at the shack. Jogging up the steps, he went inside to grab Hull's new lead, copies of the paperwork he'd recently filled out to register Hull with the local council as his dog, and Hull's favourite chew toy.

And there, right in the middle of his sun-drenched entryway, he stopped dead. Looked around. And felt Avery everywhere. He felt her in the tilt of his kitchen chair, better angled to the sun. Felt her in the throw rug draped over his couch, the one she wrapped about her feet that always got cold at night.

He stared at Hull's chew toy in his hand; Avery had ordered it online—a rubber hot dog in Yankees colours.

Poor Hull who was about to get the snip. Who'd never again have the chance to find himself a girl. The *right* girl.

Jonah was running back to the car when the first raindrops hit.

Only to find Hull was gone.

"Jonah! Excellent. You staying?" Claudia asked as she saw Jonah taking the front steps of the Tropicana two at a time.

"Where?"

"Here! Storm's a coming, my friend. A big one!" Claude poked her hand outside, captured a few stray raindrops in her palm. "Can't hate a storm when it brings a town's worth of guests through my front door to use my cellar as a safe area! Would it be poor form to hand out brochures with the water?"

He shook his head. "Claude, I'm looking for Hull."

"Not here. Why?"

"Doesn't matter." Jonah rocked on his feet; half of him keen to look for Hull, the other half somewhat stuck. "Everyone's down in the cellar?"

"Everyone who's anyone. I'm thinking it's the perfect chance to show off what the Tropicana Nights is all about."

"Natural disaster management?"

"Fun," she glowered. "Submarine theme, perhaps.

Caveman, maybe. Mum and Dad had an awesome collection of faux animal skins back in the day."

A themed bunker, Jonah thought. *Heaven help them all.* And then his thoughts shifted back to where they'd been moments before. Where they constantly strayed.

He couldn't ask—he didn't have the right after what he'd done—but it came out anyway. "Avery there already?"

Claude shot him a flat stare. "She's gone, Jonah. No thanks to you."

"Gone where?"

"*Gone* gone. Back to the U. S. of A. To the bright lights and freezing winters and her suffocating mother and neglectful father. I thought we had her this time. That our beautiful butterfly had finally realised she had wings. But no. Flight to JFK leaves in…fifteen minutes. Or left fifteen minutes ago. Not sure which."

Time slowed, then came to a screeching halt. Avery was gone. Out of his life for good. As the full realisation of all that meant wrapped about him like a dark wet cloak, Jonah was amazed he could find his voice at all. "But she wasn't due to leave for a couple of days."

"Time to get back to *real life*," Claudia said, taking a moment to glare at him between happily ticking off the list on her clipboard. "I tried to make her stay despite it, but I wasn't the one who could."

"Meaning?"

"There's a *storm* a coming. I don't have time for all this. Use that brain in that pretty little head of yours and think!"

Think he did. So hard he near burst a blood vessel.

Why? Why was he making himself feel like crap when he didn't need to? Fear she'd some day make him feel like crap and he wanted to get there first? Life had taught him some hard lessons. Some at a pretty early age. And there was no certainty there wouldn't be more hard lessons to come.

Didn't mean he couldn't buck the system. He'd done it

before, in dragging himself up by his bootstraps. He could do it again. Damn well *should* do it again, if that was what it took to have the life he wanted. To be happy.

"Don't worry about Hull," Claudia said, drawing him out of the throbbing quagmire inside his head. "He'll have found a safe haven somewhere hiding out from the storm. Dogs are smart."

"What storm?"

"Storm!" she said, taking him by the cheeks and turning his face to look through the huge front doors across the street and over the water where grey clouds swarmed like an invasion from the skies.

Where the hell had that come from? How had he not known? He owned a fleet of boats, for heaven's sake. Phone already at his ear, he called Charter North. "Nora. Get Tim to—"

Jonah listened with half an ear as he pounded down the front stairs, his eyes on the menacing clouds overhead. Turned out Tim had somehow known he might not be quite on his game and had done all that had to be done. Good man. The second he next saw him the guy was getting a promotion.

Jonah hung up and looked to the skies. And his heart imploded on the spot.

Avery was flying into that?

"If you see Hull," he called out, his voice sounding as if it were coming from the bottom of a well, "get him under cover. Don't dress him up in any way, shape or form."

"Count on it!" Claudia called back. "Where are you going?"

"To bring our girl home."

"'Atta boy!" she said, then shut the front door.

Hull was strong. Hull was smart. He'd be somewhere dry, waiting out the wet. Just as Jonah had planned to wait out the heartache of letting Avery go.

Only the storm in his head, in his heart, was of his own making. And as he set off to rescue his girl, he did so with a slice of fear cutting through him the likes of which he'd never felt. And hope.

He reached his car right as raindrops hit the road with fat slaps, and when the skies opened and dumped their contents on the cove he was already headed to the airport.

Avery sat in the cab, which had been stuck in the same spot for over an hour, the rain outside lashing the windows.

"Car accident," the cabbie said.

"Mmm?"

"Radio's saying car accident. Hasn't rained here for weeks. Oil on the road gets slick. Accidents happen." He leant forward to peer through the rain-hammered window and up into the grey skies. "Any luck your flight's been cancelled."

When he realised Avery wasn't in a chatty mood, he shrugged and went back to his phone.

She didn't mind. The shushing of the rain was a background of white noise against her disorderly thoughts.

She'd been thinking about moving, actually. Farther down the island. It would be healthy to keep some of the distance the trip had given her from her family.

Her apartment was a sublet, after all. Her job freelance too, despite numerous headhunters desperate to secure her. Even her house plants were fake. Heck, she'd only bought a one-way ticket on her holiday, ambivalence stopping her from even committing to when she might return.

She'd felt holier than thou that Jonah couldn't commit to a dog? She'd never even committed to her life.

Why not some real distance? she thought, shifting her thoughts. In San Diego the weather was spectacular. And she did have a huge bikini collection she'd hate to see go to waste.

No. Not San Diego. Too much blue sky, too much sea air, too many reminders of here.

Head thunking against the head rest, Avery thought back to that afternoon in the hammock, blithely admitting to herself that she'd sure miss Jonah when she left. As if admitting she cared meant it was somehow in her control. But it never had been. From the moment he'd yanked her out of the ocean, he was doomed to invade her heart. And now that he'd retreated, her poor abandoned heart hurt like a thousand paper cuts.

What she wouldn't do to have her hands around his neck right about then. Squeezing hard. Then softening, sliding over his throat, the rasp of his stubble against her soft palms…

She sat up straight and shook her head.

A fresh start was what she needed. A clear head with which to start her own life, one not all tied up in her mother's troubles, her father's impending nuptials, or her own heartache.

She ran both hands over her eyes that felt gritty with lack of sleep.

Yep. When she got home changes would be made. She'd soak in the moments as they happened. Do work that truly satisfied. Give her mother a daughter's love, and hold the rest of herself back so that there was something left over. Enough that she could offer it to somebody else. Somebody she loved who loved her back.

Because she'd learned all too well these past weeks that home wasn't where you laid your hat; it was whose hat lay next to yours. Those mornings waking up in Jonah's bed—to find him breathing softly, his deep grey eyes drinking her in as if she was the most beautiful thing he'd ever seen—were the most real, alive moments of her life.

A half life wasn't enough for her any more. She had to be thankful for that.

A crack of thunder split the air, rocking the cab with it. "Whoa," said the cabbie with nervous laughter.

But Avery's mind was elsewhere. Flittering through the past few weeks, to the tentative way she and Jonah had begun, circling one another like dogs who'd been kicked in the teeth by love their whole lives. How they'd come together with such flash and fire, only to blithely pretend that it was everyday. That it was normal. That they could go about their daily lives afterwards.

She couldn't. Being with Jonah had pried her open, forced her to reach deep inside and grab for what she wanted. Made her feel deeply, broadly, inside outside upside down and so thoroughly there was no going back. Not even if she wanted to.

And she didn't.

She didn't want to go back at all.

She wanted Jonah. And Hull. And the cove. She wanted that life. And the Tropicana Nights. And to help Claude. And heat and sunshine. And storms that looked as if they could rip trees from the ground. She wanted passion and light and life. Even if it was dangerous. Even if it was hard.

It was her best life. Her best moments. Her happiest self. But none of that existed without him. Which was where she came full circle yet again.

Not that she'd out and out *told* him that she loved him. She'd hinted. She'd hoped he might notice and make the first move into forever.

Jonah whose mother had left him behind. Jonah whose father had never had time for him.

"Here we go," the taxi driver said, warming up the engine once more.

When they started towards the airport, Avery looked back in panic. "Wait."

"Wait what?"

"Can we please turn around?"

"Not go to the airport?"

She shook her head. "Crescent Cove," she shouted over the sound of the rain now pelting against the car from all angles. "Whatever your fare ends up being, I'll double it."

She felt the car accelerate beneath her backside, and her heart rate rose to match.

Her parents had never been fully honest with one another, which had led to ten years of suffering. No matter what else she got wrong in her life, she'd not make *that* mistake.

She was going to find Jonah, and this time she was going to tell him how she felt.

And if Jonah was so sure he didn't feel the same way he'd just have to tell her he didn't love her back. Right to her face.

"I have to call Jonah," Avery said, panting as she trudged inside the Tropicana Nights with her sopping-wet luggage in tow. She peeled a few random leaves from her skin, and wiped away as much sand as she could.

The weather was wild out there. So much so she knew the only reason the driver had been stupid enough to keep going was the double fare she'd promised at the end of it.

Claude—wearing a moth-eaten ancient faux bear-skin over her head and holding what looked mighty like a cavegirl club—quickly shut the door behind them. "He went looking for you."

Avery stopped wringing water from her hair and looked at Claude, who was by then trying to drag her into the resort. "For me? Why?"

Claude looked at her as if she were nuts. Then when Avery continued to be daft said, "Because the woman he loves was about to fly away and out of his life? The man might be stubborn as an ass, but he's not stupid."

"He told you he *loved* me?"

Avery took a step back towards the door before Claude took her by the upper arms and looked her dead in the eye. "Storm, Avery. Everything else can wait."

She looked over Claude's shoulder to the empty foyer beyond. The lights were low, the place dark as the sun was completely blocked out by the storm. "Will you be okay?"

"We'll be fine. She's a tough old place. Strong. We're a safety point," Claude said. "Wine cellar, foods storage bunkers. Enough room to fit a hundred-odd people underground."

Avery gave her a hug and without further ado walked out into the storm.

Her clothes slapped against her limbs and the sand in the swirling winds bit at her skin. The double row of palm trees lining the beach path were swaying back and forth with such ferocity it was amazing they weren't uprooted.

She was halfway down the stairs before she realised the cab had gone.

Dammit.

Dragging her slippery hair out of her face, she took two more steps down to the path, looked up the deserted beach and down, before making to turn around, go inside. To dry out her phone. To call—

Which was when she saw a figure huddled under a tree in the front yard of a cottage overlooking the beach. A wet, bedraggled, speckled four-legged figure.

"Hull?" she called. The dog glanced up then sank deeper against the tree. She called louder this time. "Hull! Come on, boy. Come inside!"

But Hull just sat there, in the squall. This dog who *hated* water. What was he doing out in this craziness?

Lifting the back of her shirt over her head, she jogged down the steps, down the footpath, and into the front yard, slowing in case Hull was hurt. In case the hurt made him lash out instead of accepting comfort. She knew his owner, after all.

"Come on, boy," she said, sliding her arm around his wet neck. He whimpered up at her, his tail giving a double beat against the sodden ground. But he dug his heels in and bayed up at the window of the house whose yard he was camped in where the curtains flickered ominously.

When she realised he had no intention of moving, Avery sat down next to him, the shade of the tree giving them no respite at all from the onslaught. Soon she was soaked through to the skin. A little later she began to shiver.

"What are we doing here, Hull?" she asked, when the rain got so hard she could no longer see the beach at all.

He whimpered and turned to look forlornly up at the house outside which they'd camped. A small, white, flat-fronted brick cabin, with a picture of a familiar dog in an oval frame on the front door.

"No, Hull. Seriously?"

A storm was raging about them, and here Hull sat, crooning outside Petunia's house, pining for his love.

"Where did you come from, kid?" she asked, hugging him tighter. "I can't even get your owner to admit he cares for me at all."

Hull gave Avery's hand a single lick. She ran her fingers down his wet snout. And there they sat, getting drenched, ducking out of the way of the occasional falling branch, watching in bemused silence as lawn furniture went tumbling down the street. Till Avery began to fear for more than her poor heart.

Yet it all faded away when she heard the throaty growl of Jonah's car before she saw it come around the bend. She waved, and the car pulled to a halt in the middle of the street, the wheels spinning as he ground to a sudden sodden halt. It screeched into Reverse, backed up, then mounted the kerb as it pulled up across the driveway.

As Jonah leapt from the car Avery pulled herself to standing, her legs frozen solid. She tripped as she tried to walk, her legs cramped into a bend.

Jonah was there to catch her.

"Jonah," she said, wanting to tell him, to ask him, to show him…

But then she was in his arms and he was kissing her and bliss sank through her limbs. He kissed her as if his life depended upon it. As if she were his breath, his blood, his everything.

When he pulled back, he drew her into his chest and rested his chin atop her head. They both breathed heavily, rain thundering down upon them, but the sound of his heart was the only thing she heard.

When she looked up, he held her face between his hands. Emotion stormed across her eyes, too deep, too violent to catch.

"I found your dog."

"I see that," he said and his eyes smiled as they roved over her face, raking in every inch as if making sure she was really real.

"I rescued him, in fact."

"You rescued him? From a little rain?"

She slapped his chest, her hand bouncing off the hard planes before settling there, her nails scraping his wet T-shirt, her heart kicking against her ribs. "From being sued by a crazy woman."

Jonah's brow furrowed. Avery tilted her head towards the cottage. "Hull's girl lives here."

Jonah's eyes finally left hers to take in the front door with its picture of a tiny, near bald, shivering scrap of flesh that was barely rat, much less a dog. Jonah's eyes swung back to her, and he used both hands, both big, warm, rough hands, to gently peel the lank hair from her cheeks.

When Avery began to shiver harder it had nothing to

do with being thoroughly drenched. And as his hands roved down her arms, and up again, she was heading very quickly from lusciously warm to scorching hot.

But knowing he'd need encouragement, a place to feel safe to tell her what she needed to hear, Avery nudged. "Is that why you were driving around? You were worried about Hull in the rain and all?"

Jonah breathed deep through his nose, his clear grey eyes glinting. "I trusted he'd take care of himself. You, on the other hand—"

"What about me?" she said, rearing back. Not far, though. Enough to show her chagrin while still being plastered well and truly against him. "I'm perfectly capable of taking care of myself."

"I know. You're plenty tough, Avery Shaw. And yet I can't seem to fight the urge to look after you. In fact, I'm done. Done fighting it. Done fighting how I feel about you."

Avery swallowed hard while her belly flipped and started singing the Hallelujah chorus.

"Avery, I barely got halfway to the airport when I heard there was an accident. The thought that it might have been you, that you might be hurt—there are no words to explain how that felt. I called Claude. And she said you were here. And I can't possibly explain the relief."

Try, she thought. "Why were you going to the airport?"

"To *find* you, woman. To haul you back here. Or, hell, to go with you, or ask if you'd care to try living transcontinentally, if that's what you wanted. So long as you were where you belong. With me."

"You'd leave the cove? For me?"

"Not for you, Miss Shaw. With you... If it meant being able to do this—" he kissed the corner of her mouth "—and this—" he kissed the other corner "—and also this—" he placed his mouth over hers with infinite gentleness, infinite subtlety, until Avery felt as if the only thing holding her cells together were his touch.

When she shivered so hard her teeth rattled, Jonah scooped her up and deposited her in the back seat of his car. He joined her there. The curtains in the cottage continued to flicker, yet Hull kept up his vigil beneath the tree.

In the dry hollow of the car, Avery turned to face Jonah. Water glistened in his gorgeous curls, turned his lashes into dark spiky clumps, and gave his lips a seductive sheen that made her clench in deep-down places.

Raindrops still sluiced down her nose, running in rivulets beneath her now-muddy clothes. She was bedraggled. And yet he didn't seem to mind. In fact he was looking at her as if she were his moon and stars.

And then he had to go and completely tear her apart by saying, "I'm in love with you, Avery Shaw. And even if you live on the other side of the world, I'm going to keep on loving you. And if you think that's something you can live with, then we have some figuring out to do."

Could she live with it? With being loved by this man? This man who made her feel so much she couldn't contain it?

She threw herself at him so thoroughly she banged her knee, rocking the car. But pain was way in the background beneath the million other far more wonderful sensations pelting her all over as she kissed the man she loved for all that she was worth.

"I'm assuming this means you're all in favour?" he asked, when he came up for air.

"I love you. I love you, I love you, I love you!" she said. Laughing, shouting, fogging up the windows with all that beautiful, *beautiful* kissing.

The storm disappeared as quickly as it had come.

When Avery and Jonah left the cocoon of the car—

having broken several public indecency laws—they managed to encourage poor Hull away, and the three of them made their way over to the beach to check out the damage only to find the cove looking as if nothing had happened at all.

But everything had happened.

Jonah took Avery's hand and pulled her down onto a patch of sand in the shade of the palms. Her cheeks hurt from smiling and with a sigh she looked out over the waves of the Pacific. It was a completely different ocean from the one back home, and yet it didn't feel so far from everything at all. Because everything she wanted more than anything else was right here.

EPILOGUE

AVERY STOOD OUTSIDE the Tropicana Nights, eyes closed, arms outstretched, soaking up the blissful warmth that made this part of the world so famous.

Jonah grunted behind her as he dragged her bags out of the car. She had more luggage this time; she was staying longer, after all. Forever, in fact.

"Avery!" Claude said, running down the stairs, her Tropicana Nights uniform shirt brighter than the sun, her clipboard flapping at her side, Hull at her ankles.

"God, am I glad to have you back! This dog of yours pined the entire month you were gone."

Hull came bounding up, spry as a puppy, with a big new collar around his neck. Avery checked the label—a doggy bone with his name engraved into the front. On the back, *Property of Jonah North*.

"Want one?" Claude said low enough for only her to hear with a grin when Avery motioned to the tag. "How was your holiday?" she added, this time for all to hear. "Did I say how glad I am you're back? Did Jonah grumble the whole time?"

Yeah, Jonah had grumbled, Avery thought, turning to watch him crouch to take his dog—*their* dog—in a huge cuddle. Hull's tongue lolled out of his mouth as Jonah boxed him about the ears, and when Jonah laughed the dog wagged his tail so hard he near dented the car.

New York was so grey, Jonah had noted, and too cold, too many people, air so thick you could choke on it, the Hudson a poor substitute for the Pacific Ocean. But then again she found his particular brand of manly grumpiness kind of hot, so she was all good.

Also, he'd completely charmed her mother, who seemed to have come blinking into the light now that her father had truly moved on. Jonah had kept toe to toe with her dad, talking baseball stats as if he were born to it. As for her father's new fiancée, she'd turned out to be pretty nice. It had been no shock when half her friends fell in lust with Jonah on the spot, and he'd let her take him to shows, and to all the tourist traps, and when they'd stayed at the top of the Empire State Building for hours it had been his idea.

Then the Yankees won their first three exhibition games three out of three, which pretty much trumped the rest.

"The place is looking great, Claude."

"Isn't it?" She looked up at the freshly whitewashed facade, gleaming in the sunlight.

"We heard there were more storms while we were away."

"Mere rain. Though it gave me the chance to do a vampire theme party in the bunker. I sent Luke the link to the blog post with all the photos. I've yet to hear back."

"So the stay of execution is still in play?"

"He's given me a year. So the work's only just begun!"

"I love work. Bring on the work." Knowing how close Claude had come to losing her business, her home, she'd forced Claude to hire her without pay—she had a trust fund after all, and no longer any compunction about using it. Not for such a good cause.

"The press we had after the party was unbelievable, and the website guy you set me up with is awesome, and we have bookings flying in. This place is going to be as amazing as it was in its heyday."

"More amazing! Is Luke back to help?"

Claudia frowned so hard her cheeks pinked up in an instant. "Forget about Luke. All we have to concern ourselves with is making this resort the premier family destination in Far North Queensland."

"That's the spirit."

"Now, I've ordered a whole bunch of uniforms in your size—"

"Oh, not necessary, really. I've brought so many great clothes—"

"Nonsense. You are one of the team now. Uniform's a must. All about the brand."

Avery grimaced at Jonah, who grinned back, and even the thought of spending her working hours in Hawaiian print shirts and polyester capris couldn't dampen her spirits. Because, oh, she loved that smile. And the man behind it. The way those deep grey eyes of his saw through her, right to the most vulnerable heart of her, and loved her in a way she'd never dared hope she could be.

"Claude," Jonah called, his voice deep with warning.

Claudia looked over Avery's shoulder at him. "Hmm?"

"Leave the woman alone. The last time she tried to do anything strenuous while dopey with jet lag she nearly drowned."

"I did no such thing," Avery started. "I'm—"

"An excellent swimmer," Jonah joined in. "Yeah, I know."

"Fine, yes, of course!" Claudia said, backing up. She clicked her fingers at Cyrus.

The lanky kid grabbed a trolley and ambled over to Jonah's car, heaving the bags into place. Cheek twitching, Jonah dragged them all off again and set about doing it right.

"Are you sure you're right to stay here?" Claudia asked as both women watched Jonah at work, arm muscles bunching, teeth gritting, the hem of his T-shirt lifting to showcase the most stunning set of abs ever created.

"Of course!" Avery said nice and loud. "Wasn't it you who said we have a lot of work to do?"

"Yeah, right," Claude muttered. "I give it a week before you're living at his place with that huge dog of his sleeping on your feet."

"Yeah," Avery said with a grin. Mention in passing the spotting of a man-eating spider in her room perhaps, and he'd turn up and throw her over his shoulder and whisk her away to his castle in the forest like her own personal knight. "I can't wait."

Claude scrunched up her nose. "Each to their own."

Claude grabbed one arm of the trolley and dragged it and Cyrus along the path around the side of the resort to settle Avery back home.

Home.

Sea air tickled Avery's nose, heat poured and prickled all over her skin. She watched Jonah lift his face to the sky, the Queensland sun glowing against his golden-brown skin, infusing him with life.

Yeah, her guy might have wowed 'em in New York City, but he wasn't built for city living. He was built for this place. This raw, majestic, lovely, warm place. Lucky for them she could handle living in paradise.

Lucky for Avery, Jonah was also built for loving her.

Sensing he was being watched, he tipped his head to look at her. All dark curls and strong jaw, might and muscle and heat and hotness. And hers.

Feeling like she was sixteen all over again, full of hope and love and zeal, Avery ran and jumped into his arms. He caught her, swung her around, and held her tight as his lips met hers in a kiss that sank through her like melted butter.

"I love you, Jonah North, and don't you ever forget it."

"Yeah," he said, his arms wrapped about her tugging

her tighter still. "Couldn't if I tried. Now, come on, princess, time to get you to bed."

"Feisty."

"Insurance. I was serious about you getting some sleep after last time. I wouldn't put it past you to get it in your head to try parasailing for the first time. Hell, I might even strap you into bed so you don't do yourself damage."

"Extra spicy feisty." The effect of her sass was dampened when the last word was swallowed by a massive yawn.

As they walked through Reception Avery noticed at the edge of her mind that the place was busier than the last time she was there. Not bustling, but better.

Isis gave her a cheery wave. She waved back before her mind focused in on more important things, like the fact that Jonah's hand had moved down her waist until his fingers were at her hip.

Cyrus was leaving the Tiki Suite as they arrived. Yawning again, she fished through her wallet for a tip, came up with a twenty and tucked it into Cyrus's pocket, then trudged to the centre of the room and fell back on the bed with a thud.

Through the slits of her eyes she saw Jonah glare at Cyrus to make him leave. Which he did. Jonah locked the door behind him.

"That kid has a thing for you," Jonah said, thumb jerking at the door.

"I know. It's sweet."

Jonah turned slowly to stare at her, his eyes flat. "Honestly, how did you survive twenty-six years on that island without getting nabbed?"

"Street smarts. And the deep-down knowledge that I'd only ever get nabbed if the right man did the nabbing."

"Oh, yeah?" Jonah said, sliding his hands into his pockets even as he edged her way.

She lifted her weary self up onto her elbows as she was suddenly not so weary after all. "A handsome man, he'd be. A little full of himself, but understandably so." Her eyes roved down his torso, his long, strong legs to his feet, which were nudging off his shoes. "A successful man too. Helicopter an absolute must. As is..." her wandering gaze landed on the impressive bulge in his jeans "...heft."

"Heft?" he coughed out, laughing in that deep, delicious *huh-huh-huh* way that made her spine tingle and then some.

"Cerebral heft. Emotional heft. General...heft."

Jonah and his heft left a mighty dent in the mattress as he lowered himself over her, a halo of sunlight around his gorgeous curls. His dark eyes on her mouth. His knee sliding between hers and up, and up.

"Whoever this perfect man is, he can shove off, because he's too damn late. From the moment I pulled you out of the water, I owned you, Avery Shaw. You're mine—" he punctuated that one with a kiss, a long, slow, hot, bone-melting kiss "—all mine."

"Okay!" she said, sliding her arms around his neck to pull him down for more.

Jet lag be damned. The only drowning she planned to do that day and every day forth was in bliss. Pure, unadulterated bliss. Starting right now.

Because saying Yes—capital *Y* intended—had never felt more right.

* * * * *

THE BILLIONAIRE'S
BORROWED BABY

JANICE MAYNARD

For the next generation: Anastasia, Ainsley,
Allie, Sydney, Olivia, Dakota and Samuel Ellis.

One

It was a hot, beautiful Georgia morning, but all Hattie Parker noticed was the taste of desperation and panic.

"I need to speak to Mr. Cavallo, please. Mr. *Luc* Cavallo," she clarified quickly. "It's urgent."

The thirtysomething administrative assistant with the ice-blue suit and matching pale, chilly eyes looked down her perfect nose. "Do you have an appointment?"

Hattie clenched her teeth. The woman had an expensive leather date book open in front of her. Clearly, she knew Hattie was an interloper and clearly she was doing her best to be intimidating.

Hattie juggled the baby on her hip and managed a smile. "Tell him it's Hattie Parker. I don't have an appointment, but I'm sure Luc will see me if you let him know I'm here."

Actually, that was a bald-faced lie. She had no clue if Luc would see her or not. At one time in her life he had been Prince Charming, willing and eager to do anything she wanted, to give her everything she desired.

Today, he might very well show her the door, but she was

hoping he would remember some of the good times and at least hear her out. They hadn't parted on the best of terms. But since every other option she had considered, legal or not, had gone bust, it was Luc or no one. And she wasn't leaving without a fight.

The woman's expression didn't change. She was sheer perfection from her ash-blond chignon to her exquisitely made-up face to her expensive French manicure. With disdain, she examined Hattie's disheveled blond hair, discount store khaki skirt and pink cotton blouse. Even without the drool marks at the shoulder, the outfit wasn't going to win any fashion awards. It was hard to maintain a neat appearance when the little one grabbed handfuls of hair at regular intervals.

Hattie's legs felt like spaghetti. The stoic security guard in the lobby had insisted that she park her stroller before entering the elevator. Seven-month-old Deedee weighed a ton, and Hattie was scared and exhausted, at the end of her rope. The last six weeks had been hell.

She took a deep breath. "Either you let me see Mr. Cavallo, or I'm going to pitch the biggest hissy fit Atlanta has seen since Scarlett O'Hara swished her skirts through the red Georgia dust." Hattie's chin trembled right at the end, but she refused to let this supercilious woman defeat her.

Scary lady blinked. Just once, but it was enough to let Hattie know that the balance of power had shifted. The other woman stood up with a pained sigh. "Wait here." She disappeared down a hallway.

Hattie nuzzled the baby's sweet-smelling head with its little tufts of golden hair. "Don't worry, my love. I won't let anyone take you, I swear." Deedee smiled, revealing her two new bottom teeth, her only teeth. She was starting to babble nonsense syllables, and Hattie fell more in love with her every day.

The wait seemed like an eternity, but when Luc's assistant finally returned, the clock on the wall showed that less than five minutes had elapsed. The woman was definitely disgruntled. "Mr. Cavallo will see you now. But he's a very busy man, and he has many other important commitments this morning."

Hattie resisted the childish urge to stick out her tongue at the woman's back as they traversed the hallway carpeted in thick, crimson plush. At the second doorway, the woman paused. "You may go in." The words nearly stuck in ice woman's throat, you could tell.

Hattie took a deep breath, no longer concentrating on her would-be nemesis. She kissed the baby's cheek for luck. "Showtime, kiddo." With far more confidence than she felt, she knocked briefly, opened the door and stepped into the room.

Luc ran a multimillion-dollar business. He was accustomed to dealing with crises on a daily basis. The ability to think on his feet was a gift he'd honed in the fires of corporate America.

So he wasn't easily thrown off balance. But when Hattie Parker appeared in his office, the first time he'd seen her in over a decade, his heart lodged in his throat, his muscles tensed and he momentarily forgot how to breathe.

She was as beautiful now as she had been at twenty. Sun-kissed porcelain skin, dark brown eyes that held hints of amber. And legs that went on forever. Her silky blond hair barely brushed her shoulders, much shorter than he remembered. He kept the width of his broad mahogany desk between them. It seemed safer that way.

As he struggled with shock, he was stunned to realize the woman he had once loved was holding an infant. Jealousy stabbed sharp and deep. Damn. Hattie was a mother. Which meant there was a man somewhere in the picture.

The sick feeling in his gut stunned him. He'd moved on a long, long time ago. So why was his chest tight and his pulse jumping like a jackrabbit?

He remained standing, his hands shoved in his pockets. "Hello, Hattie." He was proud of the even timbre of his voice.

"Hello, Luc."

She was visibly nervous. He indicated the chair closest to him and motioned for her to sit. For a brief moment, Luc caught a glimpse of sexy legs as Hattie's skirt rode up her thighs. The baby clung to her neck, and Hattie wriggled in the chair until she was modestly covered.

He examined her face, deliberately letting the silence accumulate in tense layers. Hattie Parker was the girl next door, a natural, appealing beauty who didn't need enhancement. Even dressed as she was in fairly unflattering garments, she would stand out in a room full of lovely women.

At one time, she had been his whole world.

And it irked him that the memories still stung. "Why are you here, Hattie? The last time we had sex was a lifetime ago. Surely you're not going to try and convince me that baby is mine."

The mockery and sarcasm made her pale. He felt the pinch of remorse, but a guy needed to wield what weapons he could. The man he was today would not be vulnerable. Not ever again.

She cleared her throat. "I need your help."

He lifted a brow. "I'd have thought I would be the last person on your go-to list."

"To be honest, you were. But it's serious, Luc. I'm in big trouble."

He rocked on his heels. "What's her name?"

The non sequitur made Hattie frown. "This is Deedee."

Luc studied the baby. He didn't see much of Hattie in the child. Maybe the kid took after her dad.

Luc leaned over and punched the intercom. "Marilyn… can you come in here, please?"

It was a toss-up as to which of the two women was more horrified when Luc phrased his next request. When Marilyn appeared, he motioned to the baby. "Will you please take the little one for a few minutes? Her name is Deedee. Ms. Parker and I need to have a serious conversation, and I don't have much time."

Hattie wanted to protest, he could tell. But she reluctantly handed the baby over to Luc's assistant. "Here's a bottle. She's getting hungry. And you'll need this bib and burp cloth. You don't want to let her ruin your nice suit."

Luc knew his assistant would be fine. She might be a cold fish, but she was relentlessly efficient.

When the door closed, Luc sat down in his leather office chair. It had been specially ordered to fit his long, lanky frame. He steepled his hands under his chin and leaned back. "So spill it, Hattie. What's going on in your life to make you seek me out? As I recall, it was *you* who dumped *me* and not the other way around."

She flushed and twisted her hands in her lap. "I don't think we need to go there. That was a long time ago."

He shrugged. "All right then. We'll concentrate on the present. Why are you here?"

When she bit her lip, he shifted in his chair uneasily. Why in God's name did he still have such vivid memories of kissing that bow-shaped mouth? Running his hands through that silky, wavy hair. Touching every inch of her soft, warm skin. He swallowed hard.

Hattie met his gaze hesitantly. "Do you remember my older sister, Angela?"

He frowned. "Barely. As I recall, the two of you didn't get along."

"We grew closer after our parents died."

"I didn't know, Hattie. I'm sorry."

For a moment, tears made her eyes shiny, but she blinked them back. "Thank you. My father died a few years after I graduated. Lung cancer. He was a two-pack-a-day man and it caught up with him."

"And your mother?"

"She didn't do well without Daddy. He did everything for her, and without him, the world was overwhelming to her. She finally had a nervous breakdown and had to be admitted to a facility. Unfortunately, she was never able to go back to her home. Angela and I sold the house we grew up in…everything Mom and Dad had, but it wasn't enough. I practically bankrupted myself paying for her care."

"Angela didn't help?"

"She told me I should back off and let the state look after Mother…especially when Mom retreated totally into an alternate reality where she didn't even recognize us."

"Some people would think your sister made sense."

"Not me. I couldn't abandon my mother."

"When did you lose her?"

"Last winter."

He looked at her left hand, but it was bare. Where was her husband in all this? Was the guy a jerk who bailed on Hattie rather than help with the mom? And what about the baby?

Suddenly, it became clear. Hattie needed to borrow money. She was proud and independent, and things must be really bad if she had humbled her pride enough to come to him.

He leaned forward, his elbows on the desk. No one who knew their history would blame him if he kicked her out. But though his memories of her were bitter, he didn't have it in him to be deliberately cruel, especially if a child was involved. And though it might be petty, he rather liked the idea of having Hattie in his debt…a kind of poetic justice. "You've had a rough time," he said quietly. "I'll be happy to loan you however much money you need, interest free, no questions asked. For old time's sake."

Hattie's face went blank and she cocked her head. "Excuse me?"

"That's why you're here, isn't it? To ask if you can borrow some money? I'm fine with that. It's no big deal. What good is all that cash in the bank if I can't use it to help an old friend?"

Her jaw dropped and her cheeks went red with mortification. "No, no, no," she said, leaping to her feet and pacing. "I don't need your money, Luc. That's not it at all."

It was his turn to rise. He rounded the desk and faced her, close enough now to inhale her scent and realize with pained remembrance that she still wore the same perfume. He put his hands gently on her shoulders, feeling the tremors she couldn't disguise.

They were practically nose to nose. "Then tell me, Hattie. What do you need from me? What do you want?"

She lifted her chin. She was tall for a woman, and he could see the shades of chocolate and cognac in her irises. Her breathing was ragged, a pulse beating at the base of her throat.

He shook her gently. "Spit it out. Tell me."

She licked her lips. He could see the tracery of blue veins at her temples. Their long separation vanished like mist, and suddenly he was assaulted with a barrage of memories, both good and bad.

The soft, quick kiss he brushed across her cheek surprised them both. He was so close, he could smell cherry lip gloss. Some things never changed. "Hattie?"

She had closed her eyes when he kissed her, but her lashes lifted and her cloudy gaze cleared. Astonishment flashed across her expressive features, followed by chagrin and what appeared to be resignation.

After a long, silent pause, she wrinkled her nose and sighed. "I need you to marry me."

Luc dropped his hands from her shoulders with unflattering haste. Though his expression remained guarded, for a split second some strong emotion flashed in his eyes and then disappeared as quickly as it had come. Most men would be shocked by Hattie's proposal.

Most men weren't Luc Cavallo.

He lifted a shoulder clad in an expensive suit. The Cavallo textile empire, started by their grandfather in Italy and now headquartered in Atlanta, had made Luc and his brother wealthy men. She had no doubt that the soft, finely woven wool fabric was the product of a family mill. His mouth twisted, faint disdain in his expression. "Is this a joke? Should I look for hidden cameras?"

She felt her face go even hotter. Confronting her past was more difficult than she had expected, and without the baby to run interference, Hattie felt uncomfortably vulnerable. "It's not a joke. I'm dead serious. I need you to marry me to keep Deedee safe."

He scowled. "Good Lord, Hattie. Is the father threatening you? Has he hurt you? Tell me."

His intensity made her shiver. If she really had an abusive husband, there was no doubt in her mind that Luc Cavallo would hunt him down and destroy him. She was making a hash of this explanation. "It's complicated," she said helplessly. "But no, nothing like that."

He ran two hands through his hair, mussing the dark, glossy strands. The reminder function on his BlackBerry beeped just then, and Luc glanced down at it with a harried expression. "I have an appointment," he said, his voice betraying frustration. "Obviously we're not going to resolve this in fifteen minutes. Can you get a sitter for tonight?"

"I'd rather not. Deedee has been through a lot of trauma recently. She clings to me. I don't want to change her routine any more than necessary." And the thought of being alone with Luc Cavallo scared Hattie. This brief meeting had revealed an unpalatable truth. The Hattie who had been madly in love with Luc was still lurking somewhere inside a heart that clung to silly dreams from the past.

He straightened his tie and strode to the other side of his desk. "Then I'll send a car for you." As she opened her mouth to protest, he added, "With an infant seat. We'll have dinner at my home and my housekeeper can play with the child while we talk."

There was nothing ominous in his words, but Hattie felt her throat constrict. Was she really going to try to convince Luc to marry her? Who was she kidding? He had no reason at all to humor her. Other than perhaps sheer curiosity. Why hadn't he shown her the door immediately? Why was he allowing her to play out this odd reunion?

She should be glad, relieved, down on her knees thanking the good lord that Luc wasn't already married.

But at the moment, her exact emotions were far more complicated and far less sensible.

She was still fascinated by this man who had once promised her the moon.

Two

What did one wear to a marriage proposal? While the baby was napping, Hattie rummaged through the tiny closet in her matching tiny apartment, knowing that she was not going to find a dress to wow Luc Cavallo. The only garment remotely suitable was a black, polished cotton sheath that she had worn to each of her parent's funerals. Perhaps with some accessories it would do the trick.

In a jewelry box she'd had since she was a girl, her hand hovered over the one piece inside that wasn't an inexpensive bauble. The delicate platinum chain was still as bright as the day Luc had given it to her. She picked it up and fastened it around her neck, adjusting the single pearl flanked by small diamonds.

Though there had been many days when the wolf was at the door, she had not been able to bring herself to sell this one lovely reminder of what might have been. She stroked the pearl, imagining that it was warm beneath her fingers....

They had skipped their afternoon classes at Emory and escaped to Piedmont Park with a blanket and a picnic basket.

She was a scholarship student...his family had endowed the Fine Arts Center.

As they sprawled in the hot spring sunshine, feeling alive and free and deliciously truant, Luc leaned over her on one elbow, kissing her with teasing brushes of his lips that made her restless for more. He grinned down at her, his eyes alight with happiness. "I have an anniversary present for you."

"Anniversary?" *They'd been dating for a while, but she hadn't kept track.*

He caressed her cheek. "I met you six months ago today. You were buying a miniature pumpkin at Stanger's Market. I offered to carve it for you. You laughed. And that's when I knew."

"Knew what?"

"That you were the one."

Her smile faded. "College guys are supposed to be counting notches on their bedposts, not spouting romantic nonsense."

A shadow dimmed the good humor in his gaze. "I come from a long line of Italians. Romance is in our blood." *His whimsical shrug made her regret tarnishing the moment. Lord knew she wanted it to be true, but her mother had drummed into her head that men only wanted one thing. And Hattie had given that up without a qualm.*

Being Luc Cavallo's lover was the best thing that had ever happened to her. He was her first, and she loved him so much it hurt. But she was careful to protect herself. She had a degree to finish, grades to keep up. A woman had to stand on her own two feet. Depending on a man led to heartbreak.

Luc reached into the pocket of his jeans and withdrew a small turquoise box. He handed it to her without speaking.

If she had been able to think of a polite refusal, she would have handed it back unopened. But he looked at her with such naked anticipation that she swallowed her misgivings and removed the lid. Nestled inside the leather box was a necklace, an exquisite, expensive necklace.

Hattie knew about Tiffany's, of course. In fact, back in the fall she'd been in the store at Phipps Plaza with one of her girlfriends who was in search of a wedding gift. But even on that day, Hattie had felt the sting of being out of place. She couldn't afford a key chain in those swanky glass cases, much less anything else.

And now this.

Luc ignored her silence. He took the necklace from the box and fastened it around her neck. She was wearing a pink tank top, and the pearl nestled in her modest cleavage. He kissed her forehead. "It suits you."

But it didn't. She was not that woman he wanted her to be. Luc would take his place one day with the glitterati. And Hattie, with or without the necklace, would wish him well. But she wasn't "the one"...and she never would be.

A car backfired out on the street, the loud sound dragging Hattie back to the present. With a mutinous scowl at her own reflection, she closed the jewelry box with a defiant click. Luc probably didn't even remember the silly necklace. He'd no doubt bought pricey bling for a dozen women in the intervening years.

The afternoon dragged by, the baby fussy with teething... Hattie nervous and uncertain. It was almost a relief when a nicely dressed chauffeur knocked at the door promptly at six-thirty.

The pleasant older man took Hattie's purse and the diaper bag while she tucked Deedee into the top-of-the-line car seat. It was brand-new and not smeared with crusty Cheerios and spit-up. The baby was charmed by the novelty of having Hattie sit across from her. A game of peekaboo helped distract them both as the car wound its way from the slightly run-down neighborhood where Hattie lived to an upscale part of town.

Though it had been ten years since Hattie and Luc's college breakup, they had never crossed paths after graduation. It was a big city, and they moved in far different spheres.

West Paces Ferry was one of the premier addresses in Atlanta. Decades-old homes sat side by side with new construction created to resemble historic architecture. Even the governor's mansion called the narrow, winding avenue home. Luc had recently purchased an entire estate complete with acreage. Hattie had seen the renovation written up in a local magazine.

The article, accompanied by photos of Luc, had no doubt been responsible for this crazy decision to throw herself on Luc's mercy. Seeing his smiling face after so many years had resurrected feelings she believed to be long dead.

Perhaps it was a sign....

The old home was amazing. Azaleas and forsythia bloomed in profusion on the grounds. A lengthy driveway culminated in a cobblestone apron leading to the imposing double front doors. Luc stepped out to meet them almost before the engine noise had died. His dark hair and eyes betrayed his Mediterranean heritage.

He held out a hand. "Welcome, Hattie."

She felt him squeeze her fingers, and her skin heated. "Your home is beautiful."

He stepped back as she extracted Deedee. "It's a work in progress. I'll be glad when the last of it is finished."

Despite his disclaimer, and despite the small area of scaffolding at the side of the house where workmen had been repairing stonework, the interior of the house was breathtaking. A sweeping staircase led up and to the right. The foyer floor was Italian marble, and above a walnut chair rail, the walls were papered in what appeared to be the original silk fabric, a muted shade of celadon. A priceless chandelier showered them in shards of warm light, and on a console beneath an antique mirror on the left wall, a massive bouquet of flowers scented the air.

Hattie turned around in a circle, the baby in her arms quiet for once, as if she, too, was awed. "It's stunning, Luc."

His smile reflected quiet satisfaction. "It's starting to feel like home. The couple who lived here bought it in the 1920s. They're both gone now, but I inherited Ana and Sherman. He wears many hats...driver is only one of them."

"He was very sweet. I felt pampered. And Ana?"

"His wife. You'll meet her in a moment. She's the housekeeper, chef, gardener...you name it. I tried to get them both to retire with a pension, but I think they love this house more than I do. I get the distinct feeling that I'm on probation as the new owner."

As promised, Ana entertained Deedee during dinner while Luc and Hattie enjoyed the fruits of the housekeeper's labors—lightly breaded rainbow trout, baby asparagus and fruit salad accompanied by rolls so fluffy they seemed to melt in the mouth.

Luc served Hattie and himself, with nothing to disturb the intimacy of their meal. Surprisingly, Hattie forgot to be self-conscious. Luc was a fascinating man, highly intelligent, well-read, and he possessed of a sneaky sense of humor. As the evening progressed, sharp regret stabbed her heart. She was overwhelmed with a painful recognition of what she had lost because of her own immaturity and cowardice.

He refilled her wineglass one more time. "I suppose you're not nursing the baby."

She choked on a sip of chardonnay. An image of Luc in her bed, watching her feed a baby at her breast, flashed through her brain with the force of a runaway train. Her face was so hot she hoped he would blame it on the wine. She set the glass down gently, her hand trembling. Unwittingly, he had given her the perfect opening.

"The baby's not mine," she said softly. "My sister Angela was her mother."

"Was?"

Hattie swallowed, the grief still fresh and raw. "She was killed in a car crash six weeks ago. My brother-in-law, Eddie, was driving…drunk and drugged out of his mind. He got out and left the scene when he hit a car head-on. Both people in the other vehicle died. Angela lingered for a few hours…long enough to tell me that she wanted me to take Deedee. I was babysitting that night, and I've had the baby ever since."

"What happened to the baby's father?"

"Eddie spent a few days behind bars. He's out on bail awaiting trial. But I guarantee you he won't do any time. His family has connections everywhere. I don't know if we have the Mob in Georgia, but I wouldn't be surprised. Eddie's family is full of cold, mean-spirited people. Frankly, they scare me."

"I can tell."

"At first, none of them showed any sign of acknowledging Deedee's existence. But about two weeks ago, I was summoned to the family compound in Conyers."

"Eddie wanted to see his child?"

She laughed bitterly. "You'd think so, wouldn't you? But no. He was there when I arrived with her. A lot of them were there. But not one single person in that entire twisted family even looked at her, much less asked to hold her. They kept referring to her as 'the kid' and talked about how she was one of theirs and so should be raised by them."

"That doesn't make any sense given their lack of enthusiasm for the baby."

"It does when you realize that Eddie thinks Deedee will be his ace in the hole with the judge. He wants to portray the grieving husband and penitent dad. Having Deedee in the courtroom will soften him, make him more sympathetic to the jury."

"Ah. I take it you didn't go along with their plan?"

"Of course not. I told them Angela wanted me to raise her daughter and that I would be adopting Deedee."

"How did that go?"

She shivered. "Eddie's father said that no custody court would give a baby to a single woman with few financial means when the father wanted the child and had the resources to provide for her future."

"And you said…?"

She bit her lip. "I told them I was engaged to my college sweetheart and that you had a boatload of money and you loved Deedee like your own. And then I hightailed it out of there."

Luc actually had the gall to laugh.

"It's not funny," she wailed, leaping to her feet. "This is serious."

He topped off her wineglass once again. "Relax, Hattie. I have more lawyers than a dog has fleas. Deedee is safe. I give you my word."

Her legs went weak and she plopped into her chair. "Really? You mean that?" Suspicion reared its ugly head. "Why?"

He leaned back, studying her with a laserlike gaze that made her want to hide. He saw too much. "My motivation shouldn't matter…right, Hattie? If I really am your last resort?" Something in his bland words made her shiver.

She licked her lips, feeling as if she was making a bargain with the devil. "Are you sure you're willing to do this?"

"I never say anything I don't mean. You should know that. We'll make your lie a reality. I have the best legal counsel in Atlanta. Angela's wishes will prevail."

"I'll sign a prenup," she said. "I don't want your money."

His gaze iced over. "You made that clear a decade ago, Hattie. No need to flog a dead horse."

Her stomach clenched. Why was it that he could make her feel so small with one look?

When she remained silent, he stood up with visible impatience. "I know you need to get the little one in bed before it gets any later. I'll have my team draw up some documents, and then in a few days, you and I can go over the details."

"Details?" she asked weakly.

His grin was feral. "Surely you know I'll have a few stipulations of my own."

Her throat tightened and she took one last swallow of wine. It burned going down like it was whiskey. "Of course. You have to protect your interests. That makes sense." For some reason she couldn't quite fathom, the specter of sex had unexpectedly entered the room. Her mouth was so dry she could barely speak.

Surely lawyers didn't use legalese to dictate sex…did they?

Suddenly an unpalatable thought struck her. "Um…Luc…I should have asked. Is there anyone who will… I mean…who is…um…"

He cocked his head, one broad shoulder propped against the door frame. His face was serious, but humor danced in his eyes. "Are you asking if I'm seeing anyone, Hattie? Isn't it a bit late to worry about that…now that you've told everyone I'm your fiancé?"

Mortified didn't begin to describe how she felt. "Not everyone," she muttered.

"Just the Mob?" He chuckled out loud, enjoying her discomfiture a little too much. Finally, he sobered. "You let me worry about my personal life, Hattie. Your job is to take care of yourself and that little girl—" He stopped abruptly. "Speaking of jobs…what happened? Why aren't you teaching?" She had majored in math at Emory and had gone directly from college to a high school faculty position.

"I had to take a leave of absence for the rest of the year when the accident happened."

He sobered completely now, stepping close enough to run a hand over her hair. She'd worn it loose tonight. "You've been through a hell of a lot," he said softly, their bodies almost touching. "But things will get better."

She smiled wistfully. "Somedays it seems as if nothing will ever be the same."

"I didn't say it would be the same."

For some reason, the words struck her as a threat. She looked up at him, their breath mingling. "What do you get out of this? Why did you agree to back up an impulsive lie by a woman you haven't seen in ten years?"

"Are you trying to talk me out of it?"

"Tell me why you agreed. I was ninety percent sure you'd throw me out of your office on my fanny."

"I can be kind on occasion." The sarcasm was impossible to miss.

She searched his face. It hurt knowing that it was as familiar to her as if they had parted yesterday. "There's something more," she said slowly. "I can see it in your eyes."

His expression shuttered. "Let's just say I have my reasons." His tone was gruff and said more loudly than words that he was done with the conversation.

He was shutting her out. And it stung. But they were little more than strangers now. Strangers who had once made love with passionate abandon, but strangers nevertheless.

"I have to go."

He didn't argue. He ushered her in front of him until they entered a pleasant room outfitted as a den. Ana, despite her years, was down on an Oriental rug playing with a sleepy Deedee.

Hattie rushed forward to scoop up the drowsy baby and nuzzle her sweet-smelling neck. "Did she nap for you at all?"

Ana stood with dignity and straightened the skirt of her floral cotton housedress. "She slept about forty-five minutes…enough to keep her awake until you can get her home and in bed. Your daughter is precious, Ms. Parker, an absolute angel."

"She's not my daughter, she's my niece…but thank you." Did the housekeeper think Luc had brought his love child home for a visit?

Her host grew impatient with the female chitchat. "I'll walk you out, Hattie."

Sherman waited respectfully by the car door, making any sort of personal conversation awkward. Luc surprised Hattie by taking Deedee without ceremony and tucking her expertly into the small seat.

She lifted an eyebrow. "You did that well."

He touched the baby's cheek and stepped aside so Hattie could enter the limo. "It's not rocket science." He braced an arm on the top of the car and leaned in. "I'll look forward to seeing you both again soon."

"You'll call me?"

"I'll get Marilyn to contact you and set up a meeting. It will probably only take a couple of days. You need to go ahead and start packing."

"Packing?" She was starting to sound like a slightly dense parrot. What had she gotten herself into? Luc was helping her, but with strings attached. She had known his every thought at one time. Now he was an enigma.

His half smile made her think of a predator anticipating his prey. "You and Deedee will be moving in here as soon as the wedding is over."

Three

Two days later, Luc tapped briefly at his brother's office door and entered. Leo, his senior by little more than a year, was almost hidden behind piles of paperwork and books. A genius by any measure, Leo masterminded the financial empire, while Luc handled R & D. Luc enjoyed the challenge of developing new products, finding the next creative venture.

Leo was the one who made them all rich.

It was a full thirty seconds before his brother looked up from what he was doing. "Luc. Didn't expect to see you today."

The brothers met formally twice a month, and it wasn't unusual for them to lunch together a few times a week, but Luc rarely dropped by his brother's sanctum unannounced. Their offices were on different floors of the building, and more often than not, their customary mode of communication was texting.

Luc ignored the comfortable, overstuffed easy chair that flanked Leo's desk and instead, chose to cross the room and stand by the window. He never tired of gazing at Atlanta's distinctive skyline.

He rolled his shoulders, unaware until that moment that his neck was tight. He turned and smiled. "What are you doing on May 14?"

Leo tapped a key and glanced at his computer screen. "Looks clear. What's up?"

"I thought you might like to be my best man."

Now Luc had Leo's full attention. His older sibling, though still a couple inches shorter than Luc's six-three, was an imposing man. Built like a mountain, he looked more like a lumberjack than a numbers whiz.

He escaped the confines of his desk and cleared a front corner to lean on his hip and stare at his brother. "You're pulling my chain, right?"

"Why would you say that?"

"Three weeks ago I suggested you bring a date to Carole Ann's party, and you told me you weren't seeing anyone."

Luc shrugged. "Things happen."

Leo scowled, a black expression that had been known to make underlings quake in terror. "I can read you like a book. You're up to something. The last time I saw that exact look on your face, you were trying to convince Dad to let you take the Maserati for a weekend trip to Daytona."

"I have my own sports cars. I'm not trying to pull anything."

"You know what I mean." He changed tack. "Do I know her?"

Luc shrugged. "You've met."

"How long have *you* known her? It's not like you to go all misty-eyed over a one-night stand."

"I can assure you that I've known her for a very long time."

"But you've just now realized you're in love."

"A man doesn't have to be in love to want a woman."

"So it's lust."

"I think we've gotten off track. I asked if you would be my best man. A simple yes or no will do."

"Damn it, Luc. Quit being so mysterious. Who is she? Will I get to see her anytime soon?"

"I haven't decided. We've been concentrating on each other. I don't want to spoil things. Just promise me you'll show up when and where I say on the fourteenth. In a tux."

The silence was deafening. Finally, Leo stood up and stretched. "I don't like the sound of this. When it all goes to hell, don't come crying to me. Your libido is a piss-poor businessman. Be smart, baby brother. Women are generally not worth the bother."

Luc understood his brother's caution. They had both been burned by love at a tender age, but thankfully had wised up pretty fast. What Leo didn't know, though, was that Luc had a plan. *Revenge* was a strong word for what he had in mind. He didn't hate Hattie Parker. Quite the contrary. All he wanted was for her to understand that while he might still find her sexually attractive, he was completely immune to any emotional connection. No hearts and flowers. No protestations of undying devotion.

He was no longer a kid yearning for a pretty girl. This time *he* had the power. *He* would be calling all the shots. Hattie needed him, and her vulnerability meant that Luc would have her in his house…in his bed…under his control. Perhaps *revenge was* too strong a word. But when all was said and done, Hattie Parker would be out of his system… for good.

Hattie was ready to scream. Moving anytime was a huge chore, but add a baby to the mix, and the process was darned near impossible. She'd finally gotten Deedee down for a nap and was wrapping breakables in the kitchen when her cell phone rang. She jerked it up and snarled, "What?"

The long silence at the other end was embarrassing.

"Sorry," she said, her throat tight with tears of frustration.

Luc's distinctive tones were laced with humor. "I don't think I've ever heard you lose your temper. I kind of like it."

"Don't be silly," she said, shoving a lock of damp hair from her forehead. "What do you want?"

"Nothing in particular. I was checking in to see if you needed anything."

"A trio of muscular guys would be nice."

Another silence. "Kinky," he said, his voice amused but perhaps a tad hoarse.

Her face flamed, though he couldn't see her. "To help with moving," she muttered. "I wouldn't know what else to do with them. This mothering thing is hard work."

"Why, Hattie Parker. Are you hinting for help?"

"Maybe." Deedee was a good baby, but being a single parent was difficult. Hattie no longer felt as panicked as she had in the beginning. Much of the daily routine of dealing with an infant seemed easier now. But Deedee had been restless the three nights since Hattie had dined with Luc. Perhaps the baby was picking up on Hattie's unsettled emotions. And to make matters worse, Eddie had begun sending a harassing string of vague emails and texts. Clearly to keep Hattie on edge. And it was working.

Luc sighed audibly. "I would have hired a moving crew already, but you're always so damned independent, I thought you would pitch a fit and insist on doing it yourself."

"I've grown up, Luc. Some battles simply aren't worth fighting. I know when I'm in over my head."

"I'm sorry. I made a stupid assumption. It won't happen again."

The conversation lagged once more. She looked at the chaos in her kitchen and sighed. "Do you know yet when we're going to sit down and go over the finer points of our marriage agreement?"

"I thought perhaps tomorrow evening. When does Deedee go down for the night?"

"Usually by eight…if I'm lucky."

"What if I come over to your place then, so she won't have to be displaced. I'll bring food."

"That would be great."

"Have you heard any more from your brother-in-law?"

"Nothing specific." No need at the moment to involve Luc in Eddie's bluster. "He likes to throw his weight around. Right now, he's got the perfect setup. I'm babysitting for him, but when he's ready, he'll grab Deedee."

"I hope you don't mean that literally."

"He's not that stupid. At least, I don't think he is."

"Try not to worry, Hattie. Everything is going to fall into place."

For once, it seemed as if Luc was right. Deedee went to sleep the following evening without a whimper. Hattie found an unworn blouse in the back of her closet with the tags still attached. She'd snagged it from a clearance rack at Bloomingdale's last January, and the thin, silky fabric, a pale peach floral, was the perfect weight for a spring evening.

Paired with soft, well-worn jeans, the top made her look nice but casual…not like she was trying too hard to impress. Unfortunately, Luc showed up ten minutes early, and she was forced to open the door in her bare feet.

His eyes flashed with masculine appreciation when he saw her. "You don't look frazzled to me, Hattie."

She stepped back to let him in. "Thanks. Today was much calmer, maybe because the moving company you hired promised to be here first thing in the morning. And I was able to actually take a shower, because the baby took a two-hour morning nap."

As she closed the door, he surveyed her apartment. "No offense, but I don't see any point in storing most of this stuff. Let the movers take the bulk of it to charity, and bring only the things that are personal or sentimental with you."

She bit her lip. It had occurred to her that this subject would have to be broached, but she hadn't anticipated it would come so soon. "The thing is…"

"What are you trying to say?" He tossed the duffel bag he'd been carrying in a chair and deposited two cloth grocery bags in the kitchen. Then he turned to face her. "Is there a problem?"

She shifted from one foot to the other. Luc was wearing a suit and tie, and she felt like Daisy Duke facing off with Daddy Warbucks. "This union won't last forever. After all the money you're spending to help Deedee and me, you shouldn't have to finance the next phase of my life, as well. I thought it might be prudent to have something to fall back on in the future."

He nudged a corner of her navy plaid futon/chair with the toe of his highly polished wing tip, giving the sad, misshapen piece a dismissive glance. "When that happens, I won't cast off you and the child to live with cheap, secondhand furniture. I have a reputation to uphold in this town. Image is everything. You're going to have to face the truth, Hattie. You're marrying a rich man—whether you like it or not."

The mockery in his words and on his face was not veiled this time. He was lashing out at her for what she'd done in the past. Fair enough. Back then she had made a big deal about their stations in life. Luc's money gave him power, and Hattie had been taught at her mother's knee never to let a man have control.

The man Hattie called "daddy" was really her stepfather.

As a nineteen-year-old, her mother had been that most naive of clichés…the secretary who had an affair with her boss. When Hattie's mom told her lover she was pregnant, he tossed her aside and never looked back.

Hattie lifted her chin. "It was never about the money," she insisted. "Or not *only* the money. Look at what your life has become, Luc. You're the CEO of a Fortune 500 company. I'm a public school teacher. I clip coupons and drive a ten-year-old car. Even before I began helping with my mother's finances, I lived a very simple lifestyle."

He curled a lip. "Is this where I cue the violins?"

"Oh, forget it," she huffed. "This is an old argument. What's the point?"

He shrugged. "What's the point indeed?" He picked up the duffel bag. "Dinner will keep a few minutes. Do you mind if I change clothes? I came straight from the office."

"The baby is asleep in my room, but the bathroom's all yours. I'll set out the food."

She had rummaged in the bags only long enough to see that Luc's largesse was nothing as common as pizza, when a loud knock sounded at the door. She glanced through the peephole and drew in a breath. Eddie. Good grief. Reluctantly, she opened the door.

He reeked of alcohol and swayed slightly on his feet. "Where's my baby girl? I want to see her."

She shushed him with a quick glance over her shoulder. "She's in bed. Babies sleep at this hour of night. Why don't you call me in the morning, and we'll agree on a time for you to come by?"

He stuck a foot in the doorway, effectively keeping her from closing him out. "Or why don't I call the police and tell them you've kidnapped my kid?"

It was an idle threat. They both knew it. Hattie had already consulted a lawyer, and a nurse at the hospital had heard

Angela's dying request. Nevertheless, Eddie's bluster curled Hattie's stomach. She didn't want to be in the middle of a fight with Deedee as the prize.

"Go away, Eddie," she said forcefully, her voice low. "This isn't a good time. We'll talk tomorrow."

Without warning, he grabbed her shoulders and man-handled her backward into the apartment. "Like hell." He shoved her so hard, she stumbled into the wall. Her head hit with a muffled thud, and she saw little yellow spots.

He lunged for her again, but before his meaty fists could make contact, Luc exploded down the hallway, grabbed the intruder by the neck and put a chokehold on him. Eddie's face turned an alarming shade of purple before Hattie could catch her breath.

Luc was steely-eyed. "Call the cops."

"But I don't want…"

His expression gentled. "It's the right thing to do. Don't worry. I'm not leaving you to deal with this alone."

The response to the 911 call was gratifying. Just before the two uniformed officers arrived, Luc stuck his face nose to nose with Eddie's. "If I ever see you near my fiancée again, I'll tear you apart. Got it?"

Eddie was drunk enough to be reckless. "Fiancée? Yeah, right. If she was telling my daddy the truth about you and her, then where's the fancy diamond ring?"

"I had to order it," Luc responded smoothly. "It happens to be in my pocket even as we speak. But some jackass has ruined our romantic evening."

The conversation ended abruptly as Hattie opened the door to the police. They took Luc's statement, handcuffed Eddie and were gone in under twenty minutes.

In the sudden silence, Hattie dropped into a chair, her legs boneless and weak in the aftermath of adrenaline. Thank God the baby hadn't been awakened by all the commotion.

Luc crouched beside her, his eyes filled with concern. "Let me see your head." He parted her hair gently, exclaiming when he saw the goose egg that had popped up.

She moved restlessly. "I'm fine. Really. All I need is some Tylenol. And a good night's sleep."

Luc cursed under his breath. "Don't move." After bringing her medicine and water with which to wash down the tablets, he created a makeshift ice bag with a dish towel and pressed it to the side of her head. "Hold this." He lifted her in his arms and laid her gently on the ugly sofa. "Rest. I'll fix us a couple of plates."

He was back in no time. The smells alone made Hattie want to whimper with longing. Her stomach growled loudly.

He put a hand on her shoulder. "No need to get up yet. I'll feed you."

"Don't be ridiculous." But when she tried to sit upright, her skull pounded.

He eased her back down. "You don't have to fight me over every damn thing. Open your mouth." He fed her small manageable bites of chicken piccata and wild rice. While she chewed and swallowed, he dug into his own portion.

Hattie muttered in frustration when one of her mouthfuls landed on the sofa cushion. "See what you made me do…"

"Don't worry," he deadpanned. "A few stains could only help this monstrosity."

She eyed him, openmouthed, and then they both burst into laughter. Hattie felt tears sting the backs of her eyes. She told herself it was nothing more than delayed reaction. But in truth, it was Luc. When he forgot to be on his guard with her, she saw a glimpse of the young man she had loved so desperately.

She wondered with no small measure of guilt if her long-ago defection had transformed the boy she once knew so well into the hard-edged, sardonic Luc. A million times over the years she had second-guessed her decision. It had been gratifying to establish a career and to stand on her own two feet. Her mother had been proud of Hattie's independence and success in her chosen field.

But at what cost?

When the last of the food was consumed, the mood grew awkward. Luc gathered their empty plates. "Stay where you are. You have to deal with Deedee in the morning, so you might as well rest while you can."

She lay there quietly, wondering bleakly how her life had unraveled so quickly. Two months ago she'd been an ordinary single woman with a circle of friends, a good job and a pleasant social life. Now she was a substitute parent facing a custody battle and trying to combat a tsunami of feelings for the man who had once upon a time been her other half, her soul mate. Was it any wonder she felt overwhelmed?

A trickle of water from melting ice slid down her cheek. She sat up and sucked in a breath when a hammer thudded inside her skull. The food she had eaten rolled unpleasantly in her stomach.

Luc frowned as he rejoined her, pausing only to take the wet dish towel and toss it on a kitchen counter. "We probably should make a trip to the E.R. to make sure you don't have a concussion."

"I'll be fine." She knew her voice lacked conviction, but it was hard to be stoic with the mother of all headaches.

Luc put his hands on his hips, his navy polo shirt stretching taut over broad shoulders and a hard chest. "I'll stay the night."

Four

Hattie gaped. "Oh, no. Not necessary."

"We have the baby to think of, too. You probably won't rest very well tonight, and you'll likely need an extra hand in the morning. I'll sleep on the couch. It may be ugly as sin, but it's long and fairly comfortable. I'll be fine."

Hattie was torn. Having Luc in her small apartment was unsettling, but the encounter with Eddie had shaken her emotionally as well as physically, and she was dead on her feet.

She shrugged, conceding defeat. "I'll get you towels and bedding." She brushed by him, inhaling for a brief instant the tang of citrusy aftershave and the scent of warm male.

When she returned moments later, he was on the phone with Ana, letting her know he wouldn't be home that evening. It touched her that he would be so considerate of people who were in his employ. He was a grown man. He had no obligation to let anyone know his schedule or his whereabouts.

But wasn't that what had drawn her to him in the beginning?

His kindness and his humor? Sadly, his personality had an edge now, a remoteness that had not existed before.

She began making up the sofa, but he stopped her as soon as he hung up. "Go to bed, Hattie. I'm not a guest. I don't need you waiting on me. I can fend for myself."

She nodded stiffly. "Good night, then."

He lifted a shoulder, looking diffident for a moment. "May I see her?"

"The baby?" Well, duh. Who else could he mean?

"Yes."

"Of course."

He followed her down the short hallway into the bedroom. A small night-light illuminated the crib. Luc put his hands on the railing and stared down at the infant sleeping so peacefully. Hattie hung back. Her chest was tight with confused emotions. Had things gone differently in the past, this scene might have played out in reality.

A couple, she and Luc, putting their own daughter to bed before retiring for the night.

Luc reached out a hand, hovered briefly, then lightly stroked Deedee's hair. She never stirred. He spoke softly, his back still toward Hattie. "She doesn't deserve what has happened to her."

Hattie shook her head, eyes stinging. "No. She doesn't. I can't let Eddie take her. She's so innocent, so perfect."

Luc turned, his strong, masculine features shadowed in the half-light. His somber gaze met her wary one, some intangible link between them shrouding the moment in significance. "We'll keep her safe, Hattie. You have my word."

Quietly, he left the room.

Hattie changed into a gown and robe. Ordinarily, she slept in a T-shirt and panties, but with Luc in the house, she needed extra armor.

She folded the comforter and turned back the covers before

heading for the bathroom. Well, shoot. She'd forgotten to give Luc even the basics. Taking a new toothbrush from the cabinet, she returned to the living room. "Sorry. I meant to give you this. There's toothpaste on the counter, and if you want to shave in the morning—"

She stopped dead, her pulse jumping. Luc stood before her wearing nothing but a pair of gray knit boxers, which left little to the imagination. Every inch of his body was fit and tight. His skin was naturally olive-toned, and the dusting of fine black hair on his chest made her want to stroke it to see if it was as soft as she remembered.

Long muscular thighs led upward to… She gulped. As she watched in fascination, his erection grew and flexed. She literally couldn't move. Luc didn't seem at all embarrassed, despite the fact that her face was hot enough to fry an egg.

"Thank you for the toothbrush." A half smile lifted one corner of his mouth.

She extended the cellophane-wrapped package gingerly, making sure her fingers didn't touch his. "You're welcome."

And still she didn't leave. The years rolled away. She remembered with painful clarity what it was like to be held tightly to that magnificent chest, to feel those strong arms pull her close, to experience the hard evidence of his arousal thrusting against her abdomen.

His gaze was hooded, the line of his mouth now almost grim. "Like what you see?"

The mockery was deliberate, she had no doubt…as if to say *you were so foolish back then. Look what you gave up.*

Heat flooded her body. The robe stifled her. She wanted to tear it off, to fling herself at Luc. But her limbs couldn't move. She was paralyzed, caught between bitter memories of the past and the sure knowledge that Luc Cavallo was still the man who could make her soar with pleasure.

"Answer me, Hattie," he said roughly. "If you're going

to look at me like that, I'm damn sure going to take the invitation."

Her lips parted. No sound came out.

The color on his cheekbones darkened and his eyes flared with heat. "Come here."

No soft preliminaries. No tentative approach.

Luc was confident, controlled. He touched only her face, sliding his hands beneath her hair and holding her still so his mouth could ravage hers. His tongue thrust between her lips—invading, dominant, taking and not giving. She was shaking all over, barely able to stand. He kissed her harder still, muttering something to himself she didn't quite catch.

She felt the push of his hips. Suddenly, her body came to life with painful tingles of heat. Her arms went around his waist, and she kissed him back. But when his fingers accidentally brushed the painful knot on her skull, she flinched.

Instantly, he cursed and thrust her away, his gaze a cross between anger and incredulity. "Damn you. Go to bed, Hattie."

If she had been a Victorian heroine, she might have swooned at this very moment. But she was made of sterner stuff. She marshaled her defenses, muttered a strangled good-night and fled.

Aeons later it seemed, she rolled over and flung an arm over her face. Bright sunshine peeked in through a crack between the curtains. She had slept like the dead, deeply, dreamlessly. A glance at the clock stopped her heart. It was nine o'clock. Deedee. Dear heaven. The baby was always up by six-thirty.

She leaped from the bed, almost taking a nosedive when the covers tangled around her feet. The crib was empty. She sucked in a panicked breath, and then her sleep-fuddled brain began to function.

Luc. Memories of his kiss tightened her nipples and made her thighs clench with longing. She touched her lips as the hot sting of tears made her blink and sniff. Ten years was a lifetime to wait for something that was at once so terrible and so wonderful.

She opened her bedroom door and simultaneously heard the sound of childish gurgles and smelled the heavenly aroma of frying bacon. Luc stood by the stove. Deedee was tucked safely in her high chair nearby.

He glanced up, his features impassive. "Good morning."

The baby squealed in delight and lurched toward Hattie. Luc unfastened the tray and handed her off. "I fed her a bottle and half a jar of peaches. I didn't want to give her anything else until I checked with you." The words were gruff, as if he'd had to force them from his throat.

Hattie cuddled the baby, stunned that Luc had taken over with such relaxed competence. Not that she didn't think he was capable. But she had never witnessed him with children and she was shocked to see him so calm and in control, especially when Hattie herself had experienced a few rough moments in the last six weeks.

He started cracking eggs into a bowl. "This will be ready in five, and the movers will be showing up shortly. You might want to get dressed. I can handle Deedee."

Hattie held the baby close, realizing with chagrin that she had jumped out of bed and never actually donned her robe. The sheer fabric of her nightie revealed far too much. "She'll be fine with me." Suddenly she noticed the sheaf of legal papers on the nearby coffee table. "Luc...I'm so sorry. With everything that happened, we never did get around to dealing with the marriage stuff."

He popped two slices of bread into her toaster. "No worries. We'll have time later today."

She hesitated, eager to leave the room, but feeling oddly abashed that he had watched her sleeping…without her knowledge. Though they had made love many times when they were together, only once or twice had they enjoyed the luxury of spending the night together.

She cleared her throat. "Thank you for getting up with the baby. I can't believe I didn't hear her."

He shrugged. "I'm an early riser. I enjoyed spending time with her. She's a charming child."

"You haven't seen her throw a temper tantrum yet," she joked. "Batten down the hatches. She has a great set of lungs."

He paused his efficient preparations, the spatula in midair. "You're doing a great job. She's lucky to have you as her mother." His eyes and his voice were serious.

"Thanks." Despite the task he had undertaken, nothing about the setting made Luc look at all domestic: quite the opposite. Luc Cavallo was the kind of man you'd want by your side during a forced jungle march. He possessed a self-confidence that was absolute.

But that resolute belief in his own ability to direct the universe to his liking made Hattie uneasy. In asking for his help, she had unwittingly given him the very power she had refused to allow in their previous relationship. Even if she had second thoughts now, the situation was already beyond her control.

The contents of the small apartment were packed, boxes loaded and rooms emptied by 12:30. Luc had already paid out the remainder of Hattie's lease. All that was left for her to do was turn in her keys to the super and follow Luc out to the car where Sherman was waiting. But there she balked. "I'll follow you in my car."

Luc frowned. "I thought we had this discussion."

"I like my car. I'm sentimentally attached to my car. I'm not giving it away."

The standoff lasted only a few seconds. Luc shrugged, his expression resigned. "I'll see you at the house."

It was a small victory, but it made Hattie feel better. Luc had a habit of taking charge in ways that ostensibly made perfect sense, but left Hattie feeling like a helpless damsel in distress. She had *asked* for his help, but that didn't mean she'd let him walk all over her.

She strapped Deedee into the old, shabby car seat and slid into the front, turning the key in the ignition and praying the car would start. That would be the final indignity.

As their little caravan pulled away from the curb, Hattie glanced in the rearview mirror for one last look at her old life slipping away. Her emotions were not easy to define. Relief. Sadness. Anticipation. Had she sold her soul to the devil? Only time would tell.

Luc experienced a sharp but distinct jolt of satisfaction when Hattie stepped over his threshold. Something primitive in him exulted. She was coming to him of her own free will. She'd be under his roof…wearing his ring. Ten years ago he'd let his pride keep him from trying to get her back. That, and his misguided belief that he had to respect her wishes. But everything was different this time around. *He* was calling the shots.

The attraction was still there. He felt it, and he knew she did, as well. Soon she would turn to him out of sheer gratitude, or unfulfilled desire or loneliness. And then she would be his. He'd waited a long time for this. And no one could fault him. He was giving Hattie and her baby a home and security.

If he extracted his pound of flesh in the process, it was only fair. She owed him that much.

He left them to get settled in, with Sherman and Ana hovering eagerly. After changing clothes, he drove to the office and threw himself into the pile of work that had accumulated during his unaccustomed morning off.

But for once, his concentration was shot. He found himself wishing he was back at the house, watching Hattie...playing with the baby...anticipating the night to come.

He called home on the drive back. It wasn't late, only six-thirty. Hattie answered her cell.

"Hello, Luc."

He returned the greeting and said, "Ana has offered to look after Deedee this evening. I thought we might go out for a quiet dinner and discuss business."

Business? He winced. Did he really mean to sound so cavalier?

Hattie's response was cool. "I don't want to take advantage of Ana's good nature."

"You're not, I swear. It was her idea. Little Deedee has a way of making people fall in love with her. I'll be there to pick you up in twenty minutes."

It was only dinner. With a woman who had already rejected him once. Why was his heart beating faster?

Unfortunately for Hattie, the black dress had to do duty again. This time she had no inclination to wear Luc's necklace. Not for a *business* dinner. She tied a narrow tangerine scarf around her neck and inserted plain gold hoops in her ears.

She was ready and waiting in the foyer when he walked in the front door.

Luc seemed disappointed. "Where's the baby?"

Hattie grimaced, her nerves jumping. "She's taking an early evening nap. I couldn't get her to sleep much at all this afternoon…the uncertainty of a new place, I think. She was cranky and exhausted."

"Too bad. Well, in that case, I guess we can get going."

The restaurant was lovely—very elegant, and yet not so pretentious that Hattie felt uncomfortable. The sommelier chatted briefly with Luc and then produced a zinfandel that met with Luc's approval.

Hattie was persuaded to try a glass. "It's really good," she said. "Fruity but not too sweet."

He leaned back in his chair. "I thought you'd like it."

They enjoyed a quiet dinner, sticking to innocuous topics, and then afterward, Luc reached into a slim leather folder and extracted a sheaf of papers. "My lawyers have drawn up all the necessary documents. If you wish, you're welcome to have a third-party lawyer go over them with you. I know from experience that legalese is hard to wade through at times."

She took the documents and eyed them cautiously. "I have someone who has been helping me with the custody issues," she said, already skimming the lines of print. "I'll get her to take a look." Most of it was self-explanatory. When she reached page three of the prenup, her eyebrows raised. "It says here that if and when the marriage dissolves, I'll be entitled to a lump sum payment of $500,000."

He drummed the fingers of one hand on the table. His skin was dark against the snowy-white cloth. "You don't think that's fair?"

"I think it's outrageous. You don't owe me anything. You're doing me a huge favor. I don't plan to walk away with half a million dollars. Put something aside for Deedee's education if you want to, but we need to strike that line."

His jaw tightened. "The line stays. That's a deal breaker."

She studied his face, puzzled and upset. "I don't understand."

He scowled at her, his posture combative. "You've throw

my wealth in my face the entire time I've known you, Hattie. And now you're using it to protect someone you love. I don't have a problem with that. But I'll be damned when that day comes if I'll let anyone say I threw you out on the street destitute."

Her lip trembled, and she bit down on it…hard. Luc was a proud man. Perhaps until now she had never really understood just how proud he was. She was sure his heart had healed after she broke up with him. But maybe the dent to his pride was not so easily repaired.

She owed him a sign of faith. It was the least she could do after treating him so shabbily in the past. He was an honorable man. That much hadn't changed. She reached into her purse for a pen and turned to the first yellow sticky tab. With a flourish, she signed her name.

He put a hand over hers. "Are you sure you don't want someone to look over this with you?"

She shivered inwardly at his touch. "I'm sure," she said, her words ragged.

He released her and watched intently as she signed one page after another. When it was all done, she handed the documents back to him. "Is that it?"

Luc tucked the paperwork away. "I have a couple of other things I think we need to discuss, but it requires a private setting. We'll be more comfortable at home."

"Oh." Her scintillating response didn't faze him. He seemed perfectly calm. He summoned their waiter, paid the check and stood to pull out her chair. As they exited the restaurant, she was hyperaware of his warm hand resting in the small of her back.

Hattie was silent on the drive back. Her skin was hot, her stomach pitchy. What on earth could he mean? Sex? It seemed the obvious topic, but she had assumed they might work up to that gradually…after they were married. She hadn't anticipated talking about it so bluntly or openly. They had been as close as two people could be once upon a time. But that was long, long ago.

Was she willing to go to his bed? To be his wife in every sense of the word? He was well within his rights as a husband to insist.

Did she expect him to be faithful in the context of a sham marriage? And if Luc no longer wanted to be intimate with Hattie, was it fair to deny him physical satisfaction?

She wouldn't lie to herself. She wanted Luc.

Dear Lord, what was she going to say?

In a cowardly play for more time, she stalled when they got back to the house. "I'd like to check on the baby and change clothes. Is that okay? It won't take me long."

Luc dropped his keys into the exquisite Baccarat dish on the table in the foyer. "Take your time. I'll meet you in the den when you're ready."

Five

Wearing ancient jeans and a faded Emory T-shirt, Luc sprawled on the leather sofa and stared moodily at the blank television screen. Was he insane? *Power*. A nice fantasy. Clearly he was fooling himself. What man was ever really in control when his brain ceded authority to a less rational part of his body?

Just being close to Hattie these last few days had caused him to resort to cold showers. He told himself that his physical response to her was nothing more than a knee-jerk reaction to memories…to sensual images of the way he and Hattie had burned up the sheets.

She'd been a virgin when they met, a shy, reserved girl with big eyes and a wary take on the world. As if she was never quite sure someone wasn't going to pull the rug out from under her feet.

He'd been embarrassed to tell her how many girls he'd been with before meeting her. A horny teenager with unlimited money at his disposal was a dangerous combination. In high school, he'd been too concerned about keeping his body in shape for sports to dabble in drugs. And even drinking, a rite of passage for adolescent boys, didn't hold much allure. Perhaps because he had grown up in a house where alcohol was freely available and handled wisely.

But sex…hell, he'd had a lot of sex. Money equals power… even sixteen-year-old girls could figure that out. So Luc was never without female companionship, unless he chose to hang with his buddies.

When Hattie came into his life, everything changed. She was different. She liked him, but his money didn't interest her. At first, he thought her attitude might be a ploy to snag his attention. But as they got to know each other, he realized that she really didn't give a damn that he was loaded.

She expected thoughtfulness from him, attention to her likes and dislikes. She wanted him to *know* her. And that was something money couldn't buy.

It was only much, much later that he realized his money was actually a stumbling block.

A faint noise made him turn his head. Hattie hovered in the doorway, her sun-streaked blond hair pulled back into a short ponytail, her feet bare. She was dressed as casually as he was.

He patted the seat beside him. "Would you like more wine?" The upcoming conversation might flow more easily if she relaxed.

She shook her head as she perched gingerly on the far end of the couch, tucking her legs beneath her. "No, thanks. Water would be nice." Her toenails were painted pale pink. The sight of them did odd things to his gut.

He went to the fridge behind the bar, extracted two Perriers and handed her one. As he sat back down, he allowed the careful distance she had created to remain between them. It meant she was nervous, and that gave him an edge. He handed her a slim white envelope. "We'll start with this." Inside were three credit cards with her soon-to-be name, Hattie Parker Cavallo, already imprinted.

She extracted them with patent reluctance. "What are these?"

He stretched an arm along the back of the sofa. "As my wife, you'll need a large wardrobe. I entertain frequently, and I also travel often. When it's feasible, I'd like you and Deedee to accompany me. In addition, I want you to outfit the nursery upstairs. I've put a selection of baby furniture catalogs in the desk drawer in your bedroom. Ana will show you the suite I picked out for Deedee. If it doesn't meet with your approval, we'll decide on another."

She paled, her eyes dark and haunted.

He ground his teeth. "What's wrong?"

She shrugged helplessly. "I...I feel like you're taking over my life. Like I've lost all control."

His fists clenched instinctively, and he had to force himself to relax. "I understood there was some sense of urgency to the situation...that we needed to back up your lie quickly."

"There is...and we do...but..."

"But what? Do you disagree with any of the arrangements I've made thus far?"

"No, of course not."

"Then I don't understand the problem."

She jumped to her feet and paced. With her back to him, he could see the way the soft, worn jeans cupped her butt. It was a very nice butt. With an effort, he dragged his attention back to the current crisis.

She whirled to face him. "I'm used to taking care of myself." The words were almost a shout.

Something inside him went still...crouched like a tiger in waiting. He feigned a disinterest he didn't feel. "We don't have to get married at all, Hattie. My team of lawyers loves going for the kill. Custody situations aren't their usual fare, but with Eddie in self-destruct mode, it shouldn't be too hard to convince a judge that you're the obvious choice to raise Deedee." He paused, risking everything on a gamble, a single toss of the dice. "Is that what you want?"

Hattie pressed two fingers to the center of the forehead, clearly in pain. Her entire body language projected misery. "I want my sister back," she said…and as he watched, tears spilled down her wan cheeks.

He tried to leave her alone, he really did. But her heartbreak twisted something inside his chest. She didn't protest when he took her in his arms, when he pulled the elastic band from her ponytail and stroked her hair, careful not to further hurt her injury.

She felt fragile in his embrace, but he knew better. Her backbone was steel, her moral compass a straight arrow.

The quiet sobs didn't last long. He felt and sensed the moment she pulled herself together. She stiffened in his embrace. Though it went against his every inclination, he released her and returned to his seat on the sofa. He took a swig of sparkling water and waited her out.

She studied a painting on the wall. It was a Vermeer he'd picked up at an auction in New York last year. The obscure work immortalized a young woman in her tiny boudoir as she bent at the waist to fasten her small shoe. The play of light on the girl's graceful frame fascinated Luc. He'd bought it on a whim, but it had quickly become one of his favorite pieces. Impulse drove him at times—witness the way he'd agreed so quickly to this sham marriage.

But in the end, his impulses usually served him well.

He grew impatient. "I asked you a question, Hattie. Do you want this marriage? Tell me."

She turned at last, her fists clenched at her sides. "If I don't go through with this, Eddie's family will know I lied. And they'll use it against me. I don't have a choice."

Her fatalistic attitude nicked his pride. His heart hardened, words tumbling out like cold stones. "Then we'll do this my way. You can't run out on me this time, Hattie. I love irony, don't you?"

His sarcasm scraped her nerves. She was being so unfair. Luc had done everything she had asked of him and more. He didn't deserve her angst and criticism. She owed him more than she could ever calculate.

The fact that her body still ached for his only complicated matters.

Swallowing her aversion to the feeling that she was being bought and paid for, she sat back down and summoned a faint smile. "Giving a woman that much plastic is dangerous. Should we discuss a budget?"

His expression was inscrutable. "I know you pretty well, Hattie Parker. I doubt seriously if you'll bankrupt me." He reached in his pocket and pulled out a small velvet box, laying it on the cushion between them. "This is next on the agenda. I thought it was customary to make such things a surprise, but given your current mood, perhaps I should return it and let you choose your own."

She picked up the box and flipped back the lid. *This* was a flawless diamond solitaire. Clearly he understood her style, because the setting was simple in the extreme. But the rectangular stone that flashed and sparkled was easily four carats.

She bit her lip. "It's lovely," she said, squeezing the words from a tight throat. He made no attempt to take her hand and do the honors. She told herself she was glad. When she slid the ring onto her left hand, the brilliant stone seemed to take on a life of its own.

"So you don't want to exchange it? I wouldn't want to be accused of controlling your life."

His tone was bland, but she felt shame, nevertheless. "I love it, Luc. Thank you."

It was his turn to get up and pace. "I've made some preliminary wedding inquiries. Do you need or want a church wedding?"

Disappointment made her stomach leaden. Like most girls she had dreamed of her wedding day. "No. That's not necessary."

"Our family owns a small private island off the coast, near Savannah. If you're agreeable, we can have the ceremony there. The location precludes the possibility of Eddie or any of his relatives showing up to make a scene. Do you have someone you'd like to stand up with you?"

She picked at a stray thread on the knee of her jeans, her mind in a whirl of conflicting thoughts. "My best friend, Jodi, would have been my choice, but her husband is in the military, and they were transferred to Japan two months ago. With Angela gone, well, I…"

"I'm sure Ana would be honored to help us out."

It was a good choice, and a logical one given the circumstances. "I'll ask her tomorrow."

"A honeymoon will be important," he said, bending to turn on the gas logs in the fireplace. The spring evening had turned cool and damp.

"I'm not sure what you mean."

He turned to face her, his expression blank. "We can't risk any accusation that our marriage isn't real. I know you'll protest, but I really think we should go away for at least a week. Ana's niece is a college student working on her early childhood certification. I've already spoken to her, and she's willing to stay here at the house with Ana and Sherman while we're gone, to help with the baby."

Hattie gnawed her bottom lip. He'd neatly cut the ground from beneath her feet. Every argument anticipated and countered. It all made perfect sense. And it scared the heck out of her. "You seem to have thought of everything."

He shrugged. "It's what I do. As far as the wedding dress and the ceremony itself, I'll leave that to you. I have a good friend who is a justice of the peace. He's prepared to fly down with us and officiate."

"Who's going to be your best man?"

"Leo."

"Does he know about me…about Deedee?"

"I told him I was marrying someone he knew, but I left it at that. Leo will be there. But as far as he is concerned right now, this is a normal marriage. You and I will be the only people who will know the truth."

"You'd lie to your own brother?"

"I'll tell him the situation later…when it's a done deal."

"And your grandfather?"

"He's flying over for his big birthday party in the fall. I won't encourage him to come this time."

"I wonder if Leo will even remember me."

Luc chuckled. "My brother never forgets a beautiful woman. We'll get together with him for dinner when we come back from our honeymoon, and you can reminisce."

Hattie winced inwardly. Leo probably thought she was the worst kind of tease. Leading Luc on back in college and then dumping him. Leo would side with his brother, of course. Just one more thing to look forward to in her new, surreal life.

She took a deep breath. "When are we going to do this?"

"May 14 works for my schedule. I've cleared the week following for our honeymoon. Is there anywhere in particular you'd like to go? The company has a top-notch travel agent."

She smiled faintly. "Since I've never really *been* anywhere, I'll let you choose."

"I thought Key West might be nice…a luxurious villa on a quiet street. A private pool."

Her mouth dried. "Um, sure. Sounds lovely." Why did she suddenly have a vision of the two of them naked and... cavorting in the moonlight? *Dear heaven.* May 14 was two and a half weeks away. This was happening. This was real.

She couldn't wait any longer to address the elephant in the room. Or perhaps she was the only one who was worrying about it. Luc was a guy. Sex came as naturally to him as breathing. He probably thought nature would take its course.

But she needed to have things spelled out. "Luc?"

He rejoined her on the sofa, this time sitting so close to her that their hips nearly touched. Deliberately, he lifted her hand nearest him and linked their fingers. "What, Hattie? Permission to speak freely."

His light humor did nothing to alleviate her nerves. She squeezed his hand briefly and stood up again, unable to bear being so close to him when she was on edge. "I had a feeling earlier this evening...at dinner...that one of the things you wanted to discuss in private was sex. It makes sense...to talk about it, I mean. You're a virile man, and I assume you'll be faithful to our wedding vows. So no one can question the validity of our marriage. For the baby's sake."

His face darkened. "For the baby's sake...right. Because I assume that otherwise you could care less if I went to another woman for satisfaction."

He was angry, and she wasn't sure why. She picked up the elastic band he'd removed from her hair. With swift, jerky movements she put her ponytail back in place. She didn't want to think about how it felt to have his fingers combing through her hair, his hard, warm palms caressing her back.

"I'm trying to explain, Luc, that I'm okay with it."

"Okay with what?"

His black scowl terrified her. If she handled this wrong, he might back out entirely. "I understand that it makes sense for us to be intimate...while we're together. A man and a woman living in the same house…married. I'm willing.… That's all I wanted to say."

His lip curled. His dark eyes were impenetrable. "Well, you were right about one thing."

"I was?"

"I did want to talk about sex."

"I thought so."

"But while I am deeply touched by your desire to throw yourself on the sacrificial altar, I don't need your penance."

"I don't understand."

His legs were outstretched, propped on the coffee table. He feigned relaxation, but his entire body vibrated with intense emotion. "It's simple, Hattie. All I wanted to say was that it seems somewhat degrading to both of us to exchange *physical pleasure* for money."

The way he drawled the words *physical pleasure* made her belly tighten. "You're confusing me."

"Sex has nothing to do with this marriage agreement. Is that clear enough? If we end up in bed together, it will be because we both want it. I'm attracted to you, Hattie…just as I would be to any beautiful woman. And I have a normal man's needs. I'll welcome you to my bed anytime. But you'll have to come to me. Your body is not on the bargaining table."

He was being deliberately cruel. Perhaps she deserved it. But humiliation swept through her in burning waves. She had offered herself up in all sincerity, and he had reduced the possibility of marital intimacy to scratching an itch.

Dimly, apprehensively, she began to understand what Luc was going to get out of this marriage. He was going to make her dance to his tune. He was going to make her beg.

And what scared her even more than being totally at his mercy was the inescapable knowledge that she would be the one to crack. And she might not make it through the honeymoon.

Six

The days before the wedding flew by. Hattie was consumed with setting up the nursery and shopping for an appropriate dress in which to become Mrs. Luc Cavallo.

After the embarrassing scene with Luc in the den, Hattie saw little of him. He spent four days in Milan at a conference, and when he returned to Atlanta, he worked long days, ostensibly getting caught up so he could be away for a week's vacation. No one at his office knew anything about a wedding.

Deedee was thriving. There had been no further word from Eddie, and on the surface, life seemed normal.... Or at least as normal as it could be given the current situation.

Sherman and Ana adored Deedee and spoiled her with toys and other gifts. Hattie relished being part of that circle. She had never known her own grandparents, and the new relationships she was building helped fill the emotional hole in her soul. Things might become awkward when the marriage ended, but she would worry about that when the time came.

The wedding was only four days away when trouble

showed up. Not Eddie this time. A loud knock sounded at the front door midday, and Hattie answered it. Sherman was out back washing the cars, and Ana was making dinner preparations.

The man standing on the doorstep was familiar. "Leo," she said, her heart sinking. "Please come in."

"Well, isn't this nice," he sneered. "Playing lady of the manor, are we?"

She ignored his sarcasm. Clearly, he *did* remember her... and not fondly. "Luc's not home."

Leo folded his arms across his broad chest. "I came to see you." He was a physically intimidating man, and his brains more than equaled his brawn. Back in college he had played at flirting with her. Not seriously, just to get his brother's goat. But the look on his face at the moment said he'd just as soon toss her in the river as look at her.

"How did you know I was here?"

"I didn't. But I knew *something* was going on. My brother's been acting damn strangely. And now I know why."

Ana appeared, wiping her hands on a dish cloth. "Mr. Leo. How nice to see you." She turned to Hattie. "If you would like to step out back to the patio, I'd be happy to bring you a snack."

Leo smiled at the housekeeper, a warm, I'm-really-a-nice-guy smile. "Sounds wonderful, Ana. I've been running all day and missed lunch." He eyed Hattie blandly. "What a treat."

Hattie felt Leo's eyes boring into her back as they made their way through the house. She hadn't expected a warm welcome from Luc's brother, but she also hadn't anticipated this degree of antipathy from him. They sat down in wrought-iron chairs, and moments later Ana brought out a tray of oatmeal cookies and fresh coffee.

The older woman poured two cups and stepped back. "I'll

put the monitor in the kitchen, Hattie, so I'll be able to hear the baby if she wakes up."

Leo paled. As soon as the housekeeper was out of earshot, he swallowed half a cup of coffee and glared at Hattie over the rim of a bone china cup. His big hand dwarfed it. "Luc's a daddy?"

"No, of course not. Or not in the way you're thinking. Has he told you anything about my situation?" It was difficult to believe that Luc would cling to his intent of keeping Leo uninformed.

"Luc didn't tell me diddly squat. All he mentioned was that I should show up on the fourteenth wearing my tux when and where he said."

"Oh."

"Perhaps you'd like to fill me in." It wasn't a request.

"I'm sorry he's been keeping secrets from you. It's my fault." She quickly gave him the shortened version of the last two months. "I think that until the lawyers get a handle on this custody thing, Luc thinks the less said the better."

Leo ate two more cookies, eyeing her with a laserlike stare as he chewed slowly. "That's not why he didn't tell me. Luc knows I can keep my mouth shut. But he knew I would try to talk him out of this ridiculous sham of a marriage."

Hattie's heart sank. The two brothers were close. Could Leo, even now, derail what Luc and Hattie had set in motion?

She set down her cup so he wouldn't see her hand shaking. "Why would you do that? If you're worried about the money, or the company...you needn't be. I've already signed a prenup."

Leo snorted. "You may be a lot of things, Hattie, but even I know you're not a gold digger."

"Then why is this any of your business?" She heard the snap in her own voice and didn't care. What did Leo Cavallo have to gain by sticking his big Roman nose into her affairs?

He pulled his chair closer to the table, his knees almost touching hers beneath the glass. His accusatory mood made her want to run, but she refused to give him the satisfaction. He spoke softly, with menace. "Ten years ago, you almost destroyed my brother. You let him fall in love with you, encouraged it even. And then when he proposed, the first and only time he's ever done that by the way, you shut him down. A man has his pride, Hattie. You let things go too far. If you weren't going to love him back, why in the hell did you sleep with him? Why did you let him think you were his girl, his future?"

She bent her head, staring down at the crumbs on her plate. "That's just it, Leo. I did love him. I was sick with loving him."

"That's bull." He lifted her chin, his gaze boring into hers. "Women in love don't do what you did to Luc."

"That's not true," she cried. "We never would have worked out in the long term. I wasn't the right person to be his wife. I did the right thing by breaking it off. You know I did."

He let go of her and sat back, brooding, surly. "Then how do you explain this?" He waved a hand. "You damn sure appear to be enjoying the fancy house and the hired help."

"Don't be hateful."

"Not hateful, honey. Just stating the facts."

"This is all temporary."

"Does Luc know that?"

"Of course he does. When enough time has passed to make our marriage appear to be the real thing, we'll separate quietly. And I'll raise Deedee on my own."

"And what happens when my softhearted baby brother falls in love with the little girl sleeping upstairs? Will you tear his heart out again by taking her away?"

Hattie closed her eyes, regret raking her with sharp claws. "That won't happen," she said weakly.

"How do you know?" Leo asked quietly. "And how do you know he won't fall in love with *you* again?"

She laughed without amusement. "I can assure you *that* is not a possibility. Luc's helping me because he's a good man. But he's made it very clear that this is strictly business."

"And you believe him?"

"Why would he lie?"

"To protect himself perhaps?"

"From what?"

"The correct answer is *from whom*. You, Hattie. A man never forgets his first love. Why else would he turn his entire life upside down in a matter of days?"

"I think he's hoping for some payback, if you want to know the truth. I know I hurt him. I'm not stupid. This is his chance to be in control. To make me fall in line, not in love."

"How so?"

"He made it very clear that he has no feelings for me anymore."

Leo shook his head. "You don't know anything at all about men, sweetheart. If that's what he said, he's kidding himself. He sounds like a man who knows his own limits and is covering his ass."

Hattie mulled over Leo's words, torn between embarrassment and hope.

She was on the bed playing with Deedee when the master of the house came home. It surprised her that he sought her out. They had barely spoken a dozen words in the last week.

He looked tired. Not for the first time, she pondered the unfairness of what she had asked him to do. But what choice did she have? On her own, Eddie's family would have eaten her alive. And Luc had jumped at the opportunity to throw his weight around. So why did she feel guilty?

He sat down on the corner of the bed and grinned at

Deedee. She wriggled her way across the mattress toward him in a sort of commando crawl. He scooped her up and held her toward the ceiling. "Hey, kiddo. What mischief have you been up to today?"

Deedee squealed with laughter, her round cheeks pink with exertion. Luc nuzzled her tummy and lowered her to blow raspberries against her belly button.

Hattie watched them, her heart warmed by the budding connection man and infant shared. "She really likes you."

Luc glanced at Hattie. "The feeling is mutual."

His obvious enjoyment of something as simple as playing with a baby brought Leo's words rushing back. In all the time Hattie had thought about what would happen when the marriage ended, she had never considered the toll on Luc and her niece. Deedee would still be young. She wouldn't even remember Luc after a few months. But would Luc grieve?

Damn Leo for planting doubts.

Luc let the baby loose to roam the mattress again. Hattie had surrounded the edge with pillows, so Deedee couldn't go far. When the child latched on to one of her favorite toys, Luc finally spoke directly to Hattie. "How was your day?"

The prosaic question surprised her somehow. She leaned back on her elbows. "They delivered the nursery furniture early this morning. Deedee has already napped twice in the new bed and pronounced it quite satisfactory."

"Good." Long awkward silence. "Are you ready for the weekend? Do you need anything?"

She sat up. "I'm pretty much packed. Ana has been helping me."

"And the dress?"

"I finally found what I wanted yesterday. I hope it will be appropriate."

"I'm sure it's fine."

Hattie sighed inwardly. Next thing you know, they'd be

discussing the weather. She grabbed Deedee's ankle and pulled her toward the center of the bed. "Leo came by today."

That got Luc's attention. His eyes narrowed. "What did he want?"

"Well, apparently you neglected to mention that you were marrying me…or that I came with a baby. He wasn't happy."

Luc shrugged, his expression dangerous. "I don't make decisions based on Leo's likes and dislikes. If he doesn't want to come to the wedding, Sherman can do the honors."

"Don't be so pigheaded. Leo loves you."

"Leo believes his fourteen-month head start gives him the obligation to run my life."

"I think you should call him."

Luc's face went blank, wiped clean of all emotion. "I'll see him soon enough."

"Fine. Be an arrogant jerk. See if I care."

Luc stood up, gazing down at Hattie with an odd expression. "Sherman and Ana have the night off."

"I know. Did you want me to fix you something for dinner?"

"I thought we could take the baby on a picnic."

"It's kind of late."

"It won't hurt her to stay up just this once. Will it?"

"I guess not. I'll need to change, though."

He eyed her snug yellow T-shirt and khaki shorts. "You're fine. Let's go. I'm starving."

Luc had a garage full of expensive cars for every occasion. They took one of the more sedate sedans, a sporty Cadillac, and Luc moved the car seat. On the way, he dialed his favorite Chinese restaurant for takeout. Ten minutes later a helpful employee ran three bags out to the curb. The young man smiled hugely when Luc handed over a hundred and told the kid to keep the change.

Hattie wasn't prepared for their destination. Atlanta had

many lovely spots for al fresco dining, but Piedmont Park brought back too many memories. Had Luc chosen the location on purpose?

As Hattie freed Deedee from her seat, Luc gathered the food, a blanket from the trunk, a bottle of chilled wine and a corkscrew he'd added before they left the house. It was a perfect spring evening. The park was crowded, but after a few minutes' walk, they found a quiet spot away from Frisbees and footballs.

Deedee had eaten earlier, so Hattie buckled her into a small, portable seat with a tray and fed her Cheerios while Luc opened containers. The smells made Hattie's stomach growl.

She snagged an egg roll. "This looks heavenly. I'm probably going to make a pig of myself."

Luc ran his gaze from her long legs all the way up past her waist to her modest breasts. "A few extra pounds wouldn't do you any harm."

The intimacy in his voice caught her off guard. What kind of game was he playing?

They ate leisurely, rarely speaking, content to watch the action all around them. Hattie remembered their college days with wistfulness. Back then, Luc would already have had his head in her lap. She'd be stroking his hair, touching his chest.

She trembled inwardly as arousal made her weak with longing. Deedee was no help. Her little head slumped to the side as she succumbed to sleep. Hattie unbuckled her and lifted her free. Luc moved the seat, and together they tucked the baby between them.

Luc reclined on his side facing Hattie. "I heard from the lawyers today. They've spoken to their counterparts, and it seems that Eddie's trying to claim it was really your sister at the wheel that night. That he was confused by the impact and that was why he left the scene."

Hattie clenched her fists. "Please tell me that won't fly."

He propped up one knee. "The police report is pretty clear. But that doesn't mean the case won't drag on. I don't know what they're getting paid, but my guys said the other team doesn't seem to have trouble with Eddie committing perjury if it will get him off."

Hattie was stunned. Since when could a man literally murder other people by driving under the influence and not end up in prison?

Luc was attuned to her distress. He stroked the sleeping infant's back. "Try not to worry. I'm only keeping you informed. But I don't want you to obsess about this. Our bottom line is keeping Eddie away from Deedee. Some judges side with a biological parent automatically, but if it comes to a hearing—and it may not—we'll show proof that Eddie would be a danger to his own child."

Hattie shivered. "I hope you're right. Judges can be bought."

Luc's grin was feral. "Good thing I have deep pockets."

Moments later he surprised the heck out of her by falling asleep. As Hattie looked at man and baby, she realized an unpalatable truth. It would be dangerously easy to fall in love with Luc Cavallo again. The few men she had dated seriously in the last decade were shadows when held up against Luc's vibrant personality.

Hesitantly, she reached out and barely touched his hair. It was soft and thick and springy with the waviness he hated. Usually, he kept his cut conservatively short, but perhaps he'd been too busy for his customary barber visit, because she could see the beginnings of a curl at the back of his ear.

Something hot and urgent twisted in her belly. She wanted to lie down beside him, whisper in his ear, pull him on top of her and feel his powerful body mate with hers. Her hand shook as she pulled it back. She would go to him eventually. It was inevitable. And he would have the satisfaction of knowing that she had made a mistake in leaving him. He would taste her regret and know the scales had been evened.

Luc held all the power. She was helpless to stem the tide of the burgeoning desire she felt. It had only been lying dormant, waiting to be resurrected.

And no matter how much pain she would have to endure when the marriage ended, she would not be able to walk away from the temptation to once again be Luc Cavallo's lover.

<u>Seven</u>

The morning of May 14 dawned bright and clear. The entire household was up at first light. Ana brought Hattie breakfast in bed, toast and jam and half a grapefruit.

Hattie, who had been awake for some time, sat up, shoving the hair from her eyes. "You didn't have to do this."

Ana sat down on the edge of the bed. "A bride deserves special treatment on her wedding day. Sherman and Mr. Leo have taken Deedee outside for a walk in the stroller. All you need to do is relax and let the rest of us pamper you."

Hattie took a bite of toast and had trouble swallowing. Even the freshly brewed hot tea didn't help. Fear choked her. Panic hovered just offstage. She wiped her hands on a soft damask napkin and looked at Ana. "Am I doing the right thing?"

A few nights ago, Luc and Hattie had decided the older couple needed to know the truth. Luc had hired round-the-clock security to be in place during the honeymoon, but it wasn't fair to leave Deedee's caregivers out of the loop.

Ana smoothed the embroidered bedspread absently.

"Did I tell you that Mr. Luc offered Sherman and me an embarrassing amount of money if we wanted to retire?"

It seemed an odd answer to Hattie's question.

"I knew he gave you the option. But he told me you loved the house and didn't want to leave."

"As it was, he almost doubled our salaries. We're taking our first cruise this fall, nothing too fancy, but it will be a change of pace."

"Sounds like fun."

"The thing is, Hattie, I've worked my whole life. I wouldn't know what to do if I had to sit around all day. The previous owners of this grand old property were both in their nineties when they passed. They never had a family, and Sherman and I weren't able to have children, either. This is a big, wonderful house with all kinds of interesting history. But until you and Deedee moved in, it was missing something." She paused and smiled softly. "Mr. Luc wants to help you and that precious baby. What could be wrong with that?"

"But it isn't a real marriage. We're not a family."

Ana shrugged. "That may be true at the moment, but things happen for a reason. I've seen it too many times in my life not to believe that. Take it a day at a time. You'll be fine, Hattie dear. Now eat your breakfast and get in the shower. Mr. Luc's not one for running late."

Luc had chartered a private plane, and at ten-thirty sharp, it was wheels up. The short flight from Atlanta to the southeast coast of the state was a source of constant fascination for Deedee. She sat with Ana and Sherman, stuck her nose to the window and was uncustomarily still as she watched the clouds drift by.

Leo and Luc huddled together in the front row talking business and who knows what else. Luc's friend, who was to do the ceremony, sat with them. Hattie was left to chat with

Ana's niece, Patti. The young woman's eyes were almost as big as Deedee's.

She took a Coke from the flight attendant and turned to Hattie with a grin. "I've never been on a plane before, and especially not one like this. I could get used to the lifestyle. Did you know the bathroom has *real* hand towels…not paper?"

Hattie smiled at the girl's enthusiasm. "I can't thank you enough for helping out while we're gone on our honeymoon."

Patti wrinkled her nose. "Well, I love kids, and when Mr. Cavallo offered to pay my fall tuition in exchange for the week, I wasn't about to say no. My aunt and uncle and I will take such good care of Deedee. You won't have to worry about a thing."

Hattie gulped inwardly. Her debts to Luc were piling up more quickly than she could calculate.

Before Hattie could catch her breath and gird herself for what was to come, the plane landed smoothly on a small strip of tarmac. Three large SUVs sat waiting for the wedding party. Once in the cars, they were all whisked away to a nearby dock where they boarded a sleek black cabin cruiser.

At first, Luc's island was nothing more than a speck against the horizon, but as the boat cut through the choppy waves, land came into view. Down at the water's edge, a large wooden pier had been festooned with white ribbons. Uniformed staff secured a metal ramp and soon everyone stood on dry land.

Hattie looked around with wonder. They were too far north in latitude for the island to have a tropical flavor, but it was enchanting in other ways. Ancient trees graced the windswept contours of the land, and birds of every color and size nested in limbs overhead and left dainty footprints in the wet sand.

Luc appeared at her side. "What do you think?"

She smiled up at him. "It's amazing…so peaceful. I love it, Luc. It's perfect."

"We're trying to get the state to designate it as a wildlife refuge. Leo and I have no plans to develop this place. But one day, when we're gone, we want it to be protected." He took her arm. "Let's go. There's more to see."

Hattie's skin tingled where he touched her. Their hands were linked…perhaps he didn't notice. But the intimacy, intentional or not, was poignant to Hattie.

Dune buggies took the group up and over a crest to the far side of the island where a weathered but genteel guesthouse stood, built to blend into the landscape.

Luc helped her out of the fiberglass vehicle. "There's plenty of room inside for everyone to change. Will thirty minutes give you long enough? There's no real rush." He paused, and stared down at her, his expression pensive. "This is your day, Hattie. I know the circumstances aren't ideal, but you're doing a wonderful thing for Deedee."

For one brief moment, wistfulness crushed her chest as she wondered what it would have been like to marry Luc when she was twenty-one. Determinedly, she thrust aside regret. This was not the same situation at all. She lifted a hand and cupped his cheek. "Thank you, Luc. I don't know what I would have done if you had turned me away."

The space around them was ionized suddenly, the hot, sticky air heavy with unspoken emotions. She went up on her tiptoes and found his mouth with hers. Someone groaned. Maybe both of them. He tasted like all her memories combined, hot and sweet and dangerous.

But they were not alone.

Luc took a step backward, and her hand fell away. Something akin to pain flashed across his face. "We both want what's best for the baby," he said, his voice gruff. "That's the important thing."

* * *

Sherman and Patti tended to Deedee while Ana helped Hattie get dressed. Hattie disappeared into a well-appointed bathroom to freshen up and slip into an ivory bustier and matching silk panties. Ana stepped in briefly to help with buttons and then tactfully left Hattie alone.

The day was warm and humid, and Hattie was glad she had decided to wear her hair up. She tweaked the lace trim at her breasts, adjusted the deliberately casual knot of hair at the back of her head and looked into the mirror. Too bad Luc wouldn't get a chance to see her in the delicate garments. They made her feel feminine and desirable, and she had charged them to one of the new credit cards without a qualm.

Ana waited in the bedroom, the wedding dress draped over her arms. In a small exclusive boutique in Buckhead, Hattie had found exactly what she wanted. The off-white dress was made of watered silk fabric and chiffon. The halter neckline flattered her bust and the fitted drop waist fluffed out into several filmy layers that ended in handkerchief points. The ecru kid slippers she'd bought to match were trimmed in satin ribbons that laced at her ankles.

Both women blinked away tears when Ana zipped up the dress and turned Hattie to face the mirror. It was fairy-tale perfect for a beach wedding—definitely bridal, but spritely and whimsical. Truth be told, it was not really a "Hattie" sort of dress. But it was her wedding day, damn it, and she wanted to be beautiful for Luc.

Ana picked up the narrow tiara and pinned it carefully to the top of Hattie's head. It was the appropriate finishing touch.

The older woman fluffed the skirt and stepped back. "You look like an angel." Her expression sobered. "I'm so sorry your mother and sister aren't here with you."

Hattie hiccupped a sob. "Me, too."

Ana looked alarmed. "No crying, for heaven's sake. My fault. Shouldn't have said anything. Let's touch up your makeup and get outside. I'll bet good money you have an eager groom waiting for you."

Ana left to take her place, and for a moment, Hattie was alone with her thoughts. She couldn't say in all honesty that she had no doubts. But perhaps a lot of brides felt this way. Scared and hopeful.

There was a brief knock at the door. When Hattie opened it, Leo's large frame took up the entrance. He looked her over, head to toe. A tiny smile lifted a corner of his mouth. "You'll do, Parker." He handed her a beautiful bouquet of lilies and eucalyptus. "These are from my brother. He's impatient."

He held out his arm, and she put her hand on it, her palm damp. "I care about him, Leo…a lot."

"I know you do…which is the only reason I'm here. But God help me, Hattie…if you hurt him again, I'll make you pay."

Not exactly auspicious words to start a new life.

Leo escorted her to the corner of the house, just out of sight of the water's edge where the ceremony would take place. He bent and kissed her cheek, then stepped back. Perhaps he saw the sheer panic in her eyes, because he smiled again, a real smile this time. "Break a leg, princess." And then he was gone.

Hattie's cue was to be the opening notes of "Pachelbel's Canon." A sturdy boardwalk led from the porch of the house out over a small dune to the temporary platform and the wooden latticed archway where she and Luc would stand.

The music started. She clenched her fists and then deliberately relaxed them. One huge breath. Several small prayers. One foot in front of the other.

Afterward, she could not remember the exact details of her solitary journey to the altar. In keeping with the unorthodox nature of the marriage and the ceremony, she had decided to walk to Luc on her own. This was her decision, her gamble.

When she first caught sight of the groom, her breath lodged in her throat and she stumbled slightly. Though there were three other people framed against the vibrant blue-green of the ocean, she only had eyes for Luc. He was wearing a black tux…a formal morning coat and tails over a crisp white shirt and a gray vest.

His gaze locked on hers and stayed there as she traversed the final fifty feet. As she stepped beneath the arch and took her place by his side, she saw something hot and predatory flash in his dark eyes before he turned to face the justice of the peace.

Without looking at Hattie again, Luc reached out and took her right hand, squeezing it tightly. The officiant smiled at both of them. "We are gathered here today to witness the union of Luc Cavallo and Hattie Parker. Marriage is a…"

Hattie tried to listen…she really did. But her thoughts scattered in a million directions. Too many stimuli. The feel of Luc's hard, warm fingers twined with hers. The familiar tang of his aftershave, mingling with the scent of her bouquet. The muted roar of the nearby surf as waves tumbled onto shore.

If she had the power, she would freeze this moment. To take out later in the quiet of her bedroom and savor everything she missed the first time around.

Out of the corner of her eye, she could see the giant live oaks that cast shade and respite on this hot, windy day. Sherman and Patti stood guard over the stroller, which was draped in mosquito netting. Apparently, Deedee had decided to cooperate and sleep through it all.

Closer to hand, Ana smiled, her cheeks damp. She was wearing a moss-green designer suit that flattered her stocky frame and shaved ten years off her age. Hattie had no doubt that Luc had financed the expensive wedding finery.

For a split second Hattie caught Leo's eye. The resemblance between the two brothers was striking, but where Luc was classically handsome, quieter and more reserved, Leo was larger than life. He winked at her deliberately, and she blushed, turning her attention back to the words that would make her Luc's wife.

"May I have the rings?"

Ana commandeered the bouquet, Hattie and Leo complied, and moments later, Hattie slid a plain gold band onto Luc's left hand. He returned the favor, placing a narrow circlet of platinum beside the beautiful engagement ring to which Hattie had yet to grow accustomed.

More words, a pronouncement and then the moment she had unconsciously been waiting for. "You may kiss the bride."

In unison, she and Luc turned. The breeze ruffled his hair. His expression was solemn, though his eyes danced. He took Hattie's hands in his. Time stood still.

Ten years…ten long years since she had been free to kiss him whenever she wanted.

He bent his head. His mouth brushed hers, lingered, pressed more insistently. His tongue coaxed. His arms tightened around her as her skirt tangled capriciously with his pant legs.

Her heart lodged in her throat, tears stung her eyes, and she moved her mouth against his.

Aeons later it seemed, a chorus of unison laughter broke them apart. Luc appeared as dazed as Hattie felt.

Suddenly, hugs and congratulations separated them, but every moment, Luc's eyes followed her.

They led their small parade back to the house. Hattie had only seen one of the bedrooms, but now they all entered the great room on the opposite side of the building. The ambience was rustic but elegant. Exposed beams of warmly-hued wood were strung with tiny white lights. Dozens of blush-pink roses in crystal vases decorated every available surface.

A single table covered in pale pink linen was set with exquisite china, crystal and silver. When they were all seated, with Luc and Hattie at the head, Leo stood up.

As a waiter deftly poured champagne for everyone, Leo raised his glass. "Luc here, my baby brother, is and will always be my best friend. When Mom and Dad drowned, out on that damned boat they loved so much, Luc and I were shipped off to Italy to live for three years with a grandfather we barely knew. The language was strange, we were a mess, but we had each other."

He paused, and Hattie saw the muscles in his throat work with emotion. He moved to stand between and behind the bride and groom, laying a hand on each of their shoulders. "To Luc and his beautiful bride. May they always be as happy as they are today."

Applause and cheers filled the room, and moments later, the unobtrusive waitstaff began serving lunch.

Hattie knew the food was delicious. And wine flowed like water. But she couldn't taste any of it.

She was married to Luc. For some undefined period of time in order to protect the baby she had grown to love. But at what price?

When Luc put his arm around her bare shoulders, her heartbeat wobbled and sped up. He leaned over to whisper in her ear. "Are you doing okay, Mrs. Cavallo?" Gently, he tucked a wayward wisp of her hair into place.

She nodded mutely.

Luc laughed beneath his breath. "It might help if you quit looking like a scared rabbit."

She shrugged helplessly. "I'm in over my head," she admitted quietly. "What have we done, Luc?"

He stroked her back as he answered a cheerful question from across the table. "Forget reality," he murmured. "Pretend we're on Fantasy Island. Maybe this is all a dream."

Beneath the table, his hand played with hers.

The silly, childish game restored her equilibrium. Moments later their intimate circle was broken as Deedee demanded, in a loud string of nonsense syllables, to be recognized.

Luc chuckled as he stood to take the baby from Sherman and handed her to Hattie. Immediately, Deedee reached for the tiara. She yanked on it before Luc could stop her, and soon Hattie's hair was askew.

Amidst shrieks of infant temper, the tiara was rescued, the baby given one of her toys and the two at the head table became three. Luc tickled one chubby thigh, making Deedee chortle with laughter. He growled at her playfully and reached to take her in his arms.

Deedee's eyes went wide. She clung to Hattie's neck, burying her little face. And in a soft, childish, unmistakably clear voice, she said, *"Mama."*

Eight

Luc had known Hattie for a very long time. And he saw the mix of feelings that showed so clearly on her face. Shock. Fierce pride. Joy. Sorrow. Almost too much for one woman to bear, particularly on a day already filled with strong emotion.

He stood and addressed the small group. "Hattie and I are going to slip away for a few moments to spend some time with Deedee before we have to say goodbye. We'll cut the cake when we return. In the meantime, please relax and enjoy the rest of your meal."

He coaxed Hattie out of her seat, witnessing the way she held the baby so tightly to her chest. A crisis was brewing.

In the bedroom where Hattie had changed clothes, his brand-new bride faced him mutinously. "I can't leave her. It's cruel. We'll have to change our plans."

At that moment, Deedee spotted a carry-all stuffed with her favorite toys on the floor in a corner. She wiggled and squirmed and insisted on being put down. Hattie did so with patent reluctance.

Luc tugged Hattie toward the bed and sat her down. "Deedee will be fine. You know it in your heart. Aside from the fact that we need to make our marriage look absolutely real, you need a break, Hattie. Badly. This past year has been one crisis after another. You desperately need to rest and recharge your batteries."

Hattie looked up at him, her lips trembling, her big, brown eyes suspiciously shiny. "She called me *Mama*."

"She certainly did." Luc smoothed her hair where the baby had disheveled it. "And that's what you are."

Hattie bit her lip, not seeming to notice that he was touching her. "I feel guilty," she whispered.

"Why on earth would you say that?"

"I'm happy that Deedee is growing closer to me. I know that's a good thing in the long run. But does that make me disloyal to Angela? How can I be so thrilled that the baby called me *Mama* when she won't even remember Angela, her real mother…"

Luc struggled for wisdom, though he didn't have a good track record when it came to Hattie. "As Deedee grows older you'll show her pictures of your sister.… And later still, you'll explain what happened, when the time is right. Angela will live in your heart, and by your actions, in Deedee's."

"And what about Eddie? What do I tell her about him?"

Luc ground his teeth, unused to feeling helpless in any situation. Did he want to replace Eddie as the baby's father? The temptation was there—he felt it. But he had no desire to be a family man, and Hattie had made it painfully clear that his help was only needed on a temporary basis.

He tried to swallow his frustration. "None of us knows how that situation will work out, but I doubt seriously if Eddie has any interest in being a father. That truth will be hurtful when she's old enough to understand it. But if you've filled her life with love and happiness, Deedee will get through it."

"I hope so," she said softly, her gaze pensive.

He reached out with one hand and touched her bare shoulder, resisting the urge to stroke the satiny skin. "You look beautiful today." The words felt like razor blades in his throat.

Finally, he regained her attention.

A pale pink blush stained her cheeks, and she lowered her head. Her long eyelashes hid her thoughts. "Thank you. I thought this was a better choice than a traditional wedding dress."

Something in her voice made him frown. "Do you regret missing out on a church wedding?"

She shrugged. "I thought I would. It's what many women dream about. But today was…"

"Was what?" he prompted.

She touched his hand briefly, not linking their fingers… more of a butterfly brush. "It was…meaningful."

Her answer disappointed him. He'd hoped for more enthusiasm, more feminine effusiveness. But it hadn't escaped his notice that she'd been careful with the wording of the ceremony. He'd left that portion of the day in her capable hands. The printed order of service she'd handed over on the plane had notably omitted any reference to "till death do us part" or even the more modern "as long as we both shall live."

He turned his attention toward the baby, trying not to notice the way Hattie's rounded breasts filled the bodice of her gown. She hadn't worn the pearl necklace today, and the omission hurt him, though he'd chew glass before he'd admit it. The only reason he cared was because it was an outward symbol of the fact that she belonged to him. She relied on him. She needed him. No other reason.

He bent and picked up Deedee. "We'd better get back to our guests. They'll be waiting for cake."

* * *

Though the day and the room were plenty warm, Luc realized that Hattie's fingers were cold when he put his hand over hers and pressed down firmly with the knife. Hattie had insisted, in private, that having a photographer document their faux wedding was unnecessary. So at the official cake cutting, only Sherman's digital camera was available to record the moment.

Hattie's smile toward Luc was apologetic as she picked up a small square and pressed it into his mouth. He wasn't sure which he wanted to eat more: the almond-flavored dessert, or her slender, frosting-covered fingertips.

He returned the favor, being careful not to mess up Hattie's makeup or dress. He fed her a tiny piece of cake and then deliberately lifted her hand and licked each of her fingers clean. The guests and servers signaled their approval with a cheer, and Hattie's red-faced embarrassment was worth every penny Luc had spent to make his bride's day special.

Ana stepped forward with a smile. "Shall I help you change clothes, *Mrs. Cavallo?*"

Luc put an arm around Hattie's waist, drawing her closer. He kissed her cheek. "I think we can handle that," he said, his voice low and suggestive.

Once in the bedroom, an irate Hattie rounded on him. "What was that show about? Ana and Sherman know the truth. You embarrassed me."

He shrugged, his hands in his pockets to keep from stripping the deliberately tantalizing dress from her in short order. "The waitstaff and the drivers are outsiders. They may talk, and if they do…I want them to believe that you and I are so much in love we can't keep our hands off each other. Any gossip will help us, not hurt us if they think we're a normal bride and groom."

Hattie stood in the middle of the room, her expression troubled.

He lost his temper. "Oh, for God's sake. I'm not going to jump you when your back is turned. Take off that damned dress and put some clothes on."

She blanched. He felt like a heel. Sexual frustration was riding him hard, and he wondered with bleak mirth what in hell had possessed him to insist on a honeymoon. If his brand-new bride didn't soon admit she wanted him the way he wanted her, he'd be a raving, slobbering lunatic by the time they got back home.

But he couldn't let her think he was affected by the day and the ceremony. The softer, gentler Luc she had known back in college was a phantom. The real Luc was cynical to a fault. What he was feeling was lust, pure and simple. Hattie would be in his bed. Soon. But he wouldn't be weak. Never again. He had his emotions on lockdown.

He turned his back on her and looked out the window blindly, the ocean nothing but a blur. All of his senses were attuned to Hattie's movements. Even when he heard the bathroom door shut, he remained where he was. It was impossible not to imagine her nudity as she stepped out of her bridal attire.

His hands were clammy, and his gut churned.

The bathroom door opened again, and he sighed inwardly. But still he didn't turn around. It was only when Hattie appeared at his elbow that he finally spoke. "Are you ready to go?"

He turned and inhaled sharply. The tiara was gone, her hair was down, but she was still dressed.

She raised a shoulder, her face rueful. "I'm sorry. I can't unzip it. Will you help me?"

God in heaven. She turned her back to him with innocent trust. His hands shook. Inch by inch, as he lowered the zipper, the dress gaped, revealing a sexy piece of fantasy-fueling lingerie. He cleared his throat. "Do you…uh…"

Hattie nodded. "Yeah. The bustier, too."

A million tiny buttons held the confection in place. God knows how long it took him, but he finally succeeded in revealing the pale skin and delicate spine he remembered with such painful clarity. He also remembered running his tongue down that very spine, not stopping until he reached the curve of her ass. And sometimes not even then.

The exercise in torture lasted for what seemed like hours rather than minutes. At last he was finished.

Hattie held the dress to her front with a death grip.

He made himself step back. "All done," he croaked.

She nodded jerkily and scooted toward safety. But just as she reached the bathroom, her toe caught on a scatter rug, she stumbled, and Luc grabbed for her instinctively. His arms went around her from behind and his hands landed in dangerous territory.

Lush, soft breasts. Pert nipples begging to be stroked. He sucked in a breath, sucker punched by the slug of hunger. Hattie froze on the spot like an animal hoping not to be noticed by a hunter.

He nuzzled the nape of her neck. "Your skin is so soft," he muttered. He squeezed gently, cupping the mounds of flesh that he remembered in his dreams.

Her head fell back against his shoulder. "Luc…"

That was all. Just his name. But the single word fraught with what he hoped like hell was longing made him hard as stone and ready for action. He tugged the dress and undergarment from her deathlike grasp and tossed them aside. He couldn't see her face, and he didn't want to.

He continued to play with her breasts slowly. "Tell me you want me, Hattie."

"I want you, Luc…but…"

The last word made him frown. He slid one hand down her belly, between her legs. Hattie gasped audibly.

He bit gently at her earlobe. "But?"

"I don't think we're ready." Her whispered protest barely registered on his consciousness.

He pressed his aching erection against her, her beautiful round butt covered in less than nothing. "Oh, I'm ready, Hattie. Trust me."

The choked laugh she managed made him smile.

At that precise moment, when he felt paradise within his grasp, a loud shout of nearby laughter shattered the moment. They weren't alone. And they had guests waiting.

He cursed in frustration and released her abruptly, wanting to howl at the moon. His timing sucked. "Damn it.… I'm sorry."

Hattie didn't even turn around. He suspected her face was one huge blush. He reached for the discarded clothing and handed it to her. "Go," he said curtly. "We'll deal with this later."

Hattie huddled in the bathroom, her blood running hot and cold in dizzying, equal measure. She had come within inches of shoving her new husband onto the bed and pouncing on him. Feeling his hands on her bare skin had been more arousing than anything she had experienced in the last ten years.

She hadn't been celibate. But still…*holy cow.*

It took her three tries to button her lavender silk blouse. The cream linen trousers she stepped into were part of the outrageously expensive new wardrobe that now filled two large Louis Vuitton suitcases and a garment bag.

She looked in the mirror, wincing at her crazy tousled hair. Nothing to do but to put it up again. Ana had promised to collect the wedding finery and make sure it got back to the house. So all that was left for Hattie to do was to slip into low-heeled, gold leather sandals and wash her face.

She added fresh lip gloss, took the shine off her nose with a dash of powder, and spritzed her favorite perfume at her throat. What had Luc been thinking as he undressed her? Did he have any feelings left for her at all? Or was it only sex? What if she had turned in his arms and kissed him? Would she have been able to read his face?

He might feel the tug of attraction, but he was no green kid unable to control his body. Hell would probably freeze over before Luc would ever think about having a real relationship with Hattie, whether he saw her naked or not. He liked having her at his mercy. She had invited that with her artless marriage proposal. But Luc was thinking about sex…not a wistful reunion of lovers.

Luc had gained a heck of a lot of sexual experience since they parted. Hattie was old news.

Thinking of the women Luc had probably invited into his bed over the years was a bad thing to do on her wedding day. It only increased her misery. She'd had her chance. And being with Luc again made her rethink her youthful decision for the umpteenth time. Luc's money gave him power. No doubt about it. But from the perspective of ten years down the road, she admitted ruefully that he wouldn't have used the inequality in their bank accounts to control her, no matter what her mother said.

Her mother's take on life had always been hard-edged. Early disappointments had made her suspicious of people and their motives. Hattie had tried not to follow suit. But perhaps unconsciously that inherent attitude of distrust had been largely to blame for Hattie's breakup with Luc.

When she could procrastinate no longer, she slowly opened the bathroom door. Luc looked up and stared. Something arced across the room between them.

He cleared his throat. "I'll go change now. Why don't you play with the baby? I won't be long."

Before she could respond, he was gone.

Twenty minutes later, amidst the chaos of getting everything and everyone packed up for the return trip, she finally saw her husband again. He was wearing dark slacks and a pale blue dress shirt with the sleeves rolled up. His casual, masculine elegance took her breath away.

It shocked her to realize that she and Luc were not returning on the plane with the rest of the group. And Luc didn't take the time to explain, leaving Hattie to build scenarios in her head, each more unlikely than the next.

Ana stood by as Hattie said one last goodbye to the baby who had become so dear. When Angela was still alive, Hattie had been extremely fond of her tiny niece…as any doting aunt would. But now…now that Hattie played the role of mother, the bond was fierce and unbreakable. She couldn't pinpoint a single instant when it had happened. But the connection was substantial. As much as she was looking forward to spending time with Luc, it pained her to say goodbye to Deedee.

So much was still uncertain. And the baby was so helpless.

Ana patted Hattie's shoulder. "Don't worry…please. We'll watch over her as if she were our own."

Hattie handed over the sleepy child and forced a smile. "I know you will. She adores you and Sherman already. I wouldn't trust her with anyone else." The captain signaled Luc, and Luc began ushering everyone toward the boat.

Leo lingered to speak to Hattie. "I hope you know what you're doing."

She smiled wryly. "Do any of us ever really know what we're doing? I'm trying my best, Leo. It's all I can do."

He hesitated. "Call me if you need anything," he said gruffly. "And be good to my brother."

Before she could respond, he loped toward the end of the dock and boarded the cabin cruiser.

A mournful toot of the horn heralded departure. Luc rejoined Hattie, and they both watched and waved as the vessel moved away from the pilings, picked up speed and slowly skimmed out of sight.

Hattie shifted her feet restlessly. The sun was lower in the sky now, and a breeze had picked up, alleviating some of the heat. "Why didn't we go with them?"

Luc took her arm, leading her back toward the house. "It's been a long, stressful day. I thought it might be nice to relax here for the night. I've ordered a helicopter to pick us up at ten in the morning. He'll take us to the Atlanta airport, and we'll catch our flight to Key West from there."

"Oh."

He must have misread her quiet syllable as lack of enthusiasm, because he frowned. "I'm sorry I'm not taking you somewhere more exotic…like Paris, or St. Moritz. But with Eddie still a loose cannon, I thought it would be wiser to stay where we could get home quickly if need be."

"I think you're right."

Conversation evaporated as they neared the house. Hattie's heart was pounding in her breast. Two people alone on the proverbial deserted island. What happened next?

The truth was anticlimactic. Luc paused on the porch, running a hand through his hair, and for the first time that day, looking uncertain. "Are you hungry at all? We have leftovers."

Hattie had been too nervous earlier to eat much at their wedding meal. "Well, I…"

"It might be nice to sit out on the beach and watch the water while we eat."

Was that a note of coaxing in his voice? She indicated her clothes. "I dressed to travel. Do you mind if I change?"

"Roll up your pants legs. We'll go barefoot and pretend we're teenagers again."

This time there was definitely self-mockery in his words, but she was easily persuaded. They raided the kitchen, and in short order cobbled together a light meal. Luc found a large-handled tote, and they loaded it. Leaving Hattie to carry nothing but two bottles of water, Luc scooped up an old, faded tarp and swung the bag over his shoulder.

She laughed when he kicked off his shoes and rolled his trousers to his knees before they left the house. Following suit, she joined him outside, smiling when she felt the still warm boards beneath her feet.

It was her wedding day. Perhaps an unorthodox one at best, but still deserving of at least a jot of ceremony.

What had happened earlier lingered between them… unspoken, unacknowledged. But it was there, filling her veins with heady anticipation.

Luc managed to spread the ground cloth with her help, though the stiff wind made it necessary to quickly secure the corners with food containers. They sat down side by side. With no baby to act as a shield between them, either literally or figuratively, the mood was much different than it had been during the evening at the park.

Here, on an island far from land, removed from any other humans, it was more difficult to ignore the past.

Luc leaned back on his elbows, his expression pensive. "I wondered about you over the years…what you were doing… if you were happy." He turned his head suddenly and looked straight at her. "Were you?"

"Happy, you mean?"

He nodded.

"It's hard to pin down happiness, isn't it? I had a job that I liked. Friends. Family. So yes, I guess I was happy."

He frowned slightly. "I was an idiot back then. When we

were in college. Confusing lust with love. I'm not sure love exists."

Her chest hurt. "How can you not believe in love?"

His gaze returned to the sea. "I understand loving a child, a parent. Those emotions are real. But between men and women?" His lips twisted. "Mostly hormones, I think. Makes the world go round."

The deliberate cynicism scraped at her guilt. Was that his intention? She curled her legs beneath her, poking at a small crab scurrying in the nearby sand. "You've never come close to marrying before now?"

He smiled faintly. "You mean after the debacle with you? No. Once was enough."

"I'm sorry."

"Don't be. It was a lesson well learned."

She hated his current mood. He was spoiling whatever pleasure she had managed to squeeze from today's events.

Her temper sizzled. Abruptly, she stood up. "I can only apologize so many times. You hate me. I get it. But I can't change the past."

Nine

Luc cursed beneath his breath as Hattie ran from him. Had that been his subconscious intent? To make her angry? So there would be no question of appeasing the ache in his groin?

To say he was conflicted was an understatement. He wanted Hattie with a raw intensity that only increased day by day. But he wasn't willing to give up his position of power. He wouldn't let her see him as a supplicant. It was up to her to come to him. God help him.

He reached into the food bag and found a block of aged cheddar. Not bothering with a knife, he ripped off a hunk and bit into it. The cheese tasted bitter in his mouth. And since he knew all the food at the wedding was top-notch, the problem must be him.

He tossed the uneaten portion back in the bag and went to stand at the water's edge.

Until now, he hadn't allowed himself to think about the men who had shared her life in the intervening years. His fists curled, and he wished violently that he was at the gym so he could beat the crap out of a punching bag.

A swim in the rough surf might appease the beast inside him, but he couldn't take the chance. He wasn't worried about his own safety, but leaving Hattie alone if something happened to him would be the ultimate mark of irresponsibility.

And he was nothing if not responsible.

Damn it. He took off in his bare feet, running full-out, dragging air into his lungs, ignoring the shell fragments that pierced his skin. He kept up the brutal pace, rounding the point and covering mile after mile until he came full circle to where the uneaten picnic lay.

With his chest burning, his feet aching and his skin windburned, he stopped suddenly, bent at the waist and rested his hands on his knees. He was used up, worn-out, ready to stop.

But still he wanted Hattie.

Inquisitive gulls had found the bag of food. Much of it would have to be tossed. He waved them away and packed up what he and Hattie had brought to the beach.

The house was quiet and dark when he slipped through the door. He dumped everything in the kitchen and went to his own bedroom, acutely aware that Hattie's was only a few yards away. It was only nine o'clock, but he couldn't see any light from beneath her door.

He stripped off his clothes and took a blisteringly hot shower. The water felt good on his tight, salty skin, but if he had been hoping for a soothing experience, he was out of luck.

His recalcitrant imagination brought Hattie into the glass stall with him. Her generous breasts glistened with soapy water as he washed her from head to toe. His erection was painful. As he stroked himself, he imagined lifting her and filling her, wrapping her long legs around his hips.

Ah.... He came with a muffled groan, slumping at last to sit on the narrow seat and catch his breath. He ran his hands through his wet hair, massaging the pain in his temples.

He was ninety-nine percent sure that Hattie was still sexually attracted to him. And he wanted her in his bed again. But on his terms. She had nearly destroyed him once upon a time. He'd be a fool to let it happen twice. So he'd be on his guard.

Sleep was elusive. Though he'd been up before dawn, he tossed and turned until he finally gave up the pretense of reading and turned out the light. He left the window open, relishing the humid night air. It suited his mood.

The nocturnal sounds were vastly different from back home. Birds and other wildlife filled the night with muted chirps and rustles and clicks. The sea created a hushed backdrop.

At 2:00 a.m. he tossed the tangled covers aside and padded to the kitchen in his boxers to get a drink. The house was dark and silent. He might as well have been the only person on the planet.

He drained the tumbler of water and stepped outside, tempted to run on the beach again. As he moved forward on the boardwalk, his heart stopped. A slender figure in white stood silhouetted against the dark horizon. Hattie. As he closed the distance between them, unconsciously treading as silently as possible, he saw that her back was to him. Her head was lifted to the stars. Her hair danced in the breeze. That same wind plastered her satin nightgown to her shapely body, leaving little to the imagination.

He should have turned back. It was the wise choice. But retreat had never been an option for him. Jump in the deep end, full steam ahead, onward and upward. Pick your cliché— that was how he lived his life. Perhaps if he had handled things differently a decade ago, he might never have lost her.

Something in her posture screamed sadness. And loneliness. An artist would have painted her and titled the canvas *Melancholy*. Seeing Hattie like this cracked something inside him. It hurt.

She didn't flinch when he joined her. Was she as attuned to him as he was to her?

He stood beside her, their shoulders almost touching. Her freshly washed hair was a tangle of damp waves, the light scent of shampoo mingling with the faint fragrance of her perfume.

"Are you okay, Hattie?"

Her chin lowered a bit, her gaze now on the water. She shrugged, not answering in words.

"I was being an ass earlier. I'm sorry."

Her lips twisted. "I should be the one apologizing. I was painfully young and immature back then. I know I hurt you, and I regret it more than you realize. I should have done things differently."

He winced inwardly. She wasn't apologizing for the breakup…only for the way she did it. The distinction was telling.

"I think we're going to have to agree to leave the past where it belongs. We're different people now."

"Leo remembers."

"Leo?"

"He threatened to tear me limb from limb if I hurt his baby brother again. He's very loyal."

Luc snorted. "Leo's a pain in the butt when he wants to be. Forget anything he said to you. I don't need his protection. And he's hardly in a position to be giving relationship advice."

"Maybe not, but he loves you very much."

They fell silent. Luc tried to steady his breathing, but the longer he stood beside her, so close that her warmth radiated to him, the more he became aroused.

"You're sad," he accused softly. "Tell me why."

She shifted restlessly from one foot to the other. "It's not exactly the wedding night I dreamed of."

Dangerous territory. "I'm sorry, Hattie. But, hey." He forced a dry chuckle from his throat. "At least there's moonlight, a romantic beach, a million stars. Could be worse."

"Could be raining." She shot back with the famous line from *Young Frankenstein,* and they both burst into laughter.

He couldn't help himself. He touched her. It was a matter of utmost urgency to find out which was softer—the satin, or her skin. At first, all he did was take her chin in his hand. He turned her so that they were face-to-face, their pose and position mimicking that of the wedding ceremony.

Hattie moved restlessly and he dropped his hand. He sighed. "I take it you couldn't sleep?"

"No."

"Me, either. I've never had a wedding night before. Turns out this stuff is pretty stressful."

That coaxed a small smile from her. "At least you didn't have to contend with a receiving line and five hundred guests."

"Why do people do that? Sounds exhausting."

"I imagine they want to share their happiness with as many people as possible, and they want to express their appreciation to those who made the effort to show up."

"You apparently have given this some thought."

"It's a typical teenage girl fantasy."

"I wish you could have had your dream wedding."

"Can we talk about something else?" The hint of fatigued petulance made him smile. It was so unlike her.

"I could tell you that when I first looked out here, I thought I was seeing a ghost."

She touched his cheek, making him tremble. "I suppose this must seem like a bad dream to you, your whole world turned upside down. And no end in sight. I owe you, Luc."

He put his hand on hers, keeping the connection. "Perhaps I could collect an installment right now." He'd be kidding himself if he didn't admit that this had been his intent all along. Otherwise, he'd have stayed in the house. But he wouldn't force her. "I'm not the groom you would have chosen, and this sure as hell isn't what you expected from a wedding day. But at least we deserve a kiss...don't we?"

His free hand settled at her waist, caressing the satin-covered curve that led to her hip. As far as he could tell, she was bare beneath the seductive piece of lingerie.

Her eyes searched his, and she moved her hand away. Now both of his palms cupped her hips, inexorably pulling her closer. Her breasts brushed his bare chest. Someone moaned. Was it him?

He leaned his forehead on hers. "Do you want me to stop?"

Small white teeth mutilated her bottom lip. "What I want and what is wise are two different things."

He pushed his hips against hers, letting her feel the evidence of his arousal. He was going to pay like hell for this, but he couldn't stop. "I don't really give a damn about what's wise right at this moment."

They were pressed together now, and they might as well have been naked for all the modesty their thin garments afforded. Every hill and plane of her body fit with his like the most exquisite puzzle. Yin to yang. Positive to negative. Male to female.

She slid her arms around his neck.

He shuddered, struggling to keep a rein on his passion. Sexual attraction. That's all it was. Natural male urgency after a stretch of celibacy.

At first, their lips barely met, hardly touched. Some innate caution they both recognized pretended to slow the dance. But the cataclysm was building and nothing could hold it back.

When her small tongue hesitantly traced his bottom lip,

he growled and lifted her off her feet. Their mouths dueled, fumbled, smashed together again in reckless, breathless pleasure.

He had never forgotten her taste…sweet, but with a tart bite like an October apple. The month they first met. The time he'd fallen hard.

And speaking of hard. He rubbed his shaft against her soft belly, making her whimper. That sound of feminine longing went straight to his gut, destroying all semblance of sanity.

Again and again he kissed her…throat, cheeks, eyelids, and back to her soft, puffy-lipped mouth. He dropped to his knees and tongued her navel, wetting the fabric and gripping her hips so tightly he feared bruising her.

Her hands fisted in his hair. But she was holding him close, not pushing him away.

The tsunami crashed over him, an unimagined, unexpected wave of yearning so endless, his eyes stung.

But the aftermath was devastation.

He stumbled to his feet when Hattie tore herself from his embrace, her hair wild, her eyes dark and wide.

She held out a hand when he would have taken her in his arms again. "You've got to give me time," she whispered, her voice hoarse. "It's not just me anymore. I have the baby to think about. I can't afford to make another mistake."

"A mistake." He repeated it dumbly, his control in shreds. His soul froze with a whoosh of unbearable coldness. He shrugged, the studied nonchalance taking every ounce of acting skill he possessed. "You'll have to forgive me. I got carried away by the ambience. But you're right. We're both adults. We should be using our heads, not succumbing to moonlight madness. Let's chalk this up to a long day and leave it at that."

Her arms wrapped around her waist. For a moment he could swear she was going to say something of import.

But she didn't. And for the second time that day, she left him.

If Hattie slept at all, it was only in bits and snatches. Her eyes were gritty when the alarm went off at eight-thirty. And the fact that she had set an alarm for the first morning of her honeymoon made her want to laugh hysterically. She bit down on the macabre humor, afraid that if she let loose of the tight hold she had on her emotions that she would dissolve into a total mess.

She was dressed, packed and sitting on the bed by nine-fifteen. There was plenty of food in the kitchen, but the prospect of eating made her nauseous. Her stomach was tightly knotted, her mouth dry with despair.

When Luc knocked on her door just before ten, she opened it with pseudo calm. "Good morning."

He didn't return her greeting, but merely held out a cup of coffee. It was black and lightly sweet, just the way she liked it. Luc's expression was shuttered, dark smudges beneath his eyes emphasizing his lack of sleep.

As he picked up two of her bags, he spoke quietly. "I can hear the chopper. The pilot and I will load the luggage. Why don't you wait on the porch until we're ready?"

It was all accomplished in minutes. The man flying the helicopter was polite and deferential as he handed Hattie up into the large doorway. Luc followed. They buckled in, the rotors roared to life and moments later they were airborne.

Hattie gazed down at the island and had to blink back tears. It had been a fairy-tale wedding. Too bad she knew that fairy tales were nothing more than pleasant fiction.

The noise in the chopper made conversation impossible. Which was fine by Hattie. She kept her nose glued to the glass and watched the shoreline recede as they cruised across central Georgia. Ignoring Luc at the moment equaled self-preservation.

Landing at Atlanta's enormous airport was frantic. Chaos reigned in controlled waves. Luc gave her a sardonic look as they made their way into the terminal followed by their luggage. "We're flying commercial today," he said, scanning the departure board for their gate. "I know your Puritan soul would have balked if I had chartered a jet for just the two of us."

The security lines were long and slow. But finally, they were able to board. Hattie had never flown first-class. The width of the seat was generous, but still dangerously close to Luc's. She closed her eyes and pretended to sleep as the jet gathered speed and took off.

Pretense became reality. She woke up only when they touched down in Miami. Luc must have slept, as well, because his usual sartorial perfection was definitely rumpled.

Their connecting flight to Key West was a small plane with only two seats on either side of a narrow aisle. Now she and Luc were wedged hip to hip. After her long nap, it was hard to fake sleep again. So she pretended an intense interest in watching the commotion outside her window.

When they were airborne for the short flight, Luc pulled out a business magazine and buried his head in it.

Hattie and her new groom had barely spoken the entire day.

She was travel-weary, depressed and missing Deedee.

The Key West airport was as tiny as Atlanta's was huge. Nothing more than a handful of plastic chairs and a few car rental counters. Luc had taken care of every detail. Their leased vehicle, a bright, cherry-red convertible, was waiting for them.

The first humorous moment of the day arrived when they

struggled to fit their luggage into the car's small trunk. A disgruntled Luc finally conceded defeat and went inside to swap the car for a roomier sedan.

While he was gone, Hattie made a decision. They couldn't ignore each other forever. Last night was a bad mistake. He knew it, and she knew it. So it was best to start over and go from here.

She managed a smile when he returned with the new set of keys. "Sorry that didn't work out. I liked the convertible."

He thrust the last bag into the backseat and motioned for her to get in. "I'd buy you one, but it's not a great car for a mom."

His casual generosity was one thing, but hearing herself called a "mom" shocked her. It was true. She was a mother. The knowledge still had a hard time sinking into her befuddled brain.

Luc had apparently been here before or had at least memorized the route, because he drove with confidence, not bothering to consult the navigation system. When they pulled up in front of a charming two-story structure that looked like a sea captain's home from the nineteenth century, Hattie was surprised and delighted. This was so much better than an impersonal hotel.

The wooden building was painted mint-green with white trim. Neatly trimmed bougainvillea, and other flowers Hattie couldn't name, bloomed in profusion, emphasizing the tropical ambience.

Luc and Hattie had barely stepped from the car when a distinguished gentleman, perhaps in his early sixties, came out to meet them. He extended a hand to each of them. "Welcome to Flamingo's Rest. I'm the innkeeper, Marcel. We have the honeymoon suite all ready for you."

Marcel opened the weathered oak door and ushered them inside.

He grinned at Hattie, clearly happy to be welcoming guests. "You've come at a beautiful time of year."

Marcel led them up carpeted stairs and flung open the door to an apartment that took up half of the second floor. Before Hattie could do more than glance inside, their host smiled broadly. "Key West is the perfect spot for a romantic getaway. Let me know if you need anything at all."

Ten

In the wake of the innkeeper's departure, Hattie watched as Luc prowled the elegant quarters. The bedroom boasted an enormous four-poster king-size bed. Just looking at it through the doorway made Hattie tremble.

At the moment, she was ensconced in less volatile territory. The living area was furnished luxuriously, including a sofa and several chairs, a flat-screen TV, a wet bar and plush carpet underfoot.

Hattie curled up in one of the leather chairs. "This is very nice," she said, her words carefully neutral.

A brief knock at the door heralded the arrival of their luggage. Marcel and a younger employee stowed everything in the generous closets, accepted Luc's tip with pleased smiles and exited quietly.

In the subsequent silence, awkwardness grew.

Hattie waved a hand, doing her best to seem unconcerned. "I'll sleep out here. The couch is big and comfortable. I'll be fine." She tried changing the subject. "I'm going to call Ana now and see if I can talk to Deedee." She stopped and grinned wryly. "Well, you know what I mean. Do you want to say anything?"

Luc grabbed a beer from the fridge, his movements jerky. "Not right now. I have some business calls I need to make. I'll be in the bedroom if you need me."

Hattie choked on a sound that wasn't quite a giggle. She couldn't help it. After last night, his careless comment struck her as darkly funny.

Luc grimaced, his gaze flinty. "Give Ana and Sherman my regards."

Hattie sighed as he disappeared. Luc was definitely disgruntled. She didn't really blame him. Men didn't do well with sexual frustration, and Hattie herself was feeling out of sorts. What would it take to coax him back into a less confrontational mood?

Deedee chortled and babbled when Ana held the phone to the baby's ear. But Hattie couldn't really tell if Deedee recognized her voice. When the call ended, she had to wipe her eyes, but she knew that this separation wouldn't harm her niece. It was Hattie who was having a hard time.

The sitting room actually had its own bathroom, so Hattie decided to freshen up. Fortunately, she had kept her personal bag with her, so she didn't have to invade the bedroom. Knowing how airlines could lose luggage, she'd packed a pair of khaki walking shorts and a teal blouse in her carry-on. She changed out of her dress into the more casual clothes, breathing a sigh of relief.

Being Luc Cavallo's wife was going to take some adjustment. Hattie was accustomed to traveling in jeans and sneakers, not haute couture.

Her shoes were in one of the big suitcases, so she padded barefoot to the window and looked out into the courtyard. Two small pools, one behind the other, glowed like jewels in the late afternoon sun. It struck her as she glanced at her watch that she had been married an entire day already.

It was a full hour before Luc reappeared. He, too, had changed, but only into a fresh dress shirt. He had his briefcase in hand and a jacket slung over his shoulder.

Hattie's eyes widened. "What's going on?"

"I have to leave." He didn't quite manage to meet her gaze as he fiddled with his watch strap. "There's a crisis in the Miami office, and I'm the closest man on the ground. Our VP there is supposed to be signing a hot new Latin designer, and apparently things aren't going well."

"You're going to Miami?" She was stunned.

He shrugged into his jacket. "I'll talk to Marcel on the way out. Everyone understands business emergencies. He'll look out for you while I'm gone. Shouldn't be more than twenty-four hours at the most, not enough time for anyone to question our marriage. You'll enjoy the shopping here. And order dinner in if you don't feel like getting out tonight."

"You're leaving me on our honeymoon?" The reality was sinking in. She couldn't decide if she was more angry or hurt.

Luc strode to the door, opened it and looked back, his eyes empty of any emotion. "My life didn't suddenly stop when you came back, Hattie. I've done everything you asked. Deedee is safe. We both know this marriage is temporary. You'll have to make some allowances. I sure the hell am."

She curled up on the massive bed and cried for an hour. Insulting, that's what it was. So what if this wasn't a real marriage? Didn't she deserve at least a *pretend* honeymoon?

And did Luc care so little for her feelings that he could simply desert her after last night?

Her eyes were red and puffy, but she was calm when her cell phone rang at nine o'clock. She didn't recognize the number, though she knew it was an Atlanta area code.

Leo's deep voice echoed on the other end. "I need to talk to my brother. He's not answering his damn phone."

Hattie tucked a strand of hair behind her ear and scooted up on the down pillows. "He's not here, Leo."

"What do you mean he's not there?"

"He left. He's gone. Kaput. Some commotion in the Miami office about a new designer and an important contract."

"What the hell?"

Hattie winced. "I don't know what to say, Leo. He's not here."

Muffled profanity on the other end of the line was followed by Leo's long, audible sigh. "I'm sorry, Hattie. I should have gone to Miami. But I've been tied up with another deal."

"It's not your fault. I'm pretty sure this is his way of showing me he's the boss. Or maybe he's dishing out a bit of payback. He still harbors a lot of anger toward me. And I can't really blame him."

"I'm sure the Miami crisis is real."

"It probably is," she said, her voice dull. "But how many brides do you know who would put up with this? Me? I don't have a choice. He holds all the cards. Good night, Leo."

Luc stood on his balcony, staring out at the ocean and cursing his own stubbornness. He'd handled the business crisis in record time and had been ready to speed back to his lovely wife. But at the last moment he decided to stay gone overnight. It was important that Hattie understand he wouldn't be swayed by his lust.

They were going to have sex…and soon. But he wasn't a slave to his libido. And he wasn't going to fall at her knees and beg.

The irony didn't escape him. He'd been on his knees on his wedding night. But Hattie's indecision had saved him from making a fool of himself. He was back in the driver's seat.

He wondered what Hattie was doing right now. Was she at a restaurant, where available men were hitting on her? He slammed his fist on the railing and welcomed the pain. Maybe it would clear his head.

In business, he knew that the key to success was always, always keeping the upper hand. Last night had been a bad mistake. He'd allowed Hattie to see how much he still wanted her. And that knowledge was power.

She was supposed to beg *him* for sex, not the other way around. He wasn't in love with her. This gnawing ache in his gut was simple male lust. His last relationship had ended several months ago, and since then work had been all-consuming.

When Hattie showed up on his doorstep, it made sense that he would respond to her strongly, given their past and his recent stretch of celibacy. And it made sense for them to enjoy each other physically as long as they were legally man and wife. But when Deedee's situation was secure, Luc would make it clear that it was time for the two females to go.

Hattie fell into an exhausted slumber somewhere around two in the morning. So she was peeved when Marcel knocked at her suite before nine. But when she opened the door, the man standing there was not Marcel. It was Leo Cavallo. Her brand-new brother-in-law.

She ran a hand through her hair, ruefully aware that she looked a mess. "What are you doing here?"

He seemed unusually somber. "May I come in?"

Her knees went weak. "Oh, God. Is it Luc?" She grabbed his shirt. "Tell me. Is he okay?" Little yellow dots danced in front of her eyes and the world went black.

When she came to, she was lying flat on her back on the sofa with Leo hovering nearby. He patted her hand. "I'm sorry

I scared you. Luc is fine." His gaze was accusatory. "You still love him."

She sat up carefully. "Of course I don't."

"Are you pregnant? Is that why you fainted?"

"Leo. For God's sake. I didn't eat dinner and I haven't had breakfast. I got woozy. End of story."

She stood up carefully and went to the minibar for a Coke. She needed caffeine badly, and she wasn't prepared to wait for coffee to brew. "You still haven't told me why you're here." She shot him a bewildered look.

He shrugged, dwarfing the armchair in which he sat. "When you told me Luc had gone to Miami, it got me to thinking. At the wedding, only a blind man could have missed the fact that Luc still has strong feelings for you…and vice versa. I wasn't the only one who noticed."

"Your imagination is impressive."

"Deny it if you want. But regardless, it's a crappy thing to do to you…abandoning you on your honeymoon."

"And you've come to tell him that?"

"No. I'm here to get him to sign some papers. They're important, but I wouldn't have bothered him on his honeymoon except for the fact that he apparently doesn't see anything wrong with mixing business with pleasure." He held up his hands. "I'll hang out with you until he gets back."

She shook her head, smiling. "I thought I was the villainess of the piece."

"I've been known to be wrong on occasion." He shrugged, his boyish grin equally as appealing as her husband's. But Leo's smile didn't stir her heartbeat in the least.

"That's sweet of you, but not necessary. I can entertain myself."

"Quit arguing. Go put your swimsuit on. I'll do a quick change myself and get Marcel to roust us up some brunch."

Leo was as good as his word. When Hattie made her

way down to the pool in silver slides and an emerald-green maillot, her brother-in-law was already stretched out on a chaise lounge, apparently content to while away a few hours.

As she sat down beside him, she heard a quiet snore. He must have taken the red-eye. Poor guy. She'd let him sleep.

When the sun warmed her through and through, she slipped into the pool with a sigh of pleasure. Being rich definitely had its advantages. She did some laps and then floated lazily, feeling the hot rays beating down on her.

It was nice of Leo to keep her company, but Hattie wanted her husband…stripped down to nothing but his swim trunks so she could ogle his body to her heart's content.

If Marcel thought it odd that a new bride was frolicking poolside with a man who wasn't her husband, he made no sign. He was polite and unobtrusive when he brought out a tray laden with everything from scrambled eggs and bacon to fresh mangoes and homemade croissants filled with dark chocolate.

Leo roused in time to devour his share of the repast. "I was hungry," he said sheepishly as he snitched a lone strawberry.

Hattie lay back, her cup and saucer balanced on her tummy. "This coffee is to die for. I'll have to find out what brand it is." She finished her drink and turned on her stomach…drifting, half-awake, listening to birdsong and the gentle sough of the wind in the palm fronds.

Leo poked her knee. "You're turning pink, princess. Better put some sunscreen on."

Without opening her eyes, she reached for the bottle of lotion under her chair. "Will you do my back, please? I'll throw a towel over my legs, so don't bother with that."

Luc parked the car in front of the B and B and sat for ten seconds, giving himself a lecture. He was calm. He was in control. Hattie would dance to his tune.

He had a plan. One that would satisfy the hunger riding him and at the same time make it clear to his new wife that nothing had changed. Their marriage was still temporary.

It was an unpleasant shock to find their suite empty. But then he took a deep breath. Hattie was shopping, that was all. Women loved to shop. The tourist district of Key West wasn't all that big. Maybe he would take the car and drive around for a bit, see if he spotted her.

As he hurried back down the stairs, keys in hand, Marcel intercepted him. "Welcome back, Mr. Cavallo. I hope your business was transacted successfully."

"Yeah," Luc muttered, unaccountably embarrassed. "Do you happen to know if Hattie has gone to town?"

Marcel shook his head. "Your wife is out by the pool with her friend. I served them a meal not long ago. Shall I bring more food?"

"No thanks. Not hungry."

Luc's hackles rose. *Her friend?* No doubt, some handsome surfer type had taken advantage of Luc's short absence to make a move.

Well, not for long, buddy.

Luc walked outside, keeping behind the bushes until he got a clear shot of the pool. Hattie was stretched out, facedown, in a suit that made his mouth water. But the sight that took his breath away was the large man rubbing lotion into Hattie's shoulders.

Damn and double damn. The guy had his back to Luc, and at this distance, Luc couldn't really tell much about him… except that he was getting way too chummy with Luc's wife.

The man murmured something to Hattie that made her laugh. Luc's vision blurred with rage and indignation.

He burst through the shrubbery and advanced on the couple by the pool. "What in the hell is going on?"

The man turned his head and smiled…a wicked, *look what*

I'm up to smile. Leo stood up. "Well, hello, Luc. It's about damn time you got here."

Though he was stunned, Luc didn't let on. "Why are you here, Leo? If you're dying for a honeymoon, find your own damn wife."

Leo mocked him deliberately. "When I heard that you were willing to transact business this week, I brought some contracts that need your John Hancock ASAP."

By this time, Hattie had scrambled to her feet. Her sweat-sheened breasts revealed by the relatively modest décolletage of her suit gave Luc pause for a second or two, but he dragged his eyes away from his wife's erotic body and faced off with his sibling.

Luc looked pointedly at Leo's casual attire. "But nothing so urgent that you couldn't chill out by the pool," he said, irritated beyond belief. It had been years since he and Leo had tangled in a fistfight, but Luc was spoiling for a rematch.

Hattie grabbed his arm. "Sit down, Luc. You're being rude."

Leo egged him on. "It's your fault, little bro. I wouldn't be here if you hadn't been such a Type A jerk."

That was it. Luc lunged at Leo, determined to pummel him into the ground. Their bodies collided and the fight was on.

But Luc hadn't counted on Hattie.

She grabbed his shirt and clung to him. "Stop this. Right now. You're both insane."

He shrugged her off. "Get out of the way." He rammed his shoulder into Leo's chest. Leo fired back with a punch to Luc's solar plexus.

Hattie jumped on Luc's back this time, her arms around his neck in a stranglehold. "I mean it," she pleaded, her voice shaking. "He's your brother."

A second time Luc shook her off. "He's a pain in the ass."

Leo was momentarily distracted by Hattie's distress. Luc

used the brief advantage to land another right to Leo's chin, this time splitting his own knuckles.

Hattie tried a third intervention, grabbing Luc's belt with two hands. But both men were in motion and when she lost her grasp, she slipped on the wet surface of the pool deck and fell sideways, her cheek raking the edge of the glass-topped table as she went down.

Luc and Leo froze. Luc was down on his knees in seconds, scooping her into his arms. "Oh, God, Hattie. Are you okay?"

She struggled to a sitting position and said, "Yes."

But she was lying. Blood oozed down her cheek from a nasty gash.

Leo crouched with them, cursing beneath his breath. "Is it bad?"

"I can't tell," Luc said, his hands shaky. "We need to get her checked out."

Hattie waved a hand. "Hellooo. I'm right here. If you two doofuses would kiss and make up, I'll be fine."

Luc eyes his brother sheepishly. "Sorry, man."

Leo grinned. "I deserved it."

Hattie rolled her eyes. "Morons." Luc heard rueful affection in the two syllables.

He motioned to his brother. "Grab one of those cloth napkins."

Leo complied, wetting the fabric in a water glass.

When Luc pressed gently at the wound, Hattie winced. "That hurts. Let me do it."

He surrendered the makeshift swab reluctantly, watching in dismay as Hattie removed more of the blood. It was an odd cut, and one that stitches wouldn't necessarily help.

The unflappable Marcel appeared, handing over a first aid kit. He glanced quickly at Hattie's cheek. "A butterfly bandage should do the trick, I think."

Luc applied antibiotic ointment and pressed the plaster

in place as tenderly as he could. He and Leo helped her to her feet.

Now that the immediate crisis was over, Hattie was clearly flustered. She reached for her sheer cover-up and slid her arms into it. "I'm going upstairs to take a shower," she said, her eyes daring him to protest. "I suggest you two get your act together while I'm gone."

She turned with dignity to Marcel. "Thank you for your help. It's nice to know that someone around here has good sense."

As she flounced her way into the house, Leo shook his head and smiled. "Your wife is one tough cookie."

Luc nodded, sobered by what might have been. "For once, I agree with you completely."

Eleven

When Hattie stepped into the sitting room, she saw Luc ensconced on the sofa, elbows on his knees, waiting for her.

He stood and faced her. "You look nice."

She picked up her purse, fiddling with the contents. "Thanks." She was wearing a gauzy ankle-length dress in shades of taupe and gold. It was sleeveless, and the V neck dipped low front and back. A necklace and bracelet in chunky amber stones complemented the outfit.

The small bandage on her cheekbone made her self-conscious, but that was mostly vanity talking. Her ensemble was dressy but comfortable. After the last few days, relaxation was high on Hattie's list.

She bit her lip, not wanting to resurrect any bad feelings. "Where's Leo?"

Luc made a face. "Don't worry. I signed the damn papers. He's changing downstairs to give us some privacy. I thought we'd go out for a late lunch somewhere nice, and afterward, he'll head home."

Leaving us all alone on our "it-has-to-get-better-than-

this" honeymoon. The thought swept through Hattie's brain like wildfire, singeing neurons and making her legs weak. "Sounds good."

But when they got downstairs, Leo was gone. Marcel handed over a note. Luc read it, his expression blank and then passed it over to Hattie.

Don't want to intrude. Have a good week. See you in Hotlanta.

Hattie tossed the little piece of paper in a nearby trash can, her palms damp. "I guess it's just us."

Luc's gaze was hooded. "Guess so."

He ushered her out to the car, and they drove the short distance to the historic district. After squeezing into a tiny parking space on a street curb, Luc shut off the engine and came around to open Hattie's door. His hand on her elbow did amazing things to her heart rate.

She told herself not to expect too much. Nothing had changed. They weren't a normal couple by any means.

But it was hard to remember such mundane considerations amidst the tropical atmosphere of Key West. Everyone was in a good mood, it seemed. And no wonder. The view from Mallory Square was filled with cerulean seas, colorful watercraft and white, billowing triangles atop sailboats that zigged and zagged across the open waves.

Just offshore lay a palm-fringed island that looked so perfect Hattie wondered if the Chamber of Commerce had painted it against the sky to frame the sunsets.

When she said as much, Luc responded. "One of the large hotel chains owns it. You can rent one-, two- or three-bedroom cottages, and they even have their own man-made beach."

Hattie had already realized that Key West was not a typical "beach" destination. The coastline was rocky or coral-built.

The Conch Republic, as it was called, was literally the last stop before Cuba, a mere ninety miles southwest.

At a marina adjacent to one of the fabulous hotels, Luc took Hattie's hand and helped her down into a sleek speedboat. Moments later, they were cutting across the waves, bound for the island.

In minutes, they pulled up to a well-kept dock and stepped out of the boat. A uniformed attendant directed them to the restaurant. It was open air on three sides, with huge rattan ceiling fans rotating overhead as an adjunct to the natural sea breezes. Delicate potted orchids bloomed on each table. China, silver and crystal gleamed.

The food was amazing…fresh shrimp gumbo and home-made corn bread. Hattie chewed automatically.

She was ready for a showdown, but if she initiated what might turn out to be a shouting match, would it be worth it? Hattie's mother had made a life's work out of tiptoeing around Hattie's stepfather. She always acted as if he might desert her at any moment.

The truth was that the guy loved Hattie's mother and would have given her anything. But early lessons are hard to unlearn. Hattie wasn't proficient at confrontation, but then again, she was no pushover. Luc was doing her a favor, yes. But that didn't mean he could dominate her.

She waited until the server put a piece of key lime pie in front of each of them before she fired the first shot. "How was your business trip?"

Luc choked on a bite of dessert. "Fine," he muttered. "This pie is great."

She wouldn't be deterred. If she had been clearer about her feelings a decade ago, she and Luc might possibly have worked things out. Her jaw tightened. "There was no excuse for you to leave on the first day of our honeymoon. Not only was it disrespectful to me, it also endangered our pretense of a happy marriage. I think you were trying to teach me a lesson, but it backfired."

Luc set down his fork and leaned back in his chair, his face sober. He exhaled slowly, his lips twisted. "You're right, of course. And I do apologize."

She cocked her head, studying him, trying to see inside his brain. "I've never said this, but my leaving you wasn't really about money. It was about control."

Luc jerked as if she had slapped him. "I don't understand."

"As a young woman, my mother had an affair with her boss, a wealthy, powerful man. When she told him she was pregnant, he cast her off without a second thought. That shining example of a man was my father. My biological father."

Shock creased his face. "I wasn't your boss, Hattie. What does that have to do with anything? I feel sorry for your mother, but you're certainly not the kind to do something so reckless."

"You're missing the point. My whole childhood revolved around this missing mystery man. This terrible person who didn't want me. And to hear my mother tell it, money was what gave him all the power. Leaving her power*less* and alone. From the time I was old enough to understand, she drilled into me the importance of making my own way in the world and not letting any man control my destiny."

"And you thought I would do something like that to you?" He looked haunted.

"Of course not. But I was so head over heels in love with you, I was afraid I'd lose myself in your life. It's very easy to be taken care of, very addictive. And I wasn't brave enough to stick with you. In hindsight, I believe I was stronger than I realized at the time. But as a kid of twenty, all I could see was that you had the money and power to do anything you wanted. And I felt lost in your shadow."

"Despite the fact that I wanted you so badly I followed you around like a puppy."

"You were a young man at the mercy of his hormones. Sex makes men do crazy things."

They were sitting at adjoining corners of a table for four. Beneath the linen cloth, Luc took her hand and deliberately pushed it against his erection. "I'm not so young now," he growled, releasing her fingers and eating his pie as if nothing had happened.

The imprint of his rigid flesh was burned into Hattie's palm. She took a reckless swallow of wine. "Don't be crass."

He shrugged, his eyes a dangerous flash of obsidian. "What do you want from me, Hattie?"

She hesitated, torn between fascinated curiosity about his response to her and a healthy sense of caution. "Do you really think we can be intimate and then walk away?"

Luc shrugged again. "I can if you can."

Hattie frowned, licking whipped cream from her spoon. His nonchalance could be an act. Her heart beat faster.

She cocked her head and stared at him, trying to read his mind. He was as inscrutable as the great and powerful wizard of Oz. If Hattie could click her heels in ruby slippers, she'd be able to go back to that innocent time in college.

Did she want to? Or did she want to move ahead as an adult woman with adult needs? She'd be taking an enormous risk. What if she fell in love with Luc again? What if she never had really *stopped* loving him? What if they had sex and it was ho-hum?

Not likely.

She scraped one last bite of topping from her plate and ate it absently. Luc's hungry gaze followed every motion she made. Her throat dried. It was now or never.

When the waiter moved to a safe distance, Hattie rested her arms on the table and moved in close to Luc. She put her hand over his. "You said I had to be the one to say yes or no. But you have to know that my answer has nothing to do with protecting a baby…nothing to do with mistakes we made in the past. No feelings of obligation. This is about us…you and me. And I say—"

Luc put his hand over her mouth, his expression violent. "Not another word."

Luc was burning up. The tropical heat and Hattie's proximity made him sweat. Her gaze seemed to dissect him like a bug. To burrow inside his brain and discern his secrets. He lifted an impatient hand for the check, deliberately breaking their physical connection. He was too close to the edge. Hearing Hattie acquiesce to their mutual desire for sexual intimacy could push him over. And it wouldn't be smart to let her realize how desperate he was to have her. Talking about sex in a public venue had not helped in the least when it came to controlling his baser urges.

After he shoved two large bills into the folio, he took Hattie by the wrist, dragging her toward the exit. "We're going back to the house," he said. "I think you have sunstroke."

She laughed softly. They reached the dock, and it was all he could do not to crush her against one of the wooden posts and ravage her mouth with his. He damned the surroundings that forced him to act like a gentleman. He'd never felt less civilized in his life.

Other tourists joined them beneath the awning, and soon the return boat arrived. Hattie's hip and thigh were glued to Luc's in the small, crowded craft. Back on dry land, she followed him meekly to the car. Her honey-blond hair gleamed in the unforgiving sun.

Seeing her pink shoulders made him think of Leo again.

Which made him think of doing the lotion thing for Hattie, covering every inch of her creamy skin with fragrant moisture.

He knew what she was going to say, and his body said a resounding *"hell, yeah!"* But in addition to his need to remain in control, it occurred to him that he owed her some romance…to make up for his less than stellar behavior as a new groom. They had eight or nine hours to kill before bedtime. It was far too hot to walk the streets in the midday heat.

Fortunately, their rental was parked beneath a huge shade tree. Luc leaned his elbows on the top of the car and faced Hattie with the vehicle between them. "What would you like to do now?" he asked, wishing he could supply the answer.

She lifted the hair from the back of her neck and sighed. "I love the pool," she said. "Do you mind too much if we go back and swim? We can play tourist tomorrow."

"Whatever you want," he croaked, his mind racing ahead. Swimming as foreplay made as much sense as anything else to his testosterone fuddled brain.

In the bedroom there was an awkward moment when they both reached into suitcases with plans to change clothes. Luc held up his hands, gripping a pair of black swim trunks. "I'll use the other bathroom."

He was ready in four minutes. It took Hattie an extra twenty. But when she reappeared, he wasn't about to complain. Her hair was swept up on top of her head, leaving recalcitrant tendrils to cling to her damp neck. The white terry robe she wore covered her from throat to knee, but it molded to her breasts and hips with just enough cling to encourage his imagination.

He thought he had himself under control. But all bets were off when they reached the pool and Hattie ditched the cover-up. She wore a different suit this time, and he was damned glad Leo hadn't been around to see this one.

It was a neon-blue bikini. Luc was stunned. She was a sexual goddess, even more lovely than she had been in college. The bikini bottom fastened at the hips with a large gold circlet on either side. The two tiny triangles of fabric that made up the top barely met decency standards.

Luc looked around suspiciously to see if anyone else was enjoying the show, but their privacy was absolute. Nothing but flowers and water and a mermaid just for his entertainment. If there were other guests at the small inn, they were not around at the moment.

Luc made a show of selecting a chaise lounge and flipping out his towel. "I'm going to nap."

Hattie gazed at him over her shoulder, her eyes hidden behind tortoiseshell sunglasses. "Will you do me first?"

His body went rigid in shock until he saw the bottle of sunscreen she held out. "Sure."

When she was situated, he perched on his hip beside her and unscrewed the lid. Immediately, the scent of coconut assailed his nostrils. Hattie pillowed her head on her arms, a small smile tilting her lips.

Luc groaned inwardly. Giving her a taste of romance before the main event might drive him mad.

When his hands touched her back, she flinched. "It's cold."

He ran his fingers across her shoulder blades. "It won't be. Relax."

Too bad he couldn't take his own advice. Every one of his muscles was tight enough to snap. He exhaled slowly and concentrated on Hattie. His fingertips still remembered the hills and valleys of her body. His thumbs pressed on either side of her spine.

Hattie moaned.

Dear Lord.

When he hesitated, she lifted a hand and waved it lazily, her eyes closed. "Don't stop."

He smoothed one final spot of lotion into her skin and capped the bottle. "All done."

Hattie didn't answer. She was so still he suspected she had drifted off. Which irked him, because sleep was the furthest thing from his mind. He stood up and went to the deep end of the pool. After one last glance at Hattie, he dove in and started a series of punishing laps. Harder and faster, pushing his body to exhaustion.

He swam until his legs began to feel like spaghetti. And then he swam some more. When spots of light began to dance behind his eyelids, he dragged himself out of the pool and collapsed onto his lounger facedown. Hattie lay where he had left her, her almost naked body lax and limp, her skin glistening with a dewy sheen of lotion and perspiration.

Luc closed his eyes, his heart pounding in his chest. He had a painful erection. His body was clenched with desire, despite the brutal workout. He was a man, not a eunuch. He might not be in love with Hattie like he'd been as a stupid kid of twenty, but he had normal male needs. If she didn't come to him soon, he'd never be able to keep up the pretense that he was in control of the situation.

It was a shock to feel hands on his back. He'd been so caught up in his own turmoil, he never heard Hattie move. She mimicked his earlier position and was now preparing to rub sunscreen into his burning skin. Thankfully, his Italian heritage made him able to endure the sun without painful consequences, but he knew he needed the protection.

The question was—who or what would protect him from Hattie?

Her hands were small, but strong. Despite the ostensible point of the exercise, this was foreplay. And Luc was strung so tightly, he wasn't sure he could bear it.

Five minutes later, his body aching with the need to roll

over and pull Hattie down into his arms, she finished. He felt her touch on his hair, her fingers ruffling the wet strands.

She leaned in closer, her breast brushing his side. "I'm getting in the water. Why don't you join me?"

It was a dare. He recognized it as such and knew that this game of cat and mouse had only one possible conclusion. But it was up to him to write the script and make sure Hattie knew who was in control.

He swung to a sitting position. Now they were so close, he could have leaned forward a scant two inches and kissed her. But he didn't. Not yet.

He smiled grimly, cursing his body's weakness. "After you."

She didn't try to dive in, but instead used the ladder to lower herself into the pool. The water was only chest high where she stood. He executed a show-off dive from the opposite direction and came up beside her, shoving the hair from his face. Her eyes were wide.

He touched her shoulder. "Want a ride in the deep end?"

Hattie nodded, not speaking.

He took her hand. "Get on my back."

When she complied, her legs wrapping around his waist and her arms encircling his shoulders, he shuddered. "Hang on."

He walked forward, feeling the bottom of the pool fall away beneath his feet. When he could barely touch bottom, he tugged her off his back and around until she faced him. The slightly surprised look in her eyes when she realized she was out of her depth made him smile inwardly.

Her hands clenched his shoulders, her fingernails leaving marks in his skin. Their legs drifted together and apart. He knew she felt the evidence of what she did to him.

Hattie nibbled her bottom lip. "The water feels great."

She was nervous. He liked that. "A lot of things feel great," he said, deliberately taunting her.

"You didn't let me give you my answer earlier," she said, her eyes alight with mischief.

He kissed her softly, a bare brush of mouth to mouth. She tasted like warm summer fruit. "It will keep," he muttered. "No need to rush."

Need swam between them. His. Hers. It might have been a decade, but some pleasures the body never forgets.

Her eyes drifted shut.

"No. Look at me." He cupped one breast.

Hattie's eyelids fluttered open, her gaze unfocused, her cheeks flushed despite the cool water. Her soft cry went straight to his gut.

He kicked his legs rhythmically, keeping them afloat. Now he took the other breast. Two handfuls…warm, seductive, feminine bounty. He massaged gently, moving the barely-there bikini top aside to find naked flesh.

The pleasure flooding him from touching her so intimately blurred his vision. His hands settled at her waist as he took her mouth in a ravaging kiss. They were in danger of losing all rational thought. And he was sinking fast.

As fact matched thought, they slipped beneath the surface of the water. He kissed her again, and this time, he slid his hand into the bottom of her bikini and cupped her, pressing a finger into her tight passage and probing…stroking.

It lasted no more than a few seconds. He dragged them both back up for air. Hattie wrapped her legs around his waist, her ragged breathing matching his. She had a death grip on his shoulders, her breasts mashed to his chest.

She initiated the kiss this time, her small teeth nipping his bottom lip, her tongue sliding between his teeth, dazing him with an ache so intense, his head hurt. Hunger raged like a wild animal, one that hadn't been fed in a decade.

She whimpered when he cupped her bottom, pulling her closer. "Luc…Luc."

Hearing his name on her lips almost unmanned him. "What, Hattie?"

"Please," she groaned. "My answer is yes. Please, please, please make love to me."

Exultation filled his chest. That was what he needed to hear. "Ask me again," he demanded.

Her gaze filled with frustration. "No games. Take me. Now."

Twelve

Hattie stumbled as Luc dragged her toward the house, their few belongings left behind in his haste. His grip on her wrist allowed no protest. But then why would she…protest, that is?

She wanted Luc—the sooner the better.

If she had expected awkwardness in the bedroom, she was wrong. Luc was smooth, determined. He stripped off his trunks, grinning tightly when she looked her fill.

His erection was magnificent. Thick, long and ready for her…only her. His broad chest and strong arms rippled with muscles. He cupped her face in his hands. "Take it off."

His adamant tone brooked no refusal.

She trembled inside and out as she unfastened the knot at the back of her neck and reached behind to undo the clasp. For seconds, the bikini top clung damply to her breasts as she clutched it in sudden, belated hesitation.

The corner of Luc's beautiful mouth quirked in a half smile. "Don't go all shy on me now, Hattie."

She gulped inwardly and let the scraps of fabric fall. Luc inhaled sharply. The look in his eyes made her weak. In college, he had been her first love, her first lover. Now he was a mature man in his sexual prime. She felt the heat of his desire, not as quiet warmth, but as a flashpoint poised to explode.

There was the problem of what to do with her hands. She wanted to cover her breasts instinctively. But she knew Luc would have none of that. So her arms hung at her sides as she shifted from one foot to the other.

He lifted an eyebrow. "You're not finished."

She might have taken umbrage at his arrogant tone had she not been as eager as he was for the next act. Removing her last barrier of modesty proved harder than she expected.

Luc lost patience. He gripped her hips. "Too slow," he growled. He kissed her wildly, his mouth everywhere...her lips, her throat, and finally, her bare breasts. The sensation was an electric shock. Her entire body melted into him, closer and closer still.

His hard shaft bruised her hipbone. The soft, wiry hair on his chest tickled her sensitive skin. Breath by gasping breath they relearned the taste of each other—the touch, the sound, the smell. It was a smorgasbord of sensual delight. A cornucopia of excess.

He tangled his fingers in the rings at her hips and jerked hard, ripping the thin fabric from the metal. The remnants that he tossed aside represented Hattie's last resistance, if indeed she had any.

She was drunk on memories laced with present passion.

A nanosecond later he lifted her. Her legs wrapped around his waist instinctively. The intimate position made her limp with longing. He backed her up to the nearest wall and buried his face in her neck. Tremors shook his large frame. His chest heaved.

Slowly, as if giving her time to protest, he aligned their bodies and entered her with one forceful upward thrust. He was big, but she was ready for him. When he was buried inside her, he went still.

"Hattie?" His voice was hoarse.

"Hmmm?" She bit his earlobe and heard him curse.

"You okay?"

The four-letter word didn't come close to describing what she was. "Don't stop."

"Whatever the lady wants."

The last words were barely audible as he directed all his energy toward driving them both insane. Her bare butt slapped against the door as Luc pounded into her over and over.

A searing heat built inside her, coalesced at the spot where their bodies were joined. Higher. Stronger. The world ceased to exist. Her arms tightened around his neck as she felt the storm begin to break. "Luc…" Stars cartwheeled inside her head and tumbled downward to reignite when Luc's own release sent him rigid and straining against her.

When it was over at last, Luc staggered into their bedroom, still carrying her, and dropped her onto the mattress. He came down beside her and rested his head on her chest.

Her heart stopped. A perfect cocoon of intimacy enveloped them.

She might have slept for a few minutes—she wasn't sure. Luc was out, his body a heavy weight half on top of her. She wanted so badly to stroke his hair, but she resisted. A black hole of self-destruction yawned at her feet. She was far too close to the edge.

Awkwardly, she slid from beneath him and tiptoed to the bathroom. After quickly freshening up, she put on one of the soft luxurious robes that hung on the back of the door. Belting it tightly, she peeked out into the bedroom.

Luc's speculative gaze met hers. "You won't need the robe."

Five simple words. That's all he needed to make the

moisture bloom between her legs. She grasped the door frame to steady herself. "I won't?" All the starch had left her legs. She was melting, body and soul.

He crooked a finger. "Come back to bed."

Removing the robe was even more difficult than shedding her swimsuit. In the heat of the moment, her inhibitions had gone on vacation. But now they were back.

As she padded into the room, shivering, she noticed for the first time that the AC had been kicked up a notch. Luc held a string of condom packets in his hand. "We skipped a step. I'm sorry, Hattie. That was my fault."

She shrugged with what she hoped was blasé sophistication. "It's the wrong part of the month. I'm not worried."

His grin was tight. "Then let's not waste any more time."

The robe fell at her feet. Luc's amusement faded visibly to be replaced by sheer male determination. When she shivered now, it had nothing to do with the temperature in the room and everything to do with the man stretched out on his back like a sleek, not-quite-satisfied predator.

Nothing this older, more experienced Luc did was predictable. Instead of covering her with his aroused body, he pulled her on top. It was a position she had never really liked, because it made her feel too vulnerable. But when she tried to protest, Luc took care of that by lightly touching the small bud of nerves at her center.

She braced her hands on her thighs and tried not to flinch as he explored her most private recesses. In an embarrassingly short amount of time, she moaned and climaxed, the second event no less powerful than the first.

He held her close and stroked her hair, though she could feel the strength of his unappeased desire. Tears clogged her throat. "Luc, I…" *love you.* No, she didn't. It was just the sex talking. Shades of auld lang syne. An overabundance of postcoital hormones.

He kissed her cheek. "You what?"

"I wonder if we made a mistake." She felt him go still.

"Regrets already?"

Something in his tone made her cringe. She shouldn't have introduced reality into their bed. Not now. But she was compelled to answer. "This makes things complicated. When we go our separate ways."

His hands moved from her hair, her shoulders. He shifted her until they lay side by side. Already she missed his warmth.

His tone was perfectly calm when he answered. "You're making too much of nothing. There's no harm in enjoying each other. Divorces are simple nowadays. We'll deal with any complications when we have to. It's nothing to worry about."

She winced inwardly, her lovely moment shattered by her own bad timing and Luc's carelessly callous comment. No more pretending. This wasn't a honeymoon. This was sex for the sake of scratching an itch. No use dressing it up with romantic frills.

No reason for tears to sting her eyes and a painful lump to clog her throat.

She swallowed, her mouth dry. "I want to take a shower."

Luc pounced verbally. "No, Hattie. I don't think so."

He hardly noticed that she didn't answer. He'd been kicked in the gut and was left reeling. The sweat was barely dry on their bodies and she was already talking about leaving him. Damn it to hell. *He* would be the one to end this relationship... not Hattie.

He was hard as a pike, his erection painfully stiff. With jerky motions, he ripped open a packet and rolled on a rubber. A split second later he groaned aloud as he penetrated Hattie's tight, wet warmth. She lay passive beneath him, and it pissed him off.

He took her chin in his hand. "Look at me, Mrs. Cavallo." She obeyed. He had to grit his teeth to keep from coming right then. "What we do in the privacy of our bed is our own business. We're good together. Don't fight it. Don't fight me. Let yourself go, Hattie."

Big brown eyes looked up at him with a mixture of emotions he couldn't decipher even if he wasn't being driven by his baser needs. She whispered the single word. "Okay."

It was enough. He felt her hands touch his hips, recognized the moment when she arched her back and matched her rhythm to his. A red haze clouded his vision. His hips pistoned in agonized yearning for release. It was good…so good.

Hattie gave a small shocked cry as he felt her inner muscles squeeze him. Her release triggered his, and he bore down, losing himself in her welcome embrace and finding momentary oblivion.

Sometime later, sanity returned. He could hear his own jerky breathing in the silence of the room. Hattie was still and quiet again. Had he hurt her? He moved aside with a muttered apology, relieving her of his considerable weight.

Sweet mother of God. He hadn't had sex that good in he didn't know when. *Oh, yes, you do. It was back in college when Hattie was warm and willing and you were both blissfully happy.*

He shook off the memories. No need for those when he had the real thing in his arms. What was she thinking? He was too tired to pry it out of her. He'd barely slept the night before.

His eyes closed involuntarily.

Aeons later it seemed, he felt her try to escape. His fingers closed around her wrist. "Stay."

"I need a shower."

He scrubbed his hands over his face, yawning, his head muzzy. "I'll join you."

The look on her face made him laugh as he got to his feet. "Don't be so modest. It's the green thing to do."

After turning the water to a comfortable temperature, he dragged a clearly reluctant Hattie into the luxurious shower enclosure. His lovely new wife huddled in a tiled corner, her arms wrapped around her waist.

Everything about her screamed innocent seduction…from her long slender legs to her hourglass waist, to her plump, shapely breasts. If he could paint, he'd commit her to canvas exactly like this.

He picked up a bar of soap shaped like a shell. "Turn around."

Hattie was drowning in her own need. In her wildest imagination she had never invented a scenario like this. "Why?" she muttered.

His grin was lethal. "I thought you wanted to get clean."

"You're a dirty old man."

"Not old," he deadpanned.

She gave him her back reluctantly, hyperaware that she was at his sexual mercy. The first touch of the washcloth made her jump. But it was Luc's chuckle that made her blush.

As he washed from her neck down her spine, she braced her hands on the wall and hung her head. Luc had turned the spray so that it cascaded between them. The water was cool on Hattie's hot skin.

Luc moved the rag slowly, more of a massage than a simple exercise in cleanliness. He reached her bottom and squeezed. "Turn around."

She obeyed instinctively, their gazes colliding amidst the steamy air. "I can do the rest," she said.

He shook his head. "Why bother? I'm off to a hell of a

good start." He took her hands and tucked them behind her butt. "Don't move."

The hot water was enervating, draining Hattie of any will to challenge Luc's control. This time he made no pretense of using the washcloth. He took the bar of soap and ran it in circles around her breasts. Then he pressed gently over her nipples, decorating them with tiny bubbles.

When he was satisfied, he paused to kiss her…slow and deep. With one hand, he manacled her wrists behind her back with a firm grip. Now their bodies were touching chest to chest. She felt his erection throbbing between them.

He nuzzled her nose with his and ground his hips into hers. "More work to do," he muttered.

His hand holding the soap found its way south to the middle of her thighs. Her legs parted instinctively to give him access.

When the soap glided over a certain sensitive spot, Hattie cried out and struggled. But Luc kept his tight hold on her wrists as he moved the soap between her legs.

Hattie rested her forehead on his chest, panting. "Enough," she whispered. "I'm clean." She was close to the edge, but she didn't want to make the journey alone. She wanted Luc inside her, filling her, making her his.

Without warning, he dropped the soap and released her wrists. The shower boasted a roomy stone seat. Luc reached for the condom he'd tucked on a ledge, sheathed himself, and then pulled Hattie down to sit astride his lap.

Their bodies were slick and wet, and the moment when they joined was seamless…easy. Hattie threw back her head, the water still streaming over them. Her eyes were closed, intensifying the sensation of having Luc inside her.

He was strong. He lifted her up and down in a gentle rhythm, teasing them both.

Longing crescendoed, hunger peaked. Luc's hands bruised

her bare butt as he gave a muffled shout and found his release. Hattie still lingered on the knife edge of pleasure. She could stay there forever.

Luc bit her neck, ran his tongue over her tightly furled nipples. It was enough. It was too much. She arched her back and gave a choked sob as everything inside her splintered and fanned out through her veins in cascading ripples of pure joy.

Afterward, she was weak as a baby. Luc dried her tenderly and scooped her up in his arms to carry her to their bed. Hattie had lost all sense of time. And didn't really care.

Luc muttered an apology as he slid beneath the covers and moved over her and into her. She had nothing left, but this coupling was warm and lazy. He rode her forever, it seemed, pausing each time he came close to the end and making himself wait, stretching out the incredible connection, the deep, undulating eroticism.

He enveloped her, overwhelmed her. His scent, his touch, his powerful domination.

Somewhere in the deep recesses of her consciousness lingered the knowledge that she would have to pay for this day. That down the line her heart would face pain equal to the present elation.

But she refused to let such maudlin considerations ruin the present.

She put a hand to his cheek, loving him with her eyes. "You're amazing," she whispered. "I haven't felt like this in a very long time."

His cheeks were ruddy, his eyes hooded, his chin shadowed with late-day stubble. Everything about him reeked of uncivilized, ravenous male. Little was left of the suave businessman, the wealthy CEO.

And Hattie loved it…loved him. God help her, she did. This was a man she could live with…share a life with.

But the other Luc still existed outside this room. And that was the problem. Just as it had always been.

He groaned and his whole body shook as his mighty control finally snapped. "Hattie…" He climaxed in a series of long, rapid thrusts.

Despite her exhaustion, echoes of pleasure teased her once again.

In the aftermath, they slept. And as the tropical sun sank low in the sky, coaxing the stars out to play in the gathering dusk, Mr. and Mrs. Luc Cavallo were in perfect accord for one fleeting moment.

Thirteen

Luc rolled over and looked at the clock sometime around 9:00 p.m. His stomach was growling, and no wonder. Their late brunch was the last meal he had eaten.

He slung an arm above his head and yawned, his somber gaze noting that Hattie slept peacefully. Too bad he wasn't as relaxed. The sex had been nothing short of spectacular, but now that his head was in control and not his libido, he was able to think clearly. And the conclusions he drew were unsettling.

He was in danger of falling in love with Hattie all over again. Perhaps in some ways he had never fallen *out* of love... which might explain why the many women he had dated in the last ten years never quite seemed to measure up to some unknown standard. His grandfather had accused him of being too picky...of expecting a paragon of a woman to fill his bed and his life.

Turned out...his grandfather was right.

And that woman was Hattie Parker.

He watched her sleep for a long time, mulling over his

options. Right now she needed him because of the baby. Which gave him an advantage for the moment. But what happened when the kid's father was no longer a threat? What then?

Would Hattie try to bid Luc a pleasant goodbye and walk away? The possibility made his chest tight. He was no longer a naive and vulnerable kid. He'd learned his lesson well. Loving someone too much only opened the way for hurt.

Losing both of his parents at the same time had sent him and Leo into a tailspin. Only their grandfather's gruff, tough affection had rescued them. Perhaps way back in college Luc had fallen hard for Hattie because he needed so badly to fill a void in his life.

He was more self-sufficient now, able to enjoy a physical relationship without involving messy emotions. And besides, the barrier between Hattie and him remained the same: his need for control. He had let her too close once upon a time and suffered the consequences. And if his money gave him power, did she expect him to give it all away and live in a shack?

Perhaps since his embarrassment of riches was currently saving her niece, she might decide that being with a wealthy man wasn't exactly a ticket to purgatory.

He touched her arm...he couldn't help himself. The need to keep her close was all-consuming. She had come to him for help...for protection. He would keep Hattie and Deedee safe at all costs. It was the honorable thing to do. And he'd given his word.

Hattie was grateful to him...and she was attracted to him. But that wasn't enough. He wanted her to need him, to depend on him, to beg him to let her stay. How or why she initially came to him didn't really matter in the end. She was vulnerable now. And God help him, he liked it. His course was clear: enjoy the physical side of their marriage as long as it lasted, maintain his emotional distance...and then...

He refused to contemplate the future. Not now when life was close to perfect. He would keep her as long as it suited him.

The next time he awoke, it was morning; dawn to be exact. Clear, liquid light filtered into the bedroom. He stroked his wife's shoulder. She was sleeping on her stomach, her face turned away from him. "Wake up, sleepyhead. I'm starving."

She blinked her eyes and struggled up onto her elbows. One brief glance at her warm, pink breasts was all he got before she rolled onto her back and clutched the sheet to her chest.

Her eyes were wide, her honey-blond hair tousled. "What time is it?"

"Early. We slept through the night. But missing dinner was definitely worth it."

A deep blush painted her face crimson.

He took pity on her. "I'll use the other bathroom to get ready."

"Ready?"

"I thought we'd go snorkeling this morning. Out to the reef. Are you game?"

She frowned. "I've never done it. Is it difficult?"

He patted her leg. "Not really. You'll love it, I promise." Her expression was unconvinced, so he grinned at her. "Or... we could stay in bed all day."

Hattie stumbled to her feet, almost tripping over her bed-sheet toga. "Snorkeling sounds great," she said, the words breathless as she struggled to maintain her modesty. "If you'll order breakfast, I'll be dressed in a jiff." She disappeared into the bathroom.

He chuckled aloud at her discomfiture. Teasing Hattie had

always been fun. Too bad she agreed to the snorkeling. He could have been persuaded to follow option two.

Just thinking about the night before made him hard. With an inward groan, he picked up the phone and called for sustenance. It was going to be a long day, and he needed some serious calories.

Hattie dressed in a modest coral one-piece and covered it with a crisp, white poplin top and khaki walking shorts. A new pair of taupe leather sandals completed the outfit.

When she looked in the mirror, she winced. Going to bed with damp hair meant that she looked like a wild woman. It took a hairbrush and patient determination to tame the mess. Finally, she tucked it up into a ponytail, donned an Atlanta Braves cap and smoothed sheer sunscreen onto her face, neck and arms.

In addition to her new wardrobe, Luc had gifted her with an array of expensive cosmetics. Though most of it was products she would only use for fancy occasions, she had already come to appreciate the many wonderful skin-care creams and lotions.

Breakfast was just arriving when she stepped out of the bathroom. Luc, freshly shaven, his hair damp, tipped the young woman who brought up the largesse.

He spread a hand. "Let's eat."

They consumed an embarrassingly large amount of food in record time. Hattie hadn't realized how hungry she was.

Luc watched her bite into a huge strawberry. "You've got juice all over your chin. Let me…" He dabbed her sticky skin with a cloth napkin, his face close to hers. His expression was shuttered, and she wanted badly to know what he was thinking.

Her head was filled with memories of last night… experiences that were life-changing.

But men were far more cavalier about sex and intimacy. When it was over it was over. Luc might want to be with her again, but that didn't mean he'd be doodling a heart with both their names on scrap paper.

Sex was only physical as far as Luc was concerned. She'd do well to keep that fact firmly planted in the front of her brain. And that meant staying out of this suite as much as possible.

She scooted back from the table. "Let's go. I'm excited about this."

Luc had not chartered a private boat. And for that Hattie was glad. Having other people around diffused the natural awkwardness she was experiencing. She couldn't even look at Luc without remembering how his powerful body had joined with hers, how their skin had been damp with exertion, their muscles lax with pleasure.

If she let herself, she could imagine that they were like any normal newlyweds. Deeply in love, and ravenous for each other.

Luc didn't help her resolve to be sensible. He was in turns tender, affectionate and teasing. More and more she saw glimpses of the young man she had fallen in love with. Away from the pressure of business and responsibilities, Luc laughed often, was more relaxed and carefree.

He handed her a pair of flippers. "Put these on, and I'll help you with your mask." All around them, fellow passengers were doing the same thing. The large catamaran had cut its engines and was bobbing in clear blue-green water over the reef below.

Hattie and Luc had already shed their outer clothing and tucked all of it into a big raffia tote bag. She tried not to drool over her new husband. His black swim trunks were plain, but it was his sculpted torso and powerful arms that drew attention. Hattie didn't miss the fact that she wasn't the only one eyeing Luc's masculine beauty.

He wore expensive, reflective sunglasses that made him look like a movie star. It didn't seem fair for one man to have everything—looks, character and money to burn.

She sighed inwardly as he handed her a mask and snorkel tube. "What happens if I swallow water?"

"You'll be fine. I'll be right beside you."

The boat captain gave some basic instructions, including a warning to listen for the whistle that signaled time to return to the boat. Hattie was very glad she had a reliable partner.

She had assumed they would jump over the side like in the movies, but the catamaran had a ladder that could be lowered into the water between the two large hulls. Backing down the steps was a little claustrophobic, but Luc went first and was waiting for her as she descended. He took her arm, his face almost unrecognizable behind his mask. "Come on, little mermaid. We don't want to waste any time."

Hattie was not a superconfident swimmer. And learning to breathe through the tube was challenging. But Luc's patience and support, along with a life vest, erased much of her fear, and soon she was moving through the water, head down, discovering the wonders of the reef.

The colors were muted and not as dramatic as Discovery Channel specials she had seen about the Great Barrier Reef, but the experience was enchanting nevertheless. Corals bobbed and swayed in eerie dances. Multicolored fish, large and small, moved with unconcern in and around the landlubber visitors.

Much of the necessary communication involved pointing and arm touches. But when Hattie spotted a familiar shape, she gasped, swallowed water, and had to come up to catch her breath. "It was a shark," she cried, coughing as she cleared her throat.

Luc shoved his mask on top of his head and laughed. "I've never seen anyone's eyes get that big. I thought you were going to faint dead in the water."

She shuddered. "Don't say dead. I wanted to take some pictures, but he was too fast." The snorkeling package included disposable waterproof cameras. "He wasn't very big though."

Luc tugged her ponytail. "You were hoping for *Jaws?*"

She giggled, feeling happier than she had been in a long time. "Well, not really, but it would have made a great Facebook post."

He glanced at his diver's watch. "We'd better get back to it. Time's almost up."

By the time the whistle sounded, Hattie was ready to quit. The experience was amazing, but the unaccustomed exercise, combined with learning how to manipulate the equipment, had exhausted her.

Back onboard everyone dried off and deposited their gear in large barrels for cleaning. Young crew members passed out lemonade and cookies. Luc and Hattie sat side by side, the wind in their faces as the boat cut rapidly through the waves on the home journey. Their swimsuits dried rapidly in the heat.

Luc put his arm around her back. "Was it what you expected?"

She glanced up at him, controlling a shiver at the delicious feel of his warm skin on hers. "Even better," she said. The sun was making her drowsy. Her head lolled against his shoulder, and she let herself lean into his body.

As they docked in Key West, she roused. It was the work of minutes to slip back into shorts, shoes and top. Luc followed suit, and soon they disembarked with the other passengers.

They lingered at the dock for a few minutes watching

parasail enthusiasts go airborne. Hattie shaded her eyes with a hand. "That looks fun, too."

Luc took her arm. "Maybe tomorrow. Let's find a restaurant."

She punched him softly. "Is that all you ever want to do?"

He paused in the middle of the road and kissed her—hard. He brushed a stray hair from her cheek. "Actually, it's way down on the list, but I'm trying to be a considerate husband."

That shut her up. What would Luc say if she demanded to go back to the guesthouse and spend the afternoon and evening as they had the day before?

Sadly, she didn't have the guts to propose what she really wanted to do. Instead, she pretended interest in the fried plantains at the Cuban restaurant they found near the harbor. She ate mechanically. Every moment that passed brought them closer to the evening hours. When they would go to bed…together?

The uncertainty made her crazy. Was last night a one-time faux pas on their parts, or was Luc assuming they would continue to have sex for the duration of the marriage?

Hattie hated the idea of divorce, but what choice did they have? They had allowed sexual hunger and curiosity to lead them down a dangerous path, and she knew what happened to that proverbial cat.

Luc nudged her elbow. "I thought you'd be hungry. Swimming always gives me an appetite."

She shrugged. "I think it's the heat getting to me. Do you mind if we go back to our place? I'd love to take a shower and wash the seawater off my skin."

His fork stilled in midair, and his cheekbones went dark. He cleared his throat. "Of course. Whatever you want."

Hattie cursed her own artless stupidity. Did that sound like an open invitation for sex? She hadn't meant it that way.

Or had she?

Luc finished his meal and summoned the waiter for their check. Shortly after, they made their way through the crowded streets. Apparently, many tourists had arrived early to celebrate the Memorial Day holiday. Hattie barely noticed the commotion. All she could think about was how to handle the return to their luxurious bridal quarters.

The leather seats in the car were hot...no shade trees this time. She wriggled uncomfortably, and rolled down her window to let the steamy air escape. Luc was silent, his face impossible to read.

The ride was brief and silent. They exited the car. Marcel welcomed them as they strolled through the courtyard. "Are you enjoying your stay in Key West?"

Luc shook his hand, but Hattie answered. "It's lovely. So vibrant and colorful. You're lucky to live here year-round."

Marcel nodded as he trimmed an overgrown bougainvillea. "The only time I rethink my address is during hurricane season, but we are lucky here in the Keys...very few major hits."

Luc frowned. "Have you heard a forecast for tonight and tomorrow?"

"Nothing but calm, clear skies. Perfect vacation weather."

Hattie preceded Luc up the stairs, wondering what was up. Luc seemed focused on some unknown objective. And once in their room, instead of throwing her on the bed as she had hoped or expected, he seemed to be preoccupied...or at least avoiding sex at the moment. "Why were you concerned about the weather?" she asked him.

He tossed the car keys and his sunglasses on the dresser. "I have an idea."

"Uh-oh," she teased. "Should I be worried?"

He sprawled on the sofa. "Do you remember those camping trips we took in college?"

"Of course." They had journeyed to the north Georgia

mountains a number of times, spending several chilly spring and autumn nights curled together in a double sleeping bag… just the two of them. Those had been magical times, and Hattie had loved them even more because the outings were inexpensive.

His arms stretched along the back of the couch, his fingers drumming restlessly. "I thought it might be fun to do that again."

In this heat? Was Luc so spooked by the intense emotion of the night before that he was going to keep them busy, nonstop? "Umm, well…"

"There's an island with an old fort. We can camp there. It would be an adventure. What do you say?"

The boyish eagerness on his face was irresistible. Despite her better judgment, she managed an enthusiastic smile. "Sounds like fun."

Fourteen

While Luc was on the phone making arrangements for their impromptu trip, Hattie showered and then checked in with Ana.

The baby is fine. No problem. Enjoy yourselves.

Hattie ended her call and surveyed the room. Luc was paying who knew how much money for this wonderful suite, and yet he wanted to abandon it for parts unknown. Men… She found him in the sitting room, still on the phone, but now she could tell it was business. Knowing what she did of his work ethic and his drive and determination, it really surprised her that he had been willing and able to get away for a honeymoon, pretend or otherwise.

He hung up and turned to face her, jubilation on his face. "I got us two spots. They only allow a small number of campers each night. But there's one catch."

"Oh?"

He winced, gauging her reaction. "We have to leave right now."

"Seriously?"

"Yeah. Everything for the week was full except for tonight."

Gulp. "Okay. What do I need to pack?"

"Anything that's comfortable and cool. Plus a swimsuit. We'll be able to snorkel in the shallow water around the fort."

And at night? What would happen then?

Hattie pondered that question. And how did one prepare for possible seduction on a remote, uninhabited island? After dithering in the bedroom for several minutes, she dumped out her carry-on bag and began filling it methodically. One set of clean clothes and underwear. Swimsuit. A long T-shirt to sleep in. Sunscreen.

She picked up a lilac silk nightgown and held it to her cheek for a wistful moment. Not exactly camping attire. But what the heck. This was her honeymoon. She stuffed it in.

It was easy to see why Luc was so successful. In barely an hour, he had secured bags of food, all sorts of camping gear, two coolers and transportation. They found parking near the dock and unloaded. Hattie was stunned to see Luc walk toward a stylish, powerful speedboat.

He held out a hand. "Come aboard, my lady."

The vessel must have been wickedly expensive, even as a rental. Everything about it gleamed, from the hardwood deck to the shiny chrome trim. Luc stowed their supplies and tossed Hattie a yellow life jacket.

She wrinkled her nose. "Do I have to?"

He slid his arms into a navy one. "Captain's orders."

"How far are we going?"

"About seventy miles."

Her apprehension must have shown on her face, because he sobered. "It's perfectly safe, Hattie. Leo and I learned to pilot boats before we could drive cars. Grandfather's villa is on the shores of Lake Como, and as teenage boys, we spent all the time we could in and on the water. I'll take care of you, I promise."

He was as good as his word, and in his competent hands, the sleek craft ate up the miles effortlessly. Hattie had donned her baseball cap back at the dock, and she was glad, because the wind whipped and slapped them in joyous abandon.

At times, dolphins leaped beside the boat, gamboling playfully, their beautiful skin glistening in the sun. Hattie laughed in delight and sat back finally, her eyes closed, her face tilted toward the sun. If she and Luc could keep going forever into the next sunset, life would be perfect.

Or almost. She couldn't bear the thought of giving up her niece. Deedee wasn't a burden. The baby was a joy.

Hattie shook off reality with a deliberate toss of her head. She took advantage of Luc's concentration to watch him unobserved. He controlled the boat with a relaxed stance that gave testament to his comfort being on the water. When several dark shapes began growing ahead of them, she scooted up beside him. "Is that it?"

He gave her a sideways grin. "Yep. We're in Dry Tortugas National Park."

"Never heard of it."

"Well it's only been a national park since 1992, so that's not so surprising."

"Why the name?"

"*Tortugas* because they look like a group of turtles, and *Dry* because there's no fresh water on any of them."

As they neared their destination, she stared, incredulous. She and Luc were miles from civilization, literally in the middle of nowhere. Yet perched on a handkerchief-size piece of land sat a sturdy brick fort, its hexagonal walls enclosing a large grassy area, and its perimeter surrounded by a water-filled moat. Even at a distance, the evidence of crumbling decay was visible.

Luc waved a hand as he throttled back the engine. "Fort Jefferson."

Hattie leaned her hands on the railing and absorbed it all. "I can't believe this."

"You know the expression 'Your name is mud'?"

She nodded as Luc tied up to the dock. "Of course."

"Some people attribute that remark to Dr. Samuel Mudd who was incarcerated here in the 1860s."

"What did he do that was so terrible?"

"He had the misfortune to set the broken leg of John Wilkes Booth after Booth assassinated President Lincoln."

"Wow."

"Exactly. Mudd was convicted of treason and sent here to serve a life sentence."

Hattie shuddered. Knowing there was no possibility of escape must have been mentally anguishing. "How dreadful."

"The story does have a bit of a happy ending," Luc said. "As you can imagine, disease was rampant in the fort. Dysentery, malaria, smallpox…and, at one time, a terrible outbreak of yellow fever. It was so bad, the entire medical staff died."

"And that's where Dr. Mudd comes to the rescue?"

"Right. Even knowing as he did that the disease was a killer, he stepped in and began caring for the soldiers, saving dozens of lives. For his heroism, he ultimately received a full pardon and was allowed to return home."

Hattie pondered the sad story. She wasn't a superstitious person, but the island, beautiful though it was, carried an aura of past suffering. Dr. Mudd had earned a second chance. Would Hattie and Luc be as lucky?

Luc had arranged for one of the park ranger's sons to unload all their supplies and set up camp. Luc lent a hand, but even so, it took several loads to carry everything to the designated camping area, a small sandy strip of land lightly dotted with grass and shrubs. At the far end, a young family with two kids had already erected a red-and-white tent.

Luc handled the minimal paperwork with the ranger on duty and then turned to Hattie. "You ready for a swim?"

Disappointment colored her words. "I thought we were going to explore the fort."

He held up his hands and laughed. "Okay. Fine. Maybe it will be a little cooler in there."

They grabbed cameras and water bottles and headed out. The empty silent rooms in the fort almost reeked of despair. The thick walls blocked out some of the afternoon heat, but at the same time contributed to the oppressive dungeonlike atmosphere. There were no furnishings. The stark, barren chambers seemed to echo with the voices of long-ago inmates.

After wandering through several sections of the fort, Luc pointed out the entrance to Dr. Mudd's cell. Hattie read aloud the inscription over the arch. "*Whoso entereth here leaveth all hopes behind.*" She shuddered. "Gruesome. But it sounds familiar."

Luc nodded. "It's from Dante's *Inferno.*"

"I need to see the sky," she muttered. She stepped back out into the sunshine, noting again the way the bricks were slowly disintegrating as time took its toll. "Can we climb the lighthouse?"

Luc took her arm. "It's about a thousand degrees today. The lighthouse is inactive. And I need a swim."

"Wimp," she teased. But she allowed herself to be persuaded. Back at the tent, there was an awkward moment.

Luc avoided her gaze. "Not much room in there," he said gruffly. "You go first."

It didn't take her long. Later, while she waited for Luc to change, she shaded her eyes and watched the numerous boats anchored offshore. Divers were taking advantage of the opportunity to explore the reef and other items of interest on the ocean floor.

When Luc emerged from the tent, she swallowed. He was wearing black nylon racing trunks that left little to the imagination. She smiled weakly, her temples perspiring, as he tossed her a towel.

Luc slung an arm around her shoulders, his own towel around his neck. "Let's go."

The water felt blissfully cool. Hattie paddled happily in the shallow water near the fort, finding it a lot easier than her first experience, since she could occasionally stand up. Some of the boaters were snorkeling as well, but they stayed mostly to the back of the fort.

She noticed that the family with the two children was also taking advantage of an afternoon swim. It suddenly occurred to her to wonder how far sound carried on the night air. Her breathing hitched, and she shivered despite the blazing sun. Anticipation and anxiety mingled in her stomach, making her feel slightly faint. If she got in over her head tonight, she'd have no one to blame but herself.

Luc had been swimming in deeper water, but he reappeared suddenly by her side, tugging off his mask and running a hand through his hair, flinging drops of water everywhere.

He smiled lazily. "Having fun?"

She nodded. "It's amazing."

He glanced at his high tech waterproof watch. "I thought I'd go on back and set up the grill, get the fire started. Will you be okay?"

She motioned him away. "By all means. I'm working up an appetite."

Without warning, he lifted her against his wet chest, her feet dangling in the water. His head lowered. "So am I, Hattie. So am I."

His mouth found hers, and the raw sensuality of his

kiss made her dizzy. She closed her eyes, her other senses intensifying. He tasted salty, with a hint of coconut from the sunscreen he'd used. She pulled his lower lip between her teeth and bit gently.

His entire body quaked. He released her slowly, allowing her to slide the length of his virtually nude form. By the time her feet touched the sandy bottom once again, she could barely stand.

He laughed shakily. "Well, hell. I don't know if I have the strength to climb out of the water." He rested his chin on the top of her head, his arms wrapped around her waist. "You know what's going to happen tonight."

She nodded, mute, her face pressed to the muscular flesh just above his nipple.

He released her and stepped back. "Okay, then."

An hour later, they ate dinner in style. Hattie should have known that a Cavallo wouldn't prepare anything as plebian as hamburgers or hot dogs. Luc grilled T-bones and fresh shrimp over mesquite charcoal and then produced corn on the cob and potato salad to go with it.

She looked at him wryly over her heaping plate. "This isn't how I remember camping."

He shrugged. "My tastes have matured."

They lingered over their al fresco meal. Hattie was relaxed and yet keenly aware of the tension humming between them. Luc offered fresh chocolate-dipped strawberries for dessert. She bit into one carefully, licking the sweet juice from her lower lip.

He watched her constantly until she swatted his arm. "Stop it."

His wide, rakish grin was all innocence. "I don't know what you mean."

Moments later, the teenager showed up to do KP. He would

be leaving soon when his father went off duty. There was no official presence at the fort overnight.

Luc suggested a boat ride. The sun was beginning its slow decline. Hattie prepared her camera. Luc steered the boat to a perfect vantage point to get shots of the fort washed in the beautiful evening light.

Afterward they anchored in deep water and dropped the ladder over the side. Hattie climbed over the rail, but Luc made a neat dive off the rear of the boat.

They swam and played for a long time, until the light began to fade. Back on the boat, they dried off and Hattie put on a T-shirt over her suit. As they picked up speed, the stiff breeze raised goose bumps on her arms and legs.

While they were tying up once again at the boat dock, the young father from the family across the way approached them.

He shook Luc's hand and smiled ruefully. "Our youngest son has developed an earache, and we know from past experience that we'll need medicine, so we're going back to Key West. We wanted to tell someone, because the park service occasionally does a head count out here."

Luc grimaced. "That's too bad. It's going to be a beautiful night. But I'll help you load up."

Hattie walked back to the tent and stretched out on a sleeping bag. Daylight was fading fast. It was a half hour before Luc returned. Out the tent flap she could see the family pull away from the dock. The other boats she had watched offshore earlier in the day had long since lifted anchor and sailed or motored away.

For the first time since their arrival, she and Luc were completely, irrevocably alone.

He crouched and held out a hand. "Let's take a walk."

While she stretched her arms over her head and then donned a windbreaker, Luc retrieved a flashlight from his pack and zipped up the tent. They approached the fort and skirted the edge until they could step onto the sea wall. For most of the perimeter of the fort, the barrier separated the moat from the sea.

Hattie didn't need Luc's warning to watch her step. Although the wall wasn't particularly narrow, the thought of falling into the mysterious ocean was daunting.

On the far side of the fort they sat down, cross-legged, and surveyed the vast expanse of sky and sea. A tiny sliver of new moon did little to illuminate the night. As their eyes became accustomed to the dark, they could just make out the faint line of demarcation separating the silvery pewter of the ocean from the midnight-blue of the sky. Several miles away, a working lighthouse flashed a periodic caution to boats, warning of the reefs and small rocky islands.

They sat in silence for several minutes. Hattie finally whispered, "It's like we're the only two people in the entire world. I'm not sure I like the feeling."

He took her hand and squeezed it. "Do you want to go back?"

"No." She leaned her head on his shoulder. "It's beautiful and awe-inspiring, and a little frightening to be honest, but I wouldn't have missed this for anything. Can you imagine what it must be like here during a hurricane?"

Luc chuckled. "I don't even want to think about it."

They sat hand in hand for a long time, wrapped in a cocoon of darkness and the intimacy of complete isolation. Far out across the waves, traces of phosphorescence lent a ghostly aura to the night.

Eventually, by unspoken consent, they made their way back around to the campsite. After a quick visit to the Spartan toilet facilities near the dock, they met back at the tent and stood facing each other.

Luc lifted a hand and traced her chin with his thumb. "It's

not too late to change your mind. We have a perfectly good king-size bed back at the hotel. I can wait if you'd rather."

She took a step closer, leaning into his chest. "I want you, Luc…tonight."

Fifteen

She felt his chest lift and fall as a shuddering breath escaped his lungs. He wrapped his arms around her. "Do you need a few minutes in the tent to get ready?"

"Yes," she muttered, her throat tight with nervousness. He handed her the small flashlight. She unzipped the tent and knelt to climb in, carefully removing her shoes and leaving them in a corner so no sand would find its way into their comfy sleeping space.

Luc had spread thick, soft sleeping bags on top of a single, large, cushiony air mattress. Since it was too hot to sleep inside the bags, he had also procured crisp cotton sheets complete with small pillows tucked inside lace-edged cases. The resulting effect was one part *Out of Africa* and two parts *Pretty Woman,* a stage unmistakably set for seduction.

Earlier, Hattie had regarded the tent as pleasantly roomy. Now, with Luc standing somewhere outside, it felt surprisingly claustrophobic, especially when she imagined Luc's large frame dominating the enclosed space.

She picked up her overnight case and found her toiletry

bag. After quickly cleaning her face, she stripped off her clothes, thankful that the evening swim had left her skin feeling cool, if a bit salty. Luc had thought to bring a small container of fresh water, so she dampened a cloth and used it to further freshen up.

At Luc's murmured request, she passed the water container and a clean towel out to him. While he was presumably taking care of his ablutions, she found a tube of scented lotion and applied it to her elbows and legs and one or two other interesting spots.

She pulled out the lilac gown and slipped it over her head, relishing the feel of the silk against her bare skin. When she was done, she tucked the flashlight under Luc's pillow, leaving only the smallest beam of light to illuminate the tent.

Taking a deep breath and smoothing her hair, she called out. "I'm ready."

The tent flap peeled back instantly, and she saw him place his shoes and the water canister inside at the foot of the tent before he crawled in, immediately dwarfing the tiny space. He had already undressed.

Hattie's heart stopped for a split second, and then lurched back into service with an unsteady beat. Even her ploy with the flashlight didn't disguise his impressive attributes. She put a hand against her breastbone, feeling a bit like a Regency virgin in need of smelling salts.

Luc zipped the tent flap shut, tossed a few foil packets beside his pillow, and then stretched out with a sigh onto the comfortable bedding. He lay on his side facing her, leaning on his elbow with one leg propped up, looking like a centerfold.

Only, he was real. Here. In the flesh.

Hattie remained seated, her spine stiff as a poker, her legs paralyzed in a pretzel position. He patted the space beside him, and she saw him smile. "You're too far away," he complained.

She uncurled her legs and scooted closer, still leaving a healthy distance between them.

He reached out and smoothed a hand over her thigh covered in lilac silk. "I'm betting you didn't order this little number from L.L. Bean," he said, the words laced with amusement.

Suddenly, he reached behind him and picked up the flashlight, momentarily blinding her when he pointed it in her direction. He focused the tiny beam of light on her left shoulder.

His voice came out of the darkness. "Ditch the gown, Hattie, starting with that strap."

She couldn't see his face, only the outline of his body. Her fingers went to the slim strap he'd indicated, and she lowered it, slipping her arm free, but keeping her breast covered.

The beam of light moved to her other shoulder. "Now that one."

The second strap fell. She put a hand against her chest to hold the gown in place.

The light slipped down to her abdomen. He spoke again, his tone hoarse and rough. "Now all of it."

She rose to her knees, trembling, and let the fabric fall to her hips, and then, with a little shimmy, to the sleeping bag. Luc's indrawn breath was audible. The beam of light rose slowly to circle one breast and then the other. Her nipples tightened painfully. The light slid over the taut plane of her stomach to rest in the shadowed valley between her thighs.

His voice this time was barely a whisper. "Hand me the gown."

She lifted her knees, an awkward maneuver given the situation, and pulled the silk free, tossing it to him.

He buried his face in the cloth momentarily. Then the light went out. He called her name. "Hattie…come here."

She tumbled forward, her eagerness assisted by his firm grasp on her forearm. She landed half-sprawled across his chest, and one of her hands lodged in an interesting position between his legs. She found the hot, smooth length of him and stroked gently.

Luc groaned, covering her lips with his, the kiss ravenous and demanding. His tongue plundered the recesses of her mouth, exploring every crevice, nibbling and biting until she was breathless and whimpering with need.

Seconds later she sensed him trying to slow things down, but it was too late. While he fumbled for a condom, she rubbed her breasts against his chest, savoring the delicious friction. She felt his hands settle on her bottom. He lifted her until she sat astride him, and she tensed.

On and off during the last decade she had dreamed about being with him. But those fleeting fantasies didn't come close to approximating the reality of Luc Cavallo, naked, nudging with barely concealed impatience at the heart of her feminine passage.

She arched her back and felt him enter her, stretching her to an almost painful fullness. "Oh, Luc…" The sensation was incredible.

He froze, not moving an inch, his body taut and trembling. "Am I hurting you?"

She choked out a laugh, wriggling, forcing him centimeters deeper. "No." It was all she could manage. She raked his nipples with her fingernails. He heaved beneath her, burying himself to the hilt. The connection was stunning—her, adjusting to the sensation of his possession, him, clearly struggling for control.

He lifted his hands to cup her sensitive breasts. She cried out, nearing a peak so intense, she could feel it hovering just out of reach. He withdrew almost completely, but before she could voice a protest, he thrust even deeper, initiating a rhythm that sent them both tumbling into a fiery release. Somewhere in the fringes of her consciousness, she heard him shout as he emptied himself into her body, but her orgasm washed over her with such power, she was unable to focus on anything but her own pleasure.

Luc lay perfectly still, trying to recover from the effects of Hurricane Hattie. Her slender body lay draped over his in sensual abandon that filled him with a fierce masculine satisfaction overlaid by the terrifying realization that he had fallen in love with her…again. Far away from the familiar trappings of his daily life, it was all so clear. He didn't need *things* to be happy…not money or electronic toys or even the adrenaline-producing challenge of his job.

His arms tightened around her. A time machine couldn't have taken him back any more successfully than this sham marriage and this ill-conceived honeymoon. Hattie filled his life with an exhilaration he had experienced only once before. She brought *fun* into his days, joy into his home, passion into his bed.

But nothing had changed. He was still rich, and she was still wary about ceding power and control to a man like him.

The baby was the fragile glue holding this house of cards together. Unless he could convince Hattie that great sex covered a multitude of sins, it was only a matter of time until she left him.

He sighed as he felt her tongue trace his collarbone. The slightly rough caress sent trickles of heat down his torso straight to his groin. He smoothed his fingers over her bottom, guiltily aware that he might have bruised her pale skin.

She leaned on her elbow and kissed him briefly. "I think I've developed a whole new appreciation for roughing it…if I can say that with a straight face while lying on 800 thread count sheets."

He chuckled. "I never knew you liked it rough."

She punched his arm. "You're so bad. But I like that about you…" Her head found its way to his shoulder.

As her voice trailed off, he shifted her to one side. Not that he didn't enjoy having her body glued to his like wallpaper, but her proximity made it difficult to form a coherent thought. He hoped that if he handled this interlude correctly, he might be able to bind Hattie to him in such a way that she couldn't escape.

Women, unlike most men, had a hard time separating sex from emotional ties. All he had to do was convince Hattie that the compatibility they experienced in bed could carry over to life in general. That the incredible sex was only a sign of their overall rightness for each other…that they had more in common than she realized.

When Hattie slipped a hand across his thigh, he lost all interest in thinking. Her curious fingers found his partially erect shaft and began exploring. He shuddered, giving himself up to the heady pleasure of having Hattie map his body with an eagerness that was as flattering as it was arousing.

Her questing hands feathered over him like butterfly wings, brushing, touching. He clenched his teeth against a surge of lust as she found a particularly sensitive spot. "Hattie…"

She nipped his hipbone with her teeth. "Hmmm?"

His hands tangled in her hair, and he pulled her up for a hard kiss. This time, it was her tongue that demanded entrance, taunting his mouth with sweet little licks and strokes that made him groan with hunger.

Almost…almost he lifted her astride him as he had earlier, craving the sensation of filling her with one swift thrust. But at the last second, he broke the kiss and pushed her to her back, determined this time to give her the tenderness and attention she deserved.

She reached for him, but he eluded her, sliding down

the length of her body to concentrate on the source of her pleasure. His hands glided over her skin, skin softer than any silk nightgown. He traced her navel and abdomen with his tongue. She twisted restlessly.

Gripping her hips and holding her down, he bent his head lower, ignoring her incoherent protests. She stiffened at the first touch of his lips, her back arching off the sleeping bag. A panting cry escaped her. He licked gently, and seconds later she shattered in a moaning climax.

He scooped her into his arms, holding her tightly as the last tremors racked her body. She was his. He was familiar with sexual satisfaction, but this need to claim, to possess, was something he had experienced only one other time in his life.

When she stirred in his embrace, he stroked the hair from her face with an unsteady hand. He kissed her softly, tenderly, trying to tell her with his touch what he knew she wasn't ready to hear in words.

The kiss lengthened. Deepened. His own unappeased arousal clawed to the surface, reminding him that making Hattie fly moments ago was only a prelude. He rose over her, trapping both her hands in one of his and raising them above her head. His maneuver lifted her breasts in silent invitation. With his free hand, he caressed them, stroking the petal-soft curves, avoiding her nipples, deliberately building her need once again.

When her pleading whispers and writhing hips told him she was ready for his possession, he abandoned her breasts and slid his hand between her legs, testing her heat and dampness with one finger.

She turned her head and bit the tender flesh of his inner arm, silently demanding. He released her hands, scarcely noticing when they grasped his shoulders. His need had become a roaring torrent, a driving urgency toward completion. Damning the necessity, he sheathed his rock-hard erection in a condom.

With one knee, he spread her legs and settled between her thighs, positioning himself. He looked down at her, inwardly cursing the darkness, needing desperately to see her face. "Tell me you want me, Hattie," he said huskily. "Beg me."

She spread her legs even wider, seeking to join their bodies, but he held back, driven by some Neanderthal impulse. "Say it, Hattie."

Her voice, a rasping, air-starved whisper reached his ear. "Please Luc. Take me…please."

He surged forward, shuddering as her body gripped him. She was tight and hot, and her long, slender legs wrapped around his waist. He knew in an instant that once more there would be no slow, sweet loving. He drove into her again and again until the tide swept over him, pulled him under, erasing every thought but one. Hattie was his.

He tried to hold back, to prolong the exquisite sensations for a few moments more, but it was hopeless. With a hoarse shout, he came inside her for long, agonizing seconds, conscious of nothing but searing pleasure and blinding release.

In the aftermath, they clung together, breathing fractured, skin damp, hearts pounding in unison. With his last ounce of energy, he reached for the top sheet, pulled it over them. Hattie's limp body curled spoon fashion against his, her bare bottom pressed to the cradle of his thighs.

Luc surrendered to the oblivion of sleep.

Sixteen

Hattie slipped from Luc's arms and donned a long T-shirt and panties before quietly exiting the tent. Her body was stiff and sore in some interesting places, and she felt at once exhausted and exhilarated.

After a necessary trip to the bathroom, she stood in the eerie gray light of predawn, her arms clasped around her middle. Just a few hundred feet offshore, a tiny strip of land, hardly big enough to merit the designation *island,* was covered with a teeming mass of flapping, squawking birds.

Their raucous calls and noisy confusion mirrored the turmoil in her heart. What in the heck was she going to do? There was no longer any doubt about her feelings for Luc. Having sex with him last night in such an erotic and abandoned way had been at once the most perfect and the most stupid thing she had ever done in her life.

She might one day find another man as intelligent as Luc. As kind, as handsome, as funny…perhaps. But there was no doubt in her mind that the lovemaking they had shared was unique. He'd been a good lover in college, no question. But this time around, the sex was even better. She hadn't expected the intensity, the shattering intimacy, the feeling that she had bound herself to him body and soul.

He was also better at reading her. Some internal radar seemed to pick up her moods, to see inside her head and know what she was thinking. Which made him very dangerous to her peace of mind.

And his empathy was a huge problem given that this relationship was temporary and supposedly pragmatic. She didn't want to feel so connected to him. What a mess. As much as she longed to enjoy this surprising honeymoon all the way to its conclusion, another smarter Hattie said, *Go home.*

She looked over her shoulder at the small blue tent, its outline shrouded in the misty morning fog. In a short while, the cozy housing would be dismantled, much like her short-lived marriage. The campsite would be cleared, leaving no trace of the spot where Hattie Parker had given her heart to Luc Cavallo.

But hearts healed, didn't they? And life went on. She would go back to her job perhaps, settle into a new place, learn to play the role of single mom. And perhaps this ending wouldn't be as painful as the one ten years ago. Maybe Deedee's chortling smiles would be a distraction.

Hattie and Luc might remain friends…or, if not, she'd have memories…. And if she was lucky, someday a lover who didn't know that he was second best.

Luc knew the instant Hattie stirred from his embrace and left the tent. Even in his sleep he'd been aware of her warmth and softness twined in his arms, their legs tangled, her head tucked beneath his chin. Twice more during the night they had come together in exquisite lovemaking, the first a slow gentle mating, the second a hard, fast, almost desperate race to the finish.

But Hattie's recent stealthy departure said louder than words that she needed some time alone. That she hadn't wanted to face him. He understood her motivation. He just didn't like it.

The warm pillows still retained a remnant of her fragrance. He climbed out and put on his shorts. As he ran a hand over the stubble on his chin, he grimaced. Perhaps spending the night on a deserted island wasn't the greatest way to win over a woman. But Hattie had been a good sport about it all, and something about the isolation had deepened the intimacy of their lovemaking.

He exited the tent and walked over to where she stood looking out to sea. Looping his arms around her waist from behind, he rested his chin on the top of her head. "Good morning."

She turned slightly, enough for him to see that she was smiling. "Good morning, Luc."

He squeezed her gently. "You ready for some breakfast?"

She nodded. "At the risk of sounding unladylike, I could eat the proverbial horse."

They fixed the meal together, Hattie cutting up fresh fruit while he toasted bread on the grill. He had hoped to make love to her once more before they left, but it wasn't going to happen. Hattie had retreated to some distant place, and the invisible line in the sand was one he couldn't cross.

By ten o'clock everything was packed up and loaded in the boat. He suggested climbing the lighthouse, but Hattie shook her head, saying she was tired and ready to go back. He wanted to tease her about her fatigue. Lord knew neither of them had gotten much sleep, but his courage failed him. He had just experienced one of the most incredible nights of his life, but the lady involved was treating him like a favorite brother.

It was hell on a man's self-esteem.

They made the return trip to Key West mostly in silence. Hattie sat in the back of the boat on a bench seat wearing her baseball cap pulled low over her eyes and with her arms curled around her knees. Clouds had rolled in during the morning, making the sky sullen and angry. He had to keep both hands on the wheel to handle the choppy waves.

Docking, unloading and getting back to the hotel were interminable chores. He was determined to have his say, strangely afraid that if he didn't mend some unknown rift, she would slip away from him altogether.

Hattie unlocked the door to their room. He followed her in. She dumped her things on the sofa and turned to face him, a forced smile on her lips. "Thanks for taking me to the fort. It was wonderful."

His jaw clenched. "And what about us? Were we wonderful, too?"

He watched as shock followed by what could only be described as a flash of pain crossed her face.

As she took off her cap and ran her hands through her hair, she glanced at him. "What do *you* think?"

He jammed his hands in his pockets to keep from reaching for her. "I think we were pretty damn fabulous.... Wouldn't you agree?"

A rosy flush climbed from her throat to her cheeks. She nodded slowly. "We never had trouble in that department."

He laughed softly. "Hell, no." He sensed a softening in her, so he pressed his advantage. "Imagine what we could do in that big bed with wine and clean sheets and candles."

Her blush deepened. He stepped toward her, smiling inwardly as she backed up until her legs hit the sofa and she fell backward. He leaned over her, bracing his hands on the back of the couch, bracketing her with his arms. "Kiss me, Hattie."

Her dark eyes looking up at him were filled with secrets. "Do you really think we'll stop with a kiss?"

He bent to nuzzle her neck. "Does it matter?"

"We're both pretty grungy." She twisted her lips. "I could use a shower."

He nibbled the skin behind her ear, coming down beside her and scooping her into his lap. "I hadn't noticed."

She sighed as he kissed his way around to her collarbone, pushing aside the neckline of her T-shirt to gain easier access. He slid a hand beneath the hem and stroked her breast through her bra, lightly pinching the nipple. She groaned. "Luc…"

The flush on her cheeks deepened when he slipped a hand inside her shorts, finding the soft fluff between her legs. She arched into his caress, her breathing ragged.

He'd been teasing earlier. He had every intention of giving her a quick kiss and then getting some business done while she was in the shower. But Hattie was smarter than he was. Clearly a kiss wasn't enough.

He ripped at the zipper on her shorts, jerking it down and removing those and her panties in one quick maneuver. Seconds later, he had her beneath him as he settled between her legs. Hearing her chant his name in soft whispers went straight to his gut. Somewhere deep in the recesses of his brain he realized this was dangerous. This mindless, desperate urge to take her. But he couldn't stop. Didn't want to.

He entered her a bare inch and hesitated, his body racked with tremors. Her eyes fluttered shut. He touched her cheek. "Look at me, Hattie."

She complied, her eyes cloudy and unfocused. He went an inch deeper, and they groaned in unison. She panted, her chest rising and falling rapidly, but she held his gaze.

Struggling for almost nonexistent control, he stroked her cheekbone. "We have to deal with this."

Her head moved slowly in a gesture that could have been agreement or denial. "You talk too much." She grabbed a handful of his hair, pulling his head down for a kiss. "Just get on with it."

The breathless demand snapped his feeble efforts to maintain any kind of sanity. If she wanted it, he'd give it to her. No questions asked. He drove deeper into the hot, tight warmth of her, wanting desperately to make it last longer, but realizing with a sort of incredulous despair that he was losing the battle.

He gritted his teeth, holding back the scalding rush of pleasure. But Hattie's sudden cry and his own body defeated him. He surged harder, blindly emptying himself until he felt blackness close in around him.

A long time later he rolled off of her and flopped onto his back on the plush carpet, staring at the ceiling fan rotating overhead. He felt Hattie's fingers twine with his, and heard her voice, filled with unmistakable amusement. "Now I *really* need a shower."

He laughed, stung by chagrin at his emotionally reckless behavior but filled with a deep, boneless contentment. He glanced at his watch and swore. "I have to make two quick calls. But I won't be long, I promise."

She leaned over to kiss him. "It's okay, Luc. Really."

"And was it okay that I took you like a wild man?"

"You *were* pretty intense."

Remorse rode him for not even fully undressing her. "What can I say? You're a temptress."

She looked down at her rumpled clothes and rolled her eyes. "Oh, yeah…that's it."

He stood up, and she followed suit as they each adjusted

their clothing. Though he wanted nothing more than to drag her into the bedroom, he resisted the urge. Unless he knew for sure that Hattie was falling for him, he'd be well-advised to rein in his sexual enthusiasm.

But he couldn't resist the urge to woo her. "Why don't we go somewhere fancy for dinner? We can talk about your situation, maybe dance a little…"

Her expression was difficult to read. "That would be nice."

"And we can relax by the pool this afternoon. I'll get Marcel to serve us lunch out there."

"Sure."

He watched her turn toward the bedroom. "I could join you in the shower," he said, consigning his phone calls to the devil.

Hattie shook her head. "Do what you have to do. We've got plenty of time."

Luc let her go for the moment. She was his, body and soul. Perhaps she didn't know it yet, but he would fight dirty if he had to. He wouldn't lose her.… Not again.

Hattie stepped under the strong, stinging spray of the shower and luxuriated in the hot, steamy flow of water. It was amazing what twenty-four hours of deprivation could accomplish. She would never have made it on that TV survivor show. Never mind eating bugs; she would have begged to be voted off after the second day just so she could be clean again.

She dried off with one of the inn's sinfully thick towels. A nap sounded appealing, but she wasn't prepared to give up a day of sunbathing. Donning a robe, she returned to the bedroom and rummaged in her suitcase for the only swimsuit she had not yet worn. It wasn't at all skimpy by today's standards, but the shiny gold fabric clung to her body like a second skin. When Luc appeared in the doorway, his jaw actually dropped. "Tell me you're not wearing that thing outside our room."

She grinned, and then summoned a pout. "I thought you would love it."

He strode toward her. "Love it, hell. When a suit looks like that on a woman, the designer's only motivation is to drive men insane." He skimmed his hands over her body. "Good Lord. It feels like you're naked." He smoothed her bottom. "Are you sure you want to go to the pool? It's nice and quiet and cool up here in our room."

Though the coaxing note in his voice made her knees weak, Hattie held him at arm's length. "I want to go home with at least a semblance of a tan. So I refuse to be distracted by your masculine charms."

He lifted an eyebrow. "You think I'm charming?"

"I think I've made that pretty obvious this week."

He laughed, and for a brief second, she wondered if he felt anything more for her than lust. His actions seemed to indicate affection, but nothing he had said in any context contradicted his earlier plan to make their marriage temporary.

She wanted so badly to say the words swelling in her heart, but she chickened out. It was still too soon.

When Luc's cell phone rang she headed for the door. "You get that if you want to. I'll be out at the pool."

The concern in his words when he spoke with the caller stopped Hattie dead in her tracks.

The conversation was brief. Luc hung up, his expression serious.

Her skin chilled. "What's wrong?"

"The baby's running a temperature."

Hattie sank onto the sofa. "How bad?"

"A hundred and three. It's probably just a virus. They're on the way to a pediatrician right now. Ana wasn't unduly concerned, but she was sure you'd want to know."

"I do. Of course."

Luc eyed her. "What are you thinking?"

She winced, feeling ungrateful for all he had done. "Do you mind if we go home? I need to be with her…to make sure she's okay."

He nodded. "I thought as much. Start packing, and I'll see what kind of flights I can find."

Seventeen

It was almost midnight when they made it back to Atlanta and drove from the airport to the house. Leo was on hand to pick them up since they didn't have a car. He and Luc sat in the front. Hattie in the back.

Leo looked over his shoulder. "How was Key West?"

"Very nice," she replied, refusing to be baited.

The two brothers chuckled in unison. Hattie pretended a sudden interest in the passing scenery.

Leo helped unload the luggage into the foyer, shook Luc's hand and kissed Hattie on the cheek. "Let me know how Deedee is. I'll be at the office in the morning."

As he drove off, Hattie yawned. Ana met them in the hallway, not waiting to be asked for an update. "She's sleeping. The doctor says it's a bad ear infection. She may need surgery to have tubes put in."

Tears sprang to Hattie's eyes, a reaction to fatigue and the thought of having her small baby put to sleep.

Luc put his arm around her. "We'll deal with that when the

time comes. Thank you, Ana. Hattie and I will take it from here. You go get some rest."

"If you're sure. I wrote down her medication schedule on the nightstand in her room and the two bottles are there, too." In the nursery, Hattie approached the crib on tiptoe. But Deedee was sleeping peacefully, her bottom in the air as she crouched in a ball on the mattress.

Luc touched Hattie's arm. "I'll bring our bags up. Why don't you get ready for bed?"

Hattie couldn't resist stroking the baby's back. "She still feels so hot."

"The antibiotic will take a while to kick in. We can set the alarm and give her ibuprofen during the night. Go on," he urged. "You're weaving on your feet."

"Okay." Hattie took a quick shower and changed into a nightgown that was pretty but not overtly sexy. Now that they were home, her thoughts were in turmoil. She hated that she felt like an insecure teenager again, wondering if a boy liked her. Everything had seemed so simple, so natural out on the island.

But now…back on Luc's home turf, all her earlier reservations returned. Would Luc expect to share her room? Was she supposed to go to his?

The nursery was adjacent to Hattie's suite. Ana and Sherman had slept in a nearby guest room while Luc and Hattie were gone.

When Hattie returned to the baby's room, her steps faltered. She hung back in the hall, her heart wrenching painfully. In the room decorated with nursery rhyme murals, a night-light cast a soft, pink glow. Sitting in the maple rocker, his head leaned back, eyes half-closed, was Luc. And in his arms lay a sleeping baby.

Deedee was nestled against Luc's chest, one tiny hand clutching a fold of his shirt. The contrast between the big strong male and the tiny helpless baby twisted something deep in Hattie's chest. This was what Leo had feared. That Luc would fall in love with Deedee.

Luc himself had alluded to the fact that he understood the bond between parent and child. Clearly Hattie's niece had wormed her way into his heart. Seeing the two people Hattie loved most in the world…seeing them like this made her realize that she had backed herself into a difficult, if not impossible, corner.

Luc didn't believe in romantic love anymore. And Hattie alone was responsible for his cynicism. But if he loved Deedee, how could she take the baby away when the time came? How could she break Luc's heart a second time?

In the dimly lit room, Luc crooned a soft lullaby, his pleasing baritone singing of diamond rings and mockingbirds. The tender way he held the baby was poignant.

Hattie made herself step into the room. "I'll take her now so you can get cleaned up."

Luc's eyes, sleepy lidded, surveyed his wife. "Are you coming to my room to sleep?"

Wow. Trust Luc to cut straight to the chase. She steadied herself with a hand on the dresser. His meaning was crystal clear. But she had no clue how to respond. "Well, uh…"

His expression went blank, no trace of anything revealed on his classically sculpted features. "Don't sweat it, Hattie. We're both tired. But I'll be more than happy to help with the baby during the night if you need a hand."

Before Hattie could come up with words to explain the confusion in her heart, Luc gently placed Deedee in the crib, brushed by Hattie, and was gone.

Hattie rubbed her eyes with the heels of her hands, inhaling deeply. *Damn it*. Had she hurt his feelings? His male pride? She hadn't intended to say no to sleeping with him, but his artless question caught her off guard. This was uncharted territory.

They could no longer use a pretend honeymoon as an excuse to indulge in passionate sex. They were once again smack-dab in the throes of reality. Luc had married Hattie because she asked him to help protect an innocent baby. And perhaps because he could make Hattie dance to his tune and prove that she meant nothing to him. Did he also expect their physical intimacy to continue?

The baby was sleeping peacefully. Hattie made sure the volume on the monitor was adjusted and slipped out of the room, pulling the door shut as she left. Her big bed, which had seemed so luxurious and comfortable last week, was now a torture device. She tossed and turned, flipping the covers back in an effort to get cool.

She missed Luc, missed his big strong body snuggling with hers. What did he want from her? He'd seemed completely calm during their earlier conversation…not that it was much of a conversation. He'd taken her momentary confusion as a "no," and Hattie hadn't meant that at all, at least not completely.

Her befuddled brain had been scrambling to process all the pros and cons of maintaining a sexual relationship now that they were home. Ana and Sherman would know…and Leo, probably. Something like that was difficult to keep a secret.

So when the situation with Eddie was resolved and Hattie had to go, what then?

The next morning, Deedee was noticeably improved. Luc played with her for a half hour before announcing he was going to the office.

Hattie handed the baby off to Ana and frowned as she followed Luc down to the foyer. "You're still supposed to be on your honeymoon. They won't be expecting you…"

He shrugged into an immaculately tailored navy suit jacket, his expression impassive. "I'm back. Work will have piled up. I might as well get a jump start on things."

Hattie couldn't think of a thing to say to stop him from walking out the door.

As she stood at the window watching her husband's car move down the driveway, her cell phone rang. After ascertaining that it was an unknown number, she answered. "Hello."

"Mrs. Cavallo?"

"Yes."

"This is Harvey Sharpton. I work for your husband, and I have good news."

Hattie's chest tightened. "What is it? Tell me, please."

"Little Deedee's father has screwed up royally this time. Another DUI. A hit-and-run again, this time involving pedestrians. Fortunately, no one was fatally injured, but the judge threw the book at him. And when we came forward with the nurse's testimony, the one who heard Angela's request, the judge granted you sole custody."

Hattie could barely speak. "Thank you so much," she croaked.

"There are some papers you need to sign."

"I'll call you and make an appointment soon. I appreciate your calling me."

She sank down on the bottom step of the grand, sweeping staircase and put her face in her hands. The relief was overwhelming. She wanted to tell Luc immediately...needed to share her joy with the one person who would understand more than anyone else. But he was gone.

All day she rehearsed what she would say. Forty-eight hours ago, it would have been much easier. The Luc she had made love to on her honeymoon was far more approachable than the stern businessman he had reverted to upon their return.

When he didn't make it home in time for dinner, her stomach sank. Maybe she was foolishly naive. Building castles in the air instead of planning for a future without Luc.

Finally, at eleven o'clock, she went to bed and fell into a fitful sleep. Something awoke her in the wee hours—a muffled thud, perhaps a door closing. She glanced at the clock on the bedside table. It was already time to give the baby a dose of medicine. Without bothering to put on a robe, she stole down the hall in her bare feet and opened the nursery door. For the second time, she found Luc with Deedee in his arms. He was standing beside the bed, the infant on his shoulder, patting her softly on the back.

Luc was wearing nothing but thin cotton boxers. Despite the hour and her fatigue, Hattie's body responded. It was conditioned now to expect searing pleasure, and Luc's scent, his masculine beauty, triggered all sorts of dancing hormones.

He turned to face her, speaking softly. "I've already given her the medicine. I thought you were asleep."

She shrugged. "I had a lot on my mind."

Ignoring Hattie's conversational gambit, Luc kissed Deedee's head before laying her back in the bed. He yawned and stretched, the corded muscles in his arms and chest flexing and rippling. "I checked her temp. It's almost normal. You don't need to worry."

Deedee wasn't Hattie's greatest concern at the moment. Instead, it was the way Luc was acting...aloof, unconcerned— about Hattie, that is. She took a step closer to him. "I never meant to imply that I wasn't going to sleep with you. You caught me by surprise, that's all. Do you want me to come with you now? I'm glad you're home."

He stilled, his dark eyes opaque, impossible to read. His shrug spoke volumes. "The baby needs you."

And I don't.

The unspoken words hovered between them. They might as well have been an aerial banner tugged through the sky by a plane.

Hattie didn't know what to say. It seemed as if he was trying purposefully to hurt her. And he was succeeding.

But she had learned a lot about him in the last week. Deep inside the coldly confident, unemotional man was a younger Luc. One who had been hurt repeatedly. One who had learned to shield his softer side. One who built walls. She took a courageous step in his direction. "The reason I wasn't able to sleep is because you weren't beside me."

Luc teetered on the edge of his own personal hell. Hattie was offering herself to him, coming to him of her own free will.

He was almost positive she was falling in love with him. Women couldn't hide things like that. Hattie didn't sleep around. And even though he was her husband, she wouldn't have shared his bed just for sex.

So why was he hesitating?

The dark knot of remembered pain inside him said, *Do it. Tell her to go to hell. Tell her you don't need a wife who's been bought and paid for. Tell her you don't want her.*

Would she see through the lie?

Could he instead reach for the rosy future that seemed almost within his grasp? A wife, a baby, a happily-ever-after?

People he loved left him. His parents. Hattie. If he brought her and the baby into his heart and home and then lost them, he wasn't sure he'd survive.

He clenched his fists, fighting the urge to grab her and pull her close. Instead, he shrugged. "We should probably reevaluate our relationship. See where things stand with the custody situation. I have a hell of a lot to catch up on at work…and you'll be spending time with the baby."

Hattie's face went white, her expression agonized. "So you were just using me in Key West because I was convenient?"

"Don't cast me as the villain in this drama," he said roughly. Sexual desire and searing regret choked him. "If anything, we used each other. You were wet and willing."

"You're a selfish ass," she said, tears choking her voice and welling in her beautiful eyes.

"I gave you what you wanted. You and the baby are safe. Don't ask for the moon, Hattie."

Eighteen

Don't ask for the moon, Hattie. The careless words jangled in her head. She barely slept at all, and when dawn broke, she knew what she had to do. It would have to be a covert operation. Ana and Sherman couldn't be caught in the middle.

Breakfast was miserable. Despite Deedee's chortling happiness, Luc and Hattie barely spoke, concentrating on brief exchanges of information that left her grieving and heartsick.

By ten o'clock the house was empty. Ana and Sherman had gone to the market. Patti was back at school. Luc was at the office. As soon as Deedee went down for her morning nap, Hattie started packing. She walked the hallways back and forth, barely able to concentrate, her skin cold as ice. The pain was crushing. When the suitcases were in the car, she fled. Out the door, down the steps, the baby clasped to her chest.

Luc had sent Hattie's clunker car into the shop for an overhaul. The stylish new minivan that she was still learning to drive was backed into the garage. She snapped Deedee into the car seat, hands shaking, jumped into the driver's seat, put the car in gear and tore out of the driveway.

She drove on autopilot, her heart bleeding. Luc would never love her again. She had killed those feelings in him. He wanted her body, but with his iron control, he was clearly able to deny them even that.

If she stayed in his house an hour more, she might be reduced to begging. And Luc didn't deserve that. He had helped her when she needed it most, but that reason no longer existed. She and Deedee were on their own.

The miles flashed by as she cruised the interstate. Where would she go? What was the next step? She had credit cards galore, but what if Luc disabled them in order to force her home?

Hastily, she did a mental accounting of the cash in her purse…maybe four hundred dollars at the most. That wouldn't last long. But she had to go someplace where no one could find her. At least until she figured out what she was going to do.

Luc leaned back in his office chair and rubbed his neck. He had a killer headache. Thank God Leo was coming over for dinner tonight. His company would be a welcome diversion from the stilted, overly polite conversation to which he and Hattie had been reduced.

For the first time since the honeymoon, Luc arrived home at five-thirty. Leo was not far behind him.

Luc's brother wore a rumpled suit and offered a rueful apology. "Sorry for arriving unfashionably early. But I had a meeting in this part of town, and it didn't seem worth driving back to the office at rush hour."

Luc led him into the library and poured them each a finger of whiskey. "No worries. Deedee is starting to pull up on things, so Ana says she thinks Hattie and the baby went shoe shopping. They're not even back yet. We've got time to relax before dinner."

Leo settled his large frame into a spacious easy chair. After downing his drink in one gulp, he sighed, closed his eyes and spoke. "How are the two of you getting along?"

"No problems." Luc paced restlessly.

"Do you love her?"

"Who are you? Dr. Ruth? I'm not sure what love is."

"Then why did you marry her? Our lawyers have the ability to make mincemeat out of old Eddie. Tying the knot was totally unnecessary. So why did you do it?"

Luc had asked himself that same question a hundred times. The answer was clear, but it was too soon to tell his brother. Leo's propensity for mischief shouldn't be underestimated.

"It was the right thing to do. Protecting the baby."

"I'll give you that. You always did love playing the hero. But there's got to be more."

Sherman appeared in the door. "Excuse me, Mr. Luc. Ana found this note with your name on it. It was on the desk in the kitchen."

Luc ripped open the envelope and stared at the words without comprehension.

Leo came to stand beside him. "What is it? What's wrong?"

Luc had never been as scared as he was at this moment. "She's gone. She has custody, and she's gone."

His brother snatched the piece of paper and scanned it rapidly, cursing beneath his breath. "We'll find her. She can't have gone far."

But they didn't. One day passed. Then two. Then three. Hattie's cell phone was turned off, so the GPS locator was useless. None of her credit cards showed any sign of activity. It was as if she and Deedee had vanished off the face of the earth.

Luc was surviving on black coffee and three hours of sleep a night. His frustration with the police was enormous, but even he had to admit that there was no indication of foul play.

Hattie had left of her own free will. And she had taken his heart with her, dragging it in the wake of the speeding car, shredding it as the miles passed.

Leo was a rock. He moved in, and between the two of them, they hired the best detectives their considerable fortune could buy. But the P.I. reports were little comfort. When a person wanted to disappear, it could take weeks, months to track them down.

Luc lay in bed, night after night, dry-eyed, his body ice-cold. Pride. Injured pride had caused this debacle. All he'd had to do was tell Hattie he loved her more than life. Assure her that he had no plans to ever be parted from her or from Deedee.

If the lawyer had managed to give the news to Luc first instead of Hattie, Luc could have been prepared. But Luc had been too damn busy to listen to his voice mails.

On the fourth day, he caught a break. In her haste, Hattie had left behind the baby's antibiotic. Since Deedee had only been taking it a few days, there was a good chance the child's infection would return without the whole course of treatment.

Once Luc realized the omission, the detectives started monitoring the pediatrician's office with the cooperation of the doctor who was a friend of Luc's. At two-thirty in the afternoon of the fifth miserable day, a call came in requesting a replacement refill.

Luc practically grabbed the detective by the throat. "Tell me you got some information."

The grizzled sixtysomething veteran nodded, his gaze sympathetic. "The call originated from a Motel 6 in Marietta. Here's the address."

* * *

Hattie walked the floor, trying to soothe the cranky infant. Based on the last time she'd started the medicine, Deedee might not feel any better until at least forty-eight hours had passed.

Right after the honeymoon when the baby was ill, Hattie had been backed up with Luc's help and support. Now she was completely alone. The feelings of desolation and heartbreak were too much to bear. Her psyche adapted by shutting down all of Hattie's emotional pain sensors.

She was calm, too calm, but the unnatural state enabled her to function.

She had finally gotten Deedee to sleep late in the afternoon and had slumped onto the adjoining bed, craving a nap, when a loud knock hammered on the door of Room 106. Thankfully, the baby was dead asleep and didn't even stir.

Hattie peered through the peephole. *Dear God. Luc.* She wrung her hands, her brain paralyzed.

His distinctive voice sounded through the thin wood. "I see the car. I know you're in there. Open up, damn it."

Like a robot, she twisted the lock and turned the knob. As she stepped back into the room, Luc blew in with a barrage of rain and wind. A storm was brewing, the skies dark and boiling with clouds.

They faced off in the boxlike room.

He was haggard and pale, his shirt wrinkled, his hair a mess. Nothing about him suggested a successful entrepreneur.

Her heart iced over as the recollection of his deliberate cruelty flooded back.

"What do you want, Luc?" Fatigue enveloped her. She turned her back on him deliberately, sitting on the nearest bed and scooting back against the headboard. She pulled her knees to her chest, arms wrapped protectively around them.

His eyes were dark with misery. "I want *you*."

"Liar." She said it without inflection, but she saw him flinch as the insult found its mark.

He shrugged out of his jacket and swiped a hand through his wet hair. Thunder boomed, and the lights flickered. "I made a mistake. I was afraid to tell you how I felt. I never meant to drive you away."

Her fingernails dug into her legs. "I'm not stupid, Luc. I realized early on that one reason you agreed to help me was so that you could control things. You wanted the power this time. Lucky you. It worked."

He took a step toward the bed, but she stopped him with an outstretched arm.

Frustration carved grooves into his handsome face. "That idea lasted for about ten minutes. I told myself I wanted to hurt you…like you had hurt me. But I was kidding myself. I didn't want you to leave, Hattie."

"The lawyer called me. Eddie's not a threat anymore."

"I know. I read your note. It's wonderful news, but I'd rather have heard it from you face-to-face."

"You can give me part of that settlement now," she said calmly, her heart coming to life so that it could shatter into a million painful pieces. "We don't need your help anymore. We don't need you."

The look in his eyes made her ashamed. Spitefulness was not in her nature, but the need to lash out was inescapable.

He sat down at the foot of the bed, close enough for her to smell his aftershave and his natural, masculine scent. His eyes were dark, but no darker than the shadows beneath them. And he hadn't shaved. The anomaly disturbed her.

He touched her knee. A brief flash of heat tried to warm her, but he took his hand away. "What if *I* need *you*?" he asked hoarsely.

Hope flared in her chest. She smashed it ruthlessly. "You can buy anything you need."

The tired, wry twist of his lips was painful to watch. "I'm pretty sure you believed that ten years ago. It wasn't true then, and it isn't true now. My money doesn't give me control over you, Hattie. You're the one with all the power in this relationship."

"I'm a single, homeless mom with no job."

Again he winced. "You have a home," he said quietly. "And a husband who loves you more than life."

A single tear found its way down her cheek. "You never told me. Not once. We had sex a dozen times, maybe more… but you treated it like recreation. Not at all like love. And I know that's my fault. I'm sorry, Luc. Sorry I treated your love so callously back then."

He bowed his head briefly. "I should have said the words you needed to hear. But I was scared," he said. "You had the power to destroy me, Hattie. You still do."

Her lips trembled. "You've played games with my feelings. You hate me for what I did to you."

"I *tried* to hate you," he said softly. "For years. But it didn't work. When you showed up in my office that day, it was as if life had given me another chance. For a very short while, I told myself it was revenge I wanted. But I lied even to myself, Hattie. I loved you. I love you. I don't think I ever really stopped loving you. You have to believe me."

"Or what?"

"Or I'm going to buy this motel and lock you in this room until you come to your senses and admit you love me, too."

Hattie was shaking so hard, she was afraid she might fly apart. She wanted so badly to be certain he was telling the truth. "I don't want a relationship where both of us are jockeying for control. I don't want to play mind games. I need to be in an equal partnership. If I decide to go back to my career when Deedee starts school, I don't want any flack about that just because you're too rich for your own good. I'll dress up for parties and I'll hostess for you, but I may still clip the occasional coupon…" She ran out of breath.

"Is that all?"

"Isn't that enough?"

"I'll let you make all the decisions from now on."

"Liar." This time she said it with rueful humor.

He leaned forward and found her mouth in a kiss so exquisitely tender it thawed the block of ice in her chest. Tears trickled down her cheeks, but he kissed them away. He took her face in his hands, his expression grave. "I love you, Hattie Parker."

Her lips trembled. Her arms went around his neck in a stranglehold. "I love you, Luc Cavallo. And remember…my name isn't Parker anymore. I belong to you."

She felt the mighty shudder that racked his body, struggled to breathe as his arms crushed her in an unbreakable grip.

"Have you forgiven me?" she asked quietly, still feeling the sting of regret. "I cost us so much time."

He pulled back to look her in the eyes, his own deadly serious. "Maybe we both needed to grow up. Maybe we needed to be the people we are now so we could love Deedee as our own."

She sniffled, having a hard time with the juxtaposition of soaring happiness and recent despair. "Take me home, Luc. Take *us* home."

He tucked her head beneath his chin, their heartbeats thudding in unison. "I thought you'd never ask."

Epilogue

Five months later, in a small villa in the south of France, Hattie caught her breath as her husband's rigid length entered her slowly. The sensation was exquisite.

His breathing was labored, his face flushed. He loved her gently, as he had in recent weeks.

She wrapped her legs around his waist and squeezed. "I won't break," she complained.

Late-afternoon shadows painted their nude bodies with warm light. In a nearby cheval mirror, she watched as he penetrated her with a lazy rhythm. The tantalizing pace sent her soaring. He waited until her peak receded slowly and then found his own release.

Afterward, Luc ran his hand over the small bump where her flat stomach used to be. They had made a baby that very first time in Key West. A fact that Luc continually referred to with pride.

He nuzzled her belly. "I think he's a boy." Their ultrasound was scheduled soon.

She sighed, feeling sated and content. "We're going to have our hands full with two little ones so close together."

"We have Ana and Sherman to help. We'll be fine."

She brushed a lock of dark hair from his forehead. "You're my knight in shining armor. You rescued Deedee and me. I'll never forget it."

Luc rolled to his back, taking her with him to sprawl on his chest. His eyes were alight with happiness. "You've got it all wrong, my love. The two of you rescued me."

* * * * *

BEACH BAR BABY

HEIDI RICE

To all those people who asked me when I was
going to write Ella's story. Now you know.
I hope it lives up to expectations! x

CHAPTER ONE

NEXT TIME YOU BOOK a holiday of a lifetime, don't choose the world's most popular couples' destination, you muppet.

Ella Radley adjusted her backpack and flinched as it nudged the raw skin that still stung despite spending yesterday hiding out in her deluxe ocean-view room at the Paradiso Cove Resort in Bermuda—AKA Canoodle Central.

Ella sighed—nothing like getting third-degree sunburn in the one place you couldn't reach to remind you of your single status. Not that she needed reminding. She stared in dismay at the line of six couples, all in various stages of loved-up togetherness, on the dock ahead of her as she waited to board the motor cruiser at the Royal Naval Dockyards on Ireland Island for what the dive company's website had promised would be 'a two-hour snorkel tour of a lifetime'. Unfortunately, she'd booked the tour when she'd first arrived nearly a week ago, before she'd been hit on by a succession of married men and pimply pubescent boys, napalmed all the skin between her shoulder blades and generally lost the will to have anything remotely resembling a lifetime experience.

Her best friend Ruby had once told her she was far too sweet and eager and romantic for her own good. Well, she was so over that. Frankly, paradise and all its charms could get lost. She'd much rather be icing cupcakes in Touch of Frosting's cosy café kitchen in north London—and laughing about what a nightmare her dream holiday had turned out to be with her business partner and BFF Ruby—than standing in line to take a snorkelling tour of a lifetime that would probably give her a terminal case of seasickness.

Stop being such a grump.

Ella gazed out across the harbour, trying to locate at least a small measure of her usual sunny outlook on life. Yachts and motor boats—dwarfed by the enormous cruise ship anchored across the harbour—bobbed on water so blue and sparkly it hurt her eyes. She recalled the pink sand beach they'd passed on the way in, framed by lush palms and luxury beach bungalows, which looked as if it had been ripped from the pages of a tourist brochure.

She only had one more day to fully appreciate the staggering beauty of this island paradise. Maybe booking this holiday hadn't been the smartest thing she'd ever done, but she'd needed a distraction… The trickle of panic crawled over her skin, making her aware of the familiar clutching sensation in her belly. She pressed her palm to the thin cotton of her sundress, until it went away again. She needed this day trip—to get her out of her room before the panic overwhelmed her or, worse, she became addicted to US daytime soaps.

The line moved forward as a tall man appeared at the gangplank wearing ragged cut-offs and a black T-shirt with the dive company's logo on it, his face shadowed by a peaked captain's cap. Ella stopped breathing, her eyes narrowing to minimise the glare off the water, astonished to discover that the steely-haired Captain Sonny Mangold, whose weathered face beamed out from the photo on the website, appeared to be in amazing physical shape for a guy pushing sixty. Talk about a silver fox. Not that she could see his hair from this distance.

Captain Sonny began to welcome each couple aboard, his gruff American accent floating towards her on the still, muggy air, and sending peculiar shivers up Ella's spine, even though she couldn't make out what he was saying. The couple ahead of her, looking affluent and young and very much in love, were the last to block her view. As the captain helped them both aboard Ella stepped forward, anticipation making her throat dry. She took in the staggeringly broad shoulders and long muscular legs encased in denim cut-offs as his head dipped to tick off the list on the clipboard in his hand. Wisps of dark blond hair clung to lean cheeks and a square, stubbled jaw, confusing her even more, then his head lifted.

All thoughts of nightmare holidays, canoodling couples and silver foxes blasted right out of her brain.

Goodness, he's stunning. And not much over thirty.

'You're not Captain Sonny,' she blurted, the wake-up call to her dormant libido blasting away her usual shyness too.

'Captain Cooper Delaney at your service.' The rich jade of his irises twinkled, and the tanned skin round the edges of his eyes creased. His arresting gaze dipped, to check the clipboard again. 'And you must be Miz Radley.' The laconic voice caressed her name, while his gaze paused momentarily on its journey back to her face, rendering the bikini she had on under her sundress half its normal size.

A large, bronzed hand, sprinkled with sun-bleached hair, reached out. 'Welcome aboard *The Jezebel*, Miz Radley. You travelling on your own today?'

'Yes.' She coughed, distressed as the answer came out on a high-pitched squeak. Heat flared across her scalp.

Good Lord, am I having a hot flush? Can he see it?

'Is that okay?' she asked. Then realised it sounded as if she was asking his permission.

'Sure.' His wide sensual lips lifted but stopped tantalisingly short of a grin—making her fairly positive he knew exactly how he was affecting her.

The blush promptly went radioactive.

'As long as you don't have any objections to me being your snorkel buddy?' He squeezed her fingers as she stepped aboard. 'We don't let clients dive alone. It's safer that way.'

The pads of her fingertips rubbed against the thick calluses on the ridge of his palm. And the tips of her already constricted breasts tightened.

'I don't have any objections,' she said, feeling stupidly bereft when he let go of her hand—and thinking that even on their ten-second acquaintance she'd hazard a guess that Captain Cooper Delaney was the opposite of safe. Why for the first time in a long time she should find that exhilarating instead of intimidating made her wonder exactly how stressed she'd been in the last week.

'How about you sit up front with me?'

It didn't sound like a question, but she nodded, her tongue now completely numb.

His palm settled on the small of her back, just beneath the line of her sunburn. He directed her past the other passengers as she struggled not to notice the hot tingles generated by his touch and the fresh scent of saltwater and soap that clung to him. Bypassing the single space left between the couples wedged onto the benches that rimmed the hull, he escorted her to one of the two seats in front of the console in the boat's cabin.

'There you go, Miz Radley.' He tipped his cap, the gesture more amused than polite thanks to that tempting twinkle, then turned to address the other passengers.

She listened to him introduce himself and the two wiry teenage boys who were his crew for the day, then launch into a relaxed spiel about the twenty-five-minute voyage to the snorkel site called Western Blue Cut, the history of the sunken wreck they'd be exploring, the ecology of the reef and a string of safety tips. But all she really heard was the deliciously rusty texture of his voice while her mind wrestled with the question of exactly what being someone's snorkel buddy might entail.

It couldn't possibly be as intimate as it sounded. Could it?

But when he climbed into the seat beside her, his hand closed over the rounded head of the gear stick on the console and she swallowed past a constriction in her throat that felt a lot like excitement.

He adjusted the stick down, tapped a dial, pressed a button and the boat roared to life. She grabbed the rail at the edge of the console to stop from tumbling onto her butt. He slanted her an amused look as she scrambled back into her seat. Then hid his mischievous gaze behind a pair of sunglasses.

All the blood pumped back into her cheeks—not to mention the hot spot between her legs—as the motor launch kicked away from the dock, edged past the other boats in the marina, and left the walled harbour to skim over the swell towards the reef.

He flashed her an easy smile—that seemed to share a wicked secret. 'Hold on tight, miz. I'd hate to lose my snorkel buddy before we get there.'

The answering grin that flittered over Ella's lips felt like her first genuine smile in months—filling up a small part of the gaping hole that had opened up in the pit of her stomach over a week ago.

Maybe going on a holiday of a lifetime solo didn't completely suck after all.

'Well, honey, you've certainly captured Coop's attention.'

Ella's cheeks burned at the comment from the plump middle-aged woman in bright pink Bermuda shorts and an 'I Found My Heart in Horseshoe Bay' T-shirt who joined her at the rail as the boat bobbed on the reef.

They'd reached their destination ten minutes ago and were waiting for Captain Delaney and his crew to finish allocating the snorkelling equipment before they dived in.

Ella had to be grateful for the respite, because sitting in such close proximity to the man for twenty minutes had caused her usually sedentary hormones to get sort of hyperactive.

'Do you know Captain Delaney?' she asked, hoping to deflect the conversation while studiously ignoring the blip in her heartbeat.

After careful consideration, she'd figured out that Captain Delaney's attention had nothing to do with her and everything to do with his job. She was the only single passenger on the boat, and he was just being conscientious, ensuring she got her money's worth and enjoyed the trip. They hadn't been able to talk much on the ride out because of the engine noise, thankfully. Those sexy—and she was sure entirely impersonal—smiles he kept flashing at her were more than enough to tie her tongue in knots. A reaction that had propelled her back in time to the excruciating crushes of her teens when she'd always been rendered speechless in the presence of good-looking boys.

This was precisely why she preferred guys who were homely and safe rather than dangerous and super-hot. Being struck dumb on a date could get old really fast.

'We've known Coop for nearly a decade,' the woman said in her friendly mid-western drawl. 'Bill and I been coming back to St George every year since our honeymoon in ninety-two. And we never miss *The Jezebel*'s snorkel tour. Coop used to work as a deck hand for Sonny as a kid, got his captain's stripes a while back. Now he just pitches in from time to time.' The woman offered a hand. 'Name's May Preston.'

'Ella Radley, nice to meet you.' Ella shook the woman's hand, comforted by her open face, and easy manner—and intrigued despite herself by the unsolicited insight into the hot captain's past.

She recognised May from the resort. May and her husband Bill, whom she liked too, because he was one of the few married men at Paradiso Cove who didn't have a roving eye.

'You're a cute little thing, aren't you? And with that lovely accent.' May tilted her head, assessing Ella in that direct and personal way that only American tourists seemed able to do without appearing rude. 'I must say, I've always wondered what Coop's type was. But you're quite a surprise.'

The blush headed towards Ella's hairline. 'I wouldn't say I'm his type.' Perish the thought; her heart would probably stop beating if she believed that. She might find him extremely attractive, but dangerous men had never been good for her mental health. 'It's just that I'm a woman on my own and he's being polite and doing a good job.'

May let out a hearty chuckle. 'Don't you believe it, honey. Coop's not the polite type. And he usually spends his time peeling the single female clients off him, not offering them a personal service.'

'I'm sure you're wrong about that.' Far from stopping, Ella's heartbeat hit warp speed—stunned disbelief edging out her embarrassment.

'Maybe, maybe not.' May's smile took on a saucy tilt, which was about as far from doubtful as it was possible to get. 'But this is the first I've ever heard of the snorkel-buddy safety rule. And that's after twenty years of coming on this tour.'

Ella bided her time while wrestling with May's shocking comment, until the captain and his two deckhands had seen off all the other snorkellers. While fitting fins and masks, giving instructions about how far to stray from the boat, demonstrating some basic hand signals, advising people on how long they had before they should head back, and how to identify the paddle wheel from the wreck of the sunken blockade runner they'd come to see, Cooper Delaney appeared to be the consummate professional. In fact, he seemed so relaxed and pragmatic while handling the other passengers, Ella convinced herself May had to be mistaken about the snorkel-buddy rule—and wondered if she should even question him about it. Wouldn't she sound impossibly vain, bordering on delusional, suggesting he'd offered to partner her for reasons other than her own safety?

But then he turned from the rail, took off his sunglasses and his slow, seductive smile had all the blood pumping back into her nether regions.

She fanned herself with her sunhat. Goodness, either she was suffering from sunstroke or that smile had some kind of secret thermal mechanism.

He crossed the deck towards her, his emerald gaze even brighter than the dazzling expanse of crystal blue water.

'So, Miz Radley, you want to strip down to your swimsuit and I'll get you fitted up, then we can head out?'

He leaned against the console, his large capable hand very close to her hip.

She sucked in a sharp breath as her lungs constricted, only to discover the fresh sweat darkening the front of his T-shirt made his salt and sandalwood scent even more intoxicating.

Courage, Ella, just make a general enquiry so you know for sure where you stand.

'Is that absolutely necessary?' she asked.

''Fraid so. The salt water's bound to ruin that pretty dress if you don't take it off. You didn't forget your swimsuit, did you?' His smile tipped into a grin.

'No, I meant us snorkelling together.' Her nipples shot

back to the full torpedo as his gaze drifted south. 'Is that necessary?'

One dark eyebrow lifted in puzzled enquiry, the smile still in place.

'It's just that May Preston said she'd never heard of that rule.' The words tripped over themselves to get out of her mouth before her tongue knotted again. 'You know, about it being necessary for people to snorkel in pairs for safety's sake…' She began to babble, her tongue overcompensating somewhat. 'I know it matters with scuba-diving. Even though I've never actually scuba-dived myself…' She cut off as his lips curved more.

Get to the point, Ella.

'I just…I wondered if you could confirm for me, why it's necessary for us to be snorkel buddies? If I'm only going to be a few yards from the boat?'

'Right.'

The word rumbled out and seemed to echo in her abdomen. He muttered something under his breath, then tugged off his captain's cap, revealing curls of thick sun-streaked hair damp with sweat flattened against his forehead.

'What I can confirm…' he slapped the cap against his thigh, the smile becoming more than a little sheepish '…is that May Preston's got one hell of a big mouth. Which I'm going to be having words with her about as soon as she gets back aboard this boat.'

'It's true?' Ella's eyes widened, her jaw going slack. 'You really did make it up? But why would you do that?'

Cooper Delaney watched the pretty English girl's baby blues grow even larger in her delicate, heart-shaped face—and began to wonder if he was being taken for a ride.

Shy and hot and totally lost, with that tempting overbite, and her lush but petite figure, Ella Radley had looked cute and sort of sad when he'd spotted her at the back of the boarding line an hour ago. Then her skin had flushed a ruddy pink as soon as he'd so much as smiled at her and she'd totally captivated him.

That nuclear blush had been so damn cute, in fact, that he'd been momentarily mesmerised and the snorkel-buddy rule had popped into his head and then spilled out of his mouth without his brain ever even considering intervening.

But seriously? Could any woman really be this clueless? Even if she did have eyes big enough to rival one of the heroines in the manga comic books he'd been addicted to in middle school? And her nipples peaked under her sundress every time he so much as glanced at her rack? And her cheeks seemed to be able to light up on cue?

No way. No one was that cute. It had to be an act.

But if it was an act, it was a damn good one. And he could respect that, because he'd dedicated his life to putting on one act or another.

Unfortunately, act or no, she'd caught him out but good. *Thanks a bunch, May.*

He resigned himself to taking his punishment like a man, and hoped it didn't involve a slap in the face—or a sexual harassment suit.

'If I said because you looked like you could use the company,' he began, hoping that humour might soften the blow, 'would you buy it?'

The instant blush bloomed again—lighting up the sprinkle of freckles on her nose. 'Oh, yes, of course, I thought it might be something like that.' She shielded her eyes from the sun, tipping her chin up. 'That's very considerate of you, Captain Delaney. But I wouldn't want to put you out if you're busy. I'm sure I'll manage fine on my own.'

It was his turn for his eyes to widen at the earnest tone and the artless expression on her pixie face.

Damn, did she actually just buy that? Because if this was an act, it ought to be Oscar nominated.

No one had ever accused him of being considerate before. Not even his mom—and he'd worked harder at fooling her than anyone, because she'd been so fragile.

'The name's Coop,' he said, still not convinced that he'd got off the hook so easily, but willing to go with it. 'Believe me. I'd be happy to do it.' He tried to emulate her earnest expression. Although he figured it was a lost cause. He'd learnt at an early age to hide all his emotions behind a who-the-hell-cares smile, which meant he didn't have a heck of a lot of practice with earnest.

Her lips curved and her overbite disappeared. 'Okay, if you're absolutely sure it's not a bother.' The blue of her eyes brightened to dazzling. 'I accept.'

The smile struck him dumb for a moment, turning her expression from cute to super-hot but still managing to look entirely natural. Then she bounced up to pull her sundress over her head. And the punch of lust nearly knocked him sideways.

Bountiful curves in all the right places jiggled enticingly, covered by three pitifully tiny triangles of purple spandex that left not a lot to the imagination—and had that cheesy sixties tune his mom used to sing on her good days about a teeny-weeny polka dot bikini dancing through his head.

Damn but that rack was even hotter than her smile. Her nipples did that bullet-tipped thing again and he had to grit his teeth to stop one particular part of his anatomy from becoming the total opposite of teeny-weeny.

But then she turned, to drop her dress into the purse she had stowed under the dash, and he spotted the patch of sun-scorched flesh that spread out between slim shoulder blades and stretched all the way down to the line of her panties.

'Ouch, that's got to hurt,' he murmured. 'You need a

higher factor sun lotion. The rays can be brutal in Bermuda even in April.'

She whisked around, holding the dress up to cover her magnificent rack—and the nuclear blush returned with a vengeance. 'I have factor fifty, but unfortunately I couldn't reach that spot.'

He scrubbed his hand over the stubble on his chin, playing along by pretending to consider her predicament. 'Well, now, that sounds like a job for your snorkel buddy.'

A grateful smile lit up her face, and he almost felt bad for taking advantage of her...until he remembered this was all some saucy little act.

'That would be fabulous, if you don't mind?' She reached back into her tote and pulled out some lotion.

Presenting her back to him, she lifted the hair off her nape as he squeezed a generous amount of the stuff, which had the consistency of housepaint, between his palms, and contemplated how much he was going to enjoy spreading it all over her soft, supple, sun-warmed skin.

Well, hell... If he'd known the good-guy act came with these kind of benefits, he'd have given it a shot more often.

CHAPTER TWO

DO NOT PURR, under any circumstances.

Ella bit back a moan as Cooper Delaney's work-roughened hands massaged her shoulder blades. Callused fingers nudged under the knot of her bikini to spread the thick sun lotion up towards her hairline. Tingles ricocheted down her spine as his thumbs dug into the tight muscles of her neck, then edged downwards. She trapped her bottom lip under her teeth, determined to keep the husky groan lodged in her throat where it belonged.

'Okay, I'm heading into the red zone.' The husky voice brushed her nape as his magic touch disappeared and she heard the squirt of more lotion being dispensed. 'I'll be gentle as I can, but let me know if it's too much.'

I could never have too much of this.

She nodded, knowing any further attempt at speech would probably give away how close she was to entering a fugue state.

'Right, here goes.'

Light pressure hit the middle of her back as his palms flattened against the burnt patch. She shuddered, the sting nothing compared to the riot of tingles now rippling across her skin and tightening her nipples.

'You okay?' The pressure ceased, his palms barely touching her.

'Yes. Absolutely. Don't stop.' She shifted, pressing back into his palms. 'It feels…'

Glorious? Blissful? Awe-inspiring?

'Fine…' she managed, but then a low hum escaped as he began to massage more firmly. His thumbs angled into the hollows of her spine, blazing a trail of goosebumps in their wake.

She'd been far too long without the touch of a man's hands. That fabulous sensation of flesh on flesh, skin to skin. She stretched under the caress, like a cat desperate to be stroked, the tingles rippling down to her bottom as his thumbs nudged the edge of her bikini panties. She closed her eyes, willing the firm touch to delve beneath the elastic, while the hot heavy weight in her abdomen plunged.

Arousal zapped across her skin, and she had to swallow the sob as the exquisite, excruciating sensations pounded into her sex after what felt like decades on sabbatical.

Then disappeared.

'All done.'

Her eyes snapped open too fast, making her sway. His hand touched her hip, anchoring her in place—and snapping her back to reality.

'Steady there.' The amused tone had the blush firing up her neck.

Oh, no, had he heard that strangled sob? Could he tell she'd been hurtling towards a phantom orgasm?

Humiliation engulfed the need.

She was so going to unpack the vibrator Ruby had bought her for the trip, and test-drive it in her room to-night. Deciding she wasn't highly sexed enough to need artificial stimulation had obviously been way off the mark. And Ruby had once sworn by hers—before she'd found her husband, Callum.

'That should keep you from getting barbecued again, at any rate.' The rough comment intruded on her frantic debate about the merits of vibrators. And the blush went haywire.

She stretched her lips into what she hoped looked like a grateful smile—instead of the first stages of nymphomania. 'I really appreciate it.'

She watched as he snapped the cap onto the lotion bottle. Only to become momentarily transfixed by the sight of those long, blunt, capable fingers glistening in the sunlight from the oily residue.

'There you go.' He held out the lotion bottle as another inappropriate jolt of arousal pulsed into her sex.

Locating her backpack, she spent several additional seconds shoving the bottle back into it, pathetically grateful when her hands finally stopped trembling. Maybe if she drew this out long enough the blush might have retreated out of the forbidden zone too.

'Thank you, that was...' She groped for the right word—awesome being definitely the wrong word, even if it was the one sitting on the tip of her tongue.

'You're welcome.'

Her lungs seized at the glow of amusement in the deep green depths of his eyes. The blip of panic returned as she got lost in the rugged male beauty of his face—the chiselled cheekbones, the shadow of stubble on the strong line of his jaw, the tantalising dimple in his chin.

How could any man be this gorgeous? This potently male? It just wasn't fair on the female of the species.

The sensual lips twitched, as if he were valiantly suppressing a grin.

Get a flipping grip. The man offered to be your snorkel buddy, not your bonk buddy.

'So we're all set?' The rough question echoed in her sex.

'Unless you need me to return the favour?' She coughed, when the offer came out on an unladylike squeak. 'With the sun lotion, I mean. So you don't burn.'

The suggestion trailed off as his eyebrows lifted a fraction and the edge of his mouth kicked up in one of those
sensual, secret smiles that had been making her breathing
quicken all morning. It stopped altogether now.

*Shut up. You did not just say that? You sad, sad, sex-
deprived nymphomaniac.*

'Forget it, that was a silly thing to say.' She raced to
cover the gaff. 'I don't know why I suggested it.' Cooper
Delaney's sun-kissed skin had the healthy glow of a year-
round tan weathered by sea air. He'd probably never had
to use lotion in his entire life. 'I'm sure you don't need to
worry about sunburn. Perhaps we should just—'

'That sounds like a great idea.' The easy comment cut
through her manic babble.

'It does?'

His lips kicked up another notch. 'Sure, you can never
have enough protection, right?'

Was he mocking her? And could she summon the will
to care while she was barely able to breathe?

'Um, right. I'll get the lotion, then.' She dived back into
her bag, rummaging around for what felt like several decades as she tried to locate the lotion before he changed
his mind. She found it just in time to see him lift the hem
of his T-shirt over his head and throw it over the console.

All the blood rushed out of her brain as she stood,
poised like the Statue of Liberty, clutching the lotion like
Liberty's torch.

Oh. My. God. His chest is a work of art.

Sun-bleached hair curled around flat copper nipples as
if to accentuate the mounds of his exceptionally well-de-
fined pecs. She followed the trail down between the ridged
muscles of his six-pack, then swallowed convulsively as
the thin strip of hair tapered beneath the waistband of his
cut-offs, drawing her attention to the roped sinews that
stood out in bold relief against the line of his hip bones.

No wonder it's called a happy trail. I feel euphoric.

'Thanks, honey. I appreciate it.' His gruff words interrupted her reverie as he presented her with an equally breathtaking view of his back.

His spine bisected the slabs of packed muscle, sloping down to the tattoo of a Celtic Cross, inked across the base of his back, which peeked out above his shorts. Her gaze dipped lower, to absorb the sight of a perfectly toned male ass framed in battered denim.

She cleared her throat loudly, before she choked to death on her own drool. 'Is, um, is factor fifty okay?'

He lifted one muscular shoulder, let it drop. 'Whatever you've got is good.'

The low words seemed to rumble through her torso, making her pulse points vibrate.

She squeezed a lake of the viscous white liquid into unsteady palms. Taking a deep breath, she flattened her palms onto the hot, smooth skin of his back, while her lungs clogged with the tempting scent of cocoa butter and man.

The muscles tensed as she spread the thick lotion, and absorbed the heat of his skin, the steely strength beneath.

Moisture gathered in the secret spot between her thighs, which now felt as if it was swollen to twice its normal size.

As she spread the white liquid over the wide expanse of his back, and massaged it into his skin, she timed her breathing to the beat of the timpani drum in her ear, in a desperate attempt to stop herself from hyperventilating.

And passing out before the job was done.

Cooper touched Ella's arm, signalling with his index finger to draw her attention to the blue angel fish darting beneath the shelf of fiery orange coral. Her eyes popped wide behind the mask and her expressive mouth spread into a delighted grin around her mouthpiece.

As they hovered above the reef he watched her admire the brilliant aquamarine of the fish's scales, the white-tipped fins, and the pretty golden edging on the tail, while he admired the open excitement on her face and the buoyant breasts barely contained by purple spandex.

His groin twitched, the blood pumping south despite the chill of the seawater. The sudden flashback, of her stretching under his hands, her breathing coming out on a strangled groan as he caressed the firm skin, didn't do much to deter the growing erection.

He adjusted his junk, grateful for the wet denim of his shorts. Which had been holding him in check ever since he'd dived into the ocean, leaving Dwayne to fit Ella's flippers and snorkelling gear, before she spotted the tell-tale ridge in his pants.

They'd been out on the reef for over half an hour now, and he'd mostly got himself under control. But the sight of that shy, excited smile, every time he showed her some new species of fish, or the barnacled wreck of the *Montana*, had been almost as mesmerising as the feel of her fingers fluttering over his bicep whenever she wanted to point something out to him, or the sight of all those lush curves bobbing in the waves.

The woman was killing him. So much so that his golden rule about hooking up with single lady tourists was in danger of being blown right out of the water.

As she pointed delightedly to a shoal of parrot fish flicking past he recalled why he'd made his golden rule in the first place.

Single ladies on holiday generally fell into one of two categories: those on the hunt for no-strings thrills, or those on the look-out for an exotic island romance. As both scenarios invariably involved lots of sex, he'd been more than happy to indulge in hook-ups with the clients when he'd first arrived on the island a decade ago. But back then he'd been eighteen going on thirty with a chip on his shoulder the size of a forest, not a lot of money and even fewer prospects.

In the intervening years, he'd worked his butt off to leave that messed-up kid in the dust. As the owner of a lucrative and growing dive-shop franchise, he sure as hell didn't need to look for acceptance in casual sex any more—or the hassle of pretending to be interested in more.

Which meant single lady tourists had been off limits for a while, unless he knew for certain they weren't after more than the one night of fun. Usually, it was easy enough to figure that out. In fact he'd become an expert at deciding whether a woman had lust or stardust in their eyes when they hit on him. But Ella Radley didn't fit the profile for either.

For starters, she hadn't exactly hit on him despite the obvious chemistry between them. And he still hadn't figured out whether that enchanting mix of artless enthusiasm, sweet-natured kookiness and transparent hunger was all part of an act to get into his pants—or was actually real.

Unfortunately, he was fast running out of time to make up his mind on that score. Sonny had two more fully booked tours scheduled right after this one. And with the old guy's arthritis acting up again, Cooper had agreed to step in and captain them. It was a responsibility he couldn't and wouldn't duck out of. Because Sonny and he had a history.

The old guy had offered him a shift crewing on *The Jez*, when he'd been eighteen and had just spent his last dime on boat fare to the island. He'd been sleeping rough on the quayside and would have sold his soul for a burger and a side order of fries.

He'd done a half-assed job that afternoon, because he'd been weak from hunger and didn't know the first thing about boats. But for the first time since his mother's death, he'd felt safe and worth something. Sonny had given him hope, so whatever debt the old guy called in, he'd pay it.

All of which meant he had to make a decision about Ella Radley before they got back to the dockyards. Should he risk asking her out tonight without being sure about her?

She swam back towards him, her eyes glowing behind the mask, then made the sign for okay.

He gave her a thumbs up and then jerked it towards the boat. They'd run out of time ten minutes ago. Everyone else would be back on the launch by now ready to head back to the mainland. Which meant it was past time for him to make his mind up.

But as she swam ahead of him, her generous butt drawing his gaze with each kick of the flippers, heat flooded his groin again, and he knew his mind had already been made up… Because his brain had stopped making the decisions a good forty minutes ago, when those soft, trembling hands had stroked down his spine and hovered next to the curve of his ass. And he'd heard her sigh, above the rush of blood pounding in his ears.

Ella gripped the rail as the launch bumped against the dock and her snorkel buddy sent her one of his trademark smiles.

He laid his palm on her knee and gave it a squeeze, sending sensation shooting up her thigh. 'Hold up here, while I get everyone off the boat.' The husky, confidential tone had her heart beating into her throat, the way it had been doing most of the day.

She forced herself to breathe evenly, and take stock, while he and his crew docked the boat and he bid farewell to the rest of the passengers.

Do not get carried away. It's been an amazing morning, but now it's over.

The snorkel tour, the epic beauty of the reef and its sealife had totally lived up to the hype. But it had been Cooper Delaney's constant attention, his gorgeous body and flirtatious smile, that had turned the trip into a once-in-a-lifetime experience.

He'd made her feel special—and for that she couldn't thank him enough. Which meant not overreacting now and putting motivations into his actions that weren't there.

She gulped down the lump of gratitude as she watched him charm May Preston, and give her husband a hearty handshake. Once they'd gone, it would be her turn to say goodbye.

May waved, then winked—making the colour leech into Ella's cheeks—before handing a wad of bills to Cooper. He accepted the money with a quick lift of his cap.

A tip.

Shame tightened Ella's throat as Cooper folded the bills into the back pocket of the jeans he'd changed into. Of course, she should tip him. That would be the best way to thank Cooper for all his attention. And let him know what a great time she'd had.

She grabbed her backpack, found her purse, then had a minor panic attack over the appropriate amount. Was twenty dollars enough? Or thirty? No, forty. Forty, would work. After all, he'd surely need to share it out with the boys in his crew. She counted out the money, her palms sweating, hoping she'd got the amount right. She wanted to be generous, even though she knew that any amount couldn't really repay him for what he'd done.

For two amazing, exhilarating, enchanting hours she'd completely forgotten about all her troubles—and felt like a woman again, a whole, normal, fully functional woman—and for that no tip, however generous, could be big enough.

Slinging the pack over her shoulder, she approached him with the bills clutched in her fist. Now, how to hand it over without blushing like a beetroot?

He turned as she approached, that killer smile making her pulse hammer her neck. The appreciative light in his eyes as his gaze roamed over her had her bikini top shrinking again.

'Hey, there.' The killer smile became deadly. 'I thought I told you to stay put.'

She pursed her lips to still the silly tremble, unable to return the smile. 'I should get out of your way.'

'You're not in my way.' He tucked the curl of hair that had escaped her ponytail back behind her ear—in a casually possessive gesture that only made the tremble intensify. 'But I've got a couple more tours to run today. How about we meet up later? I'll be at a bar on the south side of Half-Moon Cove from around seven onwards...'

Blood thundered in her ears, so she could barely make out what he was saying.

'What d'you say?' he continued. 'You want to hang out some more?'

She nodded, but then his knuckle stroked down her cheek.

Panicked by the clutch of emotion, and the insistent throb of arousal, she shifted away from his touch. Time to make a quick getaway, before the lip quiver got any worse.

She thrust the bills towards him. 'I've had an incredible time. The tour was amazing. Thank you so much.'

His gaze dropped. 'What's this?'

'Umm, I hope it's enough.' Had she miscalculated? Was it too little? 'I wanted to thank you properly, for all the trouble you went to this morning.'

A muscle in his jaw hardened. And she had the strangest feeling she'd insulted him. But then he blinked and the flash of temper disappeared.

'Right.' He took the bills, counted them. 'Forty dollars. That's real generous.' She thought she detected the sour hint of sarcasm, but was sure she must be mistaken when he tipped his cap and shoved the bills into his back pocket.

'Thanks.' For the first time, the easy grin looked like an effort. 'I'll see you around, Miz Radley.'

The clutching feeling collapsed in her chest, at the formal address, the remote tone.

Had she just imagined the invitation for later in the evening? Or, worse, blown it out of all proportion? Obviously it had been completely casual and she'd made too much of it.

She stood like a dummy, not knowing what to do about the sudden yearning to see the focused heat one more time.

The moment stretched out unbearably as he studied her, his expression remote and unreadable.

'I suppose I should make a move,' she managed to get out at last.

Get off the boat. He probably has a ton of things he needs to be doing.

'Well, thank you again.' *You've said that already.* 'It's been so nice meeting you.' *Stop gushing, you nitwit.* 'Goodbye.' She lifted her hand in a pointless wave that immediately felt like too much.

'Yeah, sure.' He didn't wave back, the words curt, his face blanker than ever.

She rushed down the gangplank, refusing to look back and make an even bigger ninny of herself.

CHAPTER THREE

ELLA HELD THE plastic column, flipped the switch. Then yelped and dropped it when it shivered to life with a sibilant hum. She signed and flicked the switch back down to dump the vibrator back in its box.

Damn, trying out the sex toy had seemed like such a good idea when she'd been with Cooper, while all her hormones were jumping and jigging under his smouldering stare.

But after their awkward parting, she wasn't feeling all that enthusiastic about discovering the joys of artificial stimulation any more.

Plastic just didn't have the allure of a flesh and blood man. Plus the way things had ended had flatlined all the jiggling. She just felt empty now, and a little foolish, for enjoying his company so much when it hadn't meant anything. She racked her brains to figure out what had happened. Because one minute he'd been laid-back and charming, oozing sex appeal, and asking her if she wanted to 'hang out' later and the next he'd been cold and tense and dismissive.

The phone rang, jolting her out of her dismay. She groped for the handset, grateful for the distraction, especially when her best friend's voice greeted her.

'Ella, hi, how's things in paradise?'

Ella smiled, happiness at the sound of Ruby's voice tempered with a surge of homesickness. 'Ruby, I'm so glad you called.' She gripped the phone, suddenly wishing she could levitate down the phoneline.

Other than this morning's snorkelling trip of a lifetime with the gorgeous—and confusing—Captain Cooper, her trip to Bermuda had been a disaster. She wanted to go home now.

'Is everything okay? You sound a little wobbly.'

'No, everything's good. I guess I'm just over paradise now.'

Ruby laughed, that rich, throaty, naughty laugh that Ella missed so much. 'Uh-oh, so I'm assuming you still haven't met any buff guys in Bermuda shorts, then?'

'Umm, well.' The image of Cooper's exceptionally fit body, his low-slung cut-offs clinging to muscular thighs, that mouth-watering chest gilded with seawater, and the devastating heat in his eyes, popped into Ella's head and rendered her speechless.

'You have met someone, haven't you?' Ruby said, her usual telepathy not dimmed by thousands of miles of ocean. 'Fantastic! Auntie Ruby needs to know all the details.'

'It's nothing, really. He's just a cute guy who was captaining the snorkel tour I went on this morning. We flirted a bit.' At least, she thought they'd been flirting, but maybe she'd got that wrong too. 'But he's not my type at all. He's far too sexy.' She recalled his callused hands, massaging the thick suncream into her skin—and wondered if Ruby could sense her hot flush from the UK.

Ruby snorted. 'Are you on crack or something? There's no such thing as too sexy. Ever. And clarify "a bit"—does that mean there might be an option for more?'

'Well, he did sort of ask me out.'

'That's fantastic.'

'But I don't think I'll follow it up.'

Her mind snagged on their awkward parting. As flattering as Cooper's undivided attention had been, and as exciting as she'd found snorkelling with him—cocooned together in the exhilarating cool of the ocean as he used sign language to point out the different colourful fish, the sunken wreck of an old schooner and the majestic coral—it hadn't ended all that well.

She pictured again the tight line of his jaw when she'd handed him the hefty tip, and winced at the memory of his curt goodbye.

'Why not?' Ruby asked. 'I thought that was the whole point of this holiday. To have a wild, inappropriate fling and kick-start your sex life?'

'What?' Ella could feel the blush lighting her face like a Christmas tree. 'Who told you that?'

'You did. You said you needed to get away, and rethink your priorities. That you'd become too fixated on finding the right guy, when what you really needed was to find a guy,' Ruby replied, quoting words back to Ella she couldn't remember saying.

She'd been in a fog at the time, probably even in a state of mild shock after visiting her local doctor. She'd booked the holiday at the last minute, packed and headed for the airport the very next day, partly because she hadn't known how to tell Ruby her news. For the first time ever, she'd been unable to confide in her best friend, and that had been the scariest thing of all.

'I thought that's what you meant,' Ruby finished, sounding thoroughly confused now. 'That you were heading to Bermuda to get laid.'

'Not precisely.' Ella felt the weariness of keeping the secret start to overwhelm her.

'So what did you mean?' Ruby's sharp mind lasered straight to the truth. 'This has something to do with the doctor's appointment you had the day before you left, doesn't it? I knew something had freaked you out. What aren't you telling me?'

Ella could hear the urgency in Ruby's voice and knew her friend's natural tendency to create drama was about to conjure up a terminal illness.

'Whatever it is, you have to tell me, Ell. We can sort it out. Together. We always have.'

'Don't worry, Rube.' Ella began talking her friend down from the ledge. 'It's nothing terrible.' Or not that terrible.

'But it does have something to do with the appointment?'

'Yes.'

'Which is?' Ruby's voice had taken on the stern fear-of-God tone she used with her three children, which instantly made them confess to any and all infractions.

Ella knew she wouldn't last two seconds under that kind of interrogation. Even from four thousand miles away. 'Dr Patel took some tests. I'll get the results on Monday.' She blew out a breath, the hollow pressure that had dragged down her stomach a week ago feeling as if it had become a black hole. 'But given my mum's history and the fact that I haven't had a period now in over three months, she thinks I might be going into premature menopause.'

'Okay,' Ruby said carefully. 'But it's just a possibility? Nothing's certain yet?'

Ella shook her head, the black hole starting to choke her. 'I'm pretty certain.'

She'd done something cowardly in her teens, that she'd always believed she would be punished for one day. And sitting in Myra Patel's office, listening to her GP discuss the possible diagnoses, the prospect of a premature menopause had been both devastating, and yet somehow hideously fitting.

She placed her hand on her abdomen to try and contain the hollowness in her womb, and stop it seeping out and invading her whole body. 'I've left it too late, Ruby. I'm not going to be able to have children.'

'You don't know any such thing. Not until you get the tests back. And even if it is premature menopause, a couple of missed periods isn't suddenly going to make you infertile.'

She did know, she'd known ever since she was eighteen and she'd come round from the anaesthesia in the clinic to find Randall gone. She didn't deserve to be a mother, because the one time she'd had the chance she'd given it up to please a guy who hadn't given a hoot about her.

'I suppose you're right,' she said, humouring Ruby.

'Of course I am. You're not allowed to go the full drama until you get the results. Is that understood?'

'Right.' Her lips wrinkled, as she found some small measure of humour in having Ruby be the one to talk her off the ledge for a change.

'Now.' Ruby gave an exasperated sigh. 'I want to know why you didn't tell me about this? Instead of giving me all that cryptic nonsense about finding a guy to shag.'

'I never said shag.' Or at least she was fairly sure she hadn't.

'Don't change the subject. Why didn't you tell me about this before? Instead of running off to Bermuda?'

It was a valid question, because they'd always shared everything—secret crushes, first kisses, how best to fake an orgasm, even the disastrous end to her college romance with Randall, and Ruby's rocky road to romance with the sexy barrister who'd rear-ended her car on a Camden street seven years ago and turned out to be her one true love. But Ella still didn't know how to answer it.

'I just couldn't.' Her voice broke, and a tear escaped. One of the ones she'd been holding captive for over a week.

'Why couldn't you?' Ruby probed, refusing to let it go.

'I guess I was feeling shocked and panicky and inadequate…' She sucked in a breath, forcing herself to face the truth. 'And horribly jealous. Of the fact that you have such a wonderful family and three beautiful children and I may never have any.' She let the breath out. There, she'd said it. 'I felt so ashamed to be envious of you. Because everything you have with Cal and the kids, you've worked for and you deserve.'

The self-pitying tears were flowing freely now. She brushed them away with the heel of her hand. Hoping Ruby couldn't hear the hiccoughs in her breathing. 'I couldn't bear for this to come between us in any way.'

'That's the most ridiculous thing I've ever heard.'

'Why?' The question came out on a tortured sob.

'Well, for starters, you don't want Cal. He's far too uptight and bossy for you. His insistence on being right about everything would make you lose the will to live within a week.'

'Cal's not uptight and bossy. He's lovely.' Ella jumped in to defend Ruby's husband, whom she adored, if only in a purely platonic sense—because he actually was a little bossy.

'Only because he's got me to unwind him on a regular basis, and boss him about back,' Ruby replied. 'But more to the point.' Her voice sobered, the jokey tone gone. 'You don't want my kids, you want your own. And if I deserve my little treasures—not that Ally and Max were particularly treasurable this morning when they decided to declare World War Three on each other using their Weetabix as nuclear warheads—then you certainly do.'

Do I?

The question echoed in her head, but she didn't voice it, Ruby's passionate defence counteracting at least some of the guilt that had been haunting her for over a week.

'You're going to make an incredible mum one day,'

Ruby added with complete conviction. 'And, if you have to, there are lots of possible ways of achieving that.'

'How do you mean?'

'You know, like artificial insemination, IVF, donor eggs, surrogacy, adoption, that sort of thing.'

Ruby's matter-of-fact response shrank a little of the black hole in her belly. She hadn't considered any of those options yet, the prospect of infertility too shocking to get past. But why shouldn't she? If the worst came to the worst and Myra's diagnosis was correct?

'I guess you're right, I hadn't really—'

'But frankly,' Ruby interrupted, 'I think we're getting the cart before the stallion here.'

'Excuse me?'

'Ella, your biggest problem when it comes to having a child of your own is not the possibility of a premature menopause. It's the fact that every guy you've been out with since that tosser in college has been so mind-numbingly dull even I couldn't be bothered to flirt with them.'

Ella frowned, picturing the handful of guys she'd dated in the last decade. And realised that Ruby's outrageous statement might not actually be all that far off the mark—because she couldn't recall a single one of them with any degree of clarity.

When had dating become such an effort? And sex such a chore?

Was that why she'd had a rush of blood to the head at Cooper's casual suggestion of a drink later? Flirting with him had been exciting, exhilarating, and yet she'd totally freaked out when he'd offered her the chance to take it further.

What was that about? She was thirty-four, for goodness' sake, not ninety.

'The thing is, Ella,' Ruby continued, 'I know sexual

chemistry isn't everything in a relationship—and Randall the dickhead is a case in point.'

Ella winced at hearing Randall's name spoken aloud— a name they'd both avoided speaking for sixteen years. But the gaping wound her college boyfriend had caused— which she'd believed then would fester for the rest of her life—had scabbed over in the years since. Because the mention of his name didn't hurt any more; it only made her feel ashamed, that she'd fallen for him so easily, mistaken a couple of really spectacular orgasms for love, and then let him bulldoze her into doing something she would later regret.

'But sometimes chemistry can come in very handy, if you need a serious pick–me-up in the dating department,' Ruby continued. 'Which brings us right back to Captain Studly from your snorkel tour.'

Didn't it just?

'So tell me again,' Ruby continued. 'Why exactly can't you take him up on his offer of a date?'

'Because I'm not entirely sure he meant it.'

'And why would you think that? Talk me through it.'

'Well, he asked me if I'd like to hook up for a drink at this local hang-out after he finished work at seven and I panicked.' She'd chickened out, because Cooper Delaney had been more man than she'd had the guts to handle in a very long time—it all seemed so obvious now. 'And then I had to get off the boat, because he was busy. But it was all very casual, and we never agreed on anything specific.'

Even if the memory of Cooper's offer of a date thrilled her now, instead of terrifying her, the memory of his face, closed off and impassive, when she'd said that final goodbye wasn't far behind.

'Did this local hang-out have a name?' Ruby probed.

'No, but I think…' She searched her memory; hadn't he told her where it was? 'Half-Moon Cove.' The location echoed in her head in his deep American accent. 'He mentioned it was on the south side of Half-Moon Cove.'

'Fantastic. That's all we need.'

'It is?'

'Yes, now shut up and listen to Auntie Ruby.' Ruby paused, and the tickle of excitement in Ella's belly began to buzz as if she were being stroked by the vibrator. 'Captain Studly most definitely did invite you on a date. Time and location are all the specifics you need. And you are flipping well going to go on it.'

'But what if—?'

'No buts.' Ruby cut her off. 'It's way past time Ella Radley started dating the sort of man candy that might actually have some hope of exciting her enough to get her past first base.'

'I've been past first base in the past decade,' she said, indignantly—even if she couldn't remember the events in any great detail. 'But I don't think—'

'Uh-uh-uh, didn't you hear the "no buts" stipulation?' Ruby paused, but not long enough for Ella to form a suitable response. 'That goes hand in hand with the "no panicking" initiative. If you feel yourself starting to hyperventilate because Captain Studly is too Studly, just think of him as a test run. You need to get your flirt on, Ella, and he sounds like the perfect guy to practise on.'

And just like that, the buzz in Ella's belly sank even lower and became a definite hum.

CHAPTER FOUR

'YOU SURE YOU'RE okay here, ma'am? The Rum Runner isn't much for the tourists, just a local hang-out. I could take you to some nice places in Hamilton, where the cruise ships dock, no extra charge?'

'No, thank you, this is perfect, Earl.' Exhilaration fluttered in Ella's chest as she stepped out of the cab and surveyed the ramshackle bar at the end of the rutted beach road.

The twinkle of fairy lights on weathered wood added enchantment to the haphazard structure, which stood drunkenly, mounted on stilts over the water, as if it had downed one too many rum punches. The scent of the sea freshened the cloud of smoke and sweat as the customers spilled out of the saloon-style doors. The densely packed crowd smoked and chatted on the porch, while she could see couples dancing inside past the tables, swinging and swaying to the infectious soca beat, making the boardwalk pound beneath her sandals.

'You're sure this is the only place on the south side of Half-Moon Cove?' She handed Earl, her taxi driver, his fare and a generous tip through the cab window.

'Uh-huh.' Unlike Cooper, he sent her a wide smile as he tucked the money into the top pocket of his Hawaiian shirt. 'Cove's yonder.' He nodded towards a wide beach that began past the rocks at the end of the country road.

Edged by palm trees and vines and curving round the headland into the darkness, the cove lived up to its name, looking impossibly romantic as moonlight shimmered off the gently lapping surf.

'Ain't no other bars down here that I know of.' Pulling a card out of his pocket, he handed it to her. 'You give Earl a call when you need to get back. Not much traffic this way.'

After waving him off and watching the cab lights bounce out of sight down the unpaved road, she slipped the card into her bag, and slung the strap over her shoulder. Then she sucked in a fortifying breath and let it out in a rush.

Whether or not Cooper was here, she intended to enjoy herself. Ruby had given her the pep talk to end all pep talks, back at the hotel.

It was way past time she started living again, took the power back and charted her own course when it came to choosing the men she dated. And stopped boring herself to death with safe and secure and invited a little danger in. Bermuda with its colourful, chaotic nightlife and studly boat captains had to be the perfect place to start. Not least because if tonight went tits up, this particular dating disaster wouldn't be able to follow her home.

Ruby's words of dating wisdom had bolstered her courage as she'd showered, and waxed, and moisturised, and primped and perfumed. After far too much debate, she'd picked out an understated ensemble of skinny pedal-pusher jeans, heeled sandals and a lace-edged camisole. She'd pinned up her unruly hair, and plastered on a lot more make-up than she usually wore—as per Ruby's specific instructions—then dug out her favourite waterfall earrings and the cascade of cheap but cheerful bracelets she'd bought at Camden Market two weeks ago to complete the outfit.

The simple ritual of getting ready had helped temper her terror with a heady cocktail of excitement and anticipation.

Edging past the people milling around on the porch, she made her way to the bar. She'd have a couple of drinks and then, if Cooper didn't show, she could always ring Earl back and call it a night. At least she would have got to see something of the island before leaving.

The Rum Runner had a funky, relaxed vibe that reminded her of Sol's Salsa Joint on Camden Lock where Ruby and she and their wide circle of friends had once congregated on a Friday night to kick back after the working week. Ruby didn't go out much any more because of the kids, and most of their other friends had settled down and/or moved away in the last few years, so she'd slowly stopped going to Sol's too, but she'd always loved to dance and it occurred to her she'd missed the weekly ritual.

Her hips swung in time to the blast of horns and the fast infectious drum beat as the band on the stage in the far corner went into another number. She grinned as she wound her way through the packed tables—the soca rhythm an irresistible blend of joy and seduction—and felt the optimism that had always been so much a part of her personality seep back into her soul.

Slipping past a group of loudly dressed guys at the bar, she smiled back when one of them touched his beer bottle to his forehead in a silent salute.

'What'll it be, miz?' a barman addressed her once she had managed to inch past the crush of people and found a spot to rest her elbows on the bar. The thin layer of sweat on his dark skin made the red ink of the snake tattoo on his bicep glisten.

She tapped her toe to the bass guitar riff while checking out the names of the drinks scrawled on the chalkboard behind him—only a few of which she recognised. 'What would you recommend?'

'For you?' The lilting Caribbean accent matched the friendly twinkle in the barman's *café-au-lait*-coloured eyes. 'Only a Rum Swizzle will do.'

'That sounds wonderful.' She had absolutely no clue what that was. But tonight Ella Radley was on a mission, to get her flirt on and set it free. And for that, a Rum Swizzle sounded like just the ticket.

He returned a few minutes later and presented her with a tall icy glass of tangerine-coloured liquid, garnished with a chunk of pineapple, a swirl of orange peel and a maraschino cherry. She took a sip and the potent flavour of rum, fruit juice and liquor zinged off her tastebuds. So that was why they called it a Swizzle.

'Delicious,' she shouted over the music. 'How much do I owe you?'

'Not a thing.' A gold tooth winked in the pearly white of his smile. 'Your first Rum Swizzle in my place is always on the house.'

'You own this bar?'

He nodded. 'Sure do.'

A shot of adrenaline rushed through her to add to the hit from the rum. And Ruby's voice seemed to whisper in her ear.

Above all be bold—and seize the initiative—flirting is much more fun if you own it.

'Do you know a guy called Cooper Delaney?'

'Coop? Sure I know Coop. What do you want him for?' He sounded a bit put out. 'That boy's nothing but trouble.'

That was what she was counting on, she thought, the adrenaline more intoxicating than the Swizzle. She took another fortifying sip of the delicious concoction. 'Is he likely to be in tonight, do you think?'

She heard the eagerness in her tone but didn't care if it made her sound tarty. Discovering her inner flirt would be so much easier with a guy she already knew could make her hormones wake up and jiggle. And considering they'd been in hibernation, like, for ever, she needed all the help she could get.

The bartender's gaze was drawn to something past her shoulder. 'Yeah, he'll be in tonight.'

'Really, you're sure?' she said, then bit her lip.

Dial down on the tarty—that sounded a bit too eager.

'Uh-huh.' His dark gaze returned to her face.

'Back off, Henry. You're poaching.'

Ella spun round at the deep, wonderfully familiar accent—and the shot of adrenaline went into overdrive. Cooper Delaney had looked super-fit that morning in ragged denim, but he took fit to a whole new level in a dark blue polo shirt and black jeans. But then her head carried on spinning and she started to tilt.

A tanned hand shot out to grasp her upper arm and hold her upright. 'Damn it, Henry, how many of those things have you given her?'

'Only the one.' The barman, who Ella's slightly fuzzy brain had registered must be called Henry, sounded affronted.

'Oh, yeah?'

Ella blinked, hearing the edge in Cooper's usually relaxed tone. Was he mad about something? And what did it have to do with Henry, the benevolent barman?

Cooper slapped a couple of bills onto the bar with enough force to make her jump. 'That's for the rum punch, man. The lady's with me.'

Really? Fabulous.

So she hadn't imagined his offer of a date. The spurt of joy at the thought was quickly quashed, though, when his fingers tightened on her arm and he slanted her a look that didn't seem particularly pleased to see her. 'We're out of here.'

'But I haven't finished my drink.' She pivoted on her

heel, making a grab for her glass. But missed as he hauled her away from the bar.

'You've had enough.'

Henry shrugged and shouted after them, 'Sorry, miz. I told you he was no good.'

'You didn't have to pay for that,' she said, racing to keep up with his long strides as he marched past the tables and headed out into the night, dragging her along in his wake. 'Henry said it was on the house.'

'Yeah, I'll just bet he did.' Was that a snarl?

A succession of people called out a greeting to him or shouted across the crowd, but other than throwing back a quick wave of acknowledgement he barely broke stride. By the time they stepped off the deck and he swung her round to face him, she was breathless, the happy glow from her Swizzle fading fast.

'Okay, let's have it.' His shadowed face looked harsh in the half-light from the bar as he grasped both her arms, and made full use of his superior height. 'What are you doing here?'

'I…' And just like that her tongue swelled up, rendering her speechless. And all Ruby's advice about how to put her flirt on got washed away on a tidal wave of mortification.

He didn't look remote, the way he had when they'd parted that morning. He looked upset.

She'd made a terrible mistake—coming here when he hadn't really meant to…

'Because if you've come all the way out here to give me another smackdown, don't bother. I got the message the first time, sweetheart. Loud and clear.'

Smackdown? What smackdown?

'I should leave,' she blurted out, suddenly wishing that the worn floorboards of the bar's deck would crack open and swallow her whole. Or better yet whisk her back to her nice, quiet, ocean-view room at the resort.

Sticking to safe might be dull, but at least it didn't get you into these sorts of pickles. She'd never managed to piss off any of the guys she'd actually dated to this extent.

She sent a wistful glance back at The Rum Runner— the joyous dance music pumping out into the night. The lively bar had contained so many exciting possibilities less than five minutes ago. But as she stepped past him he didn't let go.

'Hey, hang on a minute.' The edge had left his voice. 'You didn't answer my question.'

'Was there a question in there?' she asked.

He didn't look mad any more, which she supposed was good.

But as his emerald gaze raked over her the focused attention made her breasts tighten. Humiliating her even more. Obviously her nipples were completely immune to his disapproval.

But then his wide lips quirked. 'It was never meant as a smackdown, was it?'

She tugged herself loose, and stepped back—starting to get annoyed. Okay, so she'd misinterpreted his offer of a date. Although how she had, she still wasn't sure. And her big coming-out party was officially a washout—but did he really have to gloat? And what was all this nonsense about a smackdown? 'I really have to go.'

She went to walk round him again. But his large hand wrapped around her wrist and drew her up short. 'Hey, don't… Don't go.'

He stood so close, the delicious scent of seawater and soap surrounded her. Making it a little hard for her to process the words. Was he apologising now? After all but biting her head off? 'Captain Delaney, I don't think—' she began.

'Call me Coop,' he murmured, the husky tone sending those tempting shivers of reaction back up her spine.

She drew in a breath, not able to recall a single one of Ruby's careful instructions as he stared down at her with the glint of appreciation in his eyes—and fairly sure she didn't want to any more. This evening had turned into a disaster.

She might as well face it, she would never be as good a flirt as Ruby, even if she took a degree course. She huffed out a breath. 'Listen, I genuinely thought you asked me here, and I had such a nice time this morning, I don't want to sour it now.' She hooked a thumb over her shoulder, feeling stupidly bereft at the thought of her party night ending so soon, and so ignominiously. 'But I really think I should go now.'

Because I'm a little concerned you might have a borderline personality disorder.

She came here to see you. You dumbass.

Warmth spread across Cooper's chest like a shot of hard liquor but was tempered by a harsh jolt of regret as he registered the wary caution in Ella's eyes—which looked even bigger accented with the glittery powder. Her lips pursed, glossy with lipstick in the half-light, as if she were determined to stop them trembling, crucifying him.

What the hell were you thinking? Behaving like such a jerk?

Even he wasn't sure what had gripped him when he'd walked into the bar and spotted her chatting with Henry, with that flushed excitement on her face. But the word that had echoed through his head had been unmistakable.

Mine.

And then everything had gone straight to hell.

Of course, his crazy reaction might have had something to do with the severe case of sexual frustration he'd been riding ever since she'd stepped aboard the boat that morning, but that hardly excused it. And the truth was he'd been handling it just fine, until the moment she'd handed him that wad of bills on the dock.

That was the precise moment he'd lost his grip on reality.

He'd been snarky and rude, acting as if she'd offered to kick him in the nuts, instead of giving him a forty-dollar tip.

He accepted tips all the time, to hand over to the kids who crewed the boat. Just the way Sonny had done for him when he was a kid.

He'd founded his business on the generosity of tourists like May Preston and her husband, who came back every year and always showed their appreciation way above the going rate. But when Ella had done the same, somehow he'd lost it. Instead of seeing her generosity and thoughtfulness for what it was, he'd been thrown back in time to the humiliation of his high-school days and the never-ending stream of dead-end jobs he'd taken on to keep him and his mom afloat. Back then, his teenage pride had taken a hit every time he had to accept a gratuity from people he knew talked trash about his mom behind his back. But he'd brushed that huge chip off his shoulder years ago, or at least he'd thought he had.

Why the weight of the damn thing had reappeared at that precise moment and soured his final few moments with Ella, he didn't have a clue, and he didn't plan to examine it too closely. All that mattered now was that he didn't blow his second chance with her.

That she'd come down to The Rum Runner at his suggestion was one hell of a balm to his over-touchy ego. The least he could do now was show her a good time. And given how cute and sexy she looked in those hip-hugger jeans and that skimpy tank it wasn't exactly going to be a hardship.

He raked his hand through his hair, trying to grab hold

of some of his usual charm with women, and think of how best to engineer his way back into her good graces after acting like such a douche.

Then he recalled how she'd been moving that lush butt while chatting to Henry, rocking her hips in time to the music. His pal Oggie's band played the opening sax solo, backed by the manic drum beat, of their best dance track. And he hoped he had his answer.

'You can't go back to the hotel. Not before you've danced to some real Bermuda soca with me.'

'I don't know…'

She glanced back at the bar, but he could hear her hesitation.

'Sure you do. It'll be fun.' He took her hand, lifted it to his lips and buzzed a quick kiss across her knuckles. 'You've come all this way. And I've acted like a jerk. So I owe you.'

'That's really not necessary.' She chewed on her bottom lip, the indecision in her voice crucifying him a little more.

'Sure it is. One dance. By way of an apology? That's all I'm asking.'

The shy smile was enough to tell him she'd forgiven him. But the sparkle of anticipation was tempered by caution. 'Okay, I don't see how one dance could hurt.'

'Awesome.' He placed his hand on her waist to direct her back into the bar, the spike of lust making his throat go dry when her hip bumped his thigh.

'It may be thirsty work, though,' she shouted above the bump and grind of drums and bass. 'Perhaps I should go back and get my Rum Swizzle?'

'Let's work up a sweat first,' he said, placing firm hands on her hips as he slotted them both into the packed dance-floor, the sweat already slick on his forehead. 'I'll buy you one later.'

Dancing with her was bound to be really thirsty work,

but he didn't plan to let her have any more Rum Swizzles. Those damn things were lethal, especially on an empty stomach—and with her tiny frame and that little stumble at the bar after only half a glass, he would hazard a guess Ella Radley was a really cheap drunk. He wanted her fully conscious for the rest of the night, so he could enjoy her company—and anything else she wanted to offer him.

Her perfume—a refreshing mix of citrus and spices—drifted over him as she placed her hands lightly on his shoulders and rolled her hips to the riotous bass beat in a natural, unaffected rhythm that was more seductive than original sin.

She grinned up at him, the cute smile a tempting mix of innocence and provocation, then jerked up on her toes to shout in his ear. 'Aye-aye, Captain. But be warned. I'm on a mission tonight to get whatever I want.'

His hands tightened on her hips as her belly bumped against him and his groin throbbed in time to the music. 'Not a problem, sweetheart.'

Because so am I.

'That's enough of that.' Coop lifted the sunshine drink out of her hand and held it easily out of reach. 'I want you able to walk out of here.'

Ella sent him a mock pout, but couldn't disguise her happiness as his gaze settled on her face. The way it had been doing all evening, with a gratifying combination of possessiveness and desire.

They'd danced until they were breathless to the band's medley of soca anthems, then eased into the seductive moves of the soul tunes when they slowed the pace later in the evening.

It was well after midnight now, and the bar had begun to empty out. His large group of friends, most of whom had come over to their table to banter with Coop or introduce themselves to her, had mostly drifted away, leaving only a small group of die-hard couples on the dance floor still bumping and grinding with gusto and a scatter of people by the bar.

She'd danced with a few of the other guys, enjoying that relaxed, casual camaraderie that reminded her of her own friendship group back in Camden. But most of all she'd enjoyed the feel of Cooper's gaze on her throughout the evening—that said to everyone they were a couple. That—how had he put it?—she was with him, for the night. It had made her feel as if she belonged here, even though she was thousands of miles from home.

But more than that, his constant attention and that quick easy smile had both relaxed her and yet held a delicious tension, a promise of what was to come. Because she had no doubts whatsoever about where this was all headed. The smouldering looks, the proprietary touches, the irresistible scent of him, tangy and salty and spicy, wrapping around her in a potent blend of pheromones and sweat. And the delicious press of his erection outlined by the slow, seductive, sinuous moves of his muscular body as they danced.

The coil of desire had been pulsing in the pit of her stomach for hours now. Ready for him to make the next move—and if he didn't, she was ready to take the unprecedented step of making the move for him.

It was official. Ella Radley's flirt was now fully operational, the intoxicating buzz of the Rum Swizzles nothing compared to the glorious buzz of anticipation.

'And where exactly would I be walking to?' She arched an eyebrow, her tone rich with a confidence she'd thought had died inside her a lifetime ago.

His thumb brushed her cheek, his irises a mesmerising moss green in the bar's half-light. Resting his forehead on hers, he closed his fingers over her nape, that wandering thumb caressing the frantic pulse in her neck. 'My hut's down at the other end of the cove. You ready to take a stroll with me in the moonlight?'

It was the invitation she'd been waiting for, but the surge of excitement still made her giddy. She could already feel those rough, capable fingers on the slick flesh between her thighs. She wanted to taste him, touch him, inhale that delicious scent, and take the impressive ridge in his pants inside her. Her sex clasped and released, hollow and aching with the need to be filled.

Touching her lips to his, she licked across the seam of the wide, sensual mouth that had been driving her wild all day. The shot of adrenaline was as stimulating as the pulse of reaction when she heard him drag in a ragged breath. His fingers plunged into her hair, then clasped her head so his tongue could plunder.

She let him in, her tongue duelling with his as they sank into the ravenous kiss.

He broke away first, the pants of his breathing as thready as her own. 'I'm going to take that as a yes.'

She nodded, not sure she could speak around the joy closing off her throat.

Standing, he gripped her hand and hauled her out of her chair. He tossed a few dollars on the table, and sent Henry a parting salute. She waved her own goodbye at the barman, who was stacking glasses, a rueful smile on his face.

'See you around, pretty lady.' Henry waved back, shouting over the murmur of goodbyes being thrown their way by the bar's other remaining patrons. 'And don't you be doing anything I wouldn't, Coop.'

Coop dragged her outside, sending her a wicked grin over his shoulder as the night closed over them. 'Given what you would do, man,' he whispered for her ears alone, 'that gives me a hell of a lot of options.'

For some strange reason she found the comment riotously funny, her chuckle blending with the fading beat of

music and the sound of the rolling and retreating tide as
they stepped off the deck onto the beach. He laid his arm
across her shoulders, tugged her into his side to lead her
along the sand and into the darkness.

Crickets and night crawlers added an acoustic accompaniment to the flickering light of the fireflies in the undergrowth and the hushed lap of the water. She kicked
off her sandals, picked them up, and let her toes seep into
the damp sand.

The walk in the moonlight he'd promised went past in
a blur, neither of them speaking, the only sound the sea,
the insects and the rhythmic bump of her own heartbeat.
A one-storey shack raised over the beach on a wraparound
deck appeared as if by magic out of the undergrowth on
the edge of the sand. A lamp suspended from the porch
rail shone like a homing beacon, illuminating the rudimentary clapboard structure.

He dropped his arm from around her shoulders, to lace
his fingers through hers and lead her up the steps onto
the porch.

'You live here?' she asked, enchanted by the spartan
dwelling.

'Yeah, mostly.' He held open the screen door to reveal a
large, sparsely furnished, but tidy room. A sofa with well-worn cushions made up the living area, while a large mattress, the sheets neatly folded across the bottom, stood in
front of the open deck. A tiny kitchenette cordoned off by
a waist-high counter took up the hut's back wall, next to a
door that she deduced must lead to a bathroom.

But it was the open deck, blending the hut's interior with
the beach outside, that took her breath away. The silvery
glow of the moon dipped over the horizon, shimmering
over the water and making the dark sand look as if it disappeared into oblivion. The fresh scent of sea and salt and

exotic blooms only added to the feeling of wild, untamed freedom that was so like Cooper himself.

'It suits you,' she said.

He huffed, the half-laugh both wry and amused. 'Why? Because it's cheap?' he said and she heard the cynical edge.

'No, because it's charming and unpretentious and un-conventional.'

He turned up the lamp, giving the modest hut a golden glow.

Walking to the open deck, he closed two large shut-ters and then slid the screen door across, cocooning them in together against the Caribbean night. Only the sparkle of moonlight and the sound of surf and chirping insects seeped through the slats.

'Don't want to risk getting our butts bitten off by mos-quitos,' he said, crossing the short distance back to her.

She laughed, the rough stubble on his jaw ticklish against her neck as he gripped her hips and nuzzled the sensitive skin beneath her ear.

'Especially such a cute butt,' he added, giving the butt in question an appreciative squeeze.

She wrapped her arms around his lean waist and slipped her fingers beneath the waistband of his jeans, to caress the tight muscles of the backside she had admired that morn-ing in wet denim. 'I can totally get behind that sentiment.'

He chuckled, warm, callused palms sneaking under her camisole to glide up to her ribcage and send a series of tremors through her body.

'Flattery will get you everywhere,' he said. Before plac-ing his mouth on hers at last.

Releasing his bum, she lifted arms lethargic with lust and draped them over his broad shoulders; driving her fin-gers into the soft curls at his nape, she let him devour her. He angled his hips and the thick ridge in his pants rubbed against her belly.

Oh, yes, I want this so much.

To be taken, to take. She wanted to let her body do the asking and have his answer, in the primordial mating ritual of two animals in need of an endorphin fix. The fact that she liked him, that he seemed a genuinely nice guy, didn't hurt. But right here, right now, as the building firestorm made the pulsing ache in her sex unbearable, and her nipples tighten into hard, swollen nubs, all she really cared about was satisfying the driving hunger.

His large hands rose from her waist to frame her face and she revelled in the primitive need making his eyes darken and the muscle in his jaw flex and release.

'Before we take this any further...' he trapped her against the hut's wall, the heavy ridge thickening even more '...I need to know if you're on the pill.'

Crushing disappointment cut through the fog of rum and arousal. 'You don't have any condoms? I don't either, I didn't think—'

'Hey, don't panic,' he interrupted. 'I've got condoms.'

'Oh, thank God.' Relief gushed like molten lava between her thighs.

'But I'm a belt and braces kind of guy. Condoms break.' He scooped her hair off her neck, pressed those clever lips to her collarbone, shattering her concentration. 'That's how I happened. I'm not looking to father another me.'

She heard the note of regret, and had the sudden urge to soothe. 'But you're so beautiful.' She cradled his lean cheeks between her palms, drew her thumb over one tawny brow and grinned into those piercing emerald eyes—which had crinkled at the corners with amusement. 'Your mother must have been so pleased to have you,' she said, loving the rasp of the manly stubble on his cheeks as all her inhibitions happily dissolved in the sweet buzz of Rum Swizzles and pheromones. 'Even if you were an accident.'

She heard his chuckle. Had she said something funny? She hadn't meant to.

'Not really.' He sent her the secret hey-there-gorgeous grin that he'd sent her when they were underwater and exploring the reef. Then it had flattered her, as if they were the only two people in the whole ocean allowed to explore its treasures; now it made her heart muscle squeeze and release, exciting her.

'Has anyone ever told you you're great for a guy's ego when you're hammered?'

'I'm not hammered,' she said, sure she wasn't. He'd only let her have two more Rum Swizzles, which he'd insisted on mixing himself behind the bar. And they hadn't tasted nearly as alcoholic as that first one. Plus she'd pigged out on the popcorn shrimp, some delicious jalapeño cheese things and the chips and dips and other nibbles that had appeared at their table as if by magic between dance sets. Right now she was pleasantly buzzed, but her senses felt heightened, more acute, not dull or fuzzy.

He touched his nose to hers. 'If you say so, miz,' he said in a perfect echo of Henry the friendly barman's Bermudan accent.

The spontaneous laugh turned to a staggered moan as his hands snuck under her camisole and cupped her breasts.

'Oh, yes.' She arched into the bold caress as his thumbs brushed her nipples, making the rigid peaks ache. 'That feels fabulous.'

He laughed. 'Stop distracting me and answer the damn question.'

She opened her mouth to ask what question, but then he plucked at one pulsating nipple, rolling it between his thumb and forefinger, and all that came out was a groaned, 'Yes.'

'Hallelujah.'

His teasing fingers left her breast to drag her top over

her head. And unclip the hook of her bra. He tugged his shirt over his head and tossed it over his shoulder, revealing the naked chest that she'd imagined touching all day.

Hallelujah indeed.

He boosted her into his arms, her back bumping the wall, as he wedged the hard ridge between her thighs, pressing it against the damp gusset of her jeans. She gripped his shoulders, her head spinning from the sensory overload. Then he ducked his head to capture one thrusting nipple between his lips and suckled hard.

Fire roared down to her core and she writhed, swivelling her hips to increase the pressure of his magnificent erection on that hot, sweet, swollen spot.

He blew across her wet breast, the cool air making it tingle and tighten more. 'Damn, but you're gorgeous.'

'So are you,' she said, admiring the bulge of his biceps as he held her up, the bunched pecs and sculpted abs, and the happy trail that bloomed into a forest of dark blond curls where his low-slung jeans had slipped down under the pressure of her clutching thighs.

'Can I see you naked? Please?' she asked.

His answering laugh sounded strained. 'I guess so, seeing as you asked so nice.' He dropped her suddenly, clutched her arm as she stumbled. 'Race you.'

She giggled as he hopped around on one foot, wrestling to get his boot off.

'Don't just stand there.' He tossed the boot across the room. 'Lose the damn pants or you'll have to pay a forfeit.'

Unbuttoning her jeans, she slipped them over her hips, going for the full stripper effect as she wiggled out of them, and loving the way his nostrils flared as he lost the other boot.

His wicked grin spread, and her heart rate accelerated, as he unhooked his trousers, shoved them down and kicked them off, not once taking his eyes off her.

Her gaze caught on the magnificent erection, standing proud in the nest of tawny curls. 'Wow…that's…really rather exceptional.'

He laughed. 'Have I told you, I love your accent?' He inclined his head towards the last piece of clothing she had on. 'Now lose the panties, before I rip them off.'

She whipped them off, twirled them on her finger and flung them away with a flourish.

'Good job.' He grabbed her wrist and dragged her to the bed, lying down beside her on the surprisingly comfy mattress.

She shivered, the light breeze coming through the shutters scented with the ocean.

His thumb trailed down her sternum. Then circled one heavy breast. She lifted up on her elbows to kiss him. The taste of the cola he'd been drinking all evening was as sweet as the weight of that exceptional erection cradled against her belly. Anticipation roared through her system. It had been so long since she'd felt this sexy, this aroused, this playful.

Ruby was right: why had she always been so serious about sex after college? She planned to correct that right now—she licked into his mouth, loving his staggered groan—with this gorgeous, hot, wonderfully reckless guy who was a gift she couldn't wait to unwrap.

His hands framed her face, his fingers plunging into her hair. She wrapped greedy fingers around the thick erection, slid her hand from root to tip, assessing its girth, its length, imagining it embedded into that aching, empty place between her legs.

But he swore softly as her thumb glided over the plump head, gathering the slick drop of moisture—and grabbed hold of her wrist, to tug her hand away.

'I'm way too close for that, sweetheart, but how about…?' His voice trailed off as he traced his thumb between her breasts, circled her belly button, then delved into the hot, aching flesh of her sex.

Moisture flooded between her thighs.

She drew her knees up, let her head drop back, her sobs of pleasure loud over the sound of surf and the rustle of the breeze against their sweat-slicked bodies.

He circled and toyed with the slick nub, teasing the perfect spot. 'That's it, baby, I want to see you come for me.'

One large, blunt finger entered her, then another pushed in beside it, stretching her, stroking the walls of her sex as his thumb continued to play, to provoke. Sensation fired across her skin, trapped her breath under her breastbone. The coil of need tightened like a vice, the pleasure turning to devastating, delicious pain as it built to impossible proportions but wouldn't let her go.

Clinging to his shoulders, urging him on, she pumped her hips into his hand, riding that wonderfully devious touch as she gave herself up to the riot of sensations.

Then he moved down on the bed, and disappeared between her knees. She shouted out in shock and delight as his tongue lapped at her swollen clitoris. Then he captured the slick nub between his lips and sucked. The coil yanked tight and then exploded in a dazzling shower of sensation. She sobbed—the long, thin cry of completion trapped in her throat as his mouth drove her through the last magnificent swell of orgasm.

She pressed her legs together as he lifted his head, collapsing back to earth. Shuddering and shaking, she opened her eyes as he grinned down at her, his lips slick with her juices.

The rumbled hum of his approval folded around her heart like a caress.

'Sweeter than a Rum Swizzle,' he whispered, the sensual, playful grin even more beautiful than the rest of him.

The sight was so unbearably erotic, gratitude swelled in her chest, turning her voice into a throaty purr. 'Thank you.'

His lips tipped up at the edges. 'No need to thank me, baby, the pleasure was all mine.' He placed a kiss on the tip of her nose. 'But we're not finished yet,' he added, reaching across her to grab a foil packet from a glass jar on the upturned crate that doubled as a bedside table. He held it up. 'You want to do the honours, or should I?'

She lifted it out of his hand, her mouth watering at the thought of exploring that magnificent erection. And silently thanking him again for keeping things light and fun. 'Let me.'

She pushed his shoulder, until he lay on his back, that proud erection jutting up towards his belly button. Holding the packet in her hand, she licked the new bead of moisture off the tip. Savouring the taste of him. And eager to torment him the way he'd tormented her.

But the guttural groan was followed by a harsh expletive and before she could take him into her mouth he clasped her cheeks to hold her back.

'I'm sorry, sweetheart, but we're going to have to save that for later. I'm not Superman—and I don't want to disappoint you.'

He couldn't possibly disappoint her, she thought. But only laughed at his look of panic. 'Are you sure you're not Superman?'

'I used to be…' The confident smile returned as he rolled on top of her and snagged the condom packet out of her hand. 'But you're zapping all my super-powers.'

Ripping the foil with his teeth, he sheathed himself quickly, before nudging her thighs apart and settling between them. She felt the bulbous head nudge at her entrance as he held her hips, angling her pelvis.

She groaned as the thick shaft speared through the tight sheath, overwhelming her senses as her slick, swollen flesh stretched to receive him.

At last he was buried deep, pushing at her cervix. She gasped, astonished at the fullness, and how right, how exquisite it felt. She stroked his nape with unsteady fingers, enjoying the weight of him, the feeling of intimacy, and unity.

'I think you've boldly gone where no man has gone before.' She laughed, surprising herself with the ridiculous comment. But her heart felt so full, her body so magnificent, impaled on his. Could she come again? So soon after an orgasm? She certainly never had before, but with Cooper anything felt possible.

He swore, panting, the sinews of his neck straining beneath her fingers as he began to move. 'Damn it, woman, don't quote *Star Trek* at me now,' he grunted, between thrusts. 'Can't you see I'm trying to Klingon here.'

She snorted a laugh that choked into a sob as he stroked a place deep inside that triggered another unstoppable rush towards orgasm.

Goodness. I have a G-spot. Who knew?

'Touch yourself,' he demanded. 'I want you to come with me.'

She spread her own folds, blindly rubbing the stiff nub as he directed, feeling wild and untamed, greedily pursuing her own pleasure as the wave became sharper, sweeter, more glorious.

She rode the crest, his ragged grunts matching her loud moans, and soared towards oblivion with tears of joy and laughter—and staggered astonishment—hovering on her lids.

She drifted back to consciousness, the euphoria of afterglow slowly replaced by discomfort from the thick penis still lodged inside her.

He lifted off her, making her groan as her tight flesh struggled to release him.

'That was seriously awesome.' Flopping over onto his back, he lay with his arm over his face. 'You're incredibly tight.'

She felt herself blush, an odd combination of pleasure and acute embarrassment at the intimate comment. 'Only because you're so big,' she said, trying to find the playful tone again.

'While my ego and I thank you for that...' he dropped his arm to find her hand and thread his fingers through hers '...I'm not that much bigger than the average guy.'

The blush glowed. Maybe it wasn't just his size that had made him feel so large. Maybe it was because she hadn't done it with anyone in at least a year. And certainly never with that much energy or enthusiasm.

He turned onto his side, and cupped her cheek, his palm cool against her heated flesh. 'Has it been a while?'

She blinked, disconcerted by the perceptive comment. 'Are you a mind-reader?'

He touched her cheek, the tender, curious smile more seductive than the tangy scent of sex that surrounded them. 'How long?'

She huffed out a laugh, the embarrassment burned away by a new surge of arousal. 'Far too long, it seems.'

He hooked his thigh over her legs, shocking her when something stiff prodded her hip.

'Is that...?' She looked down, stunned to see him hard and ready again still sheathed by the condom.

He lifted her chin, grinning. 'Yeah, it is.' The cheeky grin—not to mention his astonishing powers of recuperation—made him seem very boyish. Too boyish.

'How old are you?' she asked, before she could think better of it.

His lips tilted. 'Nearly thirty.'

She propped herself up on her elbows. Good grief, he was still in his twenties. 'How nearly?'

'I'll be twenty-nine next month. Why? You planning to give me a present?' He cupped her breast, licked at the nipple. 'I can think of something I'd love to see gift-wrapped.'

'You're twenty-eight.' She scooted back. 'But that's… practically a toy boy.'

He chuckled, then grabbed her shoulders and shoved her onto her back, anchoring her in place with one hard thigh. 'Oh, yeah? So how old are you, then?'

'I'm thirty-four,' she said, indignantly.

His gaze drifted over her face. 'You don't look it.'

There didn't seem to be any judgment in the tone, but still she felt…embarrassed. 'Well, I am.' Maybe it was only six years but it felt like the wrong six years. 'Let me up.'

'Not going to happen, old lady,' he teased.

She struggled, trying to buck him off, but he didn't budge. 'Please, this feels awkward now.'

'Why? You're at your sexual peak. And so am I.'

Given the now-prominent feel of his erection, she had to agree. 'I know, but it feels weird.'

'It's not weird, it's cool.' He rubbed his shaft against her hip—making it fairly obvious he wasn't put off in the slightest by her vintage. She looked down at the thrusting erection. 'Although FYI, I'm not a toy boy,' he added. 'You're a damn cougar.'

A laugh popped out before she could stop it, but cut off when he cupped her sex. His fingers delved, stroking her oversensitive clitoris, the touch light and fleeting but enough to send shock waves of need echoing through her.

She thrust her fingers into his hair as he opened her thighs to position the impressive erection against her entrance. 'Well, I suppose, if you put it like—'

Grasping her hips, he thrust deep in one long, smooth,

all-consuming stroke, stealing her breath and cutting off any more pointless protests.

Oh, sod it.

Six years was nothing, she decided, especially once he'd established a slow, lazy, teasing rhythm that quickly became more intoxicating than the rum.

Hours later, Ella struggled to focus on the radiant glow of dawn peeping through the shutters. Contemplating the tenderness between her thighs and the soreness in other, previously unknown and now thoroughly exercised muscle groups, she conceded that, while the years might not be a problem, the mileage definitely was.

'I should go,' she mumbled, her fuzzy brain latching onto the fact that lingering past daybreak had the potential to be a lot more awkward than their age difference.

But when she lifted one tired limb, a muscular forearm banded round her midriff from behind and hauled her back into his embrace.

'Nothing doing,' Cooper's sleep-roughened voice murmured against her hair. His big body cocooned her, his chest solid against her back, the soft hairs on his thighs brushing the backs of her legs and the softening erection still prominent against her bottom.

She debated arguing with him, but couldn't fight the thundering beat of her pulse, the fatigue dragging her into oblivion or the novelty of being held so securely. Maybe she could stay and snuggle, for a little bit? Grab one more hot memory to sustain her through the difficult truth she would have to face when she got home?

This was her holiday of a lifetime, after all, and Cooper Delaney—toy boy extraordinaire—her passport to no-holds-barred pleasure.

She relaxed, warmed by the comfort of his embrace. 'All right, but I'll go soon.'

Her lips tilted into a smile as he grunted. 'Shut up and go to sleep.' His forearm tightened under her breasts. 'You're going to need to get your strength up, my little cougar. This toy boy isn't finished with you yet.'

She choked out a laugh—that became a wistful hum as his arm became slack and her own body drifted towards sleep.

Colourful images collected behind her eyes—the glitter of pink sand beaches, the darting sparkle of blue-finned fish, the tangerine glow of fruit juice and rum, and the piercing jade of Cooper Delaney's eyes.

She swallowed to relieve the clutching sensation in her chest, and tumbled headlong into the rainbow dream.

CHAPTER FIVE

'HEY, COOP, GET your butt out of bed, it's past eleven. And I've got exciting news.'

The muffled musical voice intruded on Ella's dream. She squeezed open an eyelid, grateful when the brittle sunlight hitting her retinas didn't appear to be accompanied by any pain, despite the definite thumping in her head.

Flopping over onto her back, she squinted at the empty bed beside her, the rumpled sheets striped by the sunlight slanting through the shutters. And heard the thumping again. This time, though, it was definitely not in her head, but coming from the hut's door, which shook on its hinges as the same musical voice from her dream, lilting with the lazy rhythms of a Bermuda native, shouted: 'No use hiding, man. Henry told me you'd be here.'

Ella shot upright, clasping the bed's thin sheet to her naked breasts, and swayed as several questions bombarded her at once.

How long had she been asleep? Where were her clothes? Where was Coop? And who the heck was that woman banging on the door?

The answer to number one was hours, if the brightness of the sunlight was anything to go by. Scrambling out of bed as furtively as possible, she located her clothes in a neatly stacked pile on the arm of the sagging sofa, answering question number two. Questions three and four remained a mystery though, as she dressed as soundlessly as she could manage while continuing to scan the hut for any sign of her host.

She jumped as the banging began again.

'Hey, I can hear you in there. Avoidance won't do you a damn bit of good.'

Rats, do you have bionic hearing?

She waited a few more strained seconds, while debating opening the shutters and escaping onto the deck, but eventually discarded the idea—given the girl's hearing capabilities.

The banging continued, and her not entirely settled stomach churned. What if this girl were Cooper's girlfriend? Or his wife? Was that why he'd disappeared? Because what did she really know about Captain Studly, except that he was gorgeous, knew how to dance the soca and had magic fingers, a very inventive tongue, and a huge and permanently stiff…

Don't go there.

Squaring her shoulders, she swung the door open ready to face the consequences, to be greeted by a stunningly beautiful barefoot young woman of about twenty, wearing a pair of Daisy Dukes, a T-shirt with the message 'Don't Mess with a Libran', tightly braided hair decorated with multicoloured beads, and a stunned expression.

'Hi.' She craned her neck to search the hut's interior, having gained her composure a lot faster than Ella. 'Is Coop around?'

'Um, no, apparently not,' Ella replied, opting for the only answer she could give with any confidence.

'Uh-huh?' The girl gave her a thorough once-over that had the heat steaming into Ella's cheeks. 'I guess he's up at the big house.'

The big house? What big house?

'Sorry to wake you,' the girl said. 'Henry didn't tell me

Coop left the Runner with company last night. Just that he headed for his beach hut. Suppose Henry was messing with me. And Coop.'

And me, thought Ella, annoyed by Henry the barman's joke, and acutely embarrassed that this girl now knew she was the sort of woman who got picked up in bars.

What had seemed wildly romantic last night, now felt pretty tacky.

Ruby had encouraged her to let her inner flirt loose, but there had definitely been no mention of getting tipsy on rum cocktails, then getting nekkid with Captain Studly and jumping him four…no, five…oh, heck, make that at least a half-dozen times during the night.

'You Coop's new lady?' The girl interrupted Ella's panicked reappraisal of her behaviour.

'Um, no, we're just…' *What? Snorkel mates? Dance partners? Bonk buddies?*

The burning in her cheeks promptly hit maximum voltage as she searched for the appropriate term while recalling in X-rated detail exactly how intimately she and the invisible Coop had got acquainted last night, after very little provocation. 'Friends,' she finished lamely.

With benefits. Gold-standard benefits.

The phrase hung in the brisk morning air unspoken, but not unfigured out if the girl's frank appraisal was anything to go by. 'Do you know when he's going to be back?'

Hardly, seeing as I have no clue where he is.

'I'm afraid not.'

'Could you tell him I stopped by? I'm Sonny's daughter, Josie, and I—'

'Why don't you come in and wait for him?' Ella shoved the door wide, determined to make a fast getaway, before this situation got any more awkward. 'I was just leaving.'

Josie sent her a doubtful look as she stepped into the room. 'You sure, I—'

'Absolutely positive,' Ella replied, grabbing her bag from the hook by the door and slipping past the girl, before she could ask any more unanswerable questions.

'You want me to give Coop a message?'

Ella paused on the porch, the clutching sensation she'd had as she fell asleep the night before returning. 'Would you tell him thanks?' She cleared her throat, the stupid clutching sensation starting to squeeze her ribcage.

For being a friend when I needed one, she added silently as she jumped off the hut's porch and her feet sank into the wet sand.

Josie called out a goodbye and she waved back as she set off down the beach. But she didn't glance back again. Knowing it would only tighten the band squeezing her chest.

She'd had an amazing night. Maybe she'd gone a little off piste from Ruby's plan—and discovered the liberating powers of flirtation, soca dancing, Rum Swizzles and sweaty, no-strings sex in the process. Okay, make that a lot off piste.

But it was all good.

Give or take the odd heart murmur.

'Up you get, Sleeping Beauty, breakfast is served.' Coop bumped the hut's door open with his butt, keeping a firm hold on the tray his housekeeper had piled high with freshly sliced fruit, French toast, syrup and coffee. It had taken Inez a good half hour to assemble everything to her exacting standards—and quiz him mercilessly about his 'overnight guest'—during which time he'd got stupidly eager to see Ella again. Enough to question why he hadn't just woken her up and invited her to his place for breakfast.

The fifteen-acre estate that overlooked the cove, and the two-storey colonial he'd built on the bluff, were a symbol of who he was now. And he was super proud of it—and all he'd achieved, after ten long, back-breaking years of dawn wake-up calls refurbing second-hand equipment, long days spent out on the ocean running back-to-back dives, late nights getting his brain in a knot at the local community college studying for his MBA, all while keeping a ready smile on his face to schmooze a succession of tourists and corporate clients and bank managers and investors.

His business—Dive Guys—had made its first million-dollar turnover five years ago, and he'd celebrated by buying himself a brand-new motor launch, and the beach hut he'd been renting since his early days with Sonny. Three years later, he'd expanded the franchise across the Caribbean and had finally had enough to invest in the construction of his dream home on the land he'd bought behind the hut. He'd moved into Half-Moon House two years ago— but still couldn't quite believe that all those years of work had paid off in a wraparound deck that looked out over the ocean, five luxury en-suite bedrooms, a forty-foot infinity pool, a mile of private beach and an extremely nosey housekeeper.

Normally, he loved showing the place off to women he dated.

But when he'd woken up with Ella cuddled in his arms, he'd decided to keep the place a secret until after he'd finessed Inez into cooking a lavish breakfast for his overnight guest.

There had been something so cute and refreshing about Ella's breathless enthusiasm when she'd got a load of his first place the night before. She wasn't the only woman he'd brought to the hut, but she was the only one who had appreciated its charm and overlooked the used furniture and lack of amenities.

For some weird reason it had felt good to know all she'd seen was him—not Dive Guys, or the things it had afforded him.

'That looks real tasty, Coop. You shouldn't have bothered, though—I already grabbed a crab patty up at the
Runner.'

Coop swung round, nearly dropping the tray, to find
Sonny's daughter, Josie, perched on one of his bar stools.
With her long legs crossed at the knee and a mocking
smile on her lips, she should have looked all grown up,
but somehow all he ever saw was the fresh kid he'd met a
decade ago and who had made it her mission in life to be
a thorn in his side ever since.

'Josie, what are you doing here?' He dumped the tray on
the counter, sloshing the coffee all over the French toast, as
he took in the empty bed in the far corner, and the empty
couch where he'd folded Ella's clothes into a pile not more
than thirty minutes ago. 'And where the hell is Ella?'

Josie's grin became smug as she snagged a chunk of
fresh pineapple off the breakfast tray. 'So that's Sleeping
Beauty's name. I always wondered if she had one.'

'Ha, ha,' he said without heat, used to Josie's teasing.

'She's very pretty. But kind of shy. Not your usual type.'

'Where is she?' he asked again, not happy at the news
that Josie had met her. Somehow he didn't think someone
with Ella's insta-blush tendencies would appreciate being
caught in his bed by a smartass like Josie. 'Please tell me
you didn't say anything to make her bolt.'

Josie sucked on the pineapple, shaking her head. 'Uh-
uh. She bolted all on her own. Seemed kind of spooked
that you'd disappeared.'

He ran his fingers through his hair. Damn it, he'd only
been gone a half-hour and Ella had looked totally done
in. After the workout they'd both had last night he would
have bet she'd be comatose for hours yet. The thought had
him eyeing his uninvited guest. 'You woke her up, didn't
you, you little…?'

He made a swipe for Josie, but she leapt off the stool

and danced out of his reach, laughing. 'What's the big deal? You don't date the tourists, remember? In case they get ideas.'

Not Ella.

The thought popped into his head, and had him stopping dead in front of Josie—the quest for retribution dying a quick death.

What was with that? Sure Ella had been sweet, and eager and inventive in bed, but how had she got under his guard so easily? Knowing what he did about tourists who liked to slum it in neighbourhood bars, how come he had never thought of Ella as one of them? And why had he crept out of bed and harassed Inez into making her breakfast? He didn't have a romantic bone in his body. Not since... He stared at the ruined toast, the creeping sense of humiliation coming back in an unpleasant rush of memory.

Not since the evening of the junior prom in Garysville, Indiana, when he'd stood like a dummy on Amy Metcalfe's porch, his neck burning under the collar of the borrowed suit, and a corsage clutched in his sweating palm that had cost him ten of his hard-earned dollars, while Amy's old man yelled at him to get lost, and his prom date sent him a pitying smile from the passenger seat of his half-brother Jack Jnr's Beemer convertible.

'Don't you want to know why I'm here?' Josie stared at him, her usual mischief replaced with excitement. 'I've got news.'

Shaking off the unpleasant memory, he clamped down hard on the dumb urge to head out after Ella. 'Sure? What news?' He tossed a piece of papaya into his mouth, impressed with his own nonchalance.

The smile on Josie's face reached ear-to-ear proportions. 'Taylor popped the question last night and I said yes.'

'What question?' he said, trying to process the information while his mind was still snagged on Ella and why the hell she'd run out on him. Wasn't Taylor that pimply kid Josie'd been dating for a while?

Josie's eyes rounded. 'Damn, Coop, even you can't be that dumb. The "Will you marry me?" question. Duh.'

Coop choked on the mango chunk he'd just slung in his mouth. 'You've got to be kidding me?' His eyes watered as his aggravation over Ella's sudden departure was surpassed by horror. 'You're way too young to be getting married.' Plus marriage was for chumps—and Josie was a smart kid—what was she thinking?

Josie whacked him hard on the back, dislodging the chunk and nearly dislocating his shoulder. 'I'm twenty,' she said, indignantly. 'Taylor and I have been dating for four years.' She propped her hands on her hips, striking the Wonder Woman pose he knew meant she was about to start lecturing him. 'And we love each other. Marriage is the obvious next step. So we can think about babies.'

'Babies!' he yelped, as a blood vessel popped out on his forehead and began to throb. 'You cannot be serious?'

'Just because you're dead set on being the Oldest Player in Town,' she countered, 'doesn't mean everyone's that cynical and immature.'

'I'm immature?' he snapped. Seeing her flinch, he struggled to lower his voice, and regain some of his usual cool.

But damn it, first Ella's disappearing act, and now this? Had all the females in Bermuda been hitting the crazy sauce while he slept?

'Honey, I'm not the one planning to get hitched when I'm still in college.' Not to mention have a parcel of rugrats. Was she nuts?

The look she sent him went from pissed to pitying. 'Why does the thought of that terrify you so much, Coop? Maybe you should try it some time yourself?'

'What? Marriage? And kids?' he scoffed, barely suppressing the shudder. 'No way.'

'Not that, not yet, but...' Josie searched his face, the pitying look starting to annoy him now. 'Couldn't you at least try dating the same woman for longer than a week?' Her eyes shadowed with concern. 'Haven't you ever thought there might be more to women than just hot and sweaty sex?'

'Damn it, give me a break.' He slapped his hands over his ears. 'Don't talk to me about that stuff—my ears are bleeding.' He'd never kept his dating habits a secret, but Josie butting into his sex life was just wrong. On so many levels.

She glared at him. 'So who's being immature now?'

He dropped his hands, having to concede that point. 'Fine, you win that one, but conversations about sex are off limits, okay?' The last thing he needed was some snot-nosed kid giving him dating advice.

'Okay, truce.' She surprised him by backing down. 'I'll butt out of your business. You're a hopeless cause anyway.' She sighed, to emphasise the point. 'I didn't come here to argue with you, I came to tell you Taylor and I want to set the date for August tenth. If you're good with us using your land to do the ceremony on the cove near the Runner?'

'Sure, of course, no problem,' he said, feeling about two feet tall all of a sudden. He hadn't meant to piss on her parade; the wedding announcement had just come as a shock, that was all. How the heck had Josie grown up without him noticing?

'I also wanted to ask you to be my witness,' she added. 'If you think you can contain your horror long enough to sign the book?' The shadow of uncertainty in her gaze shaved another foot off his stature. Hell, he hadn't meant to be that much of a grouch.

'You sure you want the Oldest Player in Town there?' he murmured, relieved when she sent him a cheeky grin.

'Only if he promises not to hit on the bridesmaids.'

The thought of hitting on anyone brought back thoughts of Ella. And the pang of regret sliced under his ribs. She had to be long gone by now.

He raised his hand as if taking a mock oath. 'I do solemnly swear not to hit on the bridesmaids.'

'Cool, we're all set, then.' Josie grinned, then planted a kiss on the tip of his nose. 'I'll keep you posted on the wedding plans. I better hit the road, though.' She rolled her eyes. 'You have no idea how much work goes into organising a wedding in under four months.'

And he didn't want to know, he thought silently, but decided to keep that information to himself.

'Oh, by the way,' she said as she reached the door. 'Sleeping Beauty left you a message before she ran off.'

'Yeah?' The bubble of hope expanded under his breastbone. 'What message? Did she tell you where she's staying?' Maybe if she had, he could give her a call? Get Inez to make a fresh batch of French toast, or better yet some lunch?

Josie shook her head. 'She just said to tell you thanks.'

'That's it?' The bubble of hope deflated, making his voice sound flat and dull.

Josie nodded, her expression thoughtful as she studied him. 'If you wanted to contact her, Henry might know where she's staying if she was at the Runner last night. You know how talkative he is.'

'No, that's okay, it's no big deal,' he replied, and willed himself to believe it.

'Are you sure?'

He forced out a laugh. 'Sure, I'm sure. Not my style.' He didn't get hung up on women, even ones as cute and sexy as Ella. 'Oldest Player in Town, remember?'

Josie rolled her eyes again. 'Oh, yeah. How could I forget?'

But after Josie had left, and he had dumped the ruined breakfast spread in the trash and collapsed onto the bed, the joke nickname didn't seem all that funny any more. Especially when he got a lungful of the light, refreshing, lemony scent and the earthy smell of sex that still lingered on the sheets.

CHAPTER SIX

ELLA PLUCKED THE TRAY of Triple Indulgence Brownies out of the industrial oven and dropped it gingerly on the counter—her tummy hitching up towards her throat as the aroma of melting chocolate surrounded her. The rich decadent scent tasted like charcoal on her tongue. Clasping her hand over her mouth, she sliced the brownies into twelve chunks, perched the tray on the window sill to cool, and rushed into the café, her stomach wobbling alarmingly.

Taking deep, measured breaths, she berated herself and her stupid nervous tummy as she stacked the batch of mini-chocolate tarts she'd made earlier—which thankfully didn't smell too strongly. Ruby would be here any minute and the last thing she needed was more searching looks and probing questions from her business partner—because she'd barfed all over the shop again.

She'd been tense and out of sorts for weeks. Ever since she'd got back from Bermuda and got the diagnosis she'd been dreading from her doctor, Myra Patel. That she was no longer ovulating at regular intervals—which explained the now five months without a period—because the onset of premature menopause was now a reality.

But she thought she'd come to terms with it. Or at least found a strategy to deal with her loss. Even though her biological clock was now ticking at triple time—and Myra had told her that her chances of conceiving naturally were probably remote, and getting remoter by the second—she had referred her to a specialist. Plus she and Ruby had discussed the feasibility of other options, when and if she found a life partner.

The good news was, after her wild night with Coop, there was every reason to be a lot more cheerful about her prospects when it came to relationships. Or at least sexual relationships.

Coop.

Her stomach clutched and released, the queasiness returning.

Maybe it was about time she admitted that her fertility problems weren't the only thing that had had her down in the dumps? That her nervous stomach wasn't just a symptom of her stress over the test results she'd got from Myra two months ago, but also her ridiculous overreaction to her one night with Cooper Delaney.

Somehow, she'd got fixated on him, picking over every minute detail of their day and night together—instead of assigning the experience to its rightful place in her past, and moving on with her real life.

So what if he'd disappeared the following morning, without leaving a note to say where he'd gone? They'd had a one-night fling. He'd owed her nothing. They lived thousands of miles apart, and he was only twenty-eight, for goodness' sake. Not that their age difference had bothered him… Then again, maybe it had, more than he'd let on. Could that be why he'd disappeared so abruptly? Before she'd even woken up? Without bothering to say goodbye?

She folded the oven mitt she'd used into the drawer and slammed it shut.

Stop right there, you're doing it again.

The hollow feeling of inadequacy opened up in her stomach, and the weary ache in her chest pinched her heart.

Maybe if she had left him a note…

She sighed and glanced up to see Ruby and Cal standing together on the pavement outside the shop—bidding
each other goodbye as they did every morning before Cal
headed for the tube station and his work as a top defence
barrister in the City. The hollow weight became a gaping
hole as she watched them.

Ruby threw her head back and laughed at something
her husband had said. Callum said something else, that
seemed to make her laugh more, but then he gripped the
lapels of her coat and jerked her up onto her tiptoes, before
silencing the laughter with a hungry kiss.

Ella felt the nasty dart of envy as Ruby's arms wrapped
around Cal's neck to pull him closer. The kiss heated to
scorching, Cal's hands finding Ruby's bottom beneath
the hem of her coat. Anyone passing by would have mistaken them for newlyweds, instead of a couple who had
recently celebrated their seventh wedding anniversary and
had three very energetic children ranging in age from two
to six.

Ella dropped her chin, and concentrated on rearrang-
ing the cookies on the display, feeling like a Peeping Tom
as the nausea pitched and rolled in her belly. The door-
bell tinkled, then the creak of the café door opened and
slammed shut followed by the click of Ruby's stilettos on
the tiled floor.

'Sorry I'm late. I'll close up today to make up for it.'
Ruby's voice sounded upbeat and pleasantly mellow, as it
often did first thing in the morning. Ella frowned, dusting icing sugar over the tarts. Hard to remember now that
her business partner had once been the biggest grump on
the planet until she'd downed at least two cups of coffee
in the morning, but that was before her fender bender with
Callum Westmore nearly eight years ago.

'That man sweet-talked me back into bed,' Ruby added
with a huff. 'After Helga picked up the kids.'

'Poor you,' Ella muttered under her breath, then bit her lip to contain the sour note of sarcasm, and the bile rising up her throat.

What was the matter with her? She'd always been so happy for Ruby and Cal. It wasn't as if their path to true love had exactly been smooth. And as for Max and Ally and Art, Ruby and Cal's three irrepressible children, she adored them. And adored having a special place in their lives as their favourite 'auntie'. That relationship would only become more treasured if the possibility of a childless future became a reality.

'Ella, is everything okay?'

She put down the icing sugar to find Ruby watching her. Far too closely. Oh, no. Had she just heard that cutting remark? How was she supposed to explain it? 'Yes, of course...'

'Are you sure? You're a rather strange colour.'

'Really, I'm perfectly—' The gag reflex struck without warning, punching Ella's larynx and slamming her stomach into her throat. She slapped her hand over her mouth, and raced around the counter and into the restroom—getting there just in time to lose in the toilet the tea and dry toast she'd managed to force down that morning for breakfast.

'Okay, deep breaths.' Ruby rubbed Ella's spine as the nausea retreated. The cool cloth felt glorious on the back of her neck as she dragged in several deep breaths.

'How's your stomach? All finished puking?'

'Yes, I think so.' Ella pressed her hand to her belly to double-check. But her stomach seemed to have settled after the retching, the strong scent of the disinfectant in the toilet nowhere near as abrasive as the brownie scent had been earlier.

Ruby flushed the toilet and anchored her arm around Ella's waist. 'Good, then let's get you more comfortable.'

By the time they'd both settled in the two armchairs at the back of the café, Ruby's careful scrutiny had Ella's cheeks burning.

'Any idea what caused it?' Ruby asked.

Ella took a moment to examine the hands she had clasped in her lap.

'From that delightful shade of rosé on your cheeks I'm guessing you do know.' Ruby's hand covered hers and squeezed. 'But you don't want to say.'

'It's silly.' Ella shrugged, forced to face her friend. 'I'm totally overreacting to a stupid holiday fling—which didn't mean anything.'

'Of course it meant something. You wouldn't have slept with him if it didn't. You're not the casual-sex type.'

Ella breathed a heavy sigh. 'Kind of annoying that I didn't figure that out before I decided to jump into bed with him for a night of casual sex, isn't it?' The clutching sensation in her chest was back with a vengeance. 'I miss him. I wish I'd hung around to tell him goodbye properly. Got closure. Then maybe I could stop giving myself an ulcer thinking about him constantly.'

Ruby nodded, her expression far too intuitive. 'All excellent points. But can I suggest another possible explanation for the puking?'

Ella frowned. Why was Ruby looking at her like that? As if she was struggling to suppress a smile. 'There is no other—'

'Because you're no more the highly strung, give-yourself-an-ulcer type than you are the casual-sex type.'

'Your point?' Ella replied a little sharply.

'Look, you've been stressing about your holiday fling for weeks, I know that. But isn't it at all possible—given the extremely hot description you gave me of your bedroom aerobics with Captain Studly—that what we just witnessed might be something more substantial than a nervous tummy?'

'Such as?'

'Morning sickness.'

Ella stiffened. 'You know that's not possible.'

'According to Dr Patel it isn't impossible.'

Ella's frown became a scowl. 'It's only a very slight possibility. And we used condoms the whole time.'

'As did Cal and I before we got pregnant with Arturo,' Ruby shot straight back.

'It's not the same thing.' The sour note was back. 'You don't have any fertility issues.'

'I still think you should do a pregnancy test, just to be sure.'

Ella straightened in the chair. 'I am sure.' Sure what the result would be. And even surer that bringing back memories of another pregnancy test that she'd taken with Ruby years before would only make her current misery seem even more insurmountable.

'Well, I'm not.'

Ella threw up her hands. 'Yes, well, I don't have a pregnancy test and I don't have time to go and get one because we open in half an hour.' Maybe if Ruby wouldn't listen to her, at least she'd listen to reason.

'That's okay, because I do.' Reaching into her handbag, Ruby produced a blue and white chemist bag from which she pulled out a telltale pink box.

'Where did you get that?' Ella stared, her hurt and astonishment turning to dismay.

'Ella, you've been sick three times this week now.' Grabbing Ella's hand, Ruby slapped the box into her palm.

Ella wanted to refuse, but as she stared at the box she felt her will power crumbling in the face of Ruby's determination.

'Just go pee on the stick.' Ruby closed Ella's fingers around the box. 'Don't overthink this. Whatever the result is, we'll handle it. But denial is not the answer. I'll wait here.'

Ella stood up, her stomach folding in on itself, as the last of her will power ebbed away on a wave of exhaustion. 'Okay, fine, but you may be waiting a long time.' She frowned at her best friend. 'I am so not in the mood to pee on demand right now.'

It took fifteen torturous minutes before she could get out of the toilet.

'I left it on the vanity in there.' She washed her hands in the shop's sink and dosed them with anti-bacterial gel. 'Don't forget to dispose of it before we open,' she added, brushing the stupid sting of tears off her cheek.

'Ella, don't cry. You need to know for sure.'

She didn't dignify that with an answer, but simply set about filling the icing bag with cream-cheese frosting. She needed to be ready for the nine a.m. rush when they opened in fifteen minutes. She so did not have time for this rubbish.

She was still busy adding cream-cheese frosting in decorative swirls to the carrot cake when Ruby dashed back into the café a few minutes later. 'I think you better look at this.'

'Don't bring it in here,' she said crossly. 'It's covered in pee.'

'I know that,' Ruby replied. 'But it's not just any pee, it's pregnant-lady pee.'

'What?' Frosting squirted across the counter as her fingers fisted on the bag involuntarily. And her heart jumped into her mouth.

'You heard me.' Ruby held the pee stick in front of Ella's face like a talisman. 'See that strong blue line? That means

Ella's going to be a mummy in exactly seven months' time. You're going to be ringing in the new year with your very own bundle of fun.'

She couldn't focus, thanks to the sheen of shocked tears misting her vision. 'But that's not possible,' she murmured, her voice hoarse.

Ruby laughed. 'Um, well, clearly it is. Pregnancy tests don't lie.'

Ella's unfocused gaze raised to Ruby's smiling face. 'I should take another one. It might be wrong.'

'Take as many as you like, but there's no such thing as a false positive with these things. I took six tests with Art. And they all came out exactly the same. Assuming it was definitely you who peed on that stick, it's definitely you who's pregnant.'

Ella collapsed into the chair beside the cash register. Her knees trembling now almost as violently as her hands—which clutched the bag of frosting in a death grip as it dripped onto the floor.

'I'm going to have a baby.' The words sounded fragile and far away, as if they had been said by someone else, as if they could be extinguished if she said them too loudly.

Ruby stroked her back as she crouched beside her and wrapped her hand round Ella's wrist. 'Yes, you are.'

The tears welled and flowed, her whole body shaking now, at the memory of a similar test so long ago. The joy then had felt scary, terrifying, but so small and sweet. This time it didn't feel small, it felt huge, like a living, breathing thing that couldn't be contained within her skin, but so much more scary and terrifying too.

Dumping the pregnancy test in the bin, Ruby washed and dried her hands, then tugged a couple of wet wipes from the dispenser on the counter. 'I take it those are happy tears?' Ruby took the icing bag out of Ella's numb fingers and began cleaning the mess of cream-cheese frosting with the wipes.

Ella nodded, the lump in her throat too solid and overwhelming to talk around.

'Am I allowed to say I told you so, then?'

Ella's eyes focused at last, and she swept her arms round her friend's shoulders and clung on tight, too overwhelmed to care about the smug smile on Ruby's face.

'I don't deserve this chance.' She sobbed as Ruby hugged her.

Ruby moved back, and held her arms. 'Don't say that.' She gave her a slight shake. 'What you did then, you did for the right reasons.'

Ella folded her arms over her stomach, as if to protect the precious life within and stop the guilt from consuming the joy. 'I'm not so sure about that.'

Ruby tugged a tissue out of her pocket, to dab at Ella's eyes. 'You were eighteen years old Ella, you had your whole life ahead of you, and it was a mistake. You made the only choice you could in the circumstances.' She placed the damp tissue in the palm of Ella's hand, rolled her fist over it, and held on. 'Don't you think it's about time to forgive yourself?'

She would never be able to forgive herself, not completely, but that didn't mean she couldn't protect this child with every fibre of her being. This time she wouldn't mess it up. 'I want to.'

Ruby's lips quirked. 'Okay, next question. Because I'm going to assume the "Do you want to have this baby?" question is a no-brainer.'

Ella bobbed her head as the small smile spread. 'Yes, it is.'

'Brilliant. So next question, how do we contact Captain Studly? Do you have like a card for his tour company or something?'

'What? No.' The joy cracked, like the crumbling top of a newly baked muffin, exposing the soft centre beneath. 'We can't tell him. He doesn't need to know.'

'Calm down.' Ruby gripped her fingers tight. 'There's no need to panic. You don't have to do anything yet.'

The memory of his voice, smooth, seductive, husky, and so sexy asking, 'Are you on the pill?' seemed to float in the air around the café, mocking her.

What happened if she told him and he reacted the same way Randall had? He was still in his twenties; he lived in a beach hut; he picked up women in bars. He was exciting, reckless, charming, sexier than any one she'd ever met, and probably the least likely guy on the planet to welcome news like this.

'And he's not necessarily going to freak out the way Randall did,' Ruby said, doing her mind-reading thing.

Oh, yes, he will.

'I don't want to risk it.' She tugged her hands out of Ruby's. 'Why do I have to tell him?'

'Because it's his baby, and he has a right to know,' Ruby said, in that patient I-know-what's-best voice that she'd acquired ever since having kids. Ella had always thought it was so sweet. Now she was finding it more than a little patronising.

'But suppose he'd rather not know?'

'How can you possibly know that?' Ruby replied.

She opened her mouth to tell Ruby how he'd asked her if she was on the pill and how the correct answer had somehow got lost in the heat of the moment. But then shut it again. She didn't want Ruby to think she'd deliberately tricked him, because she hadn't. But even thinking about that conversation now made her feel as if she had, which would only tarnish the perfection of this moment.

'He lives in Bermuda. I don't need his support.' Especially as he didn't have any money. 'I'm more than solvent on my own and—'

'That's not the point. He's the baby's father. By not telling him you're not giving him the choice, or the baby the choice to know him when it gets older. Think of how much it screwed up Nick when he found out our dad wasn't his biological father,' she said, reminding Ella of her brother Nick, who had run away from home in his teens when he'd discovered the truth about his parentage and had only recently come back into Ruby's life.

'It's not the same thing at all,' Ella protested. It wasn't as if she planned never to tell her child who its father was; she just didn't see why she had to tell the father right this second.

'I know it's not, but what I'm trying to say is you can't keep those kinds of secrets. It's not fair on either one of them.'

Ella wanted to say life wasn't fair. But the truth was she'd never believed that. Life could be fair, if you made the effort to make it so.

She wanted to deny he had any right to know. This was her child. Her responsibility. And she didn't want to consider his rights, his reaction. But even as the panic sat under her breastbone, ready to leap up her throat and cut off her air supply, she pictured Coop's face, the genuine smile, those emerald eyes twinkling with humour, and knew that not telling him would be taking the coward's way out.

While she never would have planned to have a child alone, that was what she'd be doing—because fate had handed her this incredible gift. And while it was very likely that Coop wouldn't want to know about this baby, she had to at least give him the option of saying no. Because she had to give her child the chance to know its father. However slim that chance might be.

Ruby patted her hand. 'How about we leave this discussion for another day? You really don't have to do this yet.'

A loud tapping had them both turning to see the whole of the Hampstead Heath Mother and Baby Stroller Work-Out Class crowded around the door, looking sweaty and dishevelled and in desperate need of light refreshments.

Jumping up, Ella headed round the counter, to flip the sign on the door to open and welcome them in. As they smiled and wheeled their babies proudly into the café, chatting about the Hitler who ran the class, Ella smiled back, amazed to realise the lethagy that had dragged her down for days had vanished.

'Wait, Ella, are you sure you don't want to go home and rest? I can handle the Yummies,' Ruby offered as she joined her behind the counter.

Ella grinned back at her, the ball of panic lifting too.

She had time to think about how to tell Cooper; how to break the news to him without making him feel responsible. And really, while the thought of what she had to tell him wasn't easy, the fact that she had a reason to speak to him again felt surprisingly good. 'No need. I feel great.'

Ruby laughed back, her own face beaming with pleasure. 'Just wait till tomorrow morning when you're crouched over the toilet bowl again. Actually, we better get some buckets for the duration.'

Ella spent the morning chatting to the mums, serving tea and freshly baked cakes and cookies, whipping up a succession of speciality coffees, while she admired their children, and struggled to contain the silly grin at how totally amazing her life suddenly was.

She'd speak to Cooper soon. Ruby was right: it would be wrong not to. But it had been an accident. And really, she didn't need to think about all the particulars just yet. Right now, all she really had to do was bask in the miracle occurring inside her. And focus on making sure she gave her baby the best possible chance to thrive. And if that meant eventually finding the courage to tell its father about their happy accident, she'd do it, somehow.

CHAPTER SEVEN

'OUCH. DAMN IT!' Coop yanked his hand out of the casing, and threw the wrench down on the deck. Blood seeped from the shallow gash at the base of his thumb, through the thick black smear of engine grease. He sucked on it, getting a mouthful of grit to go with the metallic taste of his own blood.

'What's all the cussing for?' Sonny's head peered out from the captain's cabin.

'That damn propeller just took a chunk out of my hand,' he snarled. 'Cussing's required.' He boosted himself onto the deck. Tying the rag he'd been using to clean off the drive shaft around the injury, he sent his friend an angry glare. 'That lug nut won't budge—probably because it's been rusted on for thirty years.' With his hand now pounding in unison with his head, after one too many drinks last night at The Rum Runner, he was not in the mood to be dicking around with Sonny's ancient outboard motor.

Sonny tilted his head to one side, sending him a calm, searching look. 'Someone sure got out of bed the wrong way again this morning.'

Coop ignored the jibe. So what if he hadn't been on top form lately? Ever since a certain English girl had left him high and dry, her lush body and eager smile had got lodged in his frontal lobe and it had been interfering with his sleep patterns.

Going back to The Rum Runner last night for the first time since Ella had run out on him had been a mistake. Henry had started jerking his chain about 'his pretty lady', and he'd somehow ended up challenging the guy to a drinking contest. Staggering home at three a.m., and being violently ill in his bathroom had only added injury to the insult of too many tequila slammers and too many nights without enough sleep.

No wonder he wasn't at his sunniest.

'Isn't it about time you got rid of this bucket?' he said, letting out a little of his frustration on Sonny's boat.

Sonny stroked the console with the affection most men reserved for a lover. 'My *Jezebel*'s got plenty good years in her yet. And with Josie's wedding to pay for, she's going to have to make them count.'

Coop knotted the rag with his teeth, his temper kicking in. They both knew *The Jezebel* hadn't seen a good year since Bill Clinton had been in the White House. And that he'd offered to bankroll Josie's wedding a million times and Sonny had stubbornly refused to accept the money. But after a morning spent with a raging hangover trying to fix the unfixable when he should have been going over his business manager's projections for the new franchise in Acapulco, he wasn't in the mood to keep his reservations about Josie's nuptials to himself any longer either.

'What is Josie getting hitched for anyway? She's only twenty and they're both still in college. What are they going to live on?'

'Love will find a way,' Sonny replied with that proud paternal grin that had been rubbing Coop the wrong way for weeks. Hadn't the old guy figured out yet he was shelling out a king's ransom to kick-start a marriage that probably wouldn't last out the year?

'Will it?' he asked, the edge in his voice going razor sharp.

Sonny nodded, the probing look sending prickles of unease up Coop's spine and making his thumb throb. 'You know, you've been mighty bitchy for months now. Wanna tell me what's going on?'

Months? No way had it been months since his night with Ella. Had it? 'This isn't about me, Sonny,' he said, struggling to deflect the conversation back where it needed to be. 'This is about Josie doing something dumb and you not lifting a finger to stop her.'

'Josie's known her own mind since she was three years old,' Sonny said without any heat. 'Nothing I could say would stop her even if I wanted to.'

Coop opened his mouth to protest, but Sonny simply lifted up a silencing finger.

'But I don't want to stop them. Taylor's a good kid and she loves him. And it's not them I'm worried about.' Sonny rested his heavy frame on the bench next to Coop, his steady gaze making the prickles on Coop's spine feel as if he'd been rolling in poison ivy. 'You're the one hasn't been right ever since the night you picked up that tourist girl in the Runner.'

'What the...?' Coop's jaw went slack. How did Sonny know about Ella? The old guy was always butting into his personal life, because he was a romantic and he thought he had a right to. But he'd never spoken about Ella to anyone. Did Sonny have X-ray vision or something?

'Josie says you seemed real taken with her the next morning. But she'd run off? Is that the thing? You miss her?'

Damn Josie—so she was his source.

'It's not what you think.' Coop scowled, trying to cut the old guy off at the pass before this conversation got totally out of hand.

He didn't miss Ella, and he wasn't 'taken with her'. Whatever the heck that meant. It was nothing like that.

She'd just got under his skin, somehow. Like an itch he couldn't scratch. He could wait it out. Give it a couple more weeks and surely the almost nightly dreams he had, about those bright blue eyes wide with enthusiasm, that sunny smile, that lush butt in the itsy-bitsy purple bikini…

He thrust his fingers through his hair, annoyed by the low-level heat humming in his crotch as the erotic memories spun gleefully back—and the weird knot under his breastbone twisted.

'It was a one-night hook-up,' he continued, trying to convince himself now as much as Sonny. 'We hit it off. But only…you know.'

Just shoot me now.

He shrugged. He wasn't about to get into a discussion about his sex life with Sonny. The old guy had given him chapter and verse as a teenager about respecting women, and he didn't need that lecture again. One thing was certain, though: Josie was dead meat next time he saw her for putting him in this position. Whether she had a ten-grand wedding to attend in five weeks or not.

'I don't think Ella and I are going to be declaring any vows,' he said, going on the defensive when Sonny gave him that look that always made him feel as if he had a case to answer.

He did respect women. He respected them a lot. Sonny just had a quaint, old-fashioned idea that sex always had to mean something. When sometimes all it meant was you needed to get laid.

'She lives thousands of miles away, we only spent one night together and she wasn't looking for anything more than I was. Plus she was the one who ran out on me.'

Sonny's eyebrow winged up, and Coop knew he'd said too much.

'I see. So you're the boy that can have any woman he

wants. And she's the girl that didn't want you? Is that what's got you so upset?'

'I'm not upset.' Coop flexed his fist, his hand hurting like a son of a bitch. 'And thanks a bunch for making me sound like an arrogant jackass.'

Sonny smiled, but didn't deny it, and Coop felt the flicker of hurt. 'You're a good-looking boy with more money than you need and a charming way about you that draws women like bees to a honeypot. You've got a right to be arrogant, I guess.'

'Thanks,' Coop said wryly. He didn't kid himself, Sonny hadn't meant it as a compliment.

Money wasn't something that floated Sonny's boat; it was the one thing they still argued about. Because as far as Coop was concerned, money mattered, more than pretty much everything else. It made everything easier, oiled every cog, gave you options, and that all-important safety net that he'd lacked as a kid. He'd craved it for the first twenty years of his life. But now he had it, it meant more to him than just the luxuries, or the good times he could buy with it. It meant respect. Status. It showed people that he wasn't the worthless little trailer-trash nobody he'd once been. But best of all it meant he didn't have to rely on anyone but himself.

He liked Sonny, respected the guy more than any other guy he had ever known, but, the way he saw it, Sonny had way too many responsibilities in his life—to his five kids, his three grandkids, all his friends and acquaintances, not to mention Rhona, the wife he'd had by his side for over thirty years. Maybe that worked for Sonny, he certainly didn't seem to mind it, but, as far as Coop was concerned, that wasn't something he was looking for. A man could be an island—if he worked hard enough and had enough money to make it happen—and life was a lot easier that way.

'Aren't you headed to Europe next week?' Sonny pushed on, not taking the hint. 'Why not look this girl up and see how she's doing?'

Coop stared blankly at his friend. He'd thought about it; of course he had. He had a meeting with some financiers in St Tropez who wanted to talk about franchising options for Dive Guys in the Med. It was only a short hop from there to London, where Ella lived. But…

'I don't know. if I went all the way out to London just to hook up, she might get the wrong idea.' He sure as hell didn't want Ella thinking this was more than it was.

'Why would that be bad?' Sonny's rueful smile made Coop feel about as smart as the lug nut he'd been trying to shift all morning. 'If she's the woman of your dreams.'

'Damn, Sonny, Ella is not the woman of my dreams,' he shot back, getting exasperated.

What was with Sonny? Was all this wedding garbage messing with his head and making him even more of a romantic than usual?

He hardly knew Ella. And he didn't have dreams about women. Well, not apart from R-rated ones. For the simple reason that he was more than happy being an island.

'If you say so.' Sonny shrugged, undaunted. 'But my point is you need to go get your sunshine back.' Sonny jerked his thumb over his shoulder, indicating the glimmering turquoise water that stretched towards the horizon. 'And if it's across that ocean that's where you oughta be.' His smile thinned. 'Because until you do, you're not a heck of a lot fun for anyone to be around.'

Coop frowned as he finally got the message. So that was it. Sonny wanted him out of the way while him and his family geared up for Josie's big day.

He felt the sharp stab of hurt. But guessed the old guy had a point. He had been pretty grouchy the last couple of months. Sleepless nights and sexual frustration could do that to a guy. And whatever was going on between him and Ella, it didn't seem to be getting any better. 'Have I really been that bad?' he asked.

Resting a solid hand on his shoulder, Sonny gave it a fatherly pat. 'Boy, you've been bitchier than when you were working all hours to set up your business.'

'Sorry.'

Sonny squeezed his shoulder. 'Don't be sorry, man, go do something about it.'

Coop nodded. What the hell? Trying to talk some sense into Josie and her folks about the wedding was a lost cause. And he could do with more than the two-day break he'd planned for his trip to the Med. Why not book a flight that routed through London? Stop over for a few extra days, book a suite in a classy hotel, see the city, and if he happened to be in Ella's neighbourhood at some point, why not look her up? If she wanted to throw some more sunshine his way—and maybe give him an explanation as to why she hadn't stuck around to say goodbye—why should he object?

As Sonny had said, he'd never had a woman walk out on him before now. That was most probably all this was really about. And if that made him an arrogant jackass, so be it. He needed to do something to get himself the hell over this hump he seemed to have got hung up on. So he could come back to Bermuda ready to smile through his teeth during his best friend's daughter's wedding.

What was the worst that could happen?

'Stop eating the merchandise! I don't care if you've got a cookie craving.'

Ella hastily wiped the white chocolate and macadamia nut evidence off her mouth. 'Sorry, I can't help it.'

Ruby sent her a superior look from the cappuccino machine, where she was busy whipping up a storm of decaf lattes and skinny mochas for the tennis foursome who had just arrived after a grudge match at the heath.

'You should be sorry. I'd love to know how you've barely gained an ounce.' Her gaze dipped to Ella's cleavage, displayed in the new D half-cup bra she'd splashed out on the previous week. 'Except on the bust.' Her eyes narrowed. 'Despite having consumed your own weight in confectionery in the last week.'

Ella grinned as she arranged the freshly baked passion-fruit florentines on the 'treat of the day' display. 'I'm simply making up for lost time. I could barely keep anything down for three solid weeks.'

Ella stroked the compact bulge that made the waistband of her hip-hugger jeans dig into her tummy. Even though she could not have been more ecstatic about the pregnancy, revelling in every change it brought to her body, puking her guts up every morning had got old fairly fast. And running a cake shop, where the cloying aroma of sweetness and the bitter chicory scent of coffee had been hell on her hypersensitive sense of smell, had been a particular brand of torture she had been more than happy to see the back of. Now she could simply enjoy all the other changes—well, all except one.

Her sex drive seemed to have mushroomed at the same pace as her bosom—if the lurid dreams she had most nights, in which a certain Cooper Delaney was a key player, were anything to go by.

Only last night, she'd woken up in a pool of sweat, her skin tight and oversensitive, her already enlarged nipples swollen and her engorged clitoris pulsing with the need to be touched. She'd never been all that self-sufficient, sexually speaking, before she'd met Cooper, but she'd had to take matters into her own hands more than once in the last few weeks, while visualising Cooper's honed, ripped body driving into her and hearing his deep laconic voice growling 'touch yourself' in her ear.

Heat boiled in her cheeks, at the memory of last night's frenzied and sadly dissatisfying orgasm. And the guilt that had followed. Was it possible that her body was playing tricks on her, constantly bringing up these carnal memories of her child's father to push her into contacting him the way she'd planned to do weeks ago?

But that was before she'd done an Internet search on him. And a simple investigation to discover his contact details had brought the panic seeping back.

Because putting Cooper Delaney's name and the words 'Bermuda' and 'snorkelling' into the search engine had brought up ten whole pages of references, not just to him but to Dive Guys, the phenomenally successful franchise he owned and operated in most of the Caribbean. A company that had been listed on the New York stock exchange for over three years and was—according to an article in *Time Life* magazine—one of the fastest-growing start-ups in the region.

She'd been in shock. Then she'd been upset that he hadn't trusted her enough to tell her the truth about himself… Then she'd thought of the secret child in her womb and she'd begun shaking so hard she'd had to lie down.

Coop Delaney wasn't a part-time boat captain and all around beach bum living a free-spirited, laid-back, itinerant existence on a Bermuda beach—he was an exceptionally rich and well-connected businessman with the money and influence to buy and sell her and Ruby's little cupcake bakery several hundred times over.

How could she tell a man like that she was carrying his child? And not expect him to make demands? Demands she might not want to agree to? If he'd been the Coop she'd thought he was, she would have phoned him weeks ago. But now…

'Check out the suit in the window.' Ruby's appreciative whistle woke Ella from her stupor. 'That guy's got
shoulders even a happily married woman can appreciate.'

Ella's gaze skimmed the top of the cookie display to
see a tall man, with closely cropped hair step into the café.
Recognition tickled her spine, then thumped into her chest
as he lifted his head and shockingly familiar emerald eyes
locked on hers.

She blinked rapidly, sure this had to be an apparition
conjured up by her guilty conscience—but then his sensual
lips quirked and the warm spot between her legs ignited.

'Hi, welcome to Touch of Frosting, Camden's premiere
cupcake bakery. What's your guilty pleasure this morning?'

Ella vaguely processed Ruby's familiar greeting through
the chainsaw in her head. 'Coop?' The word came out on
a rasp of breath.

'Hey there, Ella.' The apparition winked, which had
heat flushing to her hairline, before it addressed Ruby.
'You must be Ruby. The name's Coop. I'm a friend of
Ella's.'

He held out a deeply tanned hand in greeting as Ella
heard Ruby's sharp intake of breath.

'Hi.' Ruby skirted the counter and grasped his hand in
both of hers. 'Cooper Delaney, right? It's so fabulous to
actually meet you.'

Ella heard the perk of excitement in Ruby's voice and
the laconic ease in Coop's—and everything inside her
knotted with panic.

'Ella told you about me, huh?' His voice rumbled with
pleasure as the green gaze settled on her.

Say something.

Her mind screamed as she absorbed the chiselled perfection of his cheekbones, the tawny brows, the twinkle
of amusement in those arresting eyes, and the full sensual

lips that tilted up in a confidential smile. Arousal gripped her abdomen as blood pumped into her sex.

But then she noted all the things about this man that didn't fit: the slate-grey single-breasted suit, the clean-shaven jaw, the short, perfectly styled hair that was several shades darker with fewer strands of sun-streaked blond.

She shook her head, a bolt of raw panic slamming into her chest as he passed his palm in front of her face. He was speaking to her.

'Hey there, Ella, snap out of it. How you doing?'

I'm pregnant. And I should have got in touch with you weeks ago to tell you.

She opened parched lips, but couldn't force the words out.

'Ella's great, she had her first—' Ruby began.

'Shut up, Ruby!' The high-pitched squeal shot past the boulder lodged in her throat. Ruby's eyebrows rose to her hairline but thankfully she obeyed the command, while Coop's grin took on a curious tilt.

Ella skidded round the counter, galvanised out of her trance.

Get him out of here, then you can tell him. Sensibly, succinctly, and privately, without an audience of tennis players, yummy mummies, two giggling schoolgirls and your super-nosey best friend.

She owed him that much.

'I'm taking a half-day, Rubes.'

Ruby's brow furrowed.

Oh, dear, she'd have some explaining to do to Ruby, too. But that could wait, she thought, as she came to a halt in front of Cooper.

She tilted her head back, the effect of that lazy smile shimmering down to her toes. How could she have forgotten how tall he was? Taking a deep breath in, she got a lungful of his delicious scent.

He smells the same. Hold that thought.

But then the aroma of spicy cologne and soap and man triggered a renewed pulse of heat and the shudder of re-action hit her knees.

She grasped his arm, as much to stay upright as to pro-pel him back out of the door before Ruby spilled any more confidential information. The bulge of muscle flexed be-neath the soft fabric of his designer suit—which didn't do much for her leg tremors.

He glanced at her fingers and grinned, pleased with her haste. 'It's great to see you too, Ella.' That he didn't seem particularly fazed by her fruitcake behaviour helped to calm some of the tension screaming across her shoulder blades. 'I was just in the neighbourhood,' he added. 'And I figured we could catch up over….'

'That's wonderful, Coop,' she interrupted. 'But let's go somewhere private so we can talk properly.'

'Sounds good.' His hooded gaze suggested he had made a few assumptions about her eagerness to get him alone. And talking was not at the top of his current to-do list.

The stupid tingles raced across her skin.

Do not hold that thought. You need to keep a clear head.

She crossed to the door, still clinging onto his arm, but stopped in her tracks when he didn't move with her.

She swung back, ready to beg. 'Please, my flat's just round the corner. I have coffee. And cupcakes.'

Her gaze flicked over his shoulder to Ruby, who had crossed her arms over her chest and was staring at her, the concern on her face making Ella feel small and foolish.

'Cupcakes, huh?' He laughed, but then his hands cupped her elbows, forcing her to relinquish her death grip on his arm. 'I'm a sucker for cupcakes,' he purred, then yanked her onto tiptoes. 'But first things first.' He dipped his head, bringing his lips tantalisingly close. 'Don't I rate a "wel-come to London" kiss?'

Before she had a chance to confirm or deny, his mouth settled over hers, and every thought bar one melted out of her head.

Yes, please.

His tongue coaxed her lips open in hungry strokes, then tangled with hers. The shaking in her legs shot off the Richter Scale but his arms wrapped around her waist, holding her steady against the lean, hard line of his body. His scent enveloped her, clogging her lungs as she clung to him for balance, and drank in the glorious urgency of his kiss.

As they broke apart she heard the smattering of applause from the group of mums in the corner. The heat rose up to scald her scalp—but he was smiling at her with that appreciative, sexy twist of his lips she remembered so well from Bermuda and she swallowed down the renewed bolt of panic.

She had so much to tell him, and she still had no real clue how he would respond. But kissing him again, having his arms around her, had felt so good, she refused to allow her doubts to resurface. She was having this beautiful man's baby—and it felt like fate somehow that he had come to London to see her.

He dropped his arms and slid one warm palm into hers. 'Let's get out of here.' He brushed his lips across her ear lobe. 'I'm dying to taste your cupcakes.'

She grinned, sure her cupcakes weren't the only thing he planned to taste. 'You're going to love them.'

She waved goodbye to Ruby, who sent her a wary smile back, then mouthed, 'Tell him.'

She nodded, sobering a little.

'Great to meet you, Ruby. I'll bring her back in one piece. I swear.' He sent Ruby a farewell salute as he opened the café door for her and she stepped outside. The sky was dark and overcast, a summer storm brewing, but excitement rippled.

Against all the odds, Cooper Delaney was here. And she would get the chance to tell him her news face to face. Now the initial shock had faded, she knew it was the best possible scenario. She could prepare him properly, before she told him. Explain exactly how it had happened and how much it meant to her, and make sure he understood he didn't have to be a part of the life growing inside her if he didn't want to be. That he had no obligations.

But surely him turning up here had to be a sign. Of something good. He'd come all this way to see her, and he'd kissed her with such fervour. The chemistry between them was still so strong, so hot. And there had been definite affection in his gaze too, the way his hands had steadied her, held her close.

He hadn't forgotten her, any more than she had forgotten him.

He slung an arm across her shoulders. 'Lead the way, my little cougar. But put a fire under it,' he said, casting a wary glance at the ominous thunderclouds overhead. 'It looks like we're about to get soaked.'

She chuckled, giddy with anticipation and tenderness, as a fat drop of rain landed on her cheek. 'My road is the second on the left.' The crash of thunder startled her for a moment, then the deluge of fat drops multiplied into a flood, drenching her T-shirt and jeans in seconds.

Laughing, she darted out from under his arm, the chilly summer rain plastering her hair against her cheeks and running in rivulets between her breasts. 'Come on, toy boy. I'll race you there,' she said, before sprinting off in a burst of energy.

They would work this out. Nothing bad could happen today. She was sure of it.

* * *

'Come back here…'

Cooper raced up the shadowy stairwell guided by that pert ass outlined in wet denim, his own shirt sticking to his chest.

He tripped, cursed, then finally caught up with her, his crotch throbbing now. Running with a hard-on was never a good idea, but he'd been waiting months to get his hands on her again.

Her light, infectious laugh bubbled through his blood, doing weird things to his equilibrium as he followed her into the shoebox apartment at the top of the stairs. He slammed the door behind him, taking in the compact living room, the kitchen counter, the couch covered in colourful cushions. Then grabbed a hold of one hundred pounds of wiggling, giggling female, and refused to let go.

'Got you.' He held her close, taking the time to study the open, heart-shaped face, the huge blue eyes that had haunted his dreams for weeks.

Maybe he had missed her, more than he thought.

'And you're not getting away from me any time soon,' he declared. Although she wasn't exactly trying too hard.

His lips captured hers in a hungry kiss, while he peeled off the drenched cotton T-shirt to discover the damp lemon-scented female flesh beneath.

He cupped her generous breasts, the pebbled nipples digging into his palms through her bra, then pinched the swollen tips, while his mouth drank in her soft grunts of excitement.

Her fingers threaded into his hair, tugging him back. 'I have to tell you…' Her voice came out on a whisper. 'We have to talk.'

'Later.' He nipped her bottom lip. 'Sex first. Then cupcakes. Talk after that.'

He delved to find the hook on her bra and sent up a silent prayer of thanks as it popped open. Dragging the wet hem of her T over her head, he ripped off the sodden bra.

When she was bare to the waist, her breasts heaved with her staggered breathing, the large reddened nipples like ripe berries, sweet and succulent.

'Those are even hotter than I remember.' He lifted his gaze, saw the flush of colour on high cheekbones, the blue of her eyes dilated to dark, driving need.

Cupping one heavy orb in his palm, he licked round the peak, heard her moan, then bit tenderly into the swollen tip, his erection now huge in his pants.

Her back arched as she thrust into his mouth, moaning softly as he suckled harder.

Finding the zipper of her jeans, he yanked down the tab, and delved beneath the clinging, constricting fabric to cup her. She sobbed as his fingers widened the slick folds, and touched the heart of her. She bucked, then grasped his wrist.

'Stop!' she cried. 'I'm going to come.'

'That's the general idea.' Panic clawed at his chest. If she said no now he was liable to die.

She stared at him, her need plain in the wide pupils, the staggered pants of breath. 'I want you inside me. It's been too long.'

'Not a problem.' He chuckled, relief flooding through him as the tension in his groin begged for release. 'Then let's get naked. Fast.'

The sound of frantic cursing, of tearing fabric, of buttons hitting the linoleum flooring filled the small room as they wrestled to get their wet clothes off as fast as humanly possible.

After what felt like several millennia she stood naked before him, her gaze darkening further as those bright eyes dropped to his groin. His erection twitched, the pulse throbbing at its tip, steady and relentless.

He lifted her against the wall of the apartment, wedging himself into the space between her thighs. Clasping her generous hips, he assessed those spectacular breasts. She'd gained some weight since their night in Bermuda and it suited her—the belly that had been so flat across her hip bones now pillowing his erection.

The dumb wave of regret that her body had undergone that small change and he hadn't been there to see it, to witness it, passed over like a shadow then disappeared as her breasts pressed into his chest—demanding more friction. He ducked his head, to suck at the pulse point in her neck, which beat in frantic flutters. Her addictive scent surrounded him, lemon and spice and all things nice.

His lips curved, holding her as she hooked toned legs around his waist. Her fingers threaded into the short, damp hair at his ears.

'I haven't got any condoms,' he admitted, his mind trying to engage with the need to slow the hell down. To think through the driving urge to sink into her tight heat. He hadn't had time to stop and pick any protection up because he'd come straight from the airport. And he hadn't figured things would get this hot, this quickly. But could he risk it? Just this once? She was on the pill? 'You okay with me using withdrawal? I'm clean, I swear.'

He felt her nod, and lifted his head to see her eyes, glazed with an emotion that made his heart thud against his chest wall like a sledgehammer.

'So am I,' she replied

It was all the permission he needed. His shaft jerked against her belly from the kick of desperation. Palming her buttocks, and angling her pelvis as best he could, he thrust home in one long, solid glide. Her slick, wet sex stretched to receive him, then massaged him like a velvet vice. Her head dropped back, thudding the wall, as he began to move, the thrusts jerky, desperate, the need quickly becoming too fast and furious, the need so raw and draining he couldn't slow down, couldn't stop now if his life depended on it.

She sobbed, her fingernails scraping his back as she clung on. Her muscles began to milk him, and he knew she was coming.

Don't pull out. Not yet. Hold on. Damn it.

His seed boiled, driving up from his balls, hurling him closer and closer to the cliff edge, her sobs of completion beckoning him to come faster, harder. And a tiny part of his mind screamed to the animal inside him.

Now. Pull out, now.

He wrenched himself free. Dropping his head against her shoulder, kissing the salt, sweet taste of her neck, the pain of separation as devastating as the brutal, unstoppable roll of orgasm as his seed pumped into the welcoming softness of her belly.

'Damn, that was even more awesome than I remember.'

Ella's gaze shimmered back into focus as a rough palm touched her cheek and blunt fingers sank into her hair. Those deep emerald eyes searched her face, making her chest tighten.

She nodded, gently, feeling stunned, her sex still clenching and releasing from the intensity of her orgasm. Seemed absence didn't just make the heart grow fonder.

'Yes,' she whispered, her throat raw from the wellspring of emotion.

His lips curved, and he placed a tender kiss on her forehead. 'Come on.' He hefted her into his arms, bracing his forearm under her buttocks as she held onto his shoulders. 'Let's grab a shower. Then I want a cupcake.'

'But we still need to talk,' she murmured against his neck.

'Sure. But first I want to see that magnificent rack covered in soap suds.'

She chuckled, resting her head on his shoulder, and draping her arms around his neck, her emotions too close to the surface to protest. Surely a few more minutes of intimacy, of getting reacquainted, wouldn't do any harm—she'd waited this long already?

Locating the tiny bathroom at the back of the flat, he put her down to twist on the shower. But kept one hand on her hip, as if he were afraid she'd run off. She remembered leaving him, that morning with only a thank you. And felt the renewed trickle of guilt.

The water gurgled and spurted out of the shower head, the stream thin and underwhelming.

'Is that as good as it gets?' he remarked.

She smiled. 'This is British plumbing we're talking about. That's the equivalent of Niagara Falls.'

His quick grin lifted her spirits and made the trickle of guilt dry up.

'At least it's hot,' he said, testing the temperature before he hauled her into the cubicle.

'Not for long.'

He grabbed her lemon verbena soap off the ledge, and worked up a lather, his hair plastered to his head, his eyes wicked with intent. 'Then we better get this party started.'

Gentle hands cupped her breasts, lifting and testing the weight as his thumbs glided over pebbled nipples. The heat pulsed and tugged between her thighs.

She took the soap to wash him in return, putting all the emotion she felt into the task as her hands stroked the lean, muscular slopes of his abdomen, explored the roped sinews that defined his hip bones. She took his penis into her palm, felt it lengthen and harden as she caressed it.

Blood surged into her tender clitoris, and she knew she wanted him again, already, surging deep, the delicious decadent stretching feeling of his flesh entering hers. Touching her womb where their child grew.

Soon he would know, and, whatever his reaction, surely it would be okay, when this closeness, this physical joining felt so good, so right.

But then he lifted her breasts, the cooling water sluicing away the soap, and said, 'I like the extra weight—it looks great on you.'

The approval in his gaze had the wave of guilt flopping over in her stomach. She couldn't wait any longer. It wasn't fair to him, or to their child. She drew away from him, her back wedged against the wall of the cubicle.

'We need to get dressed. I have something I have to tell you.'

'Okay.'

He flipped off the shower control, but took hold of her wrist as she opened the cubicle door. The sudden silence felt deafening, despite the blood roaring in her ears. He tugged her towards him as he stepped out behind her, tucked a finger under her chin, lifting her gaze to his. 'What's up? Is something wrong?'

'No, I just…' She gulped past the tightness.

Not yet. Get yourself together first. You need to tell him gently. Carefully.

Her gaze dropped to his erection. She certainly couldn't function, let alone think clearly, while he was standing naked in front of her, visibly aroused.

'I just need a minute.'

His grip had loosened, his gaze puzzled, but not yet wary. She pulled her hand free, headed for the door. 'Shall we get dressed? I can meet you in the living room in ten minutes? Make you that coffee I promised?'

He shrugged, grabbed a towel from the rail to wrap around his waist. 'Sure.'

She darted out of the door before he could change his mind.

* * *

'All right, let's have it, what was so important we couldn't finish what I was busy starting in the shower?'

Ella smiled at the rueful tone, and glanced up from the cupcakes she was busy arranging on a plate.

He stood with his legs crossed at the ankles, leaning against the kitchen counter. He'd changed into a pair of faded jeans and a black T-shirt, which must have been in the bag he'd had with him. Had he come straight from the airport, then, to see her? She felt a renewed spike of optimism, of hope.

She'd figured so many outcomes for what she was about to tell him, but none of them had included the possibility that he might be pleased with her news. Yes, it would be a shock, but why had she assumed it would necessarily be a disaster?

She never would have guessed he would come to London, or the chemistry between them would have remained as hot for him as it still was for her.

'Why don't you sit down?' She gestured towards the living area. 'The coffee will be ready any minute.'

His brows lifted, the rueful grin taking on a mischievous tilt. 'It's not coffee I want.' Stepping close to hold her chin, he gave her lips a quick peck. The kiss felt casual and affectionate. The hope swelled in her chest. 'But we'll play it your way, for now.'

He settled on the sofa, while she fussed over the coffee for another precious few minutes, getting her thoughts lined up.

Finally she couldn't put it off any longer. Sitting on the opposite sofa, she placed the plate of cherry-chocolate cupcakes on the coffee table and poured him a cup of coffee. She had a momentary wobble when he told her he took it black, and it occurred to her how much she didn't know about him.

Don't chicken out now. Telling him is the first step to finding out all those things you don't know.

She took a long fortifying sip of the fennel tea she'd made for herself. 'I'm not sure where to start,' she began, galvanised by the thought that she was excited about taking this new step.

He lifted a cupcake off the plate. 'Then why don't you start by telling me why you ran out on me?'

'I didn't,' she said, frowning at the slight edge in his voice. 'I woke up and you were gone. I figured you'd run out on me.'

'Damn, seriously?' He looked genuinely stunned, which was a balm to her ego.

'Well, yes. And I felt uncomfortable with your friend Josie there.' She remembered the spike of dismay and asked, 'Who is she, by the way? She seemed to know you exceptionally well.'

His eyebrows rose and his lips crinkled. 'Are you jealous?'

Colour stained her cheeks.

He chuckled. 'Josie's like a kid sister. An annoying kid sister. Believe me, you've got nothing to be jealous of.'

'I didn't say I was jealous.'

'Uh-huh.' He sent her a confident smile. And she huffed out a laugh. The tension in her chest easing.

He took a large bite of the cupcake, held it up. 'Damn, that's good.' Finishing it off in a few quick bites, he placed the paper casing on the plate. 'So why don't you spill it, whatever it is you have to talk about. Before we get back into the shower.'

The colour in her cheeks flared again, under his watchful gaze. 'Okay, it's, well, it's sort of hard to say right out.'

She gulped down the new lump in her throat.

'Yeah? That doesn't sound good.' He sent her a crooked

smile. 'I really hope you're not going to tell me you're married.'

She laughed, the tension dissolving a little. 'God, no, it's nothing like that. It's...' She examined her fingers, suddenly shy rather than scared. Wouldn't it be amazing if he was actually as excited about this as she was? 'Actually, I'm pregnant. That's why, well, I've gained some weight.'

The crooked smile remained, but the curiosity in his eyes turned to astonishment as his gaze dipped to her breasts and then her belly. He straightened on the sofa, his mouth opening. Then closing. Then opening again. 'You...? You're expecting a kid? You don't look pregnant.'

She waited for the obvious next question, but he just continued to stare at her belly.

'Well, I'm only twelve weeks, so it doesn't show much yet.' She placed her hands on the slight swelling, suddenly keen to emphasise it for his benefit.

His head lifted. She'd expected surprise, even shock when he made the connection; she'd even prepared herself for annoyance, and anger. What she hadn't prepared herself for, though, was the way the relaxed, sexy charm had been ripped away to be replaced by complete horror. 'Tell me you're not saying what I think you're saying?'

Her pulse throbbed painfully in her neck, and she cradled her abdomen, the urge to shield her child, instinctive. She couldn't speak, so she simply nodded.

He leapt up from the sofa like a puppet who had been rudely jerked on stage. The vicious swear word echoed around the tiny room. 'You have got to be kidding me? It can't be mine—you said you were on the pill.'

She'd expected this accusation, on the numerous occasions when she'd had this conversation in her head. But all the careful explanations, the reasoned arguments, the excuses absolving her all seemed to pale into insignificance in the face of his frantic denial. And all she could manage

was, 'I know, I realised when I found out you may have
got that impression, but I—'

'You lied to me?' He stepped forward, the stance threatening.

Somehow she knew he wouldn't hurt her, not physically, but she could see the turmoil of emotion and it made
her insides tangle into tight, torturous knots, the guilt that
she'd kept so carefully at bay for weeks creating a yawning chasm in the pit of her stomach.

'Why the hell did you lie?' He dug his fingers into his
hair, sending the damp strands into deep furrows. 'Unless… Hell… You wanted to get knocked up? Is this a setup? You figure I'll pay you off?'

The accusation came so far out of left-field, she hadn't
seen it coming before it had smacked into her chest and
hurled her heart into her throat. 'What? No. I never…' Her
denial choked off at the contempt in his eyes. 'You used a
condom—how could I have planned it?'

'I knew the cute and clueless act was too good to be
true. But I fell for it anyway.'

'What act? What are you talking about?'

'Drop it, okay. You've got what you wanted.' His eyes
slid back to her belly, the light in them harsh and resentful. 'My bun in your oven.'

'No, you don't understand. It was never planned.' The
justification, the explanation at last came tumbling out.
'The pregnancy was…is an accident. It was all so rushed
and…I didn't think it would matter that I wasn't on the
pill.'

'You didn't think it would matter?' His voice rose to
a shout. 'Are you nuts? I told you I didn't want to risk it.
What the hell about that did you not understand?'

'No, that's not what I meant. I didn't think I could….'
She faltered, unable to reveal the truth about her medical
history, her fertility issues, the test results she'd gone to

Bermuda to escape. She couldn't tell this stranger about any of that; it would make her too vulnerable, too raw, especially now, with her throat already aching with unshed tears.

'You don't have to be involved.' She scrambled to justify, to explain, to avert the terrible feeling of loss. 'I've made the decision to have this child. I want it. Very much.' Her hands shook, the trembling having moved up from her toes, to her knees and across her torso.

Don't you dare cry.

Why hadn't she said all of this to start with, before she'd told him about the pregnancy? He obviously thought she was some kind of gold-digger. If she could just make him understand he didn't have to feel responsible for this child, everything would be okay. But even as she told herself it, a part of her was dying inside at the knowledge that Cooper Delaney hated her now.

'I just thought you should know.'

'Right, so now I know,' he snarled. 'Thanks for that. And what the hell am I supposed to do with the information? You've told me a part of me is going to be walking around on this planet and I don't get to have any say in that?'

She shook her head, the tears drying up inside her. *Stay firm. Stay strong. Don't break, not this time.* 'No. No, you don't.' She firmed her lips to stop them trembling. 'I won't have an abortion. And nothing you can do or say will make me.'

He flinched. 'Who said anything about an abortion?'

'I won't do it. I want this baby very much. If you don't, that's okay. You never have to have anything to do with it.'

'Yeah, right.' Marching past her, he grabbed his bag off the floor. 'Like that's going to work.' He slung the leather holdall over his shoulder and opened the door. Rain slashed down in angry currents against the hall window. But the summer storm that had seemed so cleansing, so perfect, so passionate only hours before, now appeared grey and dark and oppressive.

He sent her one last scathing look over his shoulder, the look of betrayal in his eyes palpable. And then slammed the door behind him.

She sank down against the wall, her legs too shaky to hold her, and pressed her forehead into her knees. And listened to his footfalls, heavy on the stairs, fade away into nothingness.

Coop stumbled out onto the street, his heart hitting his ribcage hard enough to shatter bone. Rain slashed at his face as he dumped his bag on the sidewalk and smashed his fist into the brick wall that marked the perimeter of her apartment building.

Pain hurtled up his arm, lanced across his knuckles, but went some way to dulling the terrifying emotions consuming him.

You dumbass. What the hell were you thinking? Coming here? Trusting her?

He sucked the battered knuckles, and picked up his bag in the other hand.

He hailed a cab, jumped in out of the rain and shouted through the grill, 'Take me to a hotel.'

'How about the Renaissance, sir? It's pricey but very plush.'

'Sure, great, whatever,' he croaked, his voice hoarse, his whole body starting to shake. He didn't give a damn where he went—he just had to get away from the memory of those big eyes glossy with unshed tears.

But then he caught the glittering pink logo on the window of Ella's cupcake store as the cab sped past it. The panic boiled in his gut as the taste of her lingered on his tongue and the residual heat throbbed in his crotch. Mocking him.

He sank his head into his hands and wanted to howl with pain and frustration.

God help him, it didn't matter what he did now, or how much money he made or how fast he ran—he could never ever be an island again. And it was all his own damn fault.

CHAPTER EIGHT

Coop stared at the glittery pink lettering on the front of the diner, and then past it through the glass. He spotted Ella in front of the counter, busy chatting to a customer, her hand resting casually on her belly—and swallowed to ease the thickening in his throat.

Play it cool. No more freak-outs allowed.

He'd spent a night in the gothic splendor of the five-star hotel overlooking St Pancras Station, not sleeping a wink, as he went over every single thing she'd said, and every single thing he'd said. And he'd come to a few important—if shattering—conclusions.

He didn't have the first clue what he was supposed to do about the bomb she'd just exploded in his nice, easy, island life. Correction: his formerly nice, easy, island life. Fatherhood was something he hadn't planned for and didn't know a damn thing about.

And he hated not knowing, because it reminded him too much of his childhood. The dead weight of responsibility, the relentless pressure of being constantly trapped without a way out and that terrifying feeling of insecurity, of never knowing if he would be strong enough, smart enough, man enough to make things right for his mom.

He didn't want to live through all that again. And he hated that he would have to now.

And because of that he'd panicked yesterday, when Ella

had told him her news—and had dropped a pretty big bomb on her in return.

Because however much he might want to blame all this on Ella, he knew now—once he'd taken the time to examine all the facts—that he couldn't. He also knew he couldn't just walk away from his own kid and forget about it—the way she'd suggested—because that would make him no better than his old man. And he was pretty sure he couldn't do that and live with himself afterwards.

All of which left him with only one option. Suck it up, stop whining about what he couldn't change and try to deal with it.

And the only way he could do that was to deal with Ella first.

Forcing the trademark 'never-let-them-see-you're-scared' smile he'd perfected as a kid onto his lips, he pushed open the door. But as Ella's gaze locked on his and her eyes went wide with distress his step faltered, his heartbeat stumbled and the thickening in his throat got a hell of a lot worse.

'Coop?' Ella bit into her lip, the tremor of shock and anxiety almost as overwhelming as the wave of relief.

She'd never expected to see him again, had convinced herself that his angry departure was for the best. She'd told herself over and over again during a long night spent on the phone to Ruby, and then lying in bed staring at the crack in her ceiling, that she couldn't make Coop want to be a father—any more than she could make him forgive her for something she hadn't done. So it would be pointless and futile to contact him again.

'We need to talk,' he said, his deep voice slightly strained but with none of the explosive anger from their last encounter. 'Can you take a break?'

She nodded, too stunned to speak, then glanced round

the shop to locate her business partner. Ruby stood chatting to a young couple to whom she'd just delivered a couple of chai lattes. But then her head came up and she spotted Coop. All traces of the genial hostess disappeared as she marched back across the café.

'What do you want?' Ruby stepped behind the counter to stand shoulder to shoulder with Ella. 'Haven't you done enough?'

'I'm here to talk to Ella, honey, not you,' Coop said, the casual tone in direct contrast to the challenge in his eyes.

'Well, "honey"...' Ruby sneered the endearment, squaring up for a fight '...you're going to have to go through me to get to her after the immature way you behaved yesterday.'

'It's okay, Ruby.' Ella touched her friend's arm, emboldened by her support—even if it was counterproductive right now.

The last thing she wanted was for Coop to find out how much his accusations had hurt her, or how she'd dissolved into a quivering wreck after his departure. Showing that kind of weakness would only put her on the defensive. 'Coop's right—we need to talk. Is it okay if I take a few minutes?'

'Are you sure?' Ruby asked.

'We'll need more than a few minutes to sort this mess out,' Coop interrupted before she could reassure her friend. 'I've got a car waiting outside to take us back to my hotel, so we can have some privacy.'

This mess.

Ella's heart shrank. Her baby wasn't a mess. But if that was the way Coop saw it, then sorting out his involvement—or rather the lack of it—would be fairly clear cut. And she supposed she should be glad that he seemed prepared to do that much.

'Why do you need privacy?' Ruby interrupted again.

'So you can shag her and then have another temper tantrum like a two-year—'

'Ruby, please, don't.' Ella raised her voice, grateful for the spark of indignation. 'I'll be fine. All we're going to do is talk.' She wasn't about to make the mistake again of believing the strong physical attraction between them meant an emotional connection too.

She really didn't know this man. His volatile reaction last night had proved that. This 'talk' would be a chance to find out more about him—while also reassuring him that her expectations of him were zero as far as the baby was concerned.

Ruby continued to eyeball Coop for several pregnant seconds, but, instead of rising to the provocation, he grinned.

'You heard the lady.' He slung his hands in his pockets, the picture of nonchalance as he raised an eyebrow, the challenge unmistakable. 'All we're going to do is talk.' His gaze landed on Ella and the unwanted hum of awareness seared through her body. 'This time.'

'How are you? Is everything okay with the kid?'

Ella turned, to find Coop watching her from the opposite side of the cab as it crawled down Camden High Road. After persuading Ruby that she was woman enough to handle a private chat with her baby's father, she'd been careful to seat herself as far away as possible from him. But the tentative enquiry and the flicker of concern knocked her off balance again.

'Yes, everything's good.'

'I just wondered because…' he paused to clear his throat, looking more uncomfortable than she'd ever seen him '…I was kind of rough with you. In your apartment. You know, before you told me.'

She blinked, puzzled. He hadn't been rough, not until

after he'd heard the news and then only verbally. But then it dawned on her what he was referring to. Their frantic lovemaking against the wall. The blush climbed into her cheeks and heat pulsed in her sex at the visceral memory. While a matching, much more dangerous warmth tugged under her breastbone.

'Oh, no, everything's fine, really. Sex isn't a problem in pregnancy—as long as we don't start breaking furniture it should be okay.' The blush launched up to her hairline as it occurred to her what she had implied. 'Not that we're likely to be…well, you know.'

The sensual smile was even more unsettling. 'Yeah, I get it.' He tapped his fingers against his knee. 'Listen, I owe you another apology.'

She struggled not to be seduced by the smouldering look he appeared to be sending her, which she decided had to be an optical illusion. After their argument yesterday, he wasn't likely to jump her again. And she definitely did not plan to jump him.

'What for?' she said, unable to deny the tiny trickle of hope at his conciliatory tone. The less acrimony between them, the more chance they had of making this talk as painless as possible.

'For losing my temper. For freaking out when you told me…' his gaze dipped pointedly to her belly '…about your condition. For making out like this was all your fault.'

Relief was sharp and sweet at the heartfelt words. 'So you don't believe I got pregnant to set you up any more?'

He had the grace to look embarrassed. 'Not once I'd examined the facts. I figure opening that first condom packet with my teeth probably wasn't the smartest thing I've ever done.' His gaze fixed on her. 'And after what happened yesterday, I'm guessing even if you had told me the truth about being on the pill, I would have risked it. Things had got pretty hot by then already.'

The muscles of her thighs melted as the pesky hum of reaction shimmered down to her core.

'I appreciate your honesty.' She nodded, accepting his apology with deliberate formality, while crossing her legs in an attempt to ease the ache in her sex.

Not going there. Remember?

'I owe you an apology, too.' She heaved a sigh, knowing she was hardly blameless in the misunderstandings that had arisen between them.

'Yeah?' He arched a questioning brow.

'I should have corrected you…' The blush fired up her neck as his lips quirked, the sensual knowledge in his smile not doing a thing to cool the hot spot between her thighs. 'But I wasn't really paying a lot of attention to the conversation at that point.'

'You and me both.' The low comment was husky with intimacy.

She cleared her throat. *Hormones behave. Now.* 'But to be honest, I really didn't think it would make any difference because…' She hesitated. 'I've had some fertility issues. Believe me, the chances of me getting pregnant were extremely slim.'

He frowned. 'How slim?'

'Well, if my doctor's reaction is anything to go by when she confirmed the pregnancy, I think we might be talking lottery-winning odds.'

'Damn. Seriously?'

She nodded, smiling at his reaction. He sounded more stunned than pleased, but it still felt good to share such an important moment in their child's life with him.

'When did you find out?' he asked, and her smile faded.

Blast.

'Um…' She glanced out of the window as the pristine new Eurostar terminal at St Pancras Station inched by.

'You know, that you were knocked up?' he prompted, obviously thinking she hadn't understood the question.

She studied the station's redbrick Victorian grandeur as they turned onto Euston road, desperate to avoid his unsettling gaze and the equally unsettling question. He'd been honest with her, and she knew she owed him the same courtesy, but would telling him the truth break this momentary truce? Obviously, she should have contacted him weeks ago, and she hadn't. If only she hadn't been such a coward.

'What's the deal, Ella?' he probed, already sounding suspicious. 'How long have you known about this?'

She sighed. 'Four weeks.'

She tensed at the muffled curse as the cab stopped outside the station hotel.

'Great.' He didn't say another word, just paid the cabbie and ushered her into the Renaissance's grand lobby area.

Every time she'd passed the historic hotel since its renovation a few years ago, she'd wondered what it looked like inside. But she barely registered the lavish vaulted ceiling or the plush interior design as his palm settled on the small of her back, and he directed her to the elevators.

His suite on the third floor had a spiral wrought-iron staircase that curved onto a second level, and original Gothic arched windows that looked down onto the station concourse. But as he poured out the bottle of sparkling mineral water she'd requested into a glass filled with ice it wasn't the hotel's palatial elegance she found intimidating.

'Okay, so now I want to know—why the delay?' He helped himself to a cola from the room's bar. 'Because I've got to tell you, I'm not feeling real happy about the fact that you've known about this kid for a month and you didn't get in touch.'

She'd been expecting the question ever since they'd arrived. And had prepared an answer. But she paused to take a hasty gulp of the icy, effervescent water.

She didn't want to tell him how she'd initially panicked about his reaction. Because then she'd have to tell him about Randall, and the child she'd lost. And she didn't see how that would serve any purpose now. Except to make her look bad. And she looked bad enough already.

'Stop stalling, Ella,' he murmured, watching her over the rim of his glass. And she had the disconcerting thought again that he seemed to be able to read her a lot easier than she was able to read him.

'All right,' she huffed, perching on a bar stool. 'If you must know, I did an internet search to get your details, so I could contact you.' This wasn't lying, she justified, it was simply failing to tell the whole truth. 'And, well…' Okay, maybe this part of the truth made her seem a little pathetic. But pathetic she could live with.

'And…?' he prompted, as if he didn't already know what she was going to say.

'I thought you were a freelance boat captain who lived in a one-room beach shack. I wasn't expecting to discover your name mentioned as one of the top young entrepreneurs in the Caribbean. It was disconcerting.'

He sent her an unapologetic smile.

What was so funny?

'And totally unexpected,' she added. 'I needed time to adjust to that before contacting you. So I waited, probably a bit longer than I should have.'

'A bit?' The grin spread as he propped himself on the bar stool next to her and nudged her knee with his. Crowding her personal space. 'Four weeks is an awful lot of adjustment time, don't you think? And you never did contact me, honey. I came to you.'

'There was an awful lot to adjust to.' She raised her chin. He'd tricked her, and pretended to be someone he wasn't. Surely she was entitled to be a little miffed about that? 'It made me realise that I didn't really know anything about you, and that scared me.'

'You knew the important stuff.' He ran his thumb across her bottom lip.

'Don't.' She jerked back, the sudden touch almost as shocking as the tenderness in his eyes.

'You scare pretty easy, don't you, Ella?' The probing gaze made her feel as if he could see through her T-shirt and jeans to the naked, needy girl she'd once been. 'Why is that?'

She tried to regulate her staggered breathing, unable to take her eyes off his.

Sexual desire was something she could handle. Would handle. But she didn't want to need him. To need any man. Not again.

'Do you think we could talk about the baby now?' she said. 'I have to get back to work.'

'Sure.' Coop shrugged, the tension in his shoulder blades nothing compared to the kick of need in his crotch.

Damn, he wanted her again: that lush mouth on his, those hard nipples grinding against his chest, the hot, wet heat gripping him like a velvet glove.

And he was pretty damn sure she wanted him too.

He could smell her arousal, the spicy scent of her need, ever since she'd climbed into the cab and sat stiffly in the far corner, as if she was worried she'd spontaneously combust if she got too close.

She still fascinated him, and excited him. And even though he kept telling himself hooking up with her again had the potential to turn this mess into a total disaster—another part of him was thinking this mess couldn't get much bigger if it tried. So why should they deny themselves? Only problem was, he wasn't sure if that part of him was the part that was supposed to be doing the thinking, or a part that was positioned a lot further south.

He had to admit he was also very curious, as well as kind of touched, by her reaction when she'd discovered the truth about Dive Guys and his wealth. Wouldn't most women feel entitled to hit him for some kind of compensation? Especially once they found out how much he was worth? Instead of that she'd 'needed time to adjust'? What was with that? One thing, it sure didn't make him feel any better about having accused her of setting him up.

He poured the last of his cola into his glass, took a long swig to buy himself some time and figure out what to do now.

She hadn't said anything, the expectation in her face tempered by wariness. As if she was worried about what he was going to say, but determined to put the best possible spin on it.

'The way I see it, Ella,' he began, acknowledging that it was definitely a strike in his favour that she was so easy to read, 'however this happened, we're both going to be parents of the same kid. And you're right, we don't know nearly enough about each other.' He let his eyes wander over her torso, vindicated by the bullet points thrusting against the tight cotton of her T. 'Except in the most basic sense.' He slugged down the last of the cola, and let the cool caffeinated liquid soothe his parched throat. 'How about you come back to Bermuda for a couple of weeks?' The offer came out of his mouth before he'd really had a chance to consider it, but it instantly felt right when her eyes lit up with delighted astonishment. 'And while you're there we can iron out how we're going to handle stuff once the kid's born.'

'You want to be involved? In the baby's life?' She sounded so overjoyed, he had to bite the inside of his mouth to keep from grinning back at her. Was it really going to be that easy?

'Of course I do. It's my kid too, isn't it?'

'Well, yes. Yes, it is.' She flattened her hands across her abdomen, in that protective gesture that he was beginning to realise was entirely instinctive. And totally genuine.

His heartbeat slowed at the evidence of how much the baby meant to her already, even though it was probably no bigger than a shrimp. Then fluttered uncomfortably, at the knowledge that his child was unlikely to ever mean that much to him.

He could do responsibility, and loyalty, and commitment, up to a point. But the kind of blind faith and trust you needed to care about someone more than you cared about yourself? Forget it. He knew he'd never be able to do that again.

'What on earth do you mean you're going to Bermuda?' Ruby stared. 'For how long?'

'I'm not sure, probably only a fortnight. He suggested I get an open ticket, but I doubt it'll take longer than that.' Although she had to admit she'd been impossibly touched when he'd sounded concerned that two weeks might not be enough time to sort out 'all the baby stuff'.

'Are you completely bonkers?' Ruby propped her hands on her hips, the belligerent stance one Ella recognised.

'He's invited me and I think it's a good idea.' She sprinkled edible pink glitter onto the swirl of buttercream icing. And placed the finished cupcake onto the tower she was assembling for a nine-year-old's birthday party, refusing to make eye contact with her friend. She'd expected this reaction. It didn't mean she was going to enjoy dealing with it. She hated arguing with Ruby. 'We're having a child together. I'd like him to be involved if he wants to be, but I need to know a lot more about him to make that a realistic possibility. Especially as we live so far apart.' She'd thought it all out, and it all made perfect sense.

Ruby tapped her foot. 'So why can't he stay in London so you can sort all that out here?'

Ella sighed, and wiped sugary hands on her apron. 'He has a business to run.'

'So do you.' Ruby went straight for the jugular.

'I know it's not a good time.' Ella faced her friend, and shook off the sting of guilt. They were already having to take out a loan to cover the extra staffing costs while she went on maternity leave, but… 'It will be good for Sally and Gemma to have a trial run with you supervising before I have the baby and I've got enough saved to cover the cost of their wages while I'm away.'

'You know very well this has nothing to do with the money,' Ruby pointed out. 'What about your antenatal appointments? What if something happens with the baby?'

'Coop's arranged for the top obstetrician on the island to handle my care while I'm there.' Even if he had gone a little pale when she'd mentioned the problem. 'But it's unlikely to be more than a couple of weeks. I'll still only be four months when I get back.'

'Fine, well, now for the biggie.' Ruby threw up her hands in exasperation. 'What about the fact that Cooper Delaney is a complete jerk who accused you of being a gold-digger, and a liar and had you in floods of tears less than twenty-four hours ago? How do you know you can trust him not to be a jerk again once you're stuck in Bermuda with him?'

I don't.

Ella pushed away the doubt. He'd lost the plot when she'd told him about the baby, but he'd apologised for that and she knew he meant it. And anyway, this really wasn't about her. 'He's the father of my child and he's giving me a chance to get to know him better. Surely you can see I have to take it?'

'Umm-hmm. And you don't find it the tiniest bit suspicious that twenty-four hours after totally flipping out about this pregnancy he suddenly wants to be so intimately involved in it...' Ruby paused for effect '...and you.'

'Maybe.' Of course she'd thought about it. After the initial euphoria at his offer, she'd calmed down enough to realise his sudden interest in the baby might not be the only reason he'd asked her to come to Bermuda.

But that didn't alter the fact that he was the father of her child. And she did want him to be involved. And that going to Bermuda was the only way to find out if they could make that happen.

'You're absolutely determined to do this, aren't you?' Ruby sounded pained.

'Yes.'

Ruby cursed sharply, defeated. 'I guess it's my own fault. If I hadn't interfered and encouraged you to nail Captain Studly in the first place, you wouldn't be in this situation.'

Ella grasped Ruby's cheeks, forcing her gaze back to hers. 'What situation? Getting the chance to have a child of my own? Getting to experience the miracle of becoming a mum? Something I was sure would never be possible? That situation?'

Ruby sent her a lopsided smile. 'Okay, point taken. But do me a favour, okay?'

'What favour?'

'Don't let all your happy over the pregnancy blind you to the truth about what's really going on with him. You have a tendency to always want to see the best in people, Ella. And that's one of the things I love about you. But try to be a little bit cautious this time.'

'If this is about what happened with Randall, you don't

have to worry.' Ella threaded her fingers through Ruby's and held on. 'I'm not going into this blind. I learnt that lesson when I was eighteen I'll never fall in love that easily again.' She'd made that mistake with Randall, and her baby had paid the price. 'But I refuse to go into this scared either.'

She needed to take some risks, to solve the fascinating enigma that was Cooper Delaney. A man who had the laid-back, laconic charm of a beach bum, but had the drive and ambition to build a multimillion-dollar empire from nothing. A man who could worry about the child growing in her womb when they made love, and yet look at her with a hunger that burned right down to her soul.

She wanted to understand him—to know how he really felt about this pregnancy and this baby and her—but only so he could play an active role in her child's life.

She wasn't looking for anything else. She was sure of it.

CHAPTER NINE

'How was the trip?' Coop reached in to grab her suitcase as Ella stepped out of the air-conditioned taxi into the sheltered carport rimmed by palm trees and flowering vines at the back of his property.

She fanned her face with the wide-brimmed straw hat she'd bought at the airport as the afternoon heat enveloped her. Bermuda in April had been in the mid-seventies and pleasantly hot; in late July it was hitting the high eighties and seemed to be sucking the life-force right out of her tired limbs.

'Good. Thank you.' She huffed to stop her sweaty hair sticking to her forehead as Coop paid the driver and waved him off.

The truth was it had been better than good, when she'd arrived at Gatwick Airport to discover the economy class ticket she'd insisted on purchasing herself, despite several terse emails from Coop before she left London, had been upgraded to first class. The added benefits of a three-course cordon bleu meal and a fold-down bed had made the eight-hour flight pass in a haze of anticipation. But now she was here, the impact of seeing him again was making the crows of doubt swoop like vultures in her stomach.

'I appreciated the upgrade, but you really didn't need to do that.' She wanted to make it absolutely clear she did not expect him to bankroll her.

Picking up her suitcase, he slung her carry-on bag under his arm. 'Sure I did.' His gaze skimmed down to her midriff before he sent her an assured grin. 'No baby of mine travels coach.'

The vultures in her stomach soared upward to flap around her heart and she stood like a dummy, stupidly touched by the reference to their child.

'Come here.' Resting his hand on her waist, he directed her towards the wooden steps that led out of the carport and into the back of the house. 'Let's get you out of this heat.'

The stairs led to the wide veranda of a white, woodframed house that rose from the grove of palms to stand on a rocky outcropping. She'd admired the modern, twostorey colonial structure as they wound down the drive from the main gate. Up close, the building was dominated by the large windows covered by louvred shutters. The house appeared cool and airy even before they stepped off the veranda into a palatial, high-ceilinged living area that opened onto a wraparound porch, which looked down onto the cove below.

Dumping her bag and suitcase at the base of a curving staircase that led to the second level, Coop leaned against the balustrade and smiled. In a faded red and black Bermuda College T-shirt and ragged jeans, his bare feet bronze against the oak flooring, he looked more like the beach bum she remembered than the suited executive she'd found so intimidating in London.

'So what do you think? Better than the hut, right?'

She swung round to take in the view and give herself a moment to regain the power of speech. Expensive, luxury furnishings—including a couple of deep-seated leather sofas, a huge flatscreen TV, a bar framed in glass bricks and a walled fireplace—adorned the tidy, minimalist living area. She stepped through the open doors onto the deck, hoping that the sea breeze would cool the heat rising up her neck. And spotted the edge of an infinity pool, sparkling on the terrace below the house. Steps carved into the stone led down through the grove of palms and banana trees, probably to the beach at Half-Moon Cove.

The cosy, ramshackle beach hut where they'd conceived their child had to be down there somewhere—but felt light years away from the elegance of his real home.

'It's incredibly beautiful. You must have worked very hard to earn all this in under a decade.'

He joined her on the deck, resting his elbows on the rail beside her hip and making her heartbeat spike.

'So you've been checking up on me?'

She studied the sun-bleached hair on his muscular forearms—lost for words again.

She'd expected to be a little intimidated by his wealth—especially after the first class travel over. She hadn't expected to feel completely overwhelmed. Not just by the staggering beauty of his home, but by him too. And the staggering effect he still had on her.

'The Internet is a glorious thing,' she murmured.

Unfortunately all the articles and news clippings about the meteoric rise of his business had contained virtually no information about his personal life. Or his past—bar a few photos of him escorting model-perfect women to island events. And once she'd discovered those, her enthusiasm for playing Nancy Drew had waned considerably.

'The journalist from *Investment* magazine said you were the Rags-to-Riches King of the Islands,' she said. 'She seemed very impressed with your business model.' And not just his business model, Ella had decided, from all the detailed prose about his muscular physique and sparklingly intelligent gaze.

The grin as he glanced her way was quick and boyish. 'Yeah, I remember her. As I recall she hit on me.'

'I'm not sure I needed to know that,' she blurted, before getting control of the sting of jealousy.

He straightened away from the rail. 'Just so you know, I didn't hit on her back.' He skimmed a knuckle down her cheek. 'I like to be the one doing the chasing.' He tucked his finger under her chin. 'Except when it comes to pretty little English cougars who go trawling in beach bars.'

Her pulse sped up to thud against her neck, and the spot between her thighs melted. 'I didn't come back to Bermuda to hit on you again,' she said, trying hard to sound as if she meant it. Sleeping with him would only distract her from the real reason she was here.

He clasped the rail on either side of her hips, boxing her in.

'Then how about I hit on you?'

She gasped as he pressed warm, firm lips to her neck. Lust shot through her like a jolt of electricity—connecting the soft tissue under her chin to the bundle of nerves that lay dormant in her sex.

Except, it wasn't dormant any more.

The sensations spread like molten lava, incinerating everything they touched as he explored her mouth in bold, determined strokes.

She sucked on his tongue, savouring the tangy flavour of him, the groan of desperation. Her fingers flexed against the lean muscles of his abdomen as roughened palms stroked under her blouse. His fingers wrapped around her waist to yank her closer. She shuddered, her sensitive, pregnancy-engorged breasts pressed against the hard wall of his chest.

Sure fingers cupped her breast, then tugged at one hard peak and hot need arrowed down to her sex, the desire erupting like a volcano.

'Wait, Coop.' She wrenched herself free. 'Please, stop

a moment. I need…' She sucked in a breath, her lungs on fire, alongside the rest of her. 'I didn't come for this.'

Did she?

But as his heavy-lidded gaze met hers the heady rush that had been lapping at her senses ever since the car had pulled up to the house surged.

'So what?' He clasped her hand, and headed for the staircase.

He took the stairs two at a time. She could have resisted, could have told him no, but instead she found her feet racing to keep up with him.

He led her into a wide room on the first floor, with a huge four-poster bed draped with gauzy white curtains, and double doors that opened out onto a veranda.

He tugged her into his arms. 'I want you,' he murmured, his voice so low she almost couldn't hear it above the distant sound of the ocean, and the pounding in her eardrums. 'You want me.' His gaze dropped to her midriff. 'We've made a kid together. Why shouldn't we do this?'

She couldn't find a coherent response as the desperate desire to be touched, to be taken in that wild way only he seemed capable of, consumed her.

He jerked off his T-shirt, kicked off his jeans, and then wrestled off her clothes before lifting her, naked and yearning, onto the bed.

Her hands splayed across his wide chest, sank into the blond curls of hair across his nipples. She had to slow him down. Get her mind to engage.

Ruby had warned her not to get distracted, not to fall straight into bed with him. And here she was, less than an hour off the plane and already naked and willing.

'Shouldn't we think about this?' She struggled to hold him back, but the question broke on a soft sob as he cupped her mound. Blunt fingers probed the slick flesh, gliding over the perfect spot.

She bucked, cried out, pleasure radiating across her skin.

The light in his eyes became feral in its intensity. 'You're soaking wet, Ella. What's there to think about?'

Her breath rasped out as he stroked her into a frenzy, caressing the burning nub. Then rolled her over onto her stomach. Raising her hips, he positioned her on all fours, the thick erection nudging her entrance.

'I'll be gentle.' He lifted her hair off her neck, cradled her body with his to nip her shoulder. 'I promise.' Her heavy breasts swayed and he captured them, holding her steady. 'Now tell me you don't want this as much as I do?'

'You know I do.' She moaned, stretched unbearably, as he plunged. Her pulse thundered like an express train in her ears.

Need and desperation pummelled her. She couldn't breathe, couldn't think, the coil yanking tight inside her as he began to move. Pulling out, thrusting back, going impossibly deep, the rhythm torturously slow but steady, relentless, stealing her breath. Her hands fisted in the bed-clothes, her body battered by the building waves of pleasure. Sure fingers squeezed her nipples, then he reached down, to open her folds and touch the too-sensitive nub of her clitoris.

Pain and pleasure combined as he shot her to peak. The titanic wave crashed over her as his rhythm built and accelerated. She heard him shout, getting even bigger inside her, before the hot seed pumped into her. He let her go at last and she collapsed onto the bed, her body shaky, her mind dazed, her heart pounding against her ribs with the force and fury of a wrecking ball.

She rolled away from him, feeling stupidly fragile. 'You didn't use any protection,' she murmured.

'Not much point now. That horse has already bolted.' He whispered the words against her ear as his forearm wrapped around her waist and his body cradled her. 'You okay? I didn't hurt you, did I? I was trying to be gentle but I got kind of carried away towards the end.'

She shook her head, struggling to talk round what felt like a wad of cotton wool in her throat. 'No. It felt good.' And scarily intense.

One large hand cupped her breast, his thumb grazing the sensitive nipple. She flinched, the stiff peak too tender for attention.

'I'm sorry.' His thumbs drew back, to trace slow circles around the areola, avoiding the tip. 'The plan wasn't to jump you straight off. But I've missed you.'

'The plan…' She lurched onto her back, dislodging his hand. 'You planned this?'

'Yeah. I guess so.' He propped himself up on an elbow to look down at her, his gaze roaming over her face. 'Why? Is that a problem?'

'I don't know.' She tried to gather her thoughts and make sense of them, while the rush of afterglow still pumped through her system. 'I just thought…'

'What? That this wouldn't happen?' He brushed his fingers across her forehead, tucked the tendrils of hair that had escaped her updo behind her ear. 'Honey, I figure whenever we're on the same continent it's sort of inevitable. So why fight it?'

It wasn't the answer she had been looking for, the one she thought she should have wanted. But as soon as he said it she knew it was the truth.

'Yes, but…' She stared at him. 'That really isn't the reason I came here.'

'So why did you come?'

With her sex still aching from the intensity of their lovemaking, her breasts tender from the pinch of his fingers, and emotion coursing through her system, the answer didn't come as easily as it had when she had been lying in that fold-down bed across the Atlantic.

'To get to know you,' she murmured. 'To find out if you want to be a dad. How involved you want to be. I don't want sex to complicate that.'

'To complicate it?' He chuckled. 'The way I see it, sex is pretty much the only simple thing there is about all this. And we're good at it.' He shrugged, his gaze flicking to her midriff. 'We're going to have to work on the other stuff, because I don't have any easy answers for you there.'

For a moment he looked lost, and the lump of emotion became impossible to swallow down. Was she pushing him too hard, expecting too much, by being here?

'You don't know how you feel about the baby?' she asked, feeling foolish and a little ashamed of her naivety. Why had she been so quick to assume his decision to invite her here meant he must already have feelings for the baby? He'd been thrown into this situation against his will. Of course he'd be confused, maybe even a little resentful.

'Not really.' He flopped back on the bed, stared at the canopy above their heads. 'All I know is I don't want to mess up, like my old man did.'

She turned to him, ready to probe a little. 'How did your father mess up?'

His gaze locked with hers and for a moment she thought she saw something, but then it flicked away again. 'By not being there, I guess. I never met him. It was just my mom and me.'

'I'm sorry.' Her heart sank at the defensive 'don't go there' tone. And the news that he had been abandoned as a child by his own father. No wonder he'd reacted so violently to the news of her pregnancy. Had the horror she'd thought she'd seen been nothing more than blind panic?

She touched his forearm. 'You're not like that. If that's what you're worried about? Because you're already trying to do the right thing.'

He looked at where her fingers touched his arm, then

up at her face, his expression blank now and unreadable. 'You always this much of an optimist?'

His tone was flat, but she refused to let it bother her.

'I try to be,' she said, smiling. 'I don't consider that a bad thing.'

She wanted this child; he was still coming to terms with the fact of it. She had to remember that. Give him time. And space. And not give up hope. His cynicism made complete sense, now she'd had that brief glimpse into his childhood.

'So, what was your mother like?' she asked.

He shook his head, smiling back at her. 'Forget it, Little Miss Sunshine. How about you tell me something about your folks, first? I don't see why I have to do all the talking.'

He'd hardly told her anything, she thought, but she didn't call him on it. Surely telling him more about herself could only increase the intimacy between them, and make it easier for him to open up too?

'Okay, well…' She paused, his question triggering memories of a time in her life that she barely remembered now, but had been so painful once. 'Funnily enough, I think it was watching my parents and seeing what they went through that made me an optimist.'

'How come?'

'Because they had an incredibly acrimonious divorce when I was eight.'

His eyebrows shot up. 'And that made you an optimist?'

'Well, yes. Because it taught me how important second chances are,' she continued, choosing to ignore the sceptical expression. 'They'd tried to stay together for me and my brother and it had been a disaster. Children always see more than you think.' She sighed, remembering the whisper arguments, the bitter silences, the terror and confusion when she and her brother had been told Daddy would be moving out. 'I missed my dad terribly and it was awful to see my mum so sad and angry all the time. But then, eventually, they both found the people they were meant to be with. And I ended up with a stepmum who makes to-die-for chocolate cake and a stepdad who drove me and Ruby to cookery fairs without complaint. It totally transformed them both, made them much better people and much better parents. Because they were finally happy.'

He rolled onto his side, and suddenly she became aware of his nakedness, and hers, and the low-level hum of arousal that always seemed to be there. He placed a warm palm on her hip, slid it up to cup her breast. 'That's sweet,' he said, the comment only mildly condescending. Then he ducked his head, to lick a pouting nipple. 'But not as sweet as you are. You know, your breasts look incredible. Have they got bigger?'

Right, it seemed their deep and meaningful conversation appeared to be over. She knew a distraction technique when she heard one—and felt it hardening against her hip.

'Yes, they have…'

He leant down and sucked at the tip of her breast, gently, provocatively.

'The obstetrician says it's to do with the pregnancy hormones,' she continued, trying to focus despite the glorious feel of her nipple swelling against his tongue. 'They're much more sensitive too.'

He grinned up at her. 'Awesome.'

Wrapping his lips around the stiffened peak, he drew it against the roof of his mouth. Her fingers plunged into his hair as she held his head and gasped, the pleasure almost too intense to bear now. 'Oh, God…'

His growing erection nudged her belly, and she reached to stroke the shaft instinctively. But as she brushed her thumb across the bead of liquid at the head, rejoicing at his growl of need, her stomach rumbled loudly.

'Enough.' He gave a strained laugh, carefully dislodging her hand. Then kissed her fingers, his smile mocking. 'I guess I'm going to have to offer you food. I don't want you passing out your first day.'

At the mention of food, her stomach growled again. Colour tainted her cheeks as he laughed. 'How about you go grab a shower, and I'll put out the food my housekeeper prepared for us? We can eat out on the deck.'

'I'd like that,' she said, suddenly grateful for the respite, and the chance to examine all the emotions careering through her system.

Although she'd discovered in the last twenty minutes that he had a few 'issues' about his role as a father to overcome, it felt good to have got her first proper glimpse of the man behind the confident façade he wore so well. And exciting to know that they'd already started to establish a new intimacy between them.

Despite all Ruby's dire warnings not to confuse her joy about the pregnancy with anything else, she wasn't the least bit worried about jumping back into bed with Coop.

The one good thing about her terrible experience with Randall was, she'd never be delusional enough to mistake hot sex for love again.

Just because Coop looked great, smelled amazing, knew how to hit all her happy buttons—endorphin-wise—had sperm supersonic enough to impregnate her virtually barren body, and made everything inside her gather and tighten when he looked at her a certain way, she knew she could remain totally objective about their relationship. Such as it was.

Her main priority was the baby. And that would never change.

She lay back in the bed, and took a moment to appreciate the delicious view of Coop's naked backside as he tugged his jeans back on. And stifled the sigh as the pale strip of defined muscle disappeared behind battered denim.

Her stomach fluttered as if it were filled with hyper-active butterflies when he leaned down to press a kiss to her lips. 'Supper will be served in twenty minutes, Little Miss Sunshine. Don't be late.'

'Aye aye, Captain.'

He strolled out, and her gaze dipped back down to that beautifully tight butt—while the swooping sensation in her stomach bottomed out.

Okay, maybe sleeping with Coop would be a tiny bit distracting, but surely they were going to need some light relief from all the heavy stuff they had to deal with? And the truth was, the intimacy of sex seemed to be a great way to get him to lower his guard.

She squinted as the setting sun dipped lower and the light peaked past the four-poster's gauzy curtains onto the bed. In fact, now she thought about it, maybe she should consider it her duty to seduce him as often as possible.

Damn, you nearly blew it.

Coop put the last of the platters Inez had prepared on the outdoor table. The generous plate of lobster salad, In-ez's salted crab cakes and colourful sides of fruit salsa, fried plantain and cornbread had saliva gathering under his tongue.

Good, hopefully Inez's mouth-watering spread would keep his mouth and hands busy when Ella came down for her supper. He uncorked a chilled bottle of Pouilly Fuissé and splashed a couple of slugs into a glass before planting the bottle in the ice bucket next to the table.

Time to cool the hell down.

What the hell had got into him? He'd seen her less than a week ago. Had made love to her less than ten days ago. And yet, he'd jumped her as soon as she'd arrived.

One gasp of breath, one look from those trusting eyes and he'd been all over her like a rash. His first night with her had already caused more problems than he knew how to solve. And now he was losing all his cool points too? What the hell?

He gulped the pricey wine without tasting a single drop—the thought of the baby going some way to dousing the heat in his pants.

She loved this kid already; he could see it in the dreamy look every time she mentioned it. And then there were all those questions about how he felt about the baby. Making him pretty sure she wasn't going to be impressed with his initial thought that maybe his role in the child's life could be limited to setting up a hefty college fund and giving her a monthly allowance to cover her expenses.

On the balcony above, the white cotton curtains billowed out of the open balcony doors caught by the early evening breeze off the ocean. The sound of running water drifted down from the guest room's shower.

The image of Ella, naked and flushed, her rosy nipples begging to be sucked, swirled into his brain.

He drained the glass. Snagged one of the patties off the plate, wrapped it in some arugula and stuffed it in his mouth.

Enjoy it, Delaney, because crab cakes are the only cakes you're going to be sucking on for the rest of the night.

He needed to keep his wits about him. And not fall into the trap of getting hot and heavy about anything other than the sex. Until he had some answers to Ella's questions.

With that in mind…

Picking his smartphone off the table, he keyed in his housekeeper's home number. When Inez picked up he told her to take a holiday for a couple of weeks, all expenses paid. He could hear the suspicion in the older woman's voice—Inez had six grown kids and eight grandbabies and was nobody's fool—but after checking he'd remember to water the plants and suggesting a local girl to come in and do the laundry and cleaning while she was away, she finally took the bait.

Then he rang Sonny, listened to a lengthy update on the wedding arrangements, and then told his friend that he wouldn't be around for a while and if he needed anyone to help out with tours to contact his business manager. Then he carefully layered in a request to tell Josie he'd be mostly off island till the wedding.

He knew Josie was likely to be his biggest problem. Like any annoying little sister, that girl was more curious than the proverbial cat, had got into the bad habit of thinking she could drop in on him any time unannounced—and had an even bigger mouth than Inez.

He tucked the phone into the back pocket of his jeans. And dispelled the small tug of guilt. Ella would get to meet all his friends at Josie's wedding in three weeks' time if she was still here, but until then it would be better if they both kept a low profile.

Their little heart-to-heart and that poignant insight into her childhood had been unsettling and he didn't want any more weird moments like that again if he could avoid them.

When she'd told him about her parents' break-up, the urge to take away the unhappiness in her eyes had been dumb enough. But much worse had been the freaky feeling of connection. Because he remembered exactly what it was like to be scared, to be confused, to feel as if your world were being ripped apart and there wasn't a damn thing you could do about it. When he was a child, his mother's black moods, those dark days when she couldn't function, or when she cried—usually after his father had been by to screw her for old times' sake—had scared the hell out of him.

He'd almost told Ella about it. Thank God, he'd managed to stop himself just in time. Because the last thing he needed was them sharing confidences about stuff that meant nothing now.

He'd ridden out the storm long ago and he'd survived. And Ella had too.

But, unlike Ella, his takeaway from his childhood had been nowhere near as sunny and sweet as hers. And that made her vulnerable in a way he hadn't really considered until now.

Ella was an optimist, unrealistic expectations came with the territory, and he didn't want her getting any unrealistic ideas about him and what he was able to offer her and the kid.

But that didn't mean he didn't enjoy seeing that bright light in her eyes, or knowing she thought more of him than he knew was there. He certainly didn't plan to extinguish that light unnecessarily. Plus, after way too many bruising fights and angry words in his youth, and all those endless pointless arguments with his mom to get her to see the truth about his old man, he'd also become a big fan of avoidance when it came to talking about your feelings.

Especially if you had nothing to say on the matter.

Getting Ella together with Sonny and Josie and telling them about the baby would just create loads of unnecessary drama. He shivered as goosebumps pebbled down his spine at the thought. Because neither one of them could keep their noses out of his business and they had an opinion about every damn thing. And Inez was one of the biggest gossips on the island, so it made sense to keep her out of the loop too. He didn't want anyone knowing his business before he knew it himself.

He put the glass down at the soft pad of footsteps on the stairs and glanced up, his pulse slowing to a harsh, jerky beat as Ella walked towards him.

The filmy dress she wore blew around her legs. The

bodice only showed a small amount of cleavage, but he could still make out that magnificent rack and the bullet-tipped nipples outlined by the snug fabric.

Well, he guessed that was some compensation—however many problems this pregnancy was going to cause in the long term, he could totally get behind the changes his child was making to her body now.

He put a dampener on the thought when she opened her mouth in a jaw-breaking yawn. He needed to keep his dick under control tonight, at least until she'd slept off the effects of her flight. And suffering through another sleepless night might make him think twice before losing his cool with her again.

'Hi, this looks amazing,' she said, surveying the table. 'I'm so hungry I could eat a horse.'

'You're not the only one.'

She laughed, that musical lilt that had beguiled him from the get-go. 'Why do I have the strange feeling it's not a horse you want to eat?'

Smart girl.

He took her hand, kissed the knuckles. 'As much as I'd like to eat you, tonight, it's probably best if you stay in the guest room.' He pulled out her chair so she could take a seat. 'Alone.' He bit down on the groan as she tucked the pretty dress round that tempting butt.

'You don't have to do that.' The furrow of surprise and disappointment on her brow was almost comical. 'Unless you want to,' she added, as if his wanting her was actually in doubt.

'Honey, you've just got off an eight-hour flight.' He forced himself to be noble and ignore the growing ache in his crotch. 'It's the early hours by my count in the UK and…' He was about to point out that she was pregnant, but stopped himself. No need to bring up that topic unnecessarily. 'And I don't want to wear you out,' he finished.

The heart-pumping smile brightened her whole face. 'That's very considerate of you.' Wasn't it just? 'But I should warn you, I'm not good with jet lag. I'll probably wake up at the crack of dawn.'

He allowed himself a firm kiss, of exactly two seconds' duration. Because any longer would only increase the torment. 'Once you're awake, you'll find me in the bedroom at the end of the veranda.' Most likely wide awake and ready for action. 'I'm sure I can figure out a way to cure your jet lag.' She blushed prettily and his voice lowered. 'Sleep therapy happens to be a speciality of mine.'

'I'll bet.' The eagerness on her face crucified him. 'I'm sure that will come in handy, come cougar time.'

He chuckled, the sound rough, as he pulled up a chair and began piling the food onto their plates. He listed the different dishes Inez had prepared, reeled off some suggested activities she might like to try in the next couple of days, and neatly sidestepped a couple of questions about the snorkel tour. And Sonny.

To stay focused on eating the food and not her, he kept in mind that, while tonight would be torture, downtime now would be rewarded by lots of uptime from tomorrow morning onwards.

He quizzed her about her business and as many other generic topics as he could think of before her eyelids began to droop. He showed her back up to the guest bed after supper, and kissed her on the cheek—and had to be grateful that she was too exhausted to do more than smile sleepily back. Especially when her scent invaded his nostrils, and it took every last ounce of his will power to step back and close the door after her. Just before the door clicked shut, he heard the soft sound of her flopping onto the bed they'd shared less than an hour ago—and his knuckles whitened on the door handle.

It took a couple of seconds but he finally let go.

Tucking his clenched fists into his pockets, he headed down the hall to the library at the other end of the house, feeling more noble than Sir Galahad.

Booting up the computer on his desktop, he ran a search on the effects of pregnancy on a woman's body in the first and second trimester. Might be good to do some research—Ella said sex in pregnancy was safe, but, considering how much sex they were likely to want, he didn't want to be making any demands on her she couldn't handle.

But he couldn't concentrate on the information, his impatience for the night to be over growing as the endless minutes ticked by. The thought that every one of those minutes shortened the time they had left together only irritated him more.

What was up with that?

They had as much time as they needed. She'd agreed to buy an open ticket. And very few women had kept his interest for more than a couple of dates. So it stood to reason that, no matter how cute and fascinating and hot he found her, or how much baggage they had to sort out with the baby, having her in his home would get old soon enough.

So why the heck was he was already worrying about her departure?

CHAPTER TEN

'WOW, THAT WAS *A-MAZING*!' Ella shoved up her mask and hit the release button on her tanks. She laughed, her mind still reeling from all the images she'd seen and absorbed in the last thirty minutes. She'd thought snorkelling on the reef had been a lifetime experience, but her first scuba-dive had topped it.

Darting fish, waving coral, the dappled sunlight shining through the waves and the pure white sand sparkling under her flippers.

'Here. Let me.' Coop grabbed the air tanks and set them on the boat's deck before shrugging off his own equipment.

'I almost had a cow when I saw that shark.' She shuddered, the laugh breathless at the memory of the majestic creature gliding by beneath them. 'What kind was it? It looked enormous.'

She unzipped the snug wetsuit, struggled out of the top half.

'Tiger shark, about seven feet.' Cooper sent her a mocking smile as he climbed out of his own suit. Water glistened on his tanned chest, diverting her gaze. 'Not much more than a baby. Nothing to freak out about.'

'You're joking—that was no baby,' she replied, indignant. 'And I didn't freak out.' *Much.*

He chuckled and grabbed her wrist, to pull her into his embrace. 'I guess you handled yourself pretty well.'

His palm touched her cheek and she felt the giddy rush of pleasure from the intense study. 'For a rookie,' he whispered, before his lips covered hers and she forgot to be mad.

They were both breathless when they came up for air. Her heart beat in an even more irregular rhythm than when she'd spotted the tiger shark.

'So, you want to do that again some time?' His hands settled on her waist, his thumbs brushing her hips above the half-off wetsuit. 'Sharks notwithstanding.'

'Yes, please. And I loved the shark.' He chuckled at her enthusiasm. 'It was so beautiful and exciting.'

But not as beautiful and exciting as you, she almost added, but stopped herself just in time. She'd been on the island ten days now, and it was getting harder and harder not to let her feelings run away with themselves. With his damp hair falling across his brow, those handsome features gilded by sunlight, and the lean muscles of his six-pack rigid against her palms it was even harder to remember why she shouldn't let them.

She'd had an incredible time so far. When she'd been here in April, she'd stayed almost exclusively at the resort. And had no idea that she'd missed so much of what the island had to offer. The colonial elegance of the pastel-shaded houses and cobblestoned streets in St George, the exhilaration of a motorbike ride to a secluded cove, the luxury of an impromptu picnic lunch at a beach café.

But best of all had been Coop's attention and his willingness to spend so much time with her. Every day he'd laid on a new adventure to experience. And apart from a few hours spent in his study each day to deal with his business, he'd hardly left her side.

She hadn't expected him to be this enthusiastic about showing her around—or how much she would enjoy his company. She felt young and carefree and bold, excited at the prospect of trying out new things that she might have been too cautious to try out before.

Yesterday morning he'd announced she was learning to scuba-dive. Then he'd devoted most of the day to teaching her. Fitting her out while demonstrating all the equipment, giving her endless lessons in how to breathe through the regulator in the pool, running through all the safety routines, and the intricacies of buddy breathing.

They'd managed a short training dive yesterday from the beach, but today he'd taken her out on the motor cruiser.

And the thirty-minute dive had been spectacular. Every second of it.

But even her first scuba-dive in Bermuda couldn't top the wonder of spending her nights and the long lazy mornings in bed with Coop. The man had skills in the bedroom that were quite simply phenomenal—making love to her with care and dedication one minute and hungry intensity the next.

Of course, during all the fun and frolics, she'd been careful to keep reminding herself that this trip wasn't about her and Coop but about the baby—which hadn't been all that hard to do, for the simple reason that she hadn't made a lot of progress in that area at all.

He talked about their baby and the pregnancy, but only in very generic, impersonal ways. In fact, he was so guarded on the subject whenever it came up now, that she had begun to wonder if all the new activities, all the wonderful experiences hadn't been arranged to distract her from any mention of why she was really here.

She hated herself for being suspicious of his motives, for doubting his sincerity in any way, but most of all she didn't understand why he would even want to do that. What possible reason could he have to avoid the subject? When he'd invited her to his home specifically to talk about it? It didn't make any sense.

'You want to go back out tomorrow?' he asked, brushing her hair back from her face.

The flutter of contentment pushed aside the foolish moment of doubt.

She was being ridiculous. How could he be avoiding talking to her, when they were together so much of the time? 'Could we go out again today?'

He tapped her nose. 'No way. Half an hour's enough. You're a beginner and...' his gaze flicked to her abdomen and he took his hand from her waist '...you know.'

It was an oblique reference to the baby, but a reference nonetheless, so she decided to go with it. If she had concerns, maybe it was about time she voiced them. She knew she had a tendency to avoid confrontations. Probably a layover from her early childhood, when her parents had spent so much of the time arguing—and the hideous breakdown of her relationship with Randall.

But if the thought of the baby made Coop uncomfortable, the only way to get over that was to stop letting him avoid the subject. And when she'd Skyped Ruby the day before, her friend had told her in no uncertain terms to stop worrying and confront Coop about the issue.

'I called the obstetrician this morning,' she said as casually as she could manage. 'The one you lined up for me. She said scuba-diving would be absolutely fine.'

'Yeah, you told me. But it's still not a good idea to push it.'

'I didn't know you'd heard me,' she said, trying not to mind the abrupt dismissal as he set about hanging the air tanks on their frame. 'I arranged to go in for a check-up on Monday, by the way,' she added, but he didn't look up, engrossed in checking the gauges. 'If you want to come with me?'

That had got his attention, she thought, as his head shot

up. 'Why?' There was no mistaking the flicker of panic.
'Do I need to? Is there something wrong?'

'No, of course not, but…' While his concern warmed
her, the panic was another matter. 'I thought you might like
to come—she might do a scan and you could see the baby.'

'Right.' He turned away, went back to concentrating on
the equipment. 'Why don't you shimmy out of that wetsuit?' He threw the request over his shoulder. 'Then we can
head back before you start to burn. It's hot as hell out here.'

She inched the wetsuit down her legs, sat down on the
boat's bench seat to struggle out of the clinging black neo-
prene. 'So you'll come to the scan? On Monday?'

She handed him the suit and he draped it over the bench
seat next to his.

'Yeah, maybe, I don't know. I'll have to see how I'm
fixed.' He met her eyes at last, the 'don't get too excited'
tone in his voice loud and clear. 'When's your appointment?'

The lack of enthusiasm was almost palpable and she had
the sudden premonition that he was only asking for the information so he had time to come up with a viable excuse.

'Two-thirty.'

'Damn, that's a shame. I promised Sonny I'd come over
that afternoon. I'll have to miss it.'

Her heart stuttered. So now she knew for sure. She had
not imagined his reluctance. She drew in a deep breath,
determined not to back down again in the face of his stubbornness.

'I see.' She tugged her beach tunic on over her bikini,
the ocean breeze making her shiver despite the heat. 'I
could rearrange the appointment for later. Why don't I
come with you to see Sonny? I'd love to meet him.'

The sides of his mouth pinched—making the strain to
maintain the easy smile on his lips more visible. 'No need

for that. I'm helping him strip an old motor. It's not going to be any fun.'

She felt the dismissal like a slap that time. She'd asked before about his friends on the island. And he'd closed her down on that subject too. She'd been here for over a week and she hadn't met anyone he knew. When she'd suggested going back to The Rum Runner the previous evening, he'd explained that he didn't want Henry hitting on her again, then picked her up and dumped her in the pool. Once he'd dived in after her and then 'helped' her out of her wet clothes, the request had quickly been forgotten.

She watched as he began to pack the equipment into the box at the end of the boat. The panicked beat of her heart richocheted against her chest wall.

Stop freaking out and ask him. Avoidance isn't the answer. You can't handle this if you don't know what's going on.

'Don't you want me to meet your friends?'

He swung round on his haunches, his eyebrow arching up his forehead. 'Huh?'

'It just seems a bit strange—' she forced the comment out, past lips that had dried to parchment '—that wherever we go we never seem to bump into anyone you know.'

She saw the flash of guilt in his eyes before he was able to mask it.

'They don't even know I'm here, do they?' she asked, but from the flags of colour on his tanned cheeks she already knew the answer. The fact that he hadn't told anyone about the baby either went without saying. She clamped down on the feeling of unease though. She mustn't overreact. Just because he hadn't told them yet, didn't mean he would never tell them.

He swore softly and stood up. 'Not yet.'

'I see.' She swallowed. 'Do you plan to tell people? Eventually?'

'Yeah, sure. I just wanted to keep you to myself for a while.' He held her arm, his voice lowering to a seductive purr as he caressed the sensitive skin on the inside of her elbow with his thumb. 'You remember Josie, Sonny's daughter, the kid that woke you up when you were in the hut?'

She nodded.

'She's having a big wedding on the beach next Saturday. We'll have to go to that, I'm one of the witnesses. Everyone will be there.'

He went back to sorting out the equipment.

'Oh, okay. That's good,' she said, although the way he'd said they would 'have to go' made it sound as if he wasn't too happy at the prospect. 'But it might be nice to see them before that?' she pushed. Obviously she had overreacted, but something about the whole thing still bothered her. Was he planning to keep their relationship a secret until then? 'Because, you know, it might be a bit weird me turning up at this wedding pregnant with your child, if no one knows me.'

'Do you think they'll be able to tell?' He dropped the wetsuit he'd been packing as his eyes shot down to her tummy. 'You're not showing too much yet.'

What?

The feeling of unease was replaced by the shock of vulnerability.

'Well, no, maybe not, but…' The words got caught behind the silly lump of emotion. Which had to be the pregnancy hormones, making her feel ridiculously over-sensitive. But she couldn't stop the thoughts coming, now that the dam had broken. 'Why don't you want them to know?'

'Hey, what's the matter?' He stood up, the concern in his eyes almost making her back down again. 'It's not that big a deal. Believe me, it's just easier not to tell them yet.'

She stared at him. Was he actually serious?

Yes, it might make it easier for him, but how would it be easier for her? Wouldn't it make things awkward at this wedding if someone did notice? And asked questions about her condition? She knew they weren't a proper couple, that she shouldn't get too invested in their relationship. That they were just having fun with each other while sorting out what to do about their shared child. But the fact was, she'd been here for ten days, and they hadn't actually sorted out anything yet. Not even how he was going to introduce her to his friends.

Was she his girlfriend? His wedding date? A holiday fling? Or just another of his temporary bonk buddies? Maybe being the mother of his child didn't give her any relationship rights, but surely it ought to afford her a tiny iota of respect?

'The thing is, Coop,' she began, trying not to let the hurt show, 'I can't see how not talking about the baby is making it easier for me. I can't stay here indefinitely, you know, and—'

'Damn it, Ella, you've only been here a week. We can't rush this stuff.'

'*Rush it*? Coop, I've been here ten days!' she said, exasperated now. 'And we haven't talked about the baby at all.'

'Because we've been busy, doing…' he paused '…other stuff,' he said, so emphatically that she suddenly realised she'd been right to be suspicious of the endless round of activities. 'Stuff that you said you enjoyed,' he added, grudgingly, sounding a little hurt.

'I did enjoy them. I loved every single minute of them,' she rushed to reassure him, but then noticed he didn't actually look *that* hurt. 'But that's not the point. We could have talked about it in the mornings before we went out. Or in the evenings when we got back.'

'Uh-huh, well, we've been pretty busy then too.' His

gaze raked down her figure, making her whole body warm. And it occurred to her that the relentless schedule of day-time activities might not have been his only distraction technique. 'And I don't recall you complaining about that either,' he added. 'Especially when I had my mouth on that succulent little clit this morning.'

Hell. That did it.

She glared at him—the succulent nub in question throb-bing alarmingly now in unison with her distended nipples. 'You sod.' He'd been playing her all along. And she'd been too dazed by her own lust to see it. 'You've been seducing me deliberately, haven't you, to stop me from discussing it? I knew it.'

'Hey, calm down. I have not.' His lips quirked. 'I love sucking on your clitoris, remember?' He reached for her arm, but she jerked it out of his grasp. Not finding the joke—or the fact that her clitoris wouldn't stop throb-bing—remotely amusing any more.

'I suppose the next question is why? Why would you do that? Unless...' Her temper faded, and then collapsed, at the stubborn, defensive look on his face.

Oh, no. Not that.

She heaved a heavy sigh when he didn't say anything, scared to say it, terrified that she might be right, but know-ing she had to ask. 'If you're having second thoughts about being involved with this baby, Coop, you need to tell me.' She met his gaze, the flags of colour on his cheeks shin-ing beneath his tan. 'I want you to be part of its life, very much.'

Maybe she still didn't know much about how he really felt about parenthood, but the things she had learned about him in the last week had convinced her of that much. His generosity, his intelligence, the quick wit that always made her laugh, the care he took with her, his need to look out for her and protect her and the capable, patient way he'd taught her how to scuba-dive, not to mention that reckless, dangerously exciting streak that made her feel bold too, made her sure he would make a wonderful father. 'I'm not here to force a connection on you that you don't feel.'

She couldn't make him want to be a father, however much she might want to. That wouldn't be fair on him, and it certainly wouldn't be fair on her child.

'If you're not ready to discuss this yet, it's probably best if I just leave.'

The calm, rhythmic sound of the ocean lapping against the side of the boat stretched across the silence. She flinched as he raked his fingers through his hair and broke the silence with a bitter curse.

What the hell did he say to that?

She was looking at him with those big round trusting eyes. And he knew he hadn't been honest with her, or with himself.

But he didn't want her to leave. Not yet. He wasn't ready. And he did want to figure out what to do about the kid. But the more she'd talked about the baby, the more inadequate it had made him feel, until the problem had become so huge he'd clammed up completely. Plus, it had been so damn easy just to get lost in her and forget about all that. She was so cute and funny and engaging. Everything he showed her she loved; everything they did together she threw herself into with a complete lack of fear. She was smart and funny and resourceful and so eager and responsive. Especially in bed.

But she was right: he'd played her, even if he hadn't really intended to. And now he owed her an explanation.

'Come here, Ella.' He tried to take her into his arms, the guilt tightening his throat when she grasped his forearms to hold him off.

'Please, just give me a straight answer, Coop. Don't try to sugar-coat it, okay. I can take it.'

He wasn't so sure of that. 'I swear, no more messing you about.'

He sat on the boat's bench seat, and gently pulled her into his lap, pathetically grateful when she didn't resist him again.

'There's no need to make up excuses.' She cupped his cheek and the guilt peaked. 'I understand if you feel over-whelmed.'

He covered her hand and dragged it away from her face. 'Stop being so damn reasonable, Ella.'

She stiffened in his arms. 'This isn't about being reasonable. It's about being fair. I don't want to force you to shoulder a responsibility you don't want.'

'Damn it, Ella, who the hell ever told you life was fair?'

It scared him how easily she could be crushed, especially by a guy like him—who always looked out for himself first.

She tried to rise, but he held her tight, pressed his forehead into her shoulder. 'I'm sorry, don't go…' He sucked in a deep breath, prepared to admit at least some of the truth, even though the feel of her butt nestled against his groin was having a predictable effect.

What he wouldn't give right now to strip off the light cotton dress and feast on her lush body—and get the hell out of this conversation. But he couldn't carry on lying to her.

He rested his head back against the seat. Stared at the blue sky, the swooping seagulls, the clean bright sunlight. And felt the darkness he'd spent so long running away from descend over him like a fog.

He forced his head off the seat to look her in the face. 'Hasn't it ever occurred to you that I might not be cut out to be a dad? That you and the kid might be much better off without me?'

'No, it hasn't,' she said and the total confidence in her voice sneaked past all the defences he'd put in place over the years. 'I realise you're not as ecstatic about this pregnancy as I am. But that doesn't mean you won't be a good father when the time comes. If you're willing to try?'

'I want to try, but I just don't know if…'

'There aren't any guarantees, Coop, not when it comes to being a parent. You just have to do what comes naturally and hope for the best.'

'I guess, but you'll be a lot better at that than I am,' he said, able to appreciate the irony.

'Maybe you should ask yourself why you're so insecure about this. Would that help?'

'I doubt it.' He definitely didn't want to go there.

'Is it because of your own father? And the fact that you never knew him?' she said, going there without any help from him. 'Is that it?'

He shook his head. Damn, he'd have to tell her the truth about that too, now. 'I did know him. I guess I lied about that.'

'Oh.' She looked surprised, but not wary. Or not wary yet. 'Why did you lie?' she asked, as if it were the most natural thing in the world.

'Because I didn't exactly *know* him,' he clarified, trying to explain to her something he'd never understood. 'I knew of him. And he knew about me.'

'I don't…' she said, obviously struggling to figure it out.

'I grew up in a small place in Indiana called Garysville,' he said, reciting a story he'd denied for so long, he felt as if he were talking about some other kid's life. 'Towns like that, everyone knows everyone else's business. My old man was the police chief. A big deal with a reputation to protect, who liked to play away from home. Everyone knew I was his kid, because I looked a lot like him. And my mom didn't exactly keep it a secret.'

'But surely you must have talked to him? If it was such a small town.'

And you were his son.

He could hear her thinking it. And remembered all the times he'd tortured himself with the same question as a boy.

'Why would I?' The old bitterness surprised him a little. 'He was just some guy who came over to screw my mother from time to time. She told him I was his. He didn't want to know.'

'He never spoke to you?' She looked horrified. 'But that's hideous—how could he not want to know you?'

Like father, like son, he thought grimly. Wasn't that what he had thought about doing to his own kid? When he'd figured money would be enough to free him of any responsibility for his child.

'Actually, that's not true, I did speak to him once. Six words...' He forced the humiliating memory to the surface, to punish himself. 'You want to know what they were?'

Ella's heart clutched as Coop's face took on a cold, distant expression, the tight smile nothing like the warm, witty man she knew. She nodded, although she wasn't sure she did want to know. He seemed so unhappy.

'Do you want fries with that?' The brittle half-laugh held no amusement. 'Pretty tragic, isn't it?'

Her heart ached at the flatness of his tone. 'Oh, Coop,' she said, the sharp pain in her chest like a punch. No wonder he was so reluctant to talk about the baby. It wasn't fear of the responsibility; it was simply a lack of confidence.

'I worked nights at a drive-thru in town when I was in high school,' he continued, still talking in that flat, even tone that she was sure now was used to mask his emotions.

'My mom was finding it hard to stay in a job, she had…' he paused. '…these moods.' He shrugged. 'Anyhow we needed the money. He drove in one night with his family, about a month after I'd got the job. He ordered two chilli dogs, two chocolate malts and a side order of onion rings for his kids. Delia and Jack Jnr.'

She wondered if he realised how significant it was that he'd remembered the order exactly. 'You knew them?'

'Sure, we went to the same high school. Not that we moved in the same circles. Delia was the valedictorian, Jack Junior the star quarterback. And I hated their guts, because I was so damn jealous of the money they had, the choices.' He huffed out a bitter laugh. 'And the Beemer convertible Jack Jnr got for his sixteenth birthday.'

And the fact that they had a father, your father, and you didn't, she thought, her heart aching for him.

'He looked me right in the eye and said no, they didn't need fries, then he paid and drove on. He never came to my window again.'

She heard the yearning in his voice and the punch of pain twisted.

No wonder he'd worked so hard to get away from there, to make something out of his life. Rejection always hurt. It had nearly destroyed her when Randall had rejected her, but at least she'd been an adult. Or adult enough. She couldn't imagine suffering that kind of knock-back as a child. Every single day. To have it thrown in your face that you weren't good enough, and never knowing why.

The casual cruelty of the man who had fathered him, but had never had the guts to acknowledge him, disgusted her. But his bravery in rising above it, in overcoming it— surely that was what mattered. Why couldn't he see that?

'But you've got to understand, Ella. I'm not sure I'm a good bet as a father. Because I'm a selfish bastard, just like he was.'

She wanted to tell him that he was wrong. That he wasn't selfish, he was only self-sufficient, because he'd had to be. And that she admired him so much for having the courage to rise above the rejection. But she knew it wasn't only admiration that was making her heart pound frantically in her chest.

She touched his cheek, felt the rasp of the five o'clock shadow already beginning to grow at two in the afternoon. 'Do you really think you're the only one of us who's scared, Coop? The only one who thinks they won't measure up?'

He stared at her. 'Get real, Ella. You've loved this kid from the get-go. You've made it your number one priority from the start.' His gaze roamed over her face. 'How would you feel if I told you I'm pretty sure I only invited you here because I wanted you. Not the kid?' The desire in his heavy-lidded eyes made the heat pulse low in her abdomen. 'If that doesn't tell you what kind of father I'd be, I don't know what the hell does.'

She smiled, utterly touched by the admission. 'Actually I'm flattered. And rather turned on.'

'Seriously, Ella. For once, I'm not kidding around about—'

'I know you're not.' She cut him off, then gripped his cheeks, pressed her forehead against his, and prepared to tell him something she had never wanted him to know. 'How about if I told you that when I was eighteen I got pregnant and I had a termination? Would you still think I don't have some pretty persuasive reasons to doubt my own ability as a parent?'

She forced her gaze to his, willing him not to judge her as harshly as she had always judged herself.

His eyes widened, but he looked more stunned than disgusted. 'That's your big revelation? Big deal. You were eighteen. Why would you want a kid at that age?'

She shook her head. 'But you don't understand. I did

want it.' She rested her palm on her belly, emboldened by the new life growing there to talk for the first time about the one she'd lost. 'I wanted it very much. Which is why this child means so much to me now.'

'Okay, I get that.' He threaded his fingers through hers, the acceptance in his eyes unconditional. 'But you can't punish yourself now for a choice you made at eighteen. Having a baby at that age would have screwed up your life.'

She wanted to take his comfort, his faith in her, but she couldn't, not till he knew the whole truth. 'But that's not why I did it. I had the abortion because Randall ordered me to. He insisted. He said either I lose the baby, or I would lose him. And I chose him. Over my own child.'

A tear slipped over her lid, and he brushed his thumb across her cheek.

'Ella, don't cry.' She heard the tenderness and knew she didn't deserve it. 'This Randall was the father?'

She nodded, tucked her head onto his shoulder. 'Pretty pathetic, isn't it?'

'Not pathetic,' he said, nudging her chin up with his forefinger. 'You were young and scared. And given an impossible choice by that bastard. That's his bad, not yours.'

Ruby had always said the same thing to her, when she'd tortured herself with what ifs after the procedure. But now, for the first time, she felt herself begin to accept it.

Coop rubbed the tight muscles at the base of her neck. 'I'm guessing Randall didn't stick around once he'd got you to do what he wanted.'

'How did you know that?'

'Because the guy sounds like a selfish, manipulative jerk.' He sighed, then brushed her hair off her forehead, and his lips tilted in a wry smile. 'It takes one to know one.'

'You're nothing like him.'

'I don't know—I freaked pretty bad when you told me about Junior. And I've been doing my best to avoid the subject ever since.' He rested his hand on her belly, rubbed it gently back and forth. It was the first time he'd ever touched her there, and the flood of warmth caught her unawares.

'Yes, but you apologised for flipping out the very next day,' she pointed out. 'Even though you were still reeling from the news. And you've never tried to pressure me the way he did. That makes you a much better man than Randall ever was.'

The half-smile became rueful. 'I don't know about that.' She opened her mouth to protest, but he lifted a finger to her lips, silencing her. 'But I'm glad you think so. How about I come to the scan on Monday?'

The smile in her heart at the suggestion was even bigger than the one she could see reflected in his eyes. 'Okay, if you're sure?'

She knew what a big leap this was for him, so she was doubly pleased when he took a deep breath, then nodded. 'I guess so. I can't guarantee I'll know what I'm doing, but I'd like to be there anyway.'

'That's wonderful, Coop.'

His fingers threaded into her hair as he captured her lips in a tender kiss. But what started as gentle, coaxing, quickly heated to carnal as she opened her mouth and flicked her tongue against his.

She felt the satisfying swell of his erection, coming back to life against her bottom as she feasted on him—and let him feast on her.

He drew back first, to flick his thumb across the stiff peak of her nipple. But when she tried to reach for the front of his shorts and the stiff length inside, he grabbed her wrist to hold her off.

'Not a good idea.'

'Why not?' she said, the rush of emotion only intensifying her eagerness.

He kissed her nose. And she felt the tiny sting. 'Because you're getting a little pink around the edges, and I don't want you getting a sunburn. It's liable to cramp our style.'

He lifted her off his lap, to walk to the boat's console.

'Why don't we just go below decks?'

'For what I've got in mind, we're going to need a bigger bed.' He grinned over his shoulder and fired up the boat's engine. 'Now sit down and grab a hold of something. I'm going to see how fast I can get this thing back to base.'

She did as she was told, impossibly pleased that his eagerness matched her own, before he whisked the steering wheel round and hit the accelerator. The rush of wind lifted her hair and made the sunburn on her nose tingle as the launch bounced over the swell, hurtling them back towards the dock below his house at breakneck speed.

Her heart pumped to a deafening crescendo as she held on for dear life and watched him steer with practised ease. And the tightness that she hadn't realised had been making her chest ache for days released. Everything was going to be all right.

She faced into the wind, felt the spray of water hit her cheeks, and gave herself up to the excitement, the exhilaration pumping through her system.

She glanced back as the boat slowed to approach the small dock that stood below the back steps up to his property.

'Tie her up,' he shouted and she grabbed the thin nylon rope, climbed onto the dock and began looping the rope round the post while he switched off the engine.

His gaze locked on hers, telegraphing his hunger as she finished knotting the rope. Desire settled like a heavy weight as he stepped off the boat. The playful urge to tease hit her and she sped off towards the house.

'Hey, where the hell are you going?' he yelled, his feet

hitting the deck behind her as he gained ground. 'Come back here.'

Catching her, he swung her round in a circle. And cut off her laugh with a kiss that promised all sorts of delicious retribution.

Her tongue tangled with his as she opened her mouth to take the kiss deeper and dug greedy fingers into his damp hair. *No more doubts, no more panicking, no more holding back,* she thought as he broke the kiss to lift her into his arms.

'Got you,' he murmured.

Euphoria slammed into her at the possessive tone.

She clung onto his neck and whispered, 'Hurry up.'

'I am hurrying, damn it,' he huffed, climbing the steps two at a time with her cradled in his arms. 'You're heavier than you used to be, pregnant lady.'

She beamed at him, impossibly pleased by the silly joke.

Everything would be okay with the baby now, because she understood where his insecurities were coming from and knew he was at least willing to try to work all those problems out.

And while they were doing that, why shouldn't they see if there could be more? He'd given her a painful glimpse into his past—had let his guard down and let her in. And she'd done the same. Her heart stuttered painfully at the thought of all the possibilities that she hadn't considered, hadn't let herself consider. She'd been so cautious up to now, mindful of Ruby's warning not to let her heart run away with itself. But was it really necessary to carry on being so careful? When they'd taken such a huge step forward today?

She clung to his shoulders and kissed the soft skin beneath his chin.

'Behave,' he growled as he staggered into the living room and headed for the stairs. 'We're not there yet.'

She laughed as he boosted her in his arms to take the stairs, the euphoria intoxicating as she imagined just how far they could go, now she was ready to take the leap.

CHAPTER ELEVEN

'YOU SMELL SO GOOD.'

Strong arms wrapped around Ella's waist from behind. She shivered as Coop nipped playfully at her ear lobe, then glared into the bathroom mirror.

'For goodness' sake, I'm trying to put my face on here.' Slicking another coat of gloss on bone-dry lips, she gave him a not exactly subtle jab with her elbow, which only made him chuckle.

'Stop freaking out, you look great.' Warm palms skimmed over the light silk of the dress she'd found in a boutique shop in Hamilton after a fraught shopping expedition yesterday, then settled on the curve of her stomach. 'How's Junior?'

A little of her aggravation dissolved, pushed out by the feel of his hands, stroking where their child grew, and the tender enquiry in his gaze as it met hers in the mirror.

'Junior's fine.' She smiled back at him. She knew he was still feeling his way, still nervous about stepping into a role he hadn't prepared for, but he'd been eager and attentive during the scan five days ago, firing questions at the obstetrician.

When the doctor had asked them if they wanted to know the sex, he'd deferred to her, but she could see how keen he was to know the answer and had decided to go with it—maybe knowing the sex would make the baby more real to him. When the doctor had pointed out their child's penis, she'd been glad she had, because she hadn't been able to stop laughing when he'd whispered with stunned delight, 'For real? The kid's hung like a horse.'

She turned in his arms, pressed her hands to his cheeks. 'But Junior's not the one who's about to meet all your friends for the first time.' She dropped a hand to her stomach, the jumpy sensation nothing to do with the child growing inside her.

Because while Coop's attitude to their child had become everything she could have hoped for, the euphoria of that day a week ago, when she'd been sure they were beginning to form a more tangible bond between the two of them, had faded considerably.

'I want them to like me,' she murmured, not quite able to keep the resentment out of her voice. She'd tried in the last week to make him understand this was important to her. And he'd resolutely refused to even meet her halfway, ignoring or deflecting her repeated requests to introduce her to anyone he knew. Just as he'd continually ignored her suggestions that she should book her flight home soon.

So here they were, on the evening of his friend's wedding, and she had no idea where she stood, not just with his friends but with him too. 'I would have preferred to at least have met some of them.'

'You already met a few of them at the Runner on our first night,' he said, in a familiar argument.

'That was four months ago!' she replied, her patience straining. 'And I hardly talked to any of them.'

'Quit panicking—they're going to love you,' he murmured, dismissing her concerns again. Lifting her hand, he pressed a kiss into the palm. 'You know what you need?'

'A Valium, maybe?' she said, only half joking.

'Nuh-uh.' One warm palm settled on her leg and then

skimmed up under her dress, to cup her buttock. 'I've got a better way to help you unwind.'

His thumb sneaked under the leg of her panties, making the pulse of heat flare, as it always did. She grasped his wrist and halted the exploration—determined not to be sidetracked again. 'Stop it, Coop. We haven't got time.'

His lips curved. 'Sure we have.' Dropping his head, he kissed the pulse point in her neck, the one place he knew from experience would drive her wild. 'You're just kind of uptight. This'll help.'

'No, it won't,' she said, but the protest trailed off as he cupped her, the heel of his palm rubbing the bundle of nerves and giving them the friction they craved.

'We can't…' She gasped, blindsided by the inevitable swelling in her sex, the rush of moisture, as one thick finger snuck past the gusset of her panties and slid over her yearning clitoris. 'I don't have time to shower again.'

'Then don't.' His clever fingers played with the swollen nub. 'I love you with that just-screwed look.'

The words registered through the haze of heat, and her temper flared. Flattening her palms against his chest, she shoved him back, shaking with frustration—and no small amount of fury. 'Get off me. How old are you, for goodness' sake?'

'What the hell are you so mad about?' He looked genuinely nonplussed. 'You want to—you know you do.'

Given that his fingers were slick, he probably thought he had a point, which only made her more mad.

Feeling the threat of tears stealing over her lids, she pushed him aside to storm out of the bathroom.

'Damn it, Ella! What the hell did I do?'

She swung round, slapping her hands on her hips, desperate to keep the anger front and centre to disguise her hurt.

'I'll tell you what you did. You never once took my feelings into account about this. If I'm nervous and uptight it's because I didn't want to go to this event not knowing anyone. I realise we're not a couple, not really, but I thought...' She blinked furiously.

She had thought what exactly? That they were a couple, that there had been something developing between them in the last few weeks that had nothing to do with their child. But how could she know that, when he was so determined to avoid anything even resembling a serious conversation?

'Of course, we're a couple,' he said grumpily, making the stab of uncertainty under her breastbone sharpen. 'We're going to this damn fiasco together, aren't we? But I still don't see why we can't make love now if we both want to.'

Because we wouldn't be making love. Or at least, you wouldn't be.

The anger and frustration collapsed inside her, consumed by anxiety. She'd leapt over the cliff days ago convinced that he would catch her. But had she jumped too soon, reading far more into his actions than was actually there?

'The reason we can't make love...' she spoke the words slowly, succinctly, willing herself not to let an ounce of her distress show '...is because we don't have the time. And I'd really rather not turn up at this wedding smelling like some woman you've just screwed.'

He swore, his expression hardening, and she thanked God for it. She'd rather deal with his temper now than risk letting him see the emotion beneath.

'That's not what I meant and you damn well know it.'

She sighed, starting to feel shaky and knowing she couldn't maintain this façade for long. 'I think we should just go, I'm sure it'll be better once I get there.'

He raked his hand through his hair, the temper disappearing as quickly as it had come—as it always did with Coop.

'Okay, I guess you're right.' He pulled his smartphone from the pocket of the dark linen trousers he'd donned for the occasion and checked the time. 'The ceremony's in thirty minutes. Josie will murder me if I'm late.'

He escorted her down the steps to the beach, as if he were handling an unexploded bomb. But as they passed his beach hut, then walked together the mile along the sand towards The Rum Runner, retracing the steps they'd taken on their first night together, he threaded his fingers through hers.

Fairy lights strung through the palm trees twinkled in the distance as the strains of music and merriment drifted towards them on the breeze. Her heart lifted at the romantic sight.

No wonder she'd fallen for Coop so fast. He was such a good man, in so many ways. Easygoing, affable, charming, energetic and always striving to do his best. Unlike Randall. But she knew he also had a host of insecurities, which he worked hard to keep hidden. Maybe his attempts to keep things casual didn't come from a lack of feeling? Perhaps he just needed a little more time? She could stay a few more days before booking her flight home.

After all, she hadn't even told him yet that her feelings had deepened, intensified. Maybe if she did…?

'I've been dreading this damn wedding ever since Josie told me about it four months ago,' he murmured, interrupting her thoughts.

'Why?' she asked, sensing his nervousness, and able at last to let go of her own. Surely meeting his friends didn't have to be bad.

'At first, I thought it was because she's still just a kid,' he said, his gaze fixed on the wedding party in the distance. 'But now I think it's the thought of promising to be with someone for the rest of your life. It spooked me. Why would anyone want to do that?'

She followed the direction of his gaze to see the beautiful young woman she'd met at his hut four months ago in the middle of the crowd of people on the beach. Her long-limbed frame was displayed to perfection in a short ivory satin gown, and her face glowed with love and excitement.

'Because they love each other? And they want to be together?' she heard herself say, willing him to believe it. 'It's not hard to make a promise to love someone if they love you in return.'

'Do you really believe that?' He glanced down at her, the look on his face remote in the fading light. 'After the number that Randall guy did on you?'

She flinched at the statement. She could have said that she had never truly loved Randall, that what she'd felt for him had been infatuation, a pale imitation of what she already felt for Coop. But the cynicism in his voice was like a body blow and she hesitated.

'Come on.' He squeezed her hand, and began to walk. 'Let's get this over with, then we can go home and do something much more interesting.'

But as he drew her towards the party the red glow of dusk and the twinkle of fairy lights didn't seem quite so romantic any more.

'So she came back?'

Coop looked up from the plate he'd been piling high with Henry's famous goat curry, to find Josie, her face radiant with love, grinning at him.

'Hey, kid. Congratulations.' He scooped her up with his free arm as she giggled and kissed his cheek. 'You look amazing,' he said as he put her down again, and she did him a twirl.

'Old enough to be getting hitched?'

'All right, you've got me there,' he admitted.

The ceremony had been several hours ago, and somehow watching her and Taylor standing together before the minister, with Ella gripping his hand to stop his fingers shaking, hadn't been as bad as he'd thought. In fact, it had been kind of touching.

Or it would have been, if listening to the wedding vows hadn't made him feel like such a jerk, for taking out his frustration on Ella when they'd been walking along the beach. He didn't know what the hell had got into him, mentioning that guy she'd dated, especially after that dumb argument they'd had back at the house.

He shouldn't have tried to jump her like that, but the truth was he'd been feeling edgy and tense for days now, ever since she'd started talking about booking a flight home, and the only time that feeling went away now was when they were making love.

'So where's Mr Josie?' he asked Josie, stifling his impatience to get back to Ella.

He needed to chill out about her. He'd left her with Sonny and Rhona less then twenty minutes ago; she'd be good with them for a while. Sure, she'd been more subdued than usual tonight, but she was probably just tired—the kid had been restless last night and she hadn't been able to get comfortable. Once he'd got her something to eat he'd take her home and make slow, lazy love to her. And everything would be okay again.

'Taylor's over with his buddies,' Josie said wryly. 'Boasting about the swordfish he landed last week.'

'Damn, you already sound like an old married couple.' Coop chuckled.

'That's the general idea.' She smiled. 'Talking of couples, why didn't you tell anyone Ella was visiting?' Josie observed, wiping the easy smile off his face.

He turned back to the buffet, the direct question unsettling him. 'Maybe I didn't want anyone bothering us,' he said, trying to inject some humour into his tone, but not quite pulling it off.

Josie's fingers touched his arm. And he glanced over his shoulder to see the serious expression on her face. Uh-oh, this couldn't be good. 'Is the baby yours, Coop?'

He dumped the plate on the table, and grasped her forearm, pulling her away from the crowd of people behind them. 'How do you know about that?' he whispered furiously.

'Because it's obvious. Especially if you know how petite she was four months ago.'

He thrust his hand through his hair. 'Damn, please tell me you haven't said anything to Ella.'

He knew she'd wanted him to tell people before she met them. If she found out they'd guessed about her condition, she'd be hurt—and that had never been his intention.

'Of course I haven't. It's not something you can bring up in a conversation with someone you've only met twice.' Josie tugged her arm out of his grasp. 'But damn, Coop, why the hell didn't you say something? If the baby's yours? Why keep it a secret? And why keep Ella's being here a secret too?'

'Because...' His mind snagged—because he'd wanted to keep things as light and non-committal as possible. Because dealing with the baby had felt like enough already. But even as the excuses sprang into his head they sounded like just that. Excuses. 'Because it's complicated,' he managed at last.

'Why is it complicated?'

'Because she lives in London,' he said, reciting the reasons he'd been giving himself for weeks, but didn't seem to fit any more. 'She's only here for a couple of weeks and it was an accident. And we hardly know each other.' Although that too didn't seem true any more.

He did know Ella: he knew how much he liked to wake up and spoon with her in the morning. How much he'd come to depend on her smile, that sunny, optimistic outlook that was so unlike his own. How addicted he'd become to her company, her enthusiasm, her bright, lively chatter about anything and everything. 'She's going to have the baby…' he paused, then soldiered on '…because we both want it.'

The admission might have surprised him, but for the rush of emotion as he recalled feeling those flutters against his palm the night before, when Ella had been snuggled against him. And seeing that tiny body on the sonogram five days ago, as the doctor had counted all his son's fingers and toes.

How had that happened? Somehow, in the last few weeks, the thing that had terrified him the most didn't terrify him any more; it excited him. He actually wanted to be a dad. But more than that, he wanted to be with Ella in a few months' time, when her body became round and heavy as it cradled their baby.

Damn, was that the reason he didn't want her to leave? It seemed so obvious now he thought about it. No wonder he got edgy every time she mentioned going back to the UK. He wanted her to have the baby, his baby, here in Bermuda. He knew he could do this thing now, and he didn't want to miss a moment of it.

'We're trying to work stuff out,' he said, seeing Josie's eyes go round with astonishment at his declaration. 'And we don't need anyone butting into our business while we're doing it.'

'Okay, I get that.' Josie nodded, surprising him. 'But I still don't see why it's that complicated, if you both want to have this baby.'

'Coop!' They both turned to see Rhona, Josie's mom, descending on them.

'Hi, Mom,' Josie answered.

Rhona fanned herself with the hat she'd been wearing during the ceremony. 'Coop, honey, I thought I should tell you, Ella went off home.'

'What? Why?' The low-level feeling of panic that had been bugging him for days resurfaced in a rush. 'Is she okay?'

'I think she's just tired.' Rhona sent him a sharp look. 'Now, don't take this the wrong way, honey, but is that girl expecting?'

Oh, hell.

'I've got to go, Rhona,' he said, ignoring Josie's muffled snort of laughter and Rhona's question before he got bombarded with a million more. He'd have a lot of explaining to do next time he saw them, but that could wait.

Bidding both women a hasty goodbye, he rushed out of the bar, and broke into a run as soon as he hit the beach.

He needed to get home, and tell Ella she didn't have to go home, that he wanted her to stay—for the baby's sake. She'd be sure to welcome the news, because she always put the baby first, and having two parents had to be better than having just one.

As he jogged up the beach steps to the house he saw the light in the bedroom window and grinned.

I love it when a plan comes together.

She was still awake. He'd tell her about his plans for their future and then they could finish what he'd been trying to start before the wedding.

'Hey, Ella,' he shouted up the stairs as he heard the whizz-bang of the fireworks Sonny had organised to finish the celebrations on the beach. Glancing over his shoulder, he caught the dazzle of light and colour as a shower of golden rain cascaded into the night sky. 'You missed the fireworks—how about we watch the display from the terrace?' He bounded up the stairs, then strode down the corridor. 'I've got something I have to tell you.'

But then he pushed the door open and spotted Ella, her arms full of silk panties, and her neatly packed suitcase laid open on the bed.

His grin flatlined as all the adrenaline that had been pumping round his system during his jog home slammed full force into his chest.

'What the hell do you think you're doing?'

CHAPTER TWELVE

ELLA WHIPPED ROUND at the surly shout, her heart jumping into her throat at the sight of Cooper, looking gorgeous and annoyed, standing in the doorway, his face cast in bold relief by the coloured lights bursting in the sky outside.

She folded her underwear into the suitcase, flipped the lid closed and took several deep breaths to slow her galloping heartbeat. 'I'm packing,' she said. 'I've booked myself on the night flight to London. It leaves at eleven.'

'What the…?' The expletive echoed round the room as he slammed the door shut. 'When exactly were you planning to tell me this? Or weren't you planning to tell me? Is that why you ran off early from the wedding?'

She stiffened, stunned by the anger, and the accusation. 'No, of course not. I planned to tell you when you got back. It's just…' She chewed on her lip, determined not to fold again under the pressure of her own insecurities. She'd let him dictate the terms of this relationship— or non-relationship—right from the start. But it was only as she'd had to stand by his side and listen to his friend recite her vows, while enduring the speculative looks of all his friends, that she'd begun to realise how little she'd been prepared to settle for. Because she had lacked the courage to demand more.

'I think we need some space,' she continued. 'There's something I have to tell you and—'

'Yeah, well, I've got something to tell you.' He cut in before she could get the words out she'd been psyching herself up to say all evening. 'I want you to stay, to move in with me.'

'What?' She sat down on the bed, her legs going boneless as her insides tumbled with an odd combination of hope and astonishment at the unexpected offer. 'You want me to stay? Seriously?'

She hadn't been wrong: there had been something developing between them, and he'd seen it too. Of course, she couldn't just abandon her life in London, but that he would even suggest such a thing had to be a very good sign that his feelings had deepened too.

He took her arm, drew her up. Touching his forehead to hers, he settled his hand on her neck, to stroke the flutter of her pulse. 'Of course. You're having my kid. I want to be there for you both, not thousands of miles away.'

It took a moment for her to hear the words past the delighted buzz of anticipation. 'But that's...' She struggled to clarify, to make sure she'd understood. 'You only want me to stay because of the baby?'

His lips quirked, his brow wrinkling in a puzzled frown. 'Yeah, of course, what else is there?'

There's me. I need you to want me too.

She stepped out of his arms, the blow both shattering and painfully ironic. When she'd first arrived in Bermuda, hearing him say those words would have felt like a miracle. But now they felt desperately bittersweet. How could she accept his offer, when she wanted so much more?

She looked into those jade-green eyes that she had come to adore, but held so many secrets, and said the only words she could. 'I can't stay, Coop. It's not—'

'Why not? Is it because of your business? I get that...' He touched her waist, trying to reassure her, but only making her heart shatter a little more. 'We can work out the logistics. I'll need to be in Bermuda for the summer season, but otherwise I can come to London. I've got money, whatever we need to do to make this work—'

'That isn't it…' She placed her hand on his cheek, loving him even more if that were possible. He was a generous man, who wanted to do the right thing for his child.

'Then what is it?' he asked.

'This isn't about the baby. It's about me, and you.'

'What?'

She swallowed, knowing she needed to tell him, and hoping against hope that he wouldn't freak out when she did. 'I think I'm falling in love with you.'

He dropped his head back to hers, let out a rush of breath and then, to her total astonishment, he chuckled, the sound deep, and amused and self-satisfied. 'Damn, is that all?'

She stepped back. 'It's not funny. I'm serious.'

He shrugged, his lips tipping in that seductive smile that she had once found so endearing. 'I know you are— so what? That's good, isn't it? If you love me you've got to stay, right?'

'Not if I don't know how you feel about me?' she heard herself say, the question in her voice making her feel needy and pathetic.

'Don't be dumb. It's obvious how I feel about you. I like having you around.' He held her waist, tugged her back into his arms. 'I've invited you to move in, haven't I? At least until the kid's born.'

She braced her hands on his chest, hearing the qualification. 'But that's not enough.'

His brow furrowed. 'Why not?'

'Because I need more than that. You're asking me to make a major change in my life, to move thousands of miles away from everything I know on what sounds like a whim.' The emotion clogged in her throat at the look of total confusion on his face.

'What do you want me to say? That I love you? Is that it?' The bitter edge in his tone made the traitorous tears she'd refused to shed sting her eyes. 'If you need me to say the words I will.'

'This isn't about words.' She drew back. 'It's about emotions. It's about you being honest with me about your feelings.'

Coop stared at Ella's earnest expression, saw the glitter of tears in those trusting blue eyes and felt the panic that he had kept at bay ever since his mother's death start to choke him.

He didn't do emotion, he didn't even talk about it, because it reminded him too much of the deep, dark, inescapable hole where he'd spent most of his childhood.

'You don't know what you're asking,' he said, desperately bartering for time, scrambling around for a way to avoid the conversation. 'I'm not good at that stuff.'

'I know that, Coop.' She sighed, the sound weary and so full of despair it cut right through his heart. 'And I understand. I took a huge knock to my confidence too when Randall rejected me. If I hadn't, it wouldn't have taken me so long to tell you all this. But you have to understand. I can't come and live with you, bring up a child with you and all the time live in some kind of weird limbo where you get to call all the shots because—' she lifted her fingers to do air quotes '—you're "not good at this stuff".' She stood up, brushed her hands down her dress in a nervous gesture he recognised. 'I need to call a cab.'

She turned to pick up her case from the bed. He dived ahead of her, gripped the handle. 'You don't need a cab. You're not going tonight.'

She blinked, the sheen of tears crucifying him. 'Yes, I

am. I have to go. I'm tired and we both need space, maybe once—'

'Don't go.' His voice cracked on the word. 'It's not that I don't want to talk about it, it's that I can't.'

'Why can't you?' she asked, the tone gentle but probing, scraping at the raw wound he'd thought had healed years before.

'Because I'll mess it up. Because I'll say the wrong thing, or I'll say it in the wrong way. They're just words—they don't mean anything. What matters is what we do, not what we say to each other.'

She nodded, but he could see the concern in her gaze, and felt as if she was looking through the veneer of charm and confidence and seeing the frightened little boy cowering beneath. 'Coop, whatever made you think that there's a wrong and a right answer?'

She laid a palm on his cheek, but he jerked back. Terrified of being drawn into that dark place again.

'You say that, but there is a right answer. If there wasn't I wouldn't have given her the wrong one. I told her I loved her, that I could look after her, but it didn't change a thing.'

She watched him, her unwavering gaze so full of the love he knew he wasn't capable of giving back, all the panic imploded inside him until all that was left was the pain.

'Who are you talking about, Coop?'

His heart hammered his ribs as he dropped his chin, fisted his fingers to stop them shaking and murmured, 'My mom.'

Ella stared, unable to speak around the lump wedged in her throat. She could see the painful shadow of memory in his expression, and wished she could take it away. Reaching for his hand, she folded her fingers around his and held on. 'Can you tell me about her?'

He cleared his throat, but he didn't pull his hand out of hers. 'There's not a lot to tell. She had an affair with my old man, he gave her the standard line about leaving his wife. And she got pregnant with me, before she figured out he was lying.'

'He sounds like a very selfish person,' Ella said, then remembered how he'd once compared himself to his father. 'And nothing like you.'

'Thanks.' He sent her a half-smile, but it did nothing to dispel the shadow in his eyes. 'Anyway, he wasn't interested in me, but he carried on screwing my mom from time to time, so she convinced herself he loved her.' He shrugged, but the movement was stiff and tense, and she knew he was nowhere near as relaxed as the gesture suggested.

She pressed her hand to his chest, desperate to soothe the frantic beats of his heart. 'You don't have to tell me any more, if it upsets you. I understand.' His mother had obviously fallen in love with a man who had used her and carried on using her. Was it any wonder that after witnessing that throughout the years of his childhood, he'd be cynical about love himself? And wary about making any kind of commitment. 'I shouldn't have pushed you. It wasn't fair.'

'Yeah, you should have.' He covered her hand. 'And I don't think you do get it, Ella.' He sighed. 'The thing is, she was so fragile. She wanted something she couldn't have and she had these dark moods because she couldn't cope with that. At first, when I was really little, she'd have the odd day when she couldn't get out of bed, and she'd just cry and want to hug me. But as I got older, it got worse and worse, until she couldn't hold down a job. I tried to make things better for her. As soon as I was old enough, I got a job. I figured if I could make enough money…' He stared into the darkness, the hopelessness on his face devastating. 'But I couldn't. Whatever I did, whatever I said, it was never the right thing.'

'Coop,' she murmured, desperate to try and take the hopelessness away. 'It sounds as if she suffered from depression. Money can't cure that.' Or a child's devotion.

'I know, but…'

She leant into him, the love welling up her chest as he looped his arm round her shoulders. 'What happened to her?'

She heard him swallow, the sound loud in the stillness of the night. 'I came home from the graveyard shift at the drive-thru one night and found her in the bathroom. She'd taken too many of the pills she used to sleep. I called the paramedics, but it was too late.'

Ella pulled back, the tears soaking her lashes. 'I'm so sorry that you found her like that.' And that he'd had such a bleak childhood. No wonder he'd been so determined to protect himself—he'd suffered so much, at such a young age. 'But surely you must see that you weren't to blame. Whatever you said or didn't say, it wouldn't have made a difference.'

'Hey, don't cry.' He scooped the tear off her lashes. 'And I guess you're right. But that's not the reason I didn't want to tell you about her.'

She swallowed down the tears. 'So what is?'

'I didn't want you to know what a coward I am.'

'A coward?' She didn't understand: he'd done his best; he'd stuck by his mother and tried so hard to make her life easier, better. 'How can you say that when you did everything you could for her?'

'Maybe I did. But I'm not talking about her. I'm talking about us.' His lips tipped up in a wry smile. 'The thing is, even though I loved my mom, and I was sad when she died…' he gave his head a small shake '…you know what I felt most when I stood by her graveside?'

She shook her head, confused now. What was he trying to tell her?

'Relief.' The word came out on a huff of breath. 'I was so damn glad I didn't have to be responsible for her any more.' He cupped her cheek, brushing the tears off her lashes. 'For years after her death, I used to have this recurring nightmare that I was standing by her grave and her hand would come out and drag me in with her. Because that's what it felt like when I was growing up, being trapped in this big dark hole that I could never get out of. So I ran and I kept on running. Once I landed here, I devoted myself to making money, until I had enough to make the nightmares go away. But I never realised until this moment that in a lot of ways I never stopped running.' His hand stroked down to rest on her stomach.

'I'm sorry that I didn't tell everyone about you, and the baby. And that I'm not good with stuff like this. But if you'll just give me another chance, I'll try not to be such a damn coward again. Because I don't want to keep running any more.'

She stared at him, her heart bursting with happiness and giddy relief. Maybe it wasn't a declaration of undying and everlasting love. But she'd had one of those before and it had been a lie. Coop's declaration meant so much more.

'I think maybe we both need to stop being cowards,' she said. 'I should have had the guts to tell you straight away that my feelings were changing, that I wanted more, instead of panicking about how you would react.'

His hands framed her face, to pull her gaze back to his, and the approval she saw there was as intoxicating as the heat. 'You were just scared. Believe me, I get that. Just so long as you're not scared any more?'

She bobbed her head in answer to his question, far too emotional to speak.

'Cool.' He wrapped his arms round her waist, the solid

feel of him making heat eddy up from her core to add to the joy.

She threaded her hands through the short hair above his ears, tugged his head down to hers and poured out everything she felt for him in a kiss full of happiness and desire and the rush of emotion that no longer had to be denied.

When they finally came up for air, he cradled her cheeks. 'So will you cancel your flight? I know you've got to go home soon, but when you do I'd like to come too, until we figure out how we're going to work this out. I'm not good at making promises. But I know I want to be with you, not just because of the baby, but because...' He ducked his head, swore softly under his breath, the flags of embarrassed colour on his cheeks sweet and endearing and impossibly sexy. 'Hell, I'm pretty damn sure I'm falling for you, too.'

She laughed, the sound rich and throaty and full of hope as she clung onto his neck. 'All right, but only on one condition.'

The quick grin on his lips sparkled with a heady combination of tenderness and wickedness. 'Seriously, you've got another condition? That's pushing it.'

'I'll stay on the condition that I get to give you that just-screwed look I adore.'

He laughed. 'Yup, definitely pushing it.'

He was still chuckling when he dumped her on the bed a few minutes later and got to work giving her what she wanted.

EPILOGUE

'THAT WATER IS so warm, it's incredible,' Ruby said as she reached for one of the beach towels and patted herself dry.

Ella shielded her eyes against the sun to smile at her friend from her spot on the lounger. 'I know, but we should probably call the guys in soon, or we're going to have some very cranky kids on our hands later.'

Ruby turned towards the sea, her smile crafty. 'Yes, but they are going to sleep like the dead, once their fathers have put them to bed.'

Ella laughed, her gaze following Ruby's out to the shallow surf, where Cooper and Ruby's husband Callum were busy playing some kind of splashing war with their children. Cal ran forward, with his four-year-old Arturo clamped to his back like a limpet, while his daughter Ally shouted instructions and charged by his side. Her older brother Max seemed to be in cahoots with Cooper, who had their two-year-old son Jem slung on his hip, as he and Max launched a new offensive against the Westmore invaders. Jem's delighted chuckles were matched by the manic pumping of his little legs as his Daddy scooped up a tidal wave of water with his free arm and drenched Ally, Cal and Arturo in one fell swoop.

Ella grinned at the comical scene as Max began to do a victory dance.

She loved having Ruby and Cal and their family visiting them in Bermuda for the summer—especially now that she and Cooper had made the decision to move here permanently and sell the flat Coop had bought in Camden just before Jem's birth. It had been a major wrench finally agreeing to let that part of her life go, not least because she knew she would miss her best friend terribly, but as Jem got older they'd decided that jetting backwards and forwards between their two home bases was too confusing for him—and getting him over the jet lag every few months nothing short of a nightmare.

'Do the daddies know they're on bedtime duty?' Ella asked as the splashing war went into a new phase, Ally, Cal and Arturo apparently refusing to concede defeat. She suspected both men were going to be even more exhausted than the kids come bedtime if the war carried on much longer.

Ruby settled on the sun lounger next to her and sent her a wicked grin. 'They won't have a choice when I tell them you and I still have lots of important business to conduct concerning the new Touch of Frosting opening in Hamilton.'

'But I thought we got everything sorted yesterday?' Ella said, remembering the fabulous brainstorming session they'd had discussing recipes and displays for the opening of her new bakery in two weeks' time, which Ruby and her family were staying to attend.

'Yes, but they don't know that, do they?'

Ella laughed. 'Ruby, you're nasty.'

'I try,' Ruby replied, smiling back. Then she reached over to take Ella's hand, her smile becoming hopeful. 'So, Ella, you've been so upbeat, I'm assuming you got good news from the specialist last week?'

Ella gripped her friend's fingers, and let the moment of melancholy pass before replying. Ruby knew she and Coop had been trying for another child for over a year,

so of course she would ask. 'Actually, it wasn't the news
we wanted.'

Ruby sat upright, her smile disappearing. 'Ella, I'm so
sorry. I shouldn't have brought it up, I just assumed...'

'No, that's okay.' She tugged Ruby's hand to reassure
her. 'Really, it is. We knew it was a long shot.' She allowed
her gaze to drift over to her two precious guys, still playing like loons together in the surf with the Westmores,
and the smile that was never far away returned. 'It would
be incredibly selfish of me to expect another miracle in
my life.' She paused, the smile getting bigger. 'After the
two I already have.'

Because she considered Coop to be as much of a miracle
as their baby. He'd rescued her, she thought, in so many
ways, and she'd rescued him. They had both found something wonderful together, not just in Jem but with each
other, something made even more wonderful by the fact
that they hadn't even realised it had been missing from
their lives until they'd found it.

'Even so,' Ruby said, 'it seems such a shame it should
be so hard for you to have more children when you make
such incredible parents.'

'I know,' she said, not caring if the statement sounded
a little smug. 'Which is why we're thinking of becoming
foster parents.'

'You are?' Ruby's smile returned. 'That sounds like a
great idea.'

'We think so. It's early days yet, but we're both excited about it. Cooper runs free snorkelling classes at the
marina for kids with...' she paused '...challenging home
situations.' Something he knew far too much about himself. 'Anyway, one of the social workers who escorts the
kids suggested it to him—because she's seen how well he
handles them. So we've started the ball rolling. There's a
lot of paperwork and we have to do a...'

The sound of a toddler's crying reached them, interrupting Ella's enthusiastic reply. She sat up, seeing her husband strolling towards her across the sand, with Jem clinging to his neck and rubbing his eyes—his little head drenched in seawater.

'Oh, dear, what happened?' she said as they approached, trying not to smile, Jem looked so forlorn.

'We had to retire from the field,' Coop announced, casting a stern eye at Ruby. 'Thanks to a sneaky stealth attack from Super-Splash-Girl.'

'I should have warned you.' Ruby smiled, handing Coop a towel to wipe Jem's face. 'Ally takes no prisoners, and she always plays to win. I'm afraid it's the curse of having two brothers.'

'Want ice cream, Daddy,' Jem wailed as if he'd just undergone an extreme form of water torture.

'OK, buddy.' Coop handed Ruby back the towel. 'I guess you earned one.' He rubbed his son's back as the small head drooped onto his shoulder. 'As well as a lecture on the wiles of women.'

Ruby chuckled. 'Good luck with that.'

'Do you want me to take him?' Ella asked, reaching for the exhausted child.

'Nah, he's good. I'll see if I can sneak a scoop of strawberry past Inez, then I'll put him down for his nap.' Holding his son securely against his chest, he leant down to press a kiss to her lips, whispering as he drew back, 'Then maybe we can have *our* afternoon nap?'

The heat sizzled happily down to her core as she caressed her son's damp blond curls and grinned up at her extremely hot husband. 'Possibly, as long as I don't have to listen to a lecture on the wiles of women.'

'No problem.' He winked. 'I've got a whole other lecture planned for you, sweetheart.'

Saying goodbye to Ruby, he headed towards the beach steps up to the house.

Ella studied his broad tanned back, the muscular, capable shoulder where her drowsy son's head was securely cradled, and then let her gaze drift down to the wet board shorts clinging to tight buns.

She let out a contented sigh as her happiness combined with the hum of heat. While her husband would still rather have his teeth pulled than talk about his feelings—when it came to lectures in bed, she'd never been able to fault his energy, enthusiasm… Or his expertise.

* * * * *

LET'S TALK
Romance

For exclusive extracts, competitions
and special offers, find us online:

 facebook.com/millsandboon

@MillsandBoon

@MillsandBoonUK

Get in touch on 01413 063232

For all the latest titles coming soon, visit
millsandboon.co.uk/nextmonth